BEST LAID PLANS

THE MERCENARIES #1

STYLO FANTÔME

Best Laid Plans
Published by BattleAxe Productions
Copyright © 2015 Stylo Fantôme

Critique Partner: Ratula Roy

Editing Aides:
Barbara Shane Hoover
Ratula Roy

Cover Design
Najla Qamber Designs
www.najlaqamberdesigns.com
Copyright © 2015

Formatting: Champagne Formats
www.champagneformats.com

ISBN-13: 978-1517009359
ISBN-10: 1517009359

Other Books by the author

The Kane Trilogy
Degradation
Separation
Reparation
Completion

My Time in the Affair

DEDICATION

For R

M and K and D
all belong to you

AUTHOR'S NOTE

Every location in the following story is real. Every hotel, landmark, border, neighborhood, etc.; they are *all* based on a real location that actually exits. Customs and holidays and hazards were all researched.

That being said, creative license was taken occasionally, as a drive across western Africa would be virtually impossible in real life – geographically as well as it's simply too dangerous. The U.S. Department of State advises using extreme caution when traveling through that part of the world, and the U.N. has listed many of the cities mentioned as extremely dangerous.

LILY

Six days. Six days. Only six more days.

    Liliana Brewster unloaded her Glock 22. Racked the slide and discharged the bullet from the chamber. Disassembled the gun. Took a deep breath. Put it all back together again, as quickly as possible.

    Six more days and I never have to do this again.

    Six more days. Six more days.

MARC

Three days. Three days. Only three more days.

Marcelle De Sant hopped from foot to foot, punching the weight bag harder. As hard as he could.

Three more days and I can get the fuck out of this country.

Three more days. Three more days.

DAY ZERO

Marc smiled to himself as he strapped a shin plate onto his right leg. He could always smell her before he saw her. For almost a month, that aroma had been tempting him. Tormenting him. It was faint, the scent could be lingering from a moment earlier in the day, but he didn't think so. He thought she was somewhere close by, and getting closer.

Sure enough, a moment later and someone walked into the room.

"Hey! I didn't know you were here."

Lily. Funny, because she didn't smell like her namesake – she smelled like lavender. Not perfume, though. Maybe lotion? It was calming, and made her stand out. They were in a hellhole, one of the worst cities in the world, and here was an auburn goddess with rosy skin and a lavender scent.

At least she brightened up the scenery.

"Yeah," Marc answered, standing upright and pulling on his flak jacket. "Just suiting up."

"Oh, that's right, tonight's the night," she replied. She moved around to his side, tightening the straps on the vest for him.

"*The* night. And you leave tomorrow?" he asked, though it wasn't necessary. He knew full well she was leaving in the morning. They had spent enough time together over the past month to know the roles they each had in the little scheme the Russian *Stankovski Bratva* had going. Still, he asked, just to hear her speak. Marc was normally a loner, but over the weeks, he'd grown to enjoy her company. He hated to admit it, but he would miss her.

"Yup. Bright and early. Without me riding your ass, life is gonna be pretty boring," she teased, reading his mind.

"Life is going to be *sweet*. This time tomorrow, I'll be vacation-ing off the coast of Greece, sleeping my way through the women of Santorini," he sighed dramatically. She yanked hard on a strap and he wheezed.

"Well, try not to let the syphilis eat too much of your brain. What's left of it, that is."

With his vest in place, she came back around to his front and watched him as he loaded up the rest of his gear. Thigh holsters, shoulder holster, ankle holster; pretty much anywhere he could hang a gun, there was a holster. When he glanced at her, she had her eye-brows raised in surprise.

"What?" he looked himself over, looking to see if he'd missed anything.

"That's a lot of gear," she commented.

"Can never be too careful. I don't feel like dying tonight."

"Why are you getting ready here, anyway? Don't you have a home?" she pointed out. He snorted.

"Sweetheart, the job starts here and ends here. I don't want any-one following me back to my place – not even these fuckers. I don't let anyone see where I sleep," Marc stressed. She pouted her lips.

"Pity."

"Why?"

She stepped up close to him, standing on her tiptoes so her mouth was near his ear.

"Because I'd *love* to see where you sleep."

Before Marc could respond, could even process what she'd said, there was a knock at the door, and they both turned towards it. A large man in a black blazer and black turtle neck came into the room.

"It is time," was all he said, his Russian accent thick. Marc turned back to Lily and winked.

"Gotta go. Take it easy out there, don't break too many hearts," he cautioned her. She rolled her eyes.

"I'll try my best. Don't get shot out there."

"*I'll try my best.*"

Marc was halfway out the door when he stopped. Looked back into the room. Lily was bent in half, picking up some of the stuff he'd left on the floor. He didn't know her, not really. Marc had been hired by a Russian Mafia group, or *Bratva*, to execute a heist. A very peculiar heist, not his normal gig, but he liked a challenge.

He usually worked the EU, eastern Europe, and Russia, so getting a call to Moscow hadn't been unusual. Meeting with the *Pakhan*, or "Godfather" as it were, was also not unusual – he had met the man several times over the course of his years working with that particular group. No, it was the request itself that was unusual.

Steal diamonds from Liberia.

The blood diamond business was booming in Africa, and everyone wanted in on the action. But Africa was a dangerous place, particularly the places the diamonds were coming out of; having Bratva safe houses doing dirty deeds in Liberia was already pushing the envelope. Stealing from a Liberian gang? That would be inviting war. Every Russian in Liberia would have to fear for their lives.

That's where Marc came into the picture. Steal the diamonds. Make sure it was impossible to trace the theft back to the safe house *or* the Bratva. Give the diamonds to the *Brigadier*, the man who operated under direct orders from the big boss back in Moscow. Get paid. Get the fuck out of Africa.

Simple.

But as he watched Lily move, Marc knew it wasn't simple. There was a very real possibility he could die later in the night, and Lily could very well die the next day.

She'd shown up in Liberia a couple days after Marc had arrived. He'd been walking across the large back yard just as she was brought through, and it had been like seeing the sun after being in the rain for too long. American – he hadn't spoken to another American in longer than he could remember. A beautiful, intelligent woman – had probably been even longer since he'd talked to one of those. Who was she? He'd figured either a high end escort, or an undercover CIA agent.

She turned out to be neither. She was a transporter, and the diamonds he was going to steal, she was going to smuggle them out of Africa. How a gorgeous redhead from Cleveland became a transporter for a Bratva, in Monrovia, Liberia of all places, Marc had no clue. And she never explained it. To have gotten there, she must have been good at her job, so he'd never questioned it.

Two Americans, working for a Bratva in Monrovia, they were bound to run into each other. He was smart and funny, she was smart and funny, they got along. She was good looking, he was good looking, they flirted. They never once saw each other outside of the safe house, and they never shared any explicit info about their individual jobs.

But they chatted and they flirted and they danced around each other. Became friends. He liked her, he supposed. He didn't like many people.

"… *I'd love to see where you sleep.*"

Marc walked back across the room. Lily stood upright and smiled at him, even started to say something. But he didn't give her a chance. He grabbed her by the back of her head and pulled her in for a kiss.

Lily was a pistol, he halfway expected her to kick him in the nuts. One of the bodyguards in the house had made the mistake of grabbing her ass right after she'd gotten there. She'd broken his wrist and three of his fingers.

Luckily, she didn't do that to Marc. She grabbed the straps of his vest and yanked him even closer, sliding her tongue into his mouth before he could make that move first. They stumbled backwards, falling into a wall. She moaned and he felt her teeth against his bottom lip, and it just about had him stripping all his gear back off.

"You wait till *now* to make a move!?" she panted when he pulled away.

"I like to leave people wanting more. Take care of yourself," he replied, brushing his thumb across her lips. She went to respond, but he turned and walked away again, this time for good.

No sense in getting more attached than he already was; after that night, he'd probably never see her again.

DAY ZERO

Lily sat in an anteroom of sorts, chewing at the edge of her thumbnail. She'd never been in the safe house that late at night before; usually after nightfall, she liked to be safely tucked away in her hotel room, behind secure gates and keyed entries and multiple dead bolts.

She didn't like to be in the Bratva's house, *period*, but especially not at night. Some of the men didn't seem to understand that not all women were hookers, there solely for their pleasure and entertainment. She could handle one or two by herself, but not a whole house, not on her own, and she didn't trust the Brigadier – Oleg Ivanov wasn't exactly known for being a warm, fuzzy kind of guy.

Why the fuck am I here!?

There was a commotion outside of the room, and she turned towards a door to her left. It led to a hallway. The door to her right led into Ivanov's office. She'd only been in there once, on her first day. She hadn't expected to ever come back to it.

The commotion got louder, and suddenly the door burst open. She jumped in her seat, and was shocked to see a parade of men storming through the room. Ivanov was leading the way, waddling to his door, keys in his hand. Several *byki* trailed through the door. Bodyguards. Dumber than rocks, but loyal beyond belief. They would die before they let any harm come to Ivanov.

Between the byki and Ivanov was Marc. Lily was surprised. She really hadn't expected to see him again, either. When he'd kissed her five hours earlier, she'd figured that was goodbye.

But there he was. He was soaking wet, and muddy. Blood coated the side of his right arm, trailing out from underneath his black t-shirt sleeve. Most of his gun holsters were empty. He was breathing hard, and he looked *pissed* – she'd never seen him that way, before. Never seen him working. He was usually flirty and smiley with her, but there was no hint of that man anymore. He glanced at her once, their eyes connecting for a second, but he didn't say anything. Just followed Ivanov through the office door. The byki followed, and soon enough, Lily was alone again.

What happened? Did he get the diamonds? Is this it? Why am I here? What the fuck is going on!?

DAY ZERO

Marc ran his fingers through his hair, shaking away the wetness. When he thought of Africa, he thought of desert. Liberia was in the savanna. He felt like he was living in a sauna.

"Anyone follow you?"

"Please. I'm like a ghost. Let's hurry this up," Marc snapped at Ivanov.

"De Sant, always so impatient," the other man chuckled.

Marc wasn't actually a member of that Bratva, or *any* Bratva, in any way, but he had been hired by the Pakhan for lots of jobs, so he'd become accustomed to working around their organization. But he'd never worked around Ivanov before, and after this job, he never would again.

He did not care for the weaselly little guy.

"You were late," Ivanov was wagging his finger, but smiling, like a proud parent who liked to tease. Marc frowned.

"Yeah, they were a little more *tenacious* than I thought they would be, I had to use some interesting evasive maneuvers," Marc explained.

"Tenacious? Were you followed? De Sant, if they followed you -" Ivanov started to turn red.

"*No one followed me,*" Marc stressed.

"Good, good, good, very good. Is very good. Let me see, let me see!" Ivanov urged, waving his hand, motioning for Marc to come forward.

It took a few minutes to unstrap his gear bag from his back, and then to dig out the large velvet baggie from the bottom of it, but eventually, a sea of glistening stones was spread out across a large wooden desk. While Ivanov inspected the goods, Marc let his eyes wander around the room, taking in the faded wallpaper and peeling ceiling paint. The maps that seemed to be everywhere, and the cats that were lounging upon them.

"It's all there. I never opened the package," Marc assured him, keeping his voice loud enough for the other men in the room to hear. Ivanov nodded, but his eyes never left the diamonds.

"Yes, yes. Stunning. Absolutely stunning! The clarity! You are sure no one followed you?"

Is this guy serious?

"I'm beginning to get insulted. I've *never* been followed, and I certainly wasn't followed this time. Now give me the rest of my fee so I can get out of this fucking hellhole," Marc spit out.

"Of course, of course. *Lev!*" Ivanov snapped his fingers. A large man lumbered away from the group at the back of the room, holding out a small duffle bag. Marc took it, and was a little surprised at its weight.

"What's this?" he asked. Ivanov still hadn't looked away from the diamonds.

"Bonus. You do such good work, De Sant. No one could have done this as good as you. As quiet as you. Perfect work. Big bonus for you. Please, enjoy. Take a vacation! You have most definitely earned it," Ivanov explained.

Marc was instantly on alert. In all his years of doing mercenary work, he had never been given a bonus that hadn't been discussed in advance. Criminals weren't usually big on parting with their money – sometimes payment alone had to be taken by force. He was certainly never just *handed* extra money.

Until that moment.

Sure, it was the biggest diamond heist of Marc's nefarious career, and possibly in that Bratva's history, but still. Criminals were criminals.

Something is very, very wrong.

"We never discussed a bonus. I didn't do anything extra to earn it. Just standard protocol," Marc put out there. Ivanov waved him away.

"You got diamonds. You didn't lead them back to us. Is good enough reason. Go, go, go now, enjoy, Marcelle. For once in your miserable life, enjoy something!"

Marc paused for a second longer, but the whole situation made him so goddamned uncomfortable. He just wanted to get out of there. He gave a curt smile, nodded his head at Ivanov, then started elbowing his way through the bodyguards.

He just wanted to get away. Wanted to go home and count his money. Shower. Decompress. And then get as far away from Liberia as fucking possible. As quickly as fucking possible.

But when he stepped out of the room, it was to find Lily sitting in the anteroom. He'd forgotten about her. The last five hours had been an adrenaline ride on a roller coaster in hell. He'd been shot, he'd been chased, he'd sprinted for no less than a mile – he was *tired*. Beyond tired. He was dirty, he was angry, and he was confused by Ivanov's "*bonus*". And now the redheaded goddess herself was looking up at him with her big green eyes, all wide and confused looking.

Goddamn, she's gorgeous.

"What are you doing here?"

They both spoke in unison.

"Ivanov asked me for a meeting, but he seems to have forgotten. Your entrance was a little ... dramatic," Lily answered first.

"You think? Good thing you weren't downstairs, then," he replied.

"Why?"

"Because I broke in a backdoor and when one of those idiots tried to stop me, I beat him unconscious with my gun."

She didn't even blink.

I should marry this girl.

"Nice. You're bleeding," she pointed out.

"I know. Just a graze."

Was it getting hot in the anteroom? He felt warm.

"It could need stitches."

"It doesn't."

"A bandage?"

"Probably."

"I could bandage it for you."

And energy. It was like there was an incredible amount of energy in the room. Sparking. Causing tension. An unavoidable explosion.

I want to devour her.

"You still leaving tomorrow?" he barked out, stepping up close to her. She stood up and nodded.

"As far as I know."

"Go as fast as you can. The shit I saw tonight ... I've seen some fucked up stuff in my life, but ... goddamn. Liberian gangs don't fuck around, they make these guys look like tame little kittens," Marc gestured to the house.

"So I've gathered. I'm set to leave at six-thirty. I won't look back," she assured him.

"Good. After you're done here, meet me at the bar down the street," he told her.

For the first time, she looked caught off guard by him.

"Excuse me?"

"Bar. Down the street. Neon sign. Be there in an hour," he instructed.

"Why?"

"Because *I'm* going to be there."

He watched a blush rise in her cheeks. She was so fair. Much too pure to be in a place like Monrovia, Liberia.

"Do you think that's -" she began to counter. He covered the rest of the distance between them, pressing his chest to hers.

"It wasn't a question," he growled. She licked her lips and nodded, her fingers raising to toy with the straps on his vest.

"Okay. Okay, Marc. I'll be there. One hour," she breathed.

He couldn't resist. She was too sexy. He was too amped up. He lowered his mouth to kiss her again, but the door behind him suddenly opened.

"Oh my. I am interrupting?"

Marc turned his head to the side, actually growling a little. Ivanov stood in the doorway, staring at them. He eyeballed them carefully.

"One hour," Marc said to Lily. She nodded.

"I did not know you two were such good friends," Ivanov commented in a snide voice.

Marc didn't say a word. The contract was completed, he owed nothing to that Bratva anymore, owed no respect to that man. He glared one more time, then walked out of the room.

What a fucked up night.

DAY ZERO

As Marc walked out of the room, Lily turned back to Ivanov.

"You wanted to talk to me?" she asked. She felt short of breath. Marc had never had that effect on her before, but since he'd kissed her earlier, she felt like she hadn't been able to catch her breath once.

Focus, Liliana. Eyes on the prize. Just because you haven't had sex in almost a year doesn't mean anything. Just because the sexiest guy you've ever met clearly wants to bang you seven ways to Sunday doesn't mean anything.

"You and Marcelle are very good friends, yes?" Ivanov inquired. Lily shrugged.

"Not really."

"Just now you looked like very good friends."

"We looked like two people who want to have sex with each other, that's it," she was blunt. "What do you want?" Ivanov heaved a big laugh.

"I love your mouth, Liliana! I will miss it," he sighed.

"Look, I'm going. I'll be back in the morning," she snapped, making a move to leave.

"*Liliana!*"

She turned back.

"You will not come here tomorrow," he informed her. She raised her eyebrows in surprise. "We will come to you with goods and supplies. Stay in your hotel. Do not open door for anyone. *Not anyone but me.* Do you understand?"

She was shocked. As far as she knew, Ivanov *never* left the safe house. But she didn't question it. It was too big a job and she'd been planning for too long to mess anything up.

"I understand. No one."

"Alright. I will be at your door, at 0600 hours," he reminded her.

"0600."

"Thank you."

Lily hurried out of the anteroom, then bolted through the house. Her talk with Ivanov hadn't lasted very long and the house was large, Marc could still be in it. She dashed through hallways, pushed her way through a rowdy crowd of prostitutes. When she finally got outside, she could see him, but he was pretty far away. A tiny figure at the very end of the street, a duffle bag swinging at his side.

She chewed on her lip. It was stupid. She had a mission, something she had to do. Something she *needed* to do. Something she had been planning for five years. She couldn't risk ruining it all by chasing after a boy. *She couldn't …*

"Hey! Open the gate!" she started shouting, turning to the gated driveway that sat next to the safe house.

Something about him. For five years, she'd focused only on her goal. Men didn't even enter the picture, she wasn't looking, *at all*. Sex was a weapon, to be used just as quickly and readily as she would use a gun. A woman from America didn't get to be a transporter for Oleg Ivanov overnight. She'd had to climb and crawl and claw her way to that position. She'd had to do some things she wasn't exactly proud of.

Maybe it was time to reward herself.

She slid behind the wheel and turned the engine. The car she'd been given, the one she'd been driving around Liberia for a month, was a 1977 Mercedes. A little beat up looking, a little rough around the edges, it had clearly had a tough life. But it got the job done, and really, the worse it looked, the better. She didn't need any extra attention, considering what she'd be moving in a couple hours.

By the time Lily pulled out onto the street, he was out of sight. She got to where she'd last seen him, and it turned out to be a cross street. Again, she could make out his form in the distance. He'd taken a left, and she followed, but before she got halfway down the street, he took another left. When she got to that street, he'd disappeared.

Maybe he thought I was one of the gang members, following him?

There was a boarding house of sorts, towards the end of the block, and Lily figured it was her best bet. She was surprised that he was staying so close to the safe house, but then again, maybe that had been the idea. Anyone looking for him and guessing he was working with the Bratva would never think to look so close. She parked the car and hurried as she went into the large building.

"Hello?" she called into an entry way. It looked like someone's home. There were a multitude of people lounging about the living room, all of them watching an old black and white television. Without looking away from the screen, an old woman got up and walked towards Lily.

"Room?" she asked, still watching TV.

"No. I'm looking for my friend, he -" Lily started.

"Third floor, third room on right. You stay longer than two hours, I charge extra," the woman warned her.

"Sounds fair to me."

Lily slowly made her way up to his room. She didn't want to come off as too eager. They'd been playing cat and mouse for a month, under the assumption neither would get caught. Now that it was time to eat, she wasn't quite ready to be the mouse.

The door to the third room on the right wasn't locked. She was cautious as she opened the door, but the first thing she saw was the black duffle bag he'd taken off with, followed by the clothing he'd been wearing. She moved into the room and shut the door behind her.

She could hear water splashing around in the bathroom, so she took her time, looking over the space he'd been living in for the past month. It was simple. A room. A bed that was little more than a cot. A small table. One small chair. There had been electricity downstairs, but there didn't seem to be any in his room. Three mismatched, stout candles were burning on the table, and those were the only light source.

The sound of water diminished to just a gurgling drain, so she made her way back towards the bathroom. Just as she grasped the knob, she felt it turn from the other side and the door started to pull away. She smiled.

Samesies.

She lost her smile the same moment a hand wrapped around her neck. She let out a shriek as she was yanked around and slammed against a wall. The hand was replaced by a forearm, a much more effective body part for choking someone. She gritted her teeth, slapping at the arm that was restraining her.

"*It's me! It's me!*"

Marc looked surprised. *And* angry. He backed off a little and she sucked in gasps of air. His forearm moved to her collarbone, still holding her in place against the wall. She glared right back at him, resisting the urge to plant her knee in his testicles.   •

"What the fuck are you doing here!? How did you find me!?" he demanded, then his eyes darted around the room, as if he thought she'd brought people with her.

"You weren't exactly hard to follow, you idiot. You walked here," she growled.

"I thought you were talking with Ivanov."

"I was. It wasn't a very long conversation."

"I told you I don't let anyone know where I sleep," he reminded her, his voice low.

"Well, I didn't come here with any intentions of sleeping, so we're still good."

That got through to him and he finally smiled at her. The pressure from his arm let up, but he leaned more of his body against her, lining them up from the hips down.

"I told you to meet me at a bar," he pointed out, lowering his head to brush his cheek against the side of hers, then dipping down to rub against her neck. She heard a sharp inhale, like he was smelling her.

"Sometimes I'm not very good at listening."

"I have to be out of here in a couple hours."

"I only need a couple hours."

"That's it? I had such high hopes for you."

She snorted and moved her hands to his waist, yanking his towel away.

"And I had high hopes that your mouth would be good for something other than talking. So far, it's a disappointment."

His lips met hers in a way that made their first kiss seem like a church greeting. His tongue was present and forceful in her mouth, his hands moving to press heavily against her breasts. She moaned, reveling in the feeling of being touched. Of actually *wanting* to be touched.

She scratched her nails along his hips and went to dip down between them, but he was quicker and he grabbed her wrists, slamming her arms against the wall above her head. She gasped and automatically tried to resist, but he just squeezed tighter, pushed harder. Cat and mouse was over, the roles had been established. If he didn't want her to move, then she wasn't going to be able to move.

Does that mean I'm in the mouse trap?

He let her go, but only so he could grab her ass, lifting her off the ground. She wrapped her legs around his waist, toeing off her shoes as he carried her to the bed. She went to peel off her shirt, but he grabbed her by the hips and literally tossed her onto the mattress. She bounced a little, and before she could get her bearings, Marc was kneeling over her.

"God, do you have any idea how many times I've thought about this," he groaned. He pulled the bottom of her tank top away from her body, then ripped it clean up the middle. She sat up, helping him shove the material away from her shoulders.

"Oh yeah? How many times?" she whispered, leaning close and sucking on his earlobe.

"All the time."

"In this bed?"

"Yeah."

"Mmmm, you pictured this?"

"Yeah."

"Did you ever -"

"Stop talking."

He didn't rip her pants like her shirt, but he didn't waste any time when he pulled them free from her body, either. Then he licked and nibbled his way up the insides of her thighs. When he got to her panties he didn't bother with them at all, just pressed his tongue against her center, as hard as he could.

"Ooohhh, wow," she breathed out, combing her fingers through his hair while her eyes rolled back.

Reality was too real. Or not real enough. She could never be sure anymore. Living a lie for five years, it all got confusing. Life was shit. This felt like heaven. She didn't care that tomorrow meant war. Right now, she was in a little piece of oblivion. That's all she needed.

The friction of the lace against her slickness was almost too much. His tongue had barely done anything and she was panting sharply, whining in the back of her throat, almost yipping. Her fingers in his hair turned to clutching. Then pulling. Her thighs tightened around his head.

*How long since your last orgasm? Since the last time you had sex with someone you **wanted** to have sex with? This might stop your heart …*

"Talk about high strung, sweetheart," Marc teased her as he pulled away at a critical moment. She cried out in annoyance and tried to push him back down.

"What's that supposed to mean!?" she snapped as he evaded her hand, kissing his way up her stomach

"It means if all women came as easily as you were about to, life would be so much easier."

"Not our fault if you're normally not very good at this."

His hand slid under her bra and squeezed her breast, his fingers pinching her nipple hard. She shrieked, giving a whole body shudder.

"No one's ever taught you how to behave right, have they?"

Her bra was shoved out of the way, and while she worked at taking it off, he moved back to her underwear. Gripped the material between two fists, then *yank*, and there was nothing left. He was kneeling between her legs and she sat up quickly, gripping his waist as she kissed his skin. Worked her way across his chest. His hands went into her hair, pulling her ponytail down. He kept the auburn locks in one fist, tugging just enough to let her know he was still in charge.

If there was no tomorrow, then Lily wanted to get to know as much of right-now-Marc as she could, wanted to take her time, but he had other plans. He let go of her hair and gripped her shoulders, shoving her back down onto the mattress. One of his hands gripped her thigh and the other worked between them. He was bold, he kept eye contact as he pushed inside of her. She wanted to be his equal, wanted to be better, wanted to stare him down. But as inch after inch went by, she couldn't handle it. *No one* could be equal to that much intensity, to that much length, to that much *him*. Her eyes fluttered shut, her hands running down her body, her nails scratching at her thighs.

"Why didn't we do this a month ago?" Lily sighed, when he was finally as inside of her as he could ever be.

"Then it wouldn't be such a treat for you now. See? Being nice to me pays off."

"We'll see."

When a person met Marc for the first time, the only word that ever came to mind was "*rough*". He looked like a *rough* guy. He was an interesting sort of handsome. Not conventional. A nose that had clearly been broken at one point, a small scar on the side of his chin. He was also tall, but not overwhelmingly so. Maybe six foot. He had brown hair and a deep tan, like he'd been left out in the sun for days. It made his soft blue eyes really pop. On top of all that, he had thick arms, a solid build, and a penchant for cussing and getting angry – "rough" pretty much described him to a T.

So it wasn't a shock that sex with him turned out to be rough, as well.

As his hips pummeled her own, she didn't have time to think about how rough he was with her. He was pounding common sense and basic reasoning skills out of her. He had a way of hooking his hips, a fluid motion where he pulled away so he almost slid out, then slammed every inch home, but fast. *So fast.*

Her back began to arch, her whole body trying to reach for heaven. Reach for bliss. She cupped her breasts, holding them as they were also pushed higher and higher. Then she felt his hand in the middle of her chest and he shoved down sharply, forcing her flat. His hand stayed in place, pressing so hard she couldn't even move underneath it.

"Where you trying to go, sweetheart? You're all mine tonight," he growled, leaning down close as his hips picked up speed.

"Yes. All night. Please, all night," she echoed. His hand finally moved off her chest and he gripped her jaw, his fingers digging into her cheeks as he forced her to face him.

"Think you can handle a whole night of this?"

"I think I'd like to try."

He stopped moving, utterly shocking her. It was like he took away her oxygen. She was still searching for air when he took hold of her leg, moving it around to the other side of his body, forcing her onto her side. Figuring she knew what he wanted, she hiked her leg up, ready to move onto her knees, but he ignored her. Both of his hands held onto her hip and he was able to pound into her with an even greater force. She shrieked, gripping onto the edge of the mattress, holding on for dear life.

"Goddamn, Lily. Fuck. *Fuck,*" he groaned.

She felt like she had completely lost any kind of control, impaled on an impossibly huge dick, being fucked like she was being punished for something. It was the best feeling *ever*. She laid her cheek against the mattress, hiking her hips up a little higher. She had no leverage, there wasn't a whole lot she could do in return, but she could give him every inch of her. Try and prolong his pleasure as much as possible.

All night, he said.

Then she felt him lean over her again, his hand sliding over her hip, following the curve to the front of her body. His chest made contact with her back at the same time his fingers made contact with wetness. His free arm went across her shoulder blades, his hand holding onto her shoulder, and he used her as an anchor. Used her own body to allow him to jackhammer his hips against her ass while his fingers taught her *exactly* who was in control.

When she came, it was like an explosion. It had been so long since she'd had an orgasm, and goddamn, he'd fucked her *so good*. She screamed, her fingers clenching and unclenching, every muscle spasming, her whole body jerking around underneath him. And still, Marc didn't stop moving. He slowed down, almost massaging her with his cock, but he didn't stop. Not even when she was limp and gasping for air, one arm dangling off the bed.

"That was … everything," she managed to whisper. He laughed and kissed her behind her ear, then kissed a trail down the side of her neck.

"Sweetheart, that was *nothing.*"

He moved her onto all fours and made her put her hands flat against the wall while he pulled her hair hard, smacking her ass as he fucked her from behind. Then she was face down, ass up – every man's fave. When they moved again and he laid down on his back, she took him by surprise and went down on him. A dick that could make her feel that good deserved her mouth, she figured, and she milked him for all she was worth. But before she could finish the job, he was wrenching her hair again. It was obvious that Marc didn't know the meaning of "*gentle touch*"; the pain was sharp and real, forcing her to move away. He dragged her up his body, kissing her sloppily while he helped her shift around him, helped her take him inside of her.

She bounced up and down on top of him. He propped himself up with one arm and leaned forward to suck on her nipples. His other hand held onto her ass, helping set an almost impossible speed. He was too deep, it was too much. He was made to hit her G-spot, it seemed.

"Marc … you're gonna make me come again," she warned him, the shaking starting all over again.

"Good, good," he grunted.

He beat her to the punch, letting out a yell as he came, surprising her. His arms went around her, his hands grabbing her shoulders and yanking her down so she was flush with his pelvis. She cried out, coming at the same time.

Well. That escalated quickly.

Of course, when she'd talked to him in that anteroom, she'd known they were going to have sex. She wasn't shy about the act or her body, it just wasn't something she got to do a lot. Marc had seemed like a good partner to help her get back into the swing of things.

There's an understatement.

He helped her move off of him. While she collapsed into a sweaty mass on the mattress, too exhausted to even keep her eyes open, he wandered back into the bathroom. She could hear water sloshing around, then listened as he came back into the room, but she still didn't open her eyes. After making a rustling noise, he joined her on the bed, stretching out next to her.

"I usually save this for when I'm out of country," he said, and she opened her eyes. He had a joint between his lips and was in the process of lighting it.

"You get high in other countries?" she tried to clarify. He shook his head.

"No. When I finish a job. My reward for getting out of whatever miserable country I'm in is smoking one of these. Want?" he asked, holding it out towards her. She pinched it between her fingers and took a hit.

"Then why are you smoking it now?" she was curious, her voice hoarse as she held the smoke in her lungs. He took the joint back from her.

"I definitely need to smoke something after what we just did."

She burst out laughing, coughing on the smoke.

"Good point."

They chit chatted for a bit, lazing about on the bed. She'd always felt so comfortable with Marc. At the safe house, or even at her own hotel, she was always on edge. On guard. Ready to defend herself. With him, though, she felt like she didn't need that edge. Didn't need to defend herself.

It was nice.

"So what was the big commotion all about?" she remembered his entrance from earlier in the night.

"What do you mean?"

"Everyone was freaking out, you were bleeding, you looked pissed. Like you were gonna stomp on someone's head," she explained.

"Probably because I just had."

"Intense."

"You have no idea."

"Give me the details. It's been a boring month," she demanded.

He groaned and rolled onto his back, rubbing his hands over his eyes. She forced herself not to look down – Marc wasn't shy about his body, either, and she wasn't quite ready to get revved up again. Instead she focused on his arm, on where he'd been shot. Apparently his idea of "*bandaging his arm*" was to wrap duct tape around his bicep several times over.

"I was hired to steal those diamonds. That's what I've been doing all month, tracking the gang's movements, getting the lay of their compound. I honestly thought it would be easy. Half of those guys are hooked on drugs I've never even heard of and the other half are more scared than anything else. They've got a bunch of shitty motor-bikes and a bunch of shitty guns. Should've been an in-and-out job. Gone before they even knew I was there.

"But it was all fucked up. The shit I saw in there, goddamn. I crawled in under a fence, wound up in a garage of sorts. I'd seen cars getting hauled in and out, could tell they were stripping them in there, and figured that's all it was, just a garage. Wrong. They had bodies in there. People they were torturing. People they were killing. And I can handle that. I've tortured people, I've killed people. But god, they were butchering them. I mean, *literally* butchering them, like a cow. Preparing that shit to eat," Marc's voice went quite. Lily swallowed thickly.

"Yeah, I'd read that some gangs do that here. Food isn't exactly plentiful," she said.

"I'll never be able to un-see that shit. I got out of that place as quick as fucking possible. Blew up an oil drum, and when everyone went to investigate, I set off an EMP device. Killed their vehicles, lights, everything. Everyone was scrambling around like ants, so I slipped in and got the diamonds."

"Sounds like a perfect operation."

"Right? Only as I'm going back under the fence, all fucking hell breaks loose. It's like everyone spotted me at once. Usually on a theft job I can get out without firing a shot – I lost two guns and four clips on this job. I fucking ran through some old couple's house, had to jump off a roof, nearly broke my leg. Got shot. I fucking hate getting shot, that means my blood is on a bullet somewhere," Marc growled. Lily swallowed her laughter.

"Well, I doubt there's a '*CSI: West Point, Monrovia*', so I think you're good."

If Monrovia, Liberia was one of the worst cities on the plan-et, then the area of West Point was its epicenter of degradation. She considered herself a tough cookie, but even Lily didn't go over there. Braving a Liberian gang's compound, one that was *inside* West Point, made Marc either the bravest person she'd ever met, or the stupidest.

"I just couldn't fucking believe it. I couldn't come back to the safe house until I knew I'd shook them, and it took me *forever* to be sure. I fucking ran all over that place. Laid under a dumpster for half an hour. Do you have any idea how many people I killed tonight? Insane. Took me hours just to get back. And I knew the longer it took the more pissed off Ivanov would be," Marc added. Lily nodded in agreement. The Brigadier wasn't known for his patience and thoughtfulness.

"Sounds awful."

"You have no idea. I can't stop seeing it all in my brain."

"Is that why you were so distracted?"

"What do you mean? When?" he asked, finally glancing at her.

"I'm not exactly a detective – it was awfully easy to follow you here," she pointed out. He groaned and nodded.

"I know. I'm a little embarrassed about that; the job was done, I had my money, I just wanted to get the fuck out of there. The mood I was in, I was almost hoping someone would follow me and fuck with me. They would've been sorry," his voice lowered into a grumble, sounding evil and threatening. Lily swallowed thickly and quickly decided that she never wanted to see Marc truly angry.

"Quite the night, Marcelle De Sant. Gangs, cannibals, diamonds, killings, running for your life. I'm surprised you had any stamina left for me," she teased, deciding to lighten the mood. They both lived in darkness a majority of the time. She wanted to use their time together to make things seems shiny.

"Sweetheart, if pussy is involved, then I'll always find more stamina."

"Wish I'd known that a month ago."

"Me, too. God, look at me," he grumbled, looking down the length of his chest. Lily looked as well, taking in the sheen of sweat that covered him. "Wanna take a shower?"

"I saw your shower."

"And ...?"

"It's not a shower. It's a bucket with holes poked in the bottom that you have to keep refilling," she pointed out. "The lady has to bring the water up to you and god knows where she gets it from. No thank you, I'll wait till my hotel, where I have running water. *Hot running water.*"

Marc leaned over and bit down on her shoulder, causing her to squeal.

"I wanted to do this at your place, hence the whole '*wait for me at the bar*' bit," he reminded her.

"Awfully confident."

"No, just not stupid."

"Cheeky."

His teeth kept moving, clamping down on her bottom lip hard enough to hurt. She cried out and pulled away from him, but he moved his hand to her neck, holding her in place. As his fingers pressed down around her windpipe, she raised her knees up, rubbing her thighs together.

"Ready to play rough, princess?" he breathed against her lips. She smiled up at him.

"I thought you'd never ask."

DAY ZERO

Marc was a light sleeper and he heard movement at the edge of his bed. Before he even opened his eyes, he shot out his hand, grabbing at the person sneaking around him.

"Going somewhere?" he managed to croak out, his voice hoarse. The were was a soft laugh, making him think of magical things, like heaven and breasts, and then the smell of lavender was surrounding him again.

"Gotta go, lover boy," Lily whispered, giving him a gentle kiss. He smiled and opened his eyes, watching as she stood upright.

"I didn't realize I fell asleep, sorry," he yawned, scratching at his head as he sat up.

"No worries. I just kept going," she joked.

"Nice. Shouldn't you have at least waited till I woke back up?"

"Probably. But you liked it."

"Probably. Why the rush? I have another hour, and more tricks to show you," Marc offered, glancing at his watch.

"I'm sure you do, but it's like forty minutes to my hotel and Ivanov is supposed be meeting me in a little over an hour," Lily explained. He nodded, pulling an ashtray down from his windowsill. The half smoked joint was still in there and he lit it up.

"Wow, we've been at it that long?" he was surprised. He'd lost track of time, wandering around her lines and curves.

"Geez, don't sound so shocked," she snorted at him as she crawled over his outstretched legs. He held the roll to her lips and she took a deep breath.

"Not shocked. Sad it's over – you're a good tension reliever. So you're off soon?"

She blew a stream of smoke over his head.

"Six-thirty," she reminded him, then took another quick drag. "Ivanov is meeting me at six so we can discuss stuff, do the exchange."

"Ah, that's right. Well then …," he let his voice trail off. He wasn't sure what to say.

Thank you for a-fucking-mazing sex, and for having tits I'll dream about for years. Perfect. Sounds just like poetry.

"*Marcelle De Sant,*" she chanted off his full name as she moved to straddle his lap. "I think, just maybe, you'll miss me."

He moved his hands to her ass, squeezing her tightly and forcing her up, forcing her closer, forcing her chest against his own. She was curvy in all the right places, pliable flesh just begging to be molded under his hands. And smooth, every inch of her, as he now knew.

"I think I'll miss *this* for a long time," he whispered back, clenching his fingers. She wiggled against his hold.

"Me, too. Thanks for making Africa bearable, Marc," she said. Her voice was devoid of teasing – she sounded genuinely thankful, and even a little sad.

"Where are you going after this?" he surprised himself by asking out loud. He never discussed '*the after*', ever. With anybody. She smiled.

"Where are *you* going after this?" she returned the question.

"I don't know. Crete. Mykonos. Somewhere nice," he answered honestly.

"Ooohhh, sounds nice. Maybe when I'm done I'll come look you up, Mr. De Sant," she offered.

"Pack a bikini."

"But I like to sunbathe in the nude."

"God, you're an amazing woman."

She gave him a kiss that had him wondering if she'd leave with his tonsils, then she crawled off of him. She was wearing everything but a shirt, and he remembered that he'd ripped hers off of her. She grabbed a t-shirt off the back of a chair and held it up for his inspection. He shrugged and she slipped it on, knotting the excess material at the base of her spine.

"This was fun. I hope we get to do it again sometime," she said, standing by the door as she pulled on her shoes.

"Me, too."

"Take care of yourself, Marc."

"You, too."

"And …," her voice faltered as she opened his door. She looked back over her shoulder at him. "And be careful out there."

He was touched by her concern. There was no one left to be concerned about him, or his well being. It was a novel experience.

"Always careful, sweetheart. Take it easy out there, Africa isn't kind," he warned her. She turned away from him.

"Neither am I."

Then the door slammed shut behind her.

What a woman.

Mark took his time finishing the joint, then moved to the edge of his bed. Scratched his fingers through his hair. He was high, and, if he was completely honest, a little dumb struck. It had been the best sex he'd had in a *long* time. His only regret was that he'd gone into their night already worn out. If she thought *that* had been good, then she might die if she saw him at his best.

He finally got up, stretching so he was on his tiptoes. Then he pulled on some briefs and his pants, before heading over to his table. When he'd gotten back from the safe house, he'd grabbed a bucket of water on his way up, wanting to wash the night and the memories off his skin. He'd just stripped down and jumped in the tub.

Now it was time to see exactly how big his "bonus" really was. He over turned the duffle bag he'd been given, and his surprise at even receiving a "bonus" turned to outright shock.

It was beyond a bonus. Almost four times more than his agreed upon salary was in the bag. The money spilled out all over the floor, covering the ground between his bed and the beat up looking table.

*What **THE FUCK** is going on!?*

While he took in the bills, his ears picked up on a sound outside. A motorcycle was pulling up in front of the house; a dirt bike, with a whiny engine. Then another. Marc turned his head towards his window, but didn't move his feet. Several more pulled up, all dirt bikes and mopeds. Then more. *Even more.* He lost count. As the last candle in his room flickered out, clarity blazed through his mind.

That fucking bitch …

DAY ONE

Lily took a deep breath and glanced in her rear view mirror. No one was following her. She was on the very furthest outskirts of Monrovia. Pretty soon, she would be completely alone. There would be no one around, not for hundreds of miles.

I can't believe I'm here. I can't believe I did it. All those years. I did it.

She eased off the road and pulled up along side an ancient looking gas pump. As she climbed out of her car, a young boy came rushing out of a run down shack. He didn't say a word, just grabbed a rag out of a bucket full of rancid looking water and began washing her windshield.

"English?" Lily asked, pushing her sunglasses to the top of her head.

"Yes, little English," the boy replied. She reached her fingertips inside the top of her tank top, right where the neckline brushed against the uppermost part of her bra. She pulled out a U.S. fifty dollar bill.

"You know what this is?" she held the bill between two fingers, allowing him to see it. The boy's eyes got wide and he nodded.

"Yes, I know."

"This is yours, if you promise not to touch my car," she started. If possible, his eyes got wider, and he nodded again. "*And* if you promise not let anyone else touch my car."

"Yes, yes, no one will touch your car," he immediately began reaching for the bill. She yanked it out of his reach.

"Uh-uh, no way. *After*. If anyone touches my car, even looks at my car, you yell. Make a noise. Honk the horn. Light the building on fire. Something. Got it?"

"Yes. No one. Make noise."

Lily leaned down close and stared him very directly in the eye.

"If you mess around in my car, if you take anything from my car, I will know, and you will *not* like what happens," she lowered her voice to almost a growl. The little boy swallowed thickly.

"I promise, I won't touch," he assured her. She gave a tight lipped smile but kept her glare severe.

"Good. No touching means lots of money."

She tucked the money back into her bra as she walked towards the shack that was serving as a gas station of sorts. There was a ripped up screen door at the entrance that fell off one of its hinges when she pushed on it.

Inside wasn't any better. A man with a cloudy eye and no teeth sat on a stool, watching a black and white television that had bunny ears. Lily looked around. It wasn't exactly a seven-eleven, there weren't aisles full of shiny processed foods.

"Water?" she barked out in a loud voice. The man didn't look at her, but lifted a rail thin arm and pointed across the shop.

A large, beat up looking cooler sat at the back of the building. Its motor was loud, and a generator sat next to it, giving it power. At first she was suspicious, and was sure it would be full of "recycled" water bottles full of tap water, or worse. But surprisingly there were actual brand name bottles in the cooler. She didn't dare look at the dates, just grabbed as many as she could hold and carried them up to the front of the shop.

"U.N.?" the man asked as he slid off the stool and walked towards her. She shook her head.

"No. Globa-Doc. Food?"

A cover had been worked out long before she'd taken the job for the Bratva. Passing as a U.N. Inspector had been an option, but the U.N. was in and out of the area all the time, they didn't want to risk her running into any of them. Globa-Doc was a doctors-without-borders kind of program – doctors and nurses from all over the world, specializing in nutrition and working in third world countries. They'd recently started an operation in Monrovia and the city was crawling with western doctors and nurses and coordinators and managers and transporters. Lily had all the documentation and identification to back up the fact that she was a financial planner with the Globa-Doc organization.

The shop man offered her lunch. His mother was butchering a chicken out back, he managed to explain. Lily said no thanks, but did take the packages of beef jerky he managed to scrounge up. Their labels were in Korean, but their dates were good and their packages were sealed, and that was really all that mattered.

He named a total and Lily left the money on the counter, plus a small tip. As she walked out the front door, the young boy ran up to her, quickly grabbing her purchases out of her arms.

"Did anyone -" she started to snap, but he beat her.

"No one touched car. Money," he replied, jogging back to her car and tossing the water and jerky into the backseat for her. She sauntered up to him, glaring the whole time.

"Promise?" she asked, pulling the fifty out again.

"Promise," he answered, holding out his hand.

She'd barely begun to lower the bill when he jumped up and snatched it, running off towards the building without so much as goodbye. She chuckled, watching as he ran out of sight around the shack. It was probably the most money he'd ever seen at one time. It almost made her feel bad.

Almost.

She slid into the front seat but she didn't start the car up right away. She sat for a while, trying to go over everything in her mind. Five long years was coming to a culmination. Five years of planning.

One month of drilling for this exact drive. She should've been focused. All her attention needed to be on the road ahead of her. On pulling everything off with precision.

But she kept thinking back to the night before. Thinking of Marc. Thinking of his touch, of his tongue. His smile. The way he moved. She shivered, letting her eyes fall shut. She couldn't let herself think about it, or the drive would be *very* uncomfortable. He'd been amazing. Should've been just the thing to relieve all the pressure she'd been under.

Only now it seemed like all the pressure she'd been feeling had moved straight to between her legs.

"Three more days," Lily sighed, cracking her neck as she pulled away from the gas station. That would be her mantra. The magic words to keep a blue eyed mercenary from sneaking into her thoughts. Good sex was just good sex – *this* was her life. This was her goal. This was *everything*.

Empty road stretched out in front of her. It didn't take long before she couldn't even see the station in her rear view mirror anymore. Paranoia settled in and she looked in the mirror to double check that no one had pulled out of the gas station behind her. Looked to make sure that no one else was on the road. Looked again to -

"If you move one fucking muscle, I'll blow your goddamn brains out."

One moment, she'd been looking out her back window. The next moment, she was looking into a pair of angry blue eyes. A barrel was shoved against her temple, pressing down in a way that caused her blood to pound behind her right eye. Her hands gripped the steering wheel so hard, her knuckles turned white.

No! No! I only needed three more days!

"That little fucking liar," she growled through gritted teeth.

"A hundred bucks beats fifty, sweetheart. Pull over, this is your stop."

Sweetheart.

"Marc!?" she hissed, so shocked she almost veered off the road.

"I said pull over."

"What the fuck are you doing!? Do you know what Ivanov's gonna do when -"

He cocked the hammer and suddenly things got very serious.

"Pull the fuck over."

Something was *very* wrong. When she'd last seen him, a couple hours before, he'd been flirty and sexy. Sleepy and full of afterglow. Inviting her to join him in Greece. Now he had a cocked, and no doubt loaded, gun pressed to her head and he sounded murderous. She took a deep breath and let it out slowly, her mind racing. What to do, what to do.

"Okay. Okay," she started, keeping her voice low and calm. "I hear you. Can you tell me what's going on? What happened between now and when I last saw you?"

"I think you fucking know."

"I really, really don't."

"Fucking liar," he growled. She started to get mad.

"I've never lied to you. You're the one acting crazy. So why don't you just -"

He slapped the barrel across the back of her head and she yelped in pain, ducking away from him. She felt his fingers in her hair and he forced her back, yanking so hard her eyes watered. The gun went back to her temple.

"I didn't ask to have a goddamn conversation, I asked you to stop the car and get the fuck out."

Lily had never seen, or heard, Marc truly angry before; it was scary, and she'd been in a lot of scary situations. She took a couple more deep breaths. Appealing to their relationship was out of the question. Marc the Master of Sex from the night before was long gone. Marcelle De Sant the Mercenary was in the car, and she didn't like him very much.

"You're going to kick me out here? Do you know what happens to women left on the side of the road in Liberia?" she tried a different tactic, staring at him in the mirror. He was hugging the back of her chair so closely that she couldn't get a good look at his face. Just blue eyes hovering above the edge of her seat.

"I don't give two fucks about what happens to women in Liberia. *Stop the car.*"

No matter how badass a person claims to be, put a loaded, cocked gun to their head and they'll do just about anything they're asked. Lily wasn't really any different, except for the fact that she never stopped thinking. She'd had a whole month to train for that specific drive. A month to plan every aspect of it. To contemplate every possible scenario. So, of course, she'd thought about what she would do in the event she got carjacked. Granted, she'd never imagined that the carjacker would be a man she'd just gotten done fucking, but she figured that didn't really matter, anyway.

I can't believe he'd steal from Ivanov. **From me.** *Slept with me, got me to lower my guard. How did he even find me!? Must have followed me. Stupid, Lily. Fucking stupid. Never again.*

She pulled the car over to the side of the road. Marc ordered her to stay still while he got out of the back, pointing his gun at her the whole time. She had a split second, and could barely move, but in that second she was able to tap a button on the side of the door. He didn't notice. He ordered her to roll down her window, to put her hands where he could see them, and to open her door using the outside handle.

Lily did everything she was told, slowly climbing out of her seat, holding her hands up by her head as she stood. He ordered her to keep her back to him as he moved around her, sliding between her and the car. Then he lowered himself into her seat. She took a deep breath through her nose and closed her eyes.

You can do this. You trained for this. He's nothing to you. Sex is just sex. **He is nothing.** *Just some carjacker. Some piece of shit standing in your way.* **Get him out of your way.**

"There's a kill switch," she barked out. There was silence behind her for a moment, then she heard him shuffle around.

"Why would you tell me that?" he demanded.

"I'm only about ten miles from that gas station. I could probably make it. I want you gone. It's just a job," she replied, keeping her voice steady.

Please please please, take the bait.

"What is it?"

Thank you.

"Underneath the wheel, almost by the pedals. A switch. Three flips. Up, down, up," she completely made up the procedure as she said it. All the while, she eyed the back of the car, using of her peripherals. Estimated how many steps it would take to reach the trunk. She heard him move some more. Could picture what he was doing. Bent forward, face pressed against the steering wheel, one hand feeling down by his feet. Where was the gun? His lap? His left hand? Pointed at her spine?

"I don't feel shit. Which pedal?" he asked, grunting a little.

Gotcha.

"Clutch!" she snapped.

The moment she heard him shift to reach for the clutch, she turned and bolted. Didn't think about the gun. Didn't think about Marc. Just moved as fast as she could to the back of the car. She knew she didn't have a lot of time.

The button she'd hit on her door had popped the trunk. As she came around the end of the car, she yanked it open and immediately reached inside. She pulled back the false bottom, revealing a keypad with a digital screen. Her heart was pounding in her ears, but she didn't hesitate. Even as footsteps ran towards her, she didn't falter. She began hitting buttons and managed to push the last one before she was tackled from the side.

"*Stop it!*" Marc roared as his arms went around her waist. He dove into her with all his weight and they flew to the ground, Lily's hip bearing the brunt of the fall. She grunted as he came down on top of her. They rolled for a minute, a ball of arms and legs, before settling on the hot pavement. Her back was on the ground and he hovered over her.

"You have no idea what you've done. The Bratva is going to gut you. Make that Liberian gang look like a summer camp," she threatened him.

"What the fuck did you just do!?" he demanded, obviously not threatened at all.

"You fucking idiot. You might have just killed us both. If I don't deliver this car to a certain spot, at a certain time, they're going to -"

He backhanded her. It shocked her more than hurt her. Lily had been taking self defense classes for five years. Classes that specialized in combat training, as well as hand to hand combat. But she was pretty sure she'd never once in her life been backhanded, and certainly never by a person she had once considered a friend.

"I asked you a question, you stupid bitch. What did you do in the trunk?" he asked. She wiggled her jaw back and forth. The smack and his split personality had her head reeling – she couldn't wrap her brain around it. It was a literal one-eighty. It was like she'd never met this man before, he was so different from the Marc she knew.

"Am I dreaming?" she asked out loud.

He abruptly got off of her. She slowly sat up, rubbing her cheek. Marc was bent over the trunk, his head invisible. There was a thunking noise and he began to shout.

"No! Goddammit! What the fuck did you do!?"

She wasn't given a chance to answer. Lily was still trying to feel if all her teeth were in place when he steamed up to her. She tried to pull away from him, but he grabbed her arm, roughly hauling her to her feet. He dragged her back to the car. She struggled at first, but when he moved his hand to the back of her head and grabbed a fistful of hair, movement became difficult.

"You're hurting me," she hissed, her hands flying to the one he had in her hair. She dug her nails into his skin, but that only made him pull harder.

"*This*. What the fuck is this!?" he asked, tapping the barrel of his gun against the key pad.

"*That* is a safe."

"Open it."

"No."

"Fucking open it."

"*No.*"

This time, he pressed the barrel underneath her chin.

"Fucking open it or I shoot you right now," he informed her. She laughed. Actually laughed at him.

Alright, Marc, let's play hardball.

"*Do it.*"

"What did you just say?"

"Do it. Kill me. You'll never get it open. I'm the only one with the code."

The gun moved away from her chin, and without warning, he fired it, right at the keypad. Lily shrieked and tried to duck as the bullet ricocheted off. Marc didn't move a muscle, his hand firmly clenched in her hair.

"Are you fucking crazy!? The keypad is bulletproof, you jack ass!" she screamed at him. He scowled into the trunk.

"I can hack this safe."

"Doesn't matter."

"Or I can take it to a chop shop. Buzz right through it."

"Try it."

He yanked on her hair, forcing her head back. She took quick gasps of air through her noise.

"Why? What'll happen!?" he demanded, pulling harder still. She went onto her toes.

"*Explosives!* The safe is lined with explosives! You tamper with it, it blows. You try to crack it, it blows. You try to take it out of the car, it blows. You do *anything* to it, and everyone within a hundred feet of it will have a really shitty fucking day, now get your *fucking hand off of me!*" Lily started to lose it, clawing her nails over his wrist as she tried to jerk free of his hand. A hand that had been so soft the night before, now so rough in the light of day.

He slammed her face down into the trunk. Her nose was an inch from the keypad, his hand shoving her down against the rough up-holstery. She ground her teeth together and pressed her hands flat, pushing back against him, trying to gain some space.

"Listen to me. I need what's in that safe, I need those diamonds. *I need them.* You have to open it. *Now,*" he urged. She couldn't see him, but she narrowed her eyes.

"Why do you need them?"

Keep him talking. Distract him.

"None of your fucking business."

"Fucking thief. Steal the diamonds from the Liberians. Steal them from the Russians. From me. Gonna try to unload them on someone else, then steal them back again? Quite the racket, Marc," she called him out. He lifted her up and slammed her back down again. She squeezed her eyes shut against the pain.

"You don't get to fucking talk to me. Not after what happened, you fucking two faced bitch. *Open the goddamn safe.*"

"You're not exactly endearing yourself to me. In fact, I don't think I'll do shit for you. Go ahead and try to open it. It's too fucking hot out for this bullshit," she spit out at him. She heard him let out a sigh.

"I'm getting those diamonds one way or another, Lily," his voice went soft, which was actually almost scarier than his yelling. She tried to keep calm.

Is my left hand good enough? I should've trained more with it. Maybe I can get it to my right hand quick enough. Fuck. How quick is he? Fuck! Did he see me moving!?

"How? You a bomb expert, too? Back stabbing thief *and* a bomb defuser?" she asked, almost panting. She slid her left hand even clos-er to the side of the trunk.

"Keep 'em coming, sweetheart, I've got fifteen bullets here that are just itching to have a purpose in life. Maybe I'll start by putting one in your right foot, then move up to your left knee. Maybe when I get to your -"

Now!

In almost one fluid motion, she reached her hand underneath a flap of material that was hiding a pistol while at the same time twisting her body and driving her right elbow straight up. She caught him in the side of the face with a sharp crack. His hand moved off of her head and she rolled around, whipping her gun into her right hand as she snapped upright. He came around at the same time, shoving his arm straight out and pointing his gun into her face. Her own gun was pointed right at his throat.

Fuck, now what.

They glared at each other for a moment.

"You have two seconds to walk away from this situation," she breathed, stepping back from the bumper, not lowering her gun. Marc kept his barrel trained on her forehead as he matched her step for step.

"Not gonna happen, princess. Maybe *you* should walk away, you're in over your head," he cautioned her, his tone snide. She smirked at him and kept moving, trying to put some distance between them and the car.

"Really? This *'princess'* just outsmarted you, *twice*, in less than five minutes. I think *you're* in over *your* head, so *back the fuck off*," she growled through clenched teeth.

"Kitty has claws, I like it. But can she pull the trigger?" his tone was questioning as he cocked his head to the side.

That enraged her almost more than anything. More than his deceit. More than his treachery. More than his violence. The disrespect. He'd always treated her as an equal before – now he looked at her and spoke to her like she was a cockroach.

"Try me," Lily snapped back.

He stared at her for a second longer, then did just that – he let his gun lower and he strode forward, pushing past her as he made his way back towards the vehicle. She was stunned.

"I'm taking this car!" he called out. She whirled around, keeping her gun raised.

"No, you're not! Stop right there!" she demanded. He held up his middle finger.

"Go ahead and sto-"

Lily fired her gun right over his head. He froze in place mid-stride, then turned his head to the side so he could see her.   •

"I'm warning you," she cautioned him. He chuckled, but still didn't move.

"You don't have the balls to shoot me."

She lowered her gun a couple inches and fired again, directly between his legs. The bullet pinged into the sand at the edge of the road, right in front of him. When she sighted back on his head, he looked decidedly less confident.

"In two minutes, you won't have balls, either."

Lily didn't want to shoot him, she really didn't. She'd never killed anyone before, and didn't want to start with Marc. She was saving that damnable act for someone very specific. She didn't want to con-demn her soul to hell for some piece of shit traitor. Some con man. *Some liar.*

"Look," his voice was low, his teeth clenched. "I need what's in that trunk. Whatever deal you have with Ivanov, I can make you a better one. I *have* to take those diamonds, or I'm dead."

"And if I let you take them, *I'm* dead. Not winning me over," she replied.

"No, you can just disappear. Drive off into the sunset, find the nearest plane to take you back to L.A., or wherever you're from. Somewhere safe," he suggested.

"Not from L.A., and you have one more minute before I blow your nuts off."

"How did a sweet thing like you get caught up with Ivanov?"

"'*Sweet thing*' just threatened to shoot you in the testicles. Thirty seconds."

"Okay! Okay, just take it easy. Maybe we can work out a deal. I'll split them with you, half and half. Just take them out and we'll divide them up."

"Do you really think I'm stupid enough to fall for that?"

"Was worth a shot."

"Ten, nine, eight, seven, six -"

Lily began counting down, hoping that would scare him into moving. It worked, only not the way she'd been hoping. He abruptly dove to the side. She pulled the trigger, but it was too late. The bullet struck the ground where he'd been standing a moment before, and Marc was now laying beside the car.

Lily jumped forward, ready to run after him, when shots were fired back. She cursed and leapt into the trunk of the car, curling herself up as small as possible. There was a pop and a hiss and she felt the car lean to the side. He'd shot out the tires. More shots went off and she heard bullets ricocheting under the chassis. She screamed and pounded on the bottom of the trunk.

"Explosives! Please stop firing at the *goddamn explosives!*" she shrieked at him.

Everything went silent. Lily waited for a second, then unfolded herself. Slowly climbed out of the trunk, wary of her surroundings, her gun leading the way. Marc was back on his feet and breathing hard, his arms hanging at his sides, his own gun pointing down.

"There. Happy?" he asked, gesturing to the car.

Lily walked fully around to the side, assessing the damage. He'd shot out both tires on the driver's side and apparently shot up into the gas tank and the radiator – both water and gasoline were leaking out from underneath the vehicle. She groaned.

"That was so … stupid …," she breathed.

All of the trunk space was dedicated to the safe. There were no spare tires, and even if there had been, there certainly wasn't a spare radiator. They were ten miles or more from any sort of civilization.

"This car isn't going anywhere. *I'm* not going anywhere. You have no choice. Open the safe," Marc told her.

Lily felt her mind begin to unravel.

Three days. Three more days, and it would've been over. Three more days. And what had to happen? I had to fuck the wrong guy.

"Do you have any idea what you've done!?" she shouted, startling him. "Any idea!? Five years! Five fucking years, down the god-damn drain! *Five fucking years of my life I gave*, just for this day, and now some low life piece of shit has ruined *everything!*"

"I couldn't give a fuck about what you gave up, I need -"

"SHUT UP! SHUT THE FUCK UP!"

"Stop fucking yelling, I -"

"Five years! You think I want to be here!? You think I like working for those pieces of shit? All those days, months, years! I had to …,"

"Jesus, fuck, shut up, I need you -"

"… those fucking disgusting pigs, do you know what it's like to be a woman around them? The kind of shit I had to do to earn their respect? *Do you!?* No, you just fucking show up and flirt and lie and steal and back stab and …,"

"If you don't stop, I'm gonna -"

"… and now it was all for nothing! *Nothing!* You made it all mean nothing! I should fucking kill you! I should fucking put a bullet in your skull! I should -"

Lily was vaguely aware that she was rambling, but she couldn't stop herself. In that moment she felt like she had nothing left to give. He'd taken the last thing she had, and he'd ruined it. Now she was just bad memories and worse decisions.

She was so focused on her unspooling chain of thought that she wasn't paying attention. Mid-rant, he suddenly jabbed his hand forward. One minute, Lily was standing in the African heat, and the next, everything was black.

Which was a vast improvement to how her day was going, anyway.

DAY TWO

Marc stood with his feet wide apart, his arms crossed in front of his chest, staring down at the fire he'd built when the sun had gone down.

Fuck. Fucking bitch. Fuck.

He never shit where he slept. He never mixed business with pleasure. One time. *One time,* and look what happened. She was amazingly good at her job, she must've been hired especially for him.

Catch his attention. Flirt with him. Fuck him. Get him to lower his guard and his inhibitions.

And also lead a fucking cannibalistic group of Liberians to his front door.

"*… I didn't come here with any intentions of sleeping …*"

Clever fucking bitch, she'd come there with the intention of setting him up. Lily, leading them to him. Ivanov, with his "bonus" so big it looked as though Marc had sold the diamonds himself.

Jesus, what ever happened to honor amongst thieves!?

The Bratva didn't want any trouble with the Liberians – their presence in western Africa already wasn't appreciated. If it got out that the heist of such valuable diamonds had been orchestrated by the Bratva, a war between the two criminal organizations would break out. But if the Russians were to, say, contact the Liberians and tell them that a North American man had shown up and tried to sell them some diamonds, it would show goodwill. Of course they didn't buy them, and that would inspire more confidence. And if they even went so far as to point the Liberian's in the thief's direction, even better. That's what Marc figured.

Liberians wanted to kill me because the Russians said I stole and then sold their diamonds. I escaped. Liberians will tell the Bratva. Now both will be after me, both will want me dead – one for revenge, and the other to keep their secret safe. How did all this get so fucking complicated!? Oh yeah. A redhead with nice tits. Fuck me.

Fuck. What to do. *What to do.* He'd figured that his best option would be to convince the Liberians he'd never tried to sell their diamonds, that he'd been hired by the Bratva, and that same Bratva had set everyone up. Turn them against each other. And how to do all this? Get the diamonds back. And where were the diamonds?

He wasn't sure what exactly triggered it. Marc was a smart man, usually very intuitive. It was part of why he was good at his job. He tried to think. What were the Russians planning on doing with the diamonds? Obviously, they had to get them out of Liberia, that was a given – that's where Lily came in; unless it had all been a ruse and she'd only been a hooker hired to con him. But he didn't think so, he'd seen the way she interacted with Ivanov, he'd seen the car she was given. He believed she really was going to drive those diamonds out of Liberia.

It wasn't like a person could just walk across borders with a pocket full of gems. Smuggling blood diamonds was a full time business. A person couldn't just hop on a plane and fly with them. Driving was one of the best options. Lily had a good chance because she looked like a naughty librarian, no one would suspect her of trying to smuggle anything. But still, they wouldn't want to risk more than they had to. She would need a special route to get out of Liberia. No main roads, so definitely no driving along the coast. Would she go North? South? Which country, which way?

Think think think think.

Back at the safe house, when Ivanov had been investigating the stones, Marc had let his eyes wander around the room. There had been a lot of maps. Tons of detailed, topographical maps of Liberia, Guinea, Mali, Mauritania, Algeria, and Morocco. Why? Why would they need such detail? Wouldn't they just need a road map?

Maybe they want roads that no one else will be driving on ...

It was crazy to even imagine. Marc's brain fit the maps together in his mind's eye, like a jigsaw puzzle. North. She was heading northeast, either Morocco, or Algeria. Somewhere with a coast and easy access to boats. Easy access to the southern coast of Europe.

The Bratva were going to smuggle blood diamonds in a car and send them across the wilds of Africa, a lawless place with unforgiving terrain and harsh climates. It was insane. Before that day, Marc wouldn't have been able to picture what kind of person would take on such a feat. Now he could picture the person clearly. A feisty redhead with a bad temper and worse language would definitely be up for the job.

He'd heard her in the gas station; he'd been crouching under the window, ready to kill her. "*Globa-doc*", she'd said, referring to the aide group. It was perfect. It gave her license to move about the country, just an aide worker there to help the people.

His whole plan could have gone wrong. There were several roads out of the city of Monrovia, and Marc hadn't exactly had a lot of time to make his decision. The road he'd stopped her on had seemed like the best choice, it led to an old unused army road that would eventually lead straight into Guinea. It was a good guess, but still a guess. She could've taken another direction entirely.

But she hadn't, and the calm that had fallen over him when he saw the beat up Mercedes pull into the gas station had done wonders for his overrun nervous system. He'd pinned her to a bed the night before; he would fucking nail her to the roof of her car now. She was finished. Over. It would be like stealing candy from a baby.

Wrong.

Turned out Lily was just as feisty out of bed as she was in, and more than capable of defending anything she damn well wanted to.

She was quicker on the draw than him, he could admit that, and she was a good shot, though probably not as good as him. But she certainly wasn't as strong as him, and that's why she was laying in the back of her car, chained up and unconscious.

I don't want to have to hurt her, but I will. I don't want to have to kill her, but I will. See what happens when you play with fire, Lily? I burn down your goddamn house of lies.

Being a mercenary never got any easier.

DAY TWO

Lily woke up abruptly. No slow drift into consciousness, just *bam*, awake and eyes open. She couldn't figure out where she was for a moment. She was staring at an upholstered roof. *Car.* She was in the back of a car. *Her* car. She flicked her eyes towards the driver's side window, but the gun holster that sat above it was completely empty. What was going on?

The diamonds.

She sat up quickly and realized she had a light weight chain wrapped around her waist. Not incredibly tight, but tight enough that it wouldn't fall over her hips or wiggle over her breasts. She followed the length of chain with her eyes and realized it was hanging out the open door at her feet, so she then looked to the front of the car.

Marc was asleep in the driver's seat, and the other end of the chain was wrapped tightly around his right wrist.

Fuck! Fuck fuck fuck. **FUCK.**

It came back to her. He'd been in her backseat. There'd been guns. She'd shot at him. He'd shot at her car. She'd screamed. He'd hit her.

Asshole.

She still couldn't believe it. To go from a night of bonding and mind blowing sex, to him trying to carjack her. That's what she got for trusting a man. Never trust men, she knew the rule. She'd practically invented it. What had she been thinking!?

She had to get loose, get the diamonds, and get away.

Lily carefully got onto her knees and leaned over the seat in front of her. His head was leaned back and to the side, his mouth open. His arms were crossed, and just below them she saw the butt of a gun peeking out of the top of his pants.

Thank god.

Lily slid across the backseat and pushed the door open even further. She got out one foot at a time, moving at an excruciatingly slow pace. Marc had given them a lot of length of chain, luckily, and had strung it through the open doors, making her tangle free as she moved to the front of the car. She let a couple feet worth of chain drop to the ground before she started moving again.

Marc was still asleep, so she knelt on the seat next to him. So slowly, she leaned further towards him. Gently put a hand against the side of his seat. Watched his eyelids for any sign that he was awake. Checked his breathing. Then leaned farther forward, almost so her head was right in front of him.

It was probably the best look she'd gotten at him since she'd left his room the other night. There was dried blood on the side of his head, running from the top of his temple to just underneath his ear – he'd gotten knocked around at some point. He needed to shave. He was dirty. His fingernails were disgusting. Everything about him was *so different.*

Different from what? Not like you really knew him. He was always this disgusting person that's in front of you now, he was just really good at hiding it.

Lily tried to shake her head clear, tried to keep the anger at bay. It was all stupid, his treachery was ultimately irrelevant. It had just been sex. She had a plan to execute. If she could just get to Morocco. Even if she was late, she could still pull it off. She had to. *She had to.* A sexy hitman-slash-diamond-thief-slash-traitor wasn't going to derail her.

Pinching her lips between her teeth, she *oh so slowly* reached her right hand forward. Hovered it above his lap. Moved another inch and was over his belt. Just one more inch and she'd have the gun.

Just as she was about to cover that last inch, though, she glanced up and was faced with a pair of blue eyes watching her. In a flash, he grabbed her by her wrist and thumb, twisting them so hard to the right that she let out a shriek, almost losing her grip on his seat.

"Do you think I'm that stupid?" Marc asked, his voice hoarse.

"*Yes*," she managed to get out through teeth that were clenched in pain. He jerked her arm harder and she had no choice but to turn with the motion. It felt like he was going to break her wrist. She fell to the side, landing on his lap. He managed to hold her wrists together using only one hand and he pinned them to her chest. His other hand went around her throat, squeezing hard enough to let her know he meant business.

"I could've killed you yesterday. I could've killed you in your sleep last night. *You owe me*. I was hoping today you'd be more cooperative," he told her. She squirmed under his hold.

"Probably not going to happen," her voice was a thready whisper.

"I don't give a shit if you've got some sick fetish about playing house with the Bratva, but I'm taking those diamonds, Lily. I *need* those diamonds," he spoke in a tone that brokered no nonsense.

"You don't know shit about what I'm doing, I don't care about any of them. *I* need those diamonds to get on the boat in Morocco," she countered.

"I don't care. Open that safe back there or I'll gut you like a fucking fish."

This wasn't working. It was yesterday on repeat. She needed to change the channel. She remembered their night together and the way he'd reacted to her. Even if it had all been a scam to get close to her, he hadn't faked his hard on. He hadn't faked fucking her like he needed to do it to breathe. He liked her body, he liked her face. How she moved. Maybe she could use that to her advantage. She stopped struggling against his hold, letting herself relax. She rubbed her shoulders back and forth against his lap.

"Look. I'm sure we could work something out. I can make it *really* worth your while if you just walk away," she told him. She tried to keep her voice soft, tried not to glare.

"Really?" he questioned her, his eyebrows raising in surprise.

"We had fun, Marc. Why not have some more fun?"

"Mmmm, that does sound good. Would you strip for me?"

"Oh, yeah."

"Get completely naked?"

"Completely."

"Let me fuck your mouth?"

"Whatever you want."

"What about your ass? Ever been fucked there?"

"No, but I could let you be the first."

Suddenly, his hand squeezed her neck even harder and he yanked her up. She gasped, and for a second she thought he was going to kiss her. But he didn't. He forced her up so they were almost nose to nose.

"If I want your ass, I'll take it. If I want anything else, all I have to do is *take it*. So I don't know why you're '*offering*' yourself to me – as far as you're concerned, you're my goddamned property now, which means if I feel like fucking you, it'll happen. You think this is a fucking game, Lily, and it's not. Now shut the fuck up and *open that goddamn safe*," he growled.

She held her breath for a minute as red washed over her vision. Property!? She was going to kill him, she decided. Maybe not right that moment. Maybe not that day. But by the end of this ordeal, she was going to stand over him and she was going to put a bullet in his skull.

Breathe in. Breathe out. Patience. You waited five years to get this far. You can wait for a couple more days till you can get rid of him.

"Look. Like it or not, we need each other. You want the diamonds. I want the diamonds. I'm the only one who can get them; you're the only one who can get us out of here. You gotta give on something or I'll never open that safe," she laid everything out.

"I could have someone cut into it," he pointed out.

"Explosives."

"I don't think there really are explosives."

"Then go ahead and cut into it. Just please let me go first so I can get at least a mile between us."

The explosives weren't a bluff. The main part of the safe was surrounded by an interesting array of highly combustible materials that only became active when the safe was locked.

"Why do you need to get to Morocco?" Marc asked. She took a deep breath.

"There's a ferry from Tangier, in Morocco, to Barcelona, Spain. Once in Barcelona, I get on a plane to Moscow, where I'm supposed to deliver the diamonds to Anatoly Stankovski – the leader of the Bratva. I can't get on that ferry without showing the diamonds. I *need* to get to Moscow," she stressed. His glare grew more severe.

"Why do you need to -"

"I shared! Now it's your turn!" she shouted. There was a long pause, and she figured he wouldn't do it, but then he opened his mouth.

"Why'd you do it?"

It was a simple question that she didn't understand, but his voice made her pause. Since he'd stopped her the day before, his voice had been hard. Rough. Scary. This was softer. Like he was trying very hard to understand something.

"Do what?" she asked back, keeping her voice level as well.

"You know what you did."

"I have no clue what you're talking about."

"I'm being nice, Lily. I can go back to being mean."

"You can be mean, nice, happy, sad, and any other emotion you can think of – I still won't know what you're talking about."

The hand on her throat moved to cup her jaw, and while she struggled against him, his other hand let go of her wrists, moving to cup the back of her head. He worked his fingers into her hair, getting a good grip.

"I could snap your neck. Are you listening, *Liliana*? I'm not one of those '*no women, no kids*' mercenaries. If you stand in my way, I will get rid of you, simple as that, and right now, you're a huge fucking obstacle that has pissed me off more than should be allowed. Tell me what I want to know. Tell me Ivanov's plan for me. Tell me *everything*."

She paused again, staring up at him. He was dead serious. The way he was holding her head, she could feel it. One quick jerk and it would be over. But she still didn't know what he was asking her, what it was he thought she knew.

"Alright, *Marcelle*. Alright. Please hear me," her voice was almost a whisper. "I don't know what you're talking about, honestly. I don't know what's going on. The last thing I heard Ivanov say about you was what he said in that anteroom, when you were there. The last I saw of you or thought of you was the other night, when I left your room. That's it. I don't know what '*plan*' you're talking about, and if there is a '*plan*', I don't know anything about it."

God, he looked scary when he was mad. She felt his fingers clench and she thought, "*this is it*". She'd heard rumors about him around the safe house. How for the right price he could steal anything. Kill anyone. She held her breath and stared right back at him, refusing to close her eyes. If he was going to kill her, then he would have to live with the memory of her stare.

Not that something like that matters to a heartless killer.

"I don't believe you," he whispered. She let out the breath she'd been holding.

"Doesn't matter what you believe, it's the truth," she replied, then decided to go for it. "In fact, I don't think there's any plan from Ivanov, and I think you know that. I think *this* is your plan. You want to steal those diamonds back and pin it on me. You get away, I get stuck with the blame. Messing with my mind is your pathetic attempt to get me to open that safe."

He shocked her by bursting out laughing.

"You think I'm messing with you so I can steal the diamonds back!? You tried to have me killed! I already stole the diamonds once, why wouldn't I have just taken them then!?" he demanded.

I tried to get him … what!? What the fuck is he talking about!?

"You tell me, Marc! Maybe you waited so it would look like I stole them, or so it would look like we were in on it together, or any number of reasons! You're the con man!" she yelled back at him.

More shocking than him laughing was him letting her go. His hands released her and she didn't hesitate, she jerked upright and scooted as far away from him as the front seat of the car would allow.

"*You* think I'm trying to steal the diamonds," he double checked.

"It's obvious."

"And *I* think you helped them try to kill me."

"I … wait, what? Who? What are you talking about?"

Marc's eyes closed and he leaned his head back. Lily watched him for a second, then reached for the gun. Without looking, he snapped his arm out and his hand was back around her neck.

"Why did you come to my room last night?" he asked, finally looking at her. She pulled at his wrist, trying to break free.

"I thought I was invited," she growled.

"I *never* invited you to my place."

"*To fuck you.* I'm pretty sure the invitation for sex was clear. I went there to fuck you, *alright!?*" she snapped, slicing her nails into the skin around his fingers.

"Ivanov didn't send you?"

"No. He doesn't even know I went there, he told me to go straight to my hotel," she explained. The pressure on her neck eased a little, though he didn't let go.

"He told you that?"

"Yes. That's why he kept me there after you. To change the plan. He decided the exchange wouldn't happen at the safe house, but at my hotel, instead. He kept telling me to go there and to not open the door for anyone but him," she recounted the conversation she'd had with Ivanov.

"He didn't want it happening near the safe house," Marc mumbled, staring out the windshield.

"See? No big plot to kill you. But you – how did you even know I'd go to that gas station, huh? How long have you planning to steal from me? Before, or after, you slept with me!?" Lily demanded. He glanced at her.

"I didn't plan shit. While I was hiding in a mosque I thought about those maps in Ivanov's office. Looked at my own map. Seemed like the best route for you to take was that road. That gas station was the last place you could get water. If you hadn't stopped, I would've stolen a car and come after you. If you hadn't used that road, I would've been fucked. I got lucky," he told her.

"Me, not so much."

"Nope."

There was an awkward pause.

"Get your hand off of me," she finally broke the silence.

"Are you gonna reach for the gun?"

"At some point, yes," she was honest.

He squeezed tight one more time, but then let her go.

"I don't believe you," he said simply. She rubbed at her skin.

"I don't believe you, either," she echoed his statement.

"So we're at a stalemate."

"Yes."

"I need to get those diamonds back," Marc started in a careful voice, his hands moving to grip the steering wheel. "I want to return them to the Liberians – they think I stole the diamonds for myself and sold them to a different gang. That's what Ivanov told them, that's what it looked like when they broke into my room and saw all that fucking money Ivanov gave me. I want to explain to them that the Bratva set *all of us* up. Get me out of the picture, and start a new gang war between them and their rivals, which will make the Russian's little heist go unnoticed."

"You want the Liberians to go after the Bratva," she saw where he was going with his plan.

"Yes."

"Why? You're alive, you're home free. We're only a couple miles from Guinea. Just go away. Never come back. No one will even know," she suggested. It seemed obvious. He shook his head.

"Because a double-cross is still a double-cross. You don't do that, not to me, not in my world. Fuck with my reputation? I want them all to pay. I want to fix this and expose Ivanov. I need the Liberians to finish this, to know what's going on," Marc stated.

"I can't help you," she was honest. "Do you have any idea how long it took me to get here? A woman courier, transporting diamonds for a Bratva? Do you think I was their first choice? You have no idea the things I had to do to get to this point. They won't let me on the ferry without those diamonds, so those stones are coming with me."

Again, another long pause. She could see him struggling with a decision. He glared out the windshield, his eyebrows furrowed together, his fingers tightening even more around the wheel. The leather creaked and shifted.

"You weren't part of the plan to get me killed," he checked. She shook her head.

"No."

"You need the diamonds to get on the boat," he started. She nodded.

"Yes."

"Do you need them to get on the plane?"

She blinked. She hadn't thought about it.

"I … I don't know. I don't think so. It's a commercial plane, Air Swiss."

"So you can technically get to Moscow without them. You just need to show them to get out of Africa."

"Yes, I think that's right. The guy at the docks is supposed to check them, then he'll confirm it with Stankovski, who will then make sure there's a plane ticket waiting for me in Barcelona."

"We can make a deal," Marc began, and his fingers let go of the wheel. "I don't trust you. Even if you didn't knowingly help Ivanov, he used you to get to me, I'm positive. You're still his pawn. But I'll help you get to Morocco. Without this car, you're going to need me. You show the diamonds, you get on your ferry, you make it to Barcelona. I get the diamonds from you, I come back, I set the Liberians against the Bratva. We both get what we need."

Lily kept staring at him. It could work. It could really work. They were at an impasse – he wasn't going to let her go and she was the only one who could get the diamonds. He was right, without a car the going would be rough. She'd probably have to steal one, which would be a lot easier with his help. And having a man along to help, a man who was clearly very well versed in shooting and stealing, would make the whole journey easier.

"Why should I trust you to actually help me?" she asked the million dollar question. Neither of them had a reason to trust each other. Once that safe was open, there was no stopping him from doing whatever he wanted. He was armed. He was bigger. She was chained to his wrist. She had nothing, her only bargaining chip was the safe.

"You shouldn't. But I make a promise, I keep it. That's the best I can do," he replied.

"I want a gun."

His hand went back around her throat.

"I said I keep my promises, not that I'm fucking stupid. Now go open the goddamn safe."

He pushed her backwards, shoving her out of the car. She fell on her back and rolled around to her knees, coughing and hacking. She heard him moving behind her, then his feet were against her back, shoving her again. She growled and crawled forward, hurrying to her feet.

He coiled the chain around his arm as he walked, picking up the slack. He led her around the car, back to the trunk. He'd popped it before he'd gotten out of the car and he eased it open. The shiny key pad blinked up at them. Lily licked her lips. Once she opened it, there was no going back. The explosives would be permanently deactivated. The diamonds would be out, she would be completely at his mercy. She turned to face him.

"Marc," she breathed his name, and it seemed to have an effect on him. He frowned and wouldn't meet her eyes, just kept staring at the safe. "I'm trusting you. I *need* to get to Moscow. I *need* to get on that ferry. You can't possibly understand ... *I have to get there.*"

He simply nodded and gestured at the safe. She took a deep breath. Worst case scenario, he took the diamonds and left her there. What could she do then? Walk back to Monrovia, pray she didn't get killed along the way, and warn the Bratva of his plans. It was the only option. She couldn't sit around playing mind games with him any longer.

"Open it," he growled when she hesitated too long.

"Back away first," she ordered. He finally looked at her again. "Back away. As far as the chain will allow. I'm holding these stones. You keep your distance."

Marc looked like he wanted to argue, badly, but he complied. He slowly backed away from her, spooling out the chain and letting it drop to the ground. When he got as far as the links would allow, he made a big gesture of resting his hand on the butt of his gun. She glared and turned back to the trunk.

There were several sequences of numbers to remember and enter, but after a couple moments the safe was opened. She winced when it happened. It was like a death knoll on her plan. There was no going back to the original plan now. It was all "*winging it*" from there on out. She stared into the trunk, trying to stave off a panic attack. She'd never winged anything in her life.

"What's taking so long!?" Marc yelled, his voice angry. She reached into the safe.

"This is the bribe! For the people at the dock!" she called out, holding up tightly rolled wads of money. She began shoving them into the various pockets on her cargo pants.

After the last of the money was stashed away, she could see it. Underneath a satellite phone and wrapped up in a pashmina was a gallon Ziplock freezer bag. Durable. Waterproof. Air tight. She reached into the safe, started pulling apart the scarf. The stones came into view. Lots of them, of various sizes, a couple as big as three or four carats, though most were smaller. All had the absolute best clarity she'd ever seen.

Her hands started to shake and the panicky feeling was back. This was it. The diamonds were out. He could just snatch them from her. Take them. Take whatever he wanted. He was a man, after all, and men were awful. Men were the worst. Men could do whatever they wanted.

Men were not to be trusted.

The idea had barely formed in Lily's mind when she acted on it. She glanced at Marc while she peeled open the baggie. It was quiet out and the sound carried. She ignored it and began digging her fingers into the stones.

"Hey! *HEY!* What are you doing!?" Marc began running towards her. "We had a deal! *We had a deal!*"

Lily picked out several of the biggest stones she could find and she stood up, shoving them into her mouth at the same time. As the diamonds tumbled over her tongue, she swallowed them. Then she quickly hunched over, working fast to shove the baggie down the front of her pants, working it inside her underwear. Marc reached her just as her hand pulled free and he grabbed her by the shoulders, shaking her hard.

"*Stop it!*" she shrieked, stumbling around on her feet, gripping onto his t-shirt.

"Why would you do that!? Give me the rest!" he demanded.

"*Go fuck yourself!*"

He stopped shaking her, and for a moment she was glad, but then his hand dove down the front of her pants and gladness went away. She screamed and grabbed onto his wrist, yanking her hips back from him. They danced around, weaving back and forth. His fingers were gripping onto the front of her underwear, pulling at them, the baggie just barely out of his reach. She jammed her foot down on his instep, hoping it would get him to back away. Didn't work. He grunted and next thing she knew, she was flying through the air. He body slammed her onto the ground, knocking all the wind out of her. As she tried to catch her breath, he knelt over her and continued his search of her panties. He finally pulled the baggie free and examined it in the sunlight.

"Stupid bitch. *Goddamn stupid bitch.* Why!? I thought we had a fucking deal!" he yelled at her.

"Fuck your deal," she wheezed. He backhanded her, then grabbed her by the chin, forcing her to face him. With his free hand, he pulled a knife out of his pant leg and he pressed it against her throat.

"Fuck with me again and the deal is off. I'll cut those fucking stones out of your stomach, little girl," he hissed. She spit in his face.

Seemed the appropriate response.

One more backhand and he seemed at peace with what had happened. He crawled off her and stumbled away, looking over the remaining diamonds. Lily moaned and rubbed at her jaw for a moment. He wasn't hitting her full force, she was sure, but it was enough force to make it feel like her jaw wanted to fall off at the hinges. She finally got to her feet, keeping her distance from him.

"You can't double cross me. They know the weight of that baggie, you can be sure. They know that there were several three and four carat stones, they'll notice they're missing. Now you need me," she croaked out, dusting off her pants. He glared at her before walking back around the car and getting into the backseat.

"Only for one more day!" he called out. When he stood upright, he had some sort of bag in his hand. He shoved the diamonds into it first, then began loading it up with the bottles of water and jerky she'd bought the day before at the gas station. Her stomach growled loudly.

"What happens in a day?" she asked. He threw the bag over his shoulders. A thick strap went diagonal across his chest and he clipped it shut, securing the pack firmly in place. He yanked on the bindings, making it tighter so it was completely flush with his back.

"You have to go to the bathroom at some point, sweetheart, and any longer than that, I'll go in and get them out myself. *Now move.*"

"Where are we?" she chose to ignore him. They were in a flattened area with bushes and scrub, and she could see trees around them. They looked like they were in the middle of nowhere.

"We're about a thousand feet from the road," he answered, and she assumed it was the truth.

"A thousand feet?" she sought for clarification.

"From where you stopped the car."

"How did we get here?"

"I pushed the car here. You were in the backseat."

"Wow."

"This isn't twenty questions, I told you to move," Marc reminded her, and his hand went back to rest on his gun. She followed the movement, then stared at the gun. *Her* gun. That was *her gun* he was using, her Glock 22. The one she'd bought five years ago, the one that had traveled all over the world with her.

The one that had a very specific destiny.

"Where did you get that?" Lily asked, nodding her head at his waist. He glanced down, and when he looked up again, he was smiling.

"I knew this gun had to be special to you. There were a lot of weapons in that car. Some hidden, some in plain site, but this was the only one being kept in a locked gun case. Why? Must be pretty important to you," Marc had put the pieces together.

"It's just a gun, like any other gun," she tried to play it off.

"It's a gun that you were saving for a special occasion."

"Well, I guess it doesn't matter now, anyway."

"You're right, it doesn't. Now move."

Then he yanked on the chain hard enough to pull her to her knees.

Asshole.

They headed back to the road. Lily kept away from him at first, staying as far back as the chain would allow. She didn't like being close to him. It brought up memories she would rather forget, especially considering their new circumstances. But he didn't like her being that far behind him, so he stopped them and tightened the chain around her waist, making it so she could never be more than three feet from him.

Major asshole.

Once at the road, they started walking down it, farther away from Monrovia. He set a brisk pace, and as they went along, Lily started to feel all her injuries. Her hip hurt, her head throbbed, and she was so thirsty she could barely see straight. She didn't want to say anything to him, but her body wasn't as strong. She stumbled a couple times and managed to keep going, but when she fell to her knees it was a different story. She couldn't get back up.

"What're you playing at now?" he barked out. She shook her head, trying to clear her double vision.

"Water," she panted. He yanked on her chain, almost causing her to collapse.

"What was that!?"

"*Water!* I need … water. It's been a day and a half since I've had anything and we've been walking forever," she yelled back. There was mumbling, and she didn't expect him to comply, but then there he was, squatting in front of her and holding out a bottle of water. She grabbed it.

"Stupid, stupid, stupid. Should've said something. This heat can kill you," he grumbled. She stayed on her knees, one hand against the ground, the other tilting the bottle to her lips. While she sucked down the liquid, she was surprised to feel something cool on her neck. She opened her eyes and realized he was sprinkling water across her back.

"Why are you being nice to me?" she asked, wiping at her mouth.

"Because I don't want to drag a dead body in this heat. Keep moving."

They walked for about two hours without seeing anything. Marc stopped regularly for her, without even asking. Doled out water and jerky for them both. She still felt like shit, but she didn't quite feel like collapsing anymore. And the bastard hadn't tried to kill her yet, so that was a plus.

Yet …

Just barely into their third hour of walking, it happened. A car on the horizon. They were on a straight stretch of road with huge trees and greenery on either side of them. It was humid and hot and for a second, Lily thought it was a mirage. Or heat waves. But no, there was definitely a car headed towards them.

"Just keep walking," Marc instructed, yanking on the chain when she stopped to stare.

"What's going to happen?" she asked.

It was the first time she'd willingly engaged in conversation with him since they'd left her car. She was nervous. Liberia was a dangerous place, and Monrovia even more so – a car heading towards them wasn't necessarily a good thing. She didn't want to go from being chained to a mercenary to being chained up in some gang's basement.

"Nothing. Keep walking. Don't do anything unless I tell you to."

The car was an old beat up Volvo, and was missing a back door, with only a tarp covering it up. It was racing along, and Lily had high hopes it would pass them, but no such luck. The driver slammed on the brakes, the tires squealing and leaving rubber on the asphalt. Marc stopped walking, so Lily stopped walking, scooting behind him a little.

"Marc, what if they -" she started to whisper.

"Not a word. Do whatever I tell you," he hissed back.

Lily watched as two young men got out of the car. They could've been anywhere between eighteen years and thirty. Life hadn't been kind to them. They were sickly skinny, though whether from malnutrition or drugs, she couldn't tell. Both carried large, fully automatic rifles. Both were talking loudly to Marc while gesturing to her.

"Ah!" Marc was smiling, and it was actually scarier than the glare he'd been wearing for most of the day. "You like? You like what you see?" he asked, gesturing at her.

She almost gagged. Something was going on, the men were talking back and forth, speaking in a mish-mash of English, Pidgin, and French. A lot of looks and points and stares were being directed at her. One of the strangers stepped up close to her, reached up to touch her hair.

"I like red," he said in a baritone voice. She yanked away from him.

"What is going on!?" she demanded. They started talking louder and Marc pulled her in front of him.

"This one is dangerous, my friends! She has claws, she scratches, like a cat," he laughed, wrapping an arm around her waist and hugging her close. It was the first time he'd touched her in an intimate manner since their night together in his room.

"What the fuck are you talking about!?" she exclaimed, trying to turn her head back to look at him. The two men laughed, and one of them stretched out an arm, pointing at her chest.

"Yes! Her best feature, I agree. Even better naked, I guarantee. Want a taste?" Marc offered, and Lily was beyond shocked when both his hands came up to cup her breasts.

"*Get your fucking hands off of me!*" she spit out, thrashing around in his grip. The men just laughed even more.

"How much? How much?" they began asking, fishing around in their pants. Lily's anger turned to panic.

"You can't sell me! People know I'm here! You can't do this!" she screamed, full blown fear blossoming in her chest. Marc's hands moved to her waist and he gripped her, squeezing his fingers. She cried out in pain.

"Shut up and trust me," his voice was low near her ear.

"No! No! You fucking liar! Fucking sell me!? *You fucking liar!*" she shrieked, trying to pull away.

"The car!" Marc yelled over her. "Give me the keys, I hand you the girl!"

The men shook their heads, and arguing commenced. Lily grunted and shrieked, still trying to break free from Marc. Eventually, he cuffed her across the back of the head with the gun. The blow ricocheted around in her skull and she doubled over in pain, her hands on the back of her head.

"No deal! No deal! You take cash, or we take girl!" one of the men yelled, and he leveled his gun on Marc's head.

"You give me the car, I give you the girl!" Marc urged.

"No!"

Someone grabbed Lily's hand and she was yanked forward. She screamed and immediately tried to pull away. An arm went around her waist, she was pretty sure it was Marc's, and a tug-o-war game started. She was pulled up and off the ground, one of the stranger's getting his arm around her shoulders. She kicked out her legs and managed to wrap them around Marc's waist and she locked on, holding on for dear life.

"Lily! Calm down!" Marc's voice cut through the pandemonium.

"*ARE YOU FUCKING SERIOUS!? I'M GETTING KID-NAPPED!*" she bellowed.

Despite the commotion – the yelling, the shouting, Lily's high pitched girly shrieking – the sound of a gun being cocked was unmistakable, and it broke through the cacophony. Everyone froze, and when she lifted her head, it was to see Marc pointing her Glock straight ahead. She swallowed thickly and retightened her grip on his waist.

"As you can see, my lady friend here likes to make things difficult. We just need your car," Marc explained in a low voice.

Lily glanced behind her. During the struggle, both men had let go of their guns. Marc had the drop on them, which had possibly been his plan the whole time. Everyone held completely still, eyes bouncing off of each other.

"We put her down," one man offered, his voice quiet.

"*No!* You don't move. Lily, let go of my waist," Marc instructed.

"No, they'll pull me away."

"*Just trust me.*"

She didn't trust him, not at all. But she lowered her feet to the ground.

She'd barely made contact with the asphalt when all hell broke loose. The two men dropped her upper half as they dove for their guns. Marc shouted, then gunfire rang out. Lily cried out, covering her face with her hands.

She didn't know how long it went on for; it felt like forever, but also like it all happened in the blink of an eye. She'd curled into the fetal position, and when she felt a hand on her leg, she screamed and kicked.

"It's me! It's me, you idiot!" Marc shouted, gripping onto her ankle and pulling hard enough to drag her a couple feet towards him. She opened her eyes and he moved to stand over her.

"Where'd they go?" she asked, pushing herself upright.

"You did this," he snapped. "I want you to remember that. If you'd just shut the fuck up once and a while, listen to what I say … *fuck*." He was mumbling, almost talking more to himself than to her. She stood up and turned to face him, then gasped at the sight in front of her.

Both men were dead. One was on his front, thank god. The other, Lily wasn't as lucky. He'd been shot three times in the chest and a fourth bullet had grazed his head, taking a chunk out of his skull. She put a hand over her mouth.

"I'm gonna be sick," she groaned, trying to hold back the vomit. It was one thing to plan a man's death for over five years – it was quite another to see death and destruction laid out in front of her.

"Shut up and come help me," Marc said, yanking on her chain. She stumbled forward.

"I'm not touching them," she replied defiantly.

"Oh, yes, you are. You helped make this mess, so you're sure as shit cleaning it up," he stated.

"I did *what!?* Don't you dare put their deaths on me!" she shouted. "You didn't say anything! You were going to sell me! How did you think I'd react!?" He steamed up to her and lowered himself so his face was right in her face.

"I told you to keep your mouth shut. I told you not to do anything. I wasn't going to sell you. I was *distracting them*, so we could get the car. If you had just listened to what I said and paid attention, these men would be alive right now!"

Lily couldn't believe it. He had hit her. He had chained her to him. He had made her walk for miles. He had ruined her five-years-long plan. And now he was blaming the deaths of two men on her.

Fuck. This.

Despite losing her shit only moments before, Lily was no wilting flower. She had extensive training in hand-to-hand combat. She let out a shriek, and then she headbutted Marc as hard as she possibly could.

The move caught him off guard, and Lily took his stun and used it to her advantage, hiking her leg up and stomping down on his kneecap. He gave a strangled shout, dropping to his knees. She then knotted her fingers in his hair and slammed his forehead onto her own leg, causing him to fly backwards.

She rushed towards him, kicking him in the rib cage. Once, twice, a third and fourth time, but when she went for the fifth stomp, he managed to grab her foot. He twisted and she was completely thrown off balance, falling to the ground.

They rolled around for a minute, Marc trying to get a grip on her flailing limbs, Lily trying to throw her weight around so she could gain the upper hand. It didn't work, and soon enough he had her pinned face down on the ground, the chain wrapped around her neck. He pulled back so hard her spine arched, lifting her chest off the pavement. She gagged and coughed, fingers curling around the links.

"Fucking spit on me, fucking hit me, fucking *headbutted* me!? Where the fuck did you come from!?" he was yelling as he choked her.

Do something or you're going to black out.

He was kneeling over her hips, which put him in close rang. She rammed her elbow back into his solar plexus. He made his own weird gagging noises and pitched forward on top of her. Lily went with it, falling with his weight and letting him roll over her. She scrambled to her knees, and as she did so, she saw it. Her gun. It had fallen free of his pants and was laying on the pavement.

She jumped to her feet, scooping it up. But she didn't even have enough time to cock it before Marc was on her, yanking one of her legs out from underneath her. She fell to one knee and was treated to some of the moves she'd dished out earlier; an elbow straight to her chest. She gasped, pressing a hand to her sternum. His own hand went into her hair, pulling her into a back bend. Keeping her palm flat, she rammed her hand upwards, shoving it up into his nose. He howled and let her go.

She again got to her feet and started to run, but she forgot about the stupid chain. She'd barely made it five feet when she was violently yanked backwards. As she spun around, he slapped her across the face, causing her to fall into the side of the car. She moved quickly, racking the slide and whipping the gun out in front of her, but he grabbed her wrist, keeping the muzzle pointed away from him as she fired off two rounds. He drove his other fist straight for her face, so she jerked to the side, causing him to punch out the passenger window. Then she kneed him in the balls. She expected it to lay him out, but surprisingly, it didn't. He made a funny sound in the back of his throat and his knees buckled, but he didn't go down.

His hand was through the glass, stuck between the jagged shards. His other hand was wrapped around both of her wrists, keeping the gun at bay. When his knees had given out, they'd slammed into her own legs, effectively pinning her into place.

Another standoff.

"You were actually gonna shoot me," he was breathing heavy. She was pleased to see that his nose was bleeding.

"Only in the knee, don't be such a pussy," she panted back at him.

"What was it I said I'd do if you messed with me again?" he

asked, his eyes skating down her body. Lily swallowed thickly.

"You wouldn't," she whispered, remembering his threat to cut the diamonds out of her.

"You tested me. Maybe it's time you found out what kind of man you're dealing with."

Lily slammed all her weight against his outstretched arm, grinding his forearm into the jagged glass. He growled and his grip on her wrists lightened enough that she was able to break free. But he wasn't stunned enough to let her go, and she was knocked to the ground once more. The gun went flying.

It was a clawing, scratching, hair pulling race after that, both of them crawling towards the weapon. She climbed on his back at one point, biting down on his shoulder hard enough that the copper taste of blood stained her tongue. He flipped her over for that trick, but that was fine with her because it meant she was able to kick his legs out from underneath him. He went down as well and she scrambled to get on top of him.

She sat on his chest, her knees on either side of his head, her feet pinning his arms to his side. Then she gave him the best right hook she had, straight across his jaw. With the second punch, she drew blood, and a third, she was positive she'd loosened some teeth. She wasn't given a fourth chance, though; he yanked his arms free and grabbed her by the hips, rolling them so she was underneath him.

They landed on top of the gun. It dug painfully into her spine. They rolled from side to side, both trying to reach under her to get at it. She bucked and moved, trying to shake him off, but he didn't budge. He was even able to lock his knees down tight against her hips, managing to hold her in place. She screamed out as she felt him grip the butt of the gun. Her last hope was to possibly headbutt him again, but to her horror, just as she was lifting her forehead, he was pointing the barrel straight at her. Then he moved it a fraction of an inch and pulled the trigger twice, rapid fire, on either side of her head before pointing the muzzle straight down at her chest, so close, she could feel the heat from it.

"*Don't. Move.*"

It was not a request, and there was nothing soft in his voice. She didn't move, though she couldn't stop her panting. There was also a sharp ringing in both of her ears. She stared at the gun, then stared at his face. He was glaring again. He seemed to always be glaring.

"Do it," she whispered. "You've ruined everything, anyway. Pull the trigger. Not like killing matters to you, right? *Do it.*"

The gun was loaded, the safety was off, and it was cocked. She prepared herself for the end.

But it didn't happen.

"From here on out, *you do what I say*. Now let's get the fuck out of here."

DAY TWO

They drove for hours. They didn't speak at all, except when Lily gave him directions. She showed him where to turn onto a dirt road, which eventually led to the old unused army road. Getting out of Liberia only took a couple hours, but they didn't stop in Guinea. Marc was determined to make the trip as quickly as possible and he didn't want to stop moving, didn't want to run the risk of drawing any attention to them. He stole gas and food along the way wherever he could. He had chained Lily to her seat, not trusting her any farther than he could throw her. She stayed silent, a look of resignation painted on her face.

He could admit it – the chick was good. It wasn't so much the headbutt itself, but the sheer shock that she'd even attempted a move like that was what had stunned him. His knee, his stomach; she knew where to land her blows. After they'd gotten up and dusted themselves off, he'd had to spit out a crown that she'd managed to knock loose. *The girl could hit.* He probably would've lost that fight if she would've ever bothered to learn how to control her temper.

He glanced across the car at her. She'd finally fallen asleep. She almost looked sweet in her sleep. He'd never seen her in repose before; at the safe house she'd always been doing something, on her way in or out, or flirting with him, talking with him. In his room it had been non-stop sex, with him being the one to fall asleep. She was always moving, always going. He wondered what had happened to Lily in her life. What had turned strawberry shortcake into a fighting machine that did dirty work for a Russian Bratva?

And why does she want to get to Moscow so badly?

Whatever her reason, it must have been a doozy. He'd beaten her. He'd captured her. He'd threatened her. And still, she'd swallowed a bunch of diamonds like they were M&Ms and then done her best to kick his ass.

He was impressed.

They passed through Guinea without incident, skirting any cities, and crossed over the border into Mali. It was dark out, and he couldn't keep his eyes open, but he sure as shit wasn't going to let her drive. She'd probably lock the gas pedal in place, then drive his ass right into a lake.

They were on the outskirts of Bamako, the largest city in Mali. Marc didn't want to particularly go through the city – both the Bratva and the Liberian gang would have called allies, asking them to be on the look out for him. Even possibly *them*, at that point. There had been a phone in the safe in her car, no doubt Lily had been meant to check in. On top of that, the car probably had a tracking device in it. He could picture Ivanov losing his mind, wondering why the car was sitting in one place for so long.

Before they could enter Bamako proper, Marc took a detour, driving the car down a dark, muddy road. He was looking for something very specific, and it took about an hour of searching before he found it.

A boarding house.

Sketchy, off the beaten path "hotels", boarding houses tended to be very relaxed. Basically just normal homes, where the owners rented out their spare bedrooms for a little extra cash. The owners often looked the other way from their guests. Marc could probably walk in carrying a dead body, and as long as he paid, they wouldn't ask any questions.

It wasn't ideal. A "sketchy" boarding house was likely to draw other criminal elements, as well. Just what he was looking to avoid. But a proper hotel in a nice part of town wasn't a good idea, either. Lily could, and probably would, create a scene, and not to mention the fact that both of them were banged up and bleeding.

So boarding house it was.

Marc kept Lily close to his side as he talked to the proprietor. There was only one room left, and he took it. All he wanted was a proper shower, which he double and triple checked that they had; running water was a luxury in a lot of places in western Africa.

"*I'm not sleeping with you.*"

They were the first words Lily had spoken to him since they'd gotten off the ground, back in Liberia.

"Don't flatter yourself," he chuckled, leading the way inside their room.

"There's only one bed," she pointed out.

"I hope you like the floor."

"I honestly actually hate you."

"I can live with that," he even laughed as he took in their furniture. The bed had an old fashioned brass frame and he walked over, shoving the flimsy mattress off of it. He uncoiled her leash from his arm, then looped it around the rails of the foot board, several times over, before padlocking it into place.

"Really? Are you that scared of me?" she snapped. He nodded as he took off his pack and tossed it into the bathroom.

"Terrified," he answered. She glared at him. It was a look she wore often and he wondered if she had any idea that it wasn't scary at all. In fact, it was kind of adorable. The way she scrunched up her nose, she looked like an angry kitten.

"What if I have to pee? Or take a shower?" she demanded.

"I'm about to take a shower, feel free to join me," he replied, peeling off his t-shirt. When he pulled it clear from his head, she was looking away from him, a blush staining her cheeks. As memories from their night together rushed back to him, he knew *exactly* what she was thinking. He may have hated her, but showering together suddenly didn't sound so bad.

"I'd rather stink."

"Fine with me."

He walked into the adjoining bathroom but didn't shut the door. He wanted to be able to hear anything she might get up to; hear if she got free and decided to kill him. When he'd stripped naked, he glanced over his shoulder. She was laying on the bed with her back to him, curled into a ball.

Good, she's tired. I won't have to fight with her all night.

He let the water cascade down his body. It wasn't heated, but it felt good. He braced his forearms against the wall and the water spilled down his back. He rubbed at aching muscles and sore bones. Cleaned the blood out of his face and hair. A lot of rusty red water swirled down the drain.

All the jobs I've had over all the years, and Big Red comes the closest to taking me out of anyone I've ever known.

He spent a solid half an hour in the shower, basking in the feeling of being clean. Then he grabbed the t-shirt he'd been wearing all day, washing it as best he could using a bar of soap and rubbing it against the tiles on the wall. He only had one other t-shirt in his bag, his clothing options were limited, and he wanted to take care of them. A million different diseases and bacteria were floating around Africa, cleanliness was a necessity.

He was actually feeling pretty good when he got out of the shower, so it was an even bigger let down when he walked into the main room and saw what she'd been up to. He wasn't sure how she'd done it without him hearing, but she'd managed to get the end frame detached from the main part of the bed. The mattress was resting at a downward angle.

Lily wasn't near the bed. She was sitting in a chair by the windows, the length of chain piled in her lap. Marc was very grateful that he'd had the forethought to put his pack in the bathroom with him – it had the gun and the diamonds in it.

"I stayed," she stated in a strong voice.

"I noticed."

"I did this to prove a point. I could've left. It was a pretty stupid place to chain me. I knew the moment you did it that I could get away. But I didn't. *I stayed*. I want this thing off me, *now*," Lily demanded, yanking at the chains around her waist.

"No," he shook his head.

"I also could've snuck up behind you in the shower and stabbed you with one of these brass fittings. Brained you with one of those lamps. Or easiest of all, just tossed the radio into the water with you. *But I didn't*. I chose to sit here and wait, all to prove that I can be trusted. *Take off the chain*," she urged. Marc walked over to her, one eyebrow cocked up.

"Last time we made a deal you screwed me over," he reminded her.

"So I owe you one. Take off the chain."

"I don't want to be killed in my sleep."

"Me, neither. And I don't want to kill you. I only want to kill one man," her voice fell into a whisper.

Something had changed. Marc couldn't put his finger on it, but in the time it took him to shower, something about her had changed.

"What man?" Marc asked.

"Stankovski."

"Why!?"

"I don't have to tell you anything. Just know that it's not about you. And it's not about me. For *five years* I have been planning that man's death. Five years of my life, just to get this close to him. And where am I now? A fucking boarding house in the middle of nowhere, Mali. *Please*. Just let me do this and I will give you the diamonds," she urged.

Marc stared at her for a while. She had bruises all around her neck from where he'd strangled her with the chain. Bruising down the side of her jaw from where he'd hit her. A light bruise sat above her eyebrow from where she'd headbutted him. He knew there must be more, under her clothes. All bruises he'd put on her, all marks he'd left.

How strange, to go from one night of gentle caressing, to the next full of punches and jabs.

"Tell me why you need to get to Moscow," he replied. She sighed.

"If I tell you, will you remove the chains?"

"Probably not, but it'll get you a step closer to it."

"Fine. But first, get me something to eat."

It would shock most people to learn, but Marc could actually be a charmer when he put his mind to it. It was the middle of the night, but he convinced the owner's wife to let him troll around in their kitchen. He grabbed anything edible and carted it back up to the room. Lily had put the bed frame back together and she sat in the middle of the mattress, waiting for him. He'd chained her to a radiator before he'd left. She couldn't pull that apart.

"I found you food. Spill," he offered, dropping a plate of fruit in front of her.

She dove into the plate, moaning as she lifted the food to her lips. Marc had eaten in the kitchen, but seeing her eat the food like it was the best she'd ever had, watching her lick the juices from her fingertips, had him thinking of something other than her past. He cleared his throat, glaring harder at her.

"I need to get to Moscow," she started to talk around the food in her mouth, "because I need to kill Anatoly Stankovski."

"You know who that is, right?" he checked.

"Yup," she nodded.

"Then you know it's impossible. Stankovski is a very powerful man, and not just in his Bratva – a lot of other brotherhood's look up to him, a lot of crime rings all over the world. Not just anybody can walk up to his house and knock on his door," Marc warned her. It had taken him a lot of jobs before Marc had gotten to meet the big man.

"You think I don't know that? Why do you think I'm here? Because I thought Monrovia would be a great place to catch a tan?" she asked in a snide voice.

"Don't be cute."

"Five years, *Marcelle*. I worked at a bank in Cleveland, so I transferred to a branch in New York. Spread it around that I could launder money. When the right fish took the bait, I was in, filtering money for a gang out of Brighton Beach. I got to know people, started to insinuate myself into certain situations and events. Meanwhile, I took every kind of weapons and defense classes I could find. Eventually, I worked my way all the way to Moscow, though I was never allowed within a mile of Stankovski. This job was going to be my in, my way to prove my loyalty and my worth. Five years, one last job. Get the diamonds to him. Then shoot him in the head. Done."

"Alright, so you've '*trained*'. Why Stankovski?" Marc probed deeper. If he was going to trust her to hold up her end of the bargain, then he had to know everything.

"My sister Kaylee," she answered plainly. "She was kidnapped during a trip to Romania. The FBI and the local authorities were able to track her disappearance to a human slave trade operation being run by Stankovski's Bratva. We tracked her to Moscow, but by the time we got there … well … an autopsy showed that it had been massive trauma to the head. Someone had beaten her with a blunt object of some sort. On top of that, she had massive amounts of heroin in her system. They told us that she probably would've died within a matter of days, anyway," Lily finished her story.

Marc would've liked to have said his heart hurt for her. But he didn't have much of a heart. He'd done a lot of dastardly things in his life. He'd never sold anyone, or beaten a woman to death, but he'd killed people, he'd kidnapped people for ransom, and he'd stolen from people, and he'd never once felt bad about it.

"So your sister got killed. You got it into your head to get revenge. Why Stankovski? A lot of people operate underneath him," he pointed out. She shook her head.

"Pictures. Witnesses. He kept Kaylee for himself. The only reason he beat her was because she tried to escape. She slept in his room, and only his room. He bought her, he force fed her drugs, he raped her, and he beat her to death. I want to *end him*," Lily's voice grew hard. "That special case in the car? That gun you took, my Glock? I bought that gun five years ago, and I made a decision that I wouldn't stop until I'd used it to end him. That Glock has been on every job with me, gone to every country with me, just in case I wound up in that asshole's presence. That Glock represents *everything* I've worked for over the years. So I'd like it back, and I'd like to finish what I started."

Marc stared at her for a second. She was dead serious. She had dedicated five years of her life to killing a man, and Marc had almost ruined that plan. He could understand her frustration a little better now. She was quick with a gun, and deadly with her body, but still. There was something off. Little Lily had no clue what she was getting herself into, not really.

"That's it, huh. Done. You really think it works like that?" he asked, snatching a piece of fruit off her plate and eating it.

"Yeah, I do. Unless some asshole pops up in my backseat and carjacks me and makes me walk a million ... oh yeah, that *did* happen," she snapped.

"Killing someone isn't ever easy. You think you can shoot him in the face and just walk away?" he double checked. There was no hesitation in her answer.

"*Yes.*"

"And even then, you just walk away ... to what? Go back to Cleveland, work at that bank?"

The question seemed to throw her. She sat back as her eyebrows shot up. Clearly, she'd never thought about "*after*", she'd only focused on her anger.

"I ... I don't know. Go home, do something," she stuttered.

"You can go from living a life of crime and danger for the last five years, from kicking a mercenary's ass and killing a mob boss, back to a ranch style house and a white picket fence, two cats in the yard?" he kept pushing.

"Mercenary, huh," she replied. "Is that your polite way of saying *'low down dirty fucking thief'*?" He smirked at her, not taking the bait.

"More like my way of saying jack-of-all-trades. For the right price, I can do just about anything that needs to be done."

"So in theory, I could hire you to kill this guy," she seemed to be thinking out loud.

"No, I wouldn't take this job, not even for twice my usual price. But I could find you someone who would."

"No, thanks. I want my face to be the last one he sees."

"You're making a mistake," he sighed, pulling the now empty plate away from her. "I'm being honest with you – don't do this. It will ruin you. You've never killed anyone, have you?"

"No. But trust me, I want to do this."

"I'm sure you do, but that doesn't mean it's going to be easy, or that it'll end on his door step. That's gonna stick with you forever. You don't want that, Lily. Don't do this. Give me the diamonds, and walk away. Killing him won't bring her back. Someone else will just take his place. Don't do this," Marc urged, as he got off the bed and put the plate outside their door. When he looked back, Lily was refusing to meet his eyes.

"You don't know me, you don't know what I want."

"I know you. We were almost friends," he reminded her. She finally looked at him again.

"You only saw the parts of me I let you see. *You don't know anything.* Now unchain me," she demanded, yanking hard on her restraints. He shook his head.

"No way."

"Marc! I told you my story, I didn't kill you in the shower, what else do I have to do!?" she asked, almost yelling.

"Let me put you on a plane back to the states," he answered.

"Fuck you."

"Fine with me."

"You disgust me," she snarled.

"That's not what you said last night."

"Let's get one thing straight," she started, moving to stand on her knees. "That will *never* happen again, okay? Not only did you turn out to be the biggest asshole I've ever met, but sex just fucks everything up, *clearly*. No sex. Not between us. Not ever again."

"Agreed. Definitely a bad idea. You'd probably stab me right in the middle of an orgasm," he suggested.

"I wouldn't even let it get that far."

"No sex."

"*None*," she repeated herself as she got off the bed. "Now, at least unchain me long enough for me to use the bathroom."

"No. The door stays open, I hold the chain," he informed her. She glared and folded her arms over her chest.

"Fine. But I seriously doubt you're going to want to witness this."

It took a second for the wheels to line up in his head. She had to use the bathroom. It was the middle of the night. She'd swallowed the diamonds early that morning. Hmmm. He tried not to laugh while she continued glaring and he unchained her. As she stomped into the bathroom, he fished some plastic bags out of his backpack.

"Here. They may come in handy," he offered, not able to hold back his smile as he offered the bags. She took them, then slammed the door in his face.

There was no window in the bathroom, so she couldn't escape. He sat on the floor by the front door, in case she tried to make a dash for it. He finished off the rest of the food he'd brought up from the kitchen and waited for her to get done.

She was gone for a long time, almost half an hour. The water was running in the sink for the whole time. When she finally came out, he could feel dampness in the air just from the amount of water she'd let run. She'd washed her face and her arms, and her hair had been tamed back into a normal looking ponytail. She dropped one of the plastic bags on the floor by his feet.

"*Don't. Say. A word,*" she cautioned him before she climbed onto the bed. He leaned forward and picked up the bag, feeling at the bottom of it. There were four substantial sized diamonds sitting inside it. He cackled as he stood up.

"Does swallowing them seem like such a good idea, now?" he laughed at her. She was laying with her back to him and didn't roll over, just held up her arm, giving him the middle finger.

He thought she would put up a fight when he approached her, but she didn't say anything, so he managed to work the chain back around her waist. He then wound the other end around his wrist before laying down next to her.

He wasn't sure how long they rested there. He'd turned out the lights in the room. A flood light from the backyard cast an orange glow into the space, but that was it. He stared up at the ceiling, trying not to think about everything that had happened. Trying not to think about the woman laying next to him.

No sex. No sex. She's a harpy from hell who tried to shoot you and kicked you in the nuts. Why would you want to have sex with that!? Well, she does have nice tits, and the way she went down on - NO SEX.

"Marc," she suddenly said, startling him a little. He'd thought she'd fallen asleep.

"What?" he asked back, his voice loud in the small room.

"We only have two days. Do you really think we'll make it?" she asked.

He realized it was the first time her voice hadn't been combative since he'd made her stop her car.

"Possibly. If there's no hiccups," he answered.

"And if there is a hiccup?"

"Then we'll deal with it. Besides, there can't be only one ferry to Barcelona."

"This has to work, Marc. *You* screwed it up. Now *you* have to make it happen," she whispered. He took a deep breath.

"I don't have to do anything. I just want those diamonds."

DAY THREE

Lily woke up slowly, not sure where she was for a moment. It was warm and humid, but Africa always felt warm and humid to her. She stretched her legs and her feet came into contact with something. She froze and opened her eyes.

She was completely pressed up against Marc's side. He was sleeping on his back, his hands clasped on top of his chest. She was on her side, her forehead actually touching his bicep. She must've rolled into him in her sleep because she'd gone to bed with her back to him, with as much space between them as she could manage.

She sat up, blinking and taking in their room. She couldn't figure out what had woken her up, but there had been something. There was soft light coming in the windows, so she knew the sun was just rising. She scowled and glanced down at her sleeping captor. She reached out to push him awake.

"Marc, are you -" she began to say, but his hand snatched hers, holding it just above his chest.

"Shut up," he hissed.

"Did you hear something, too?" she whispered, ignoring his request.

"*Yes.*"

Bullets ripped through the room, just above their bed. Lily fell against the mattress and Marc's arms went around her as he rolled them off the bed. They landed on the floor, Lily on top of his chest. She covered her ears while his hands covered her head, holding her flat against him.

"What the fuck is going on!?" she shouted.

"Someone found us! Did you fucking do something while I was asleep!?" he shouted back.

"Are you kidding!? I'm chained to you, you idiot! What do you think I did, popped out for a quick phone call!?" she was shrieking.

The bullets stopped and Marc immediately shoved her to the side. He began doing a quick crawl across the floor, like a spider, staying as low as possible without actually slithering. The chain went tight and she was yanked along behind him.

"They're in the back," Marc explained, his voice low as she came up next to him, "but they won't stay there. Some are probably already in the house. We're gonna have to fight our way out. Stay close to me, stay at my back, and stay quiet. If you get in my way, I'll shoot you. If you slow me down, I'll shoot you."

"Unchain me and give me a gun!" she demanded, pulling on the chain for emphasis. He pulled two hand guns out of his bag, but neither of them went to her. One went into the back of his pants, and the other he laid at his feet. Then he pulled her Glock out and it joined the first gun at his back, the butts sticking out above his belt. He took out extra clips, storing them in his pockets. He handed two clips to her and she let out a sigh of relief, expecting a gun of her own to follow. But it didn't. He took out a set of keys and zipped his bag shut.

"Remember, stay at my back," he ordered her as he unlocked the padlock on his wrist. The chain fell free.

"What!? Gun! I need a gun! I can't go out there unarmed! They have a fucking anti-aircraft machine gun out there!" she was almost yelling.

"Deal with it. You're not getting a weapon."

And that was it, he was moving towards their door while he put the bag on his back.

"Hey! Hey! Chain!" she snapped.

He turned just enough to toss the keys at her, but at the same time the machine gun from outside started firing again. Startled, she missed the catch and the keys hit her palm, bouncing to the floor. She watched in dismay as they fell through a crack in the floorboards. She cursed and slammed her fists against the wood, listening as the gun shots died down.

"This is it, sweetheart. Keep up!"

Marc had risen to stand against the wall, a gun in his hand. He yanked open the door, waited a beat, then spun around, the gun out-stretched. Lily stayed flat against the floor, waiting for someone to fire. When nothing happened, she got up and scurried behind him, hunching down and matching him step for step as he made his way down the hall.

"Which way are we going?" she whispered.

"The front."

"Is that a good idea?"

"Have you got a better one!? Just shut up and keep moving!"

There was shouting from the end of the hall and Marc imme-diately hugged the wall closest to them. Lily followed suit, trying to coil all the excess chain around her arm. Whoever was yelling, they were speaking in a language she didn't understand, a mangled sort of French. Marc held still, his head cocked towards the voice.

"Can you understand what they're saying?" she asked.

"What part of '*shut the fuck up*' don't you fucking understand!?" he growled, not looking at her. "*Yes.* He's saying he knows we're here and he knows what I did. He's saying he wants the diamonds. Ask me another question and I'll shoot you in the leg."

Lily kept her mouth shut.

As they got closer to the voice, her breathing picked up. She'd trained in dozens and dozens of classes, but nothing ever compared to real life action. They were heading towards potential death. Those had been real bullets ripping through the building. They were sur-rounded by very angry people with very real guns. She could die. Chances were high that she *would* die.

*No. Not yet. Remember everything you were taught. You have to make it. **You have to**. Trust him to get you out of this. **You have to make it**.*

Marc once again had the gun out in front of him. They got to the end of the hall. Whoever was yelling was right next to them. Lily squeezed her eyes shut tight, pushing her forehead against Marc's shoulder blades. She would kill for a gun, but both of the other ones he had were hidden by the bag on his back. She took a deep breath and stood upright. He glanced at her and she nodded, staring straight ahead.

Well. It was a good life, for the most part. At least I got to have fantastic sex one last time before I died.

Marc held the gun up, at first at the same height as his own head, and then a couple inches higher. He moved it around for a bit, then held it in place. At first she couldn't figure out what he was doing, then she understood, and after a two count beat, he stuck the gun out around the corner.

There was silence, so Marc slowly moved out of the hall, not moving his arm at all. Lily followed suit. The barrel of his gun was pressed into the middle of a tall man's forehead. The man looked cross eyed, staring straight up. Marc cleared his throat and their attacker finally looked at them.

"You have two seconds to drop your gun," Marc warned in a low voice. The man glared.

"Fuck you, *De Sant*. We know who you are, and the whore you've got with you, and we're going -"

BANG.

Lily had heard guns fired before, of course. She'd shot guns plenty of times, in firing ranges. There, in Africa. At Marc, specifically. But it still sounded different when he pulled the trigger.

Maybe because she'd never heard a gun being fired while shoved up against someone's skull. The shot was loud, but she didn't make a peep. Not even when the man's body hit the floor.

"Move. They had to have heard that, they'll be coming," Marc told her.

Lily moved.

They went down the stairs in a crouch, the gun once again leading the way. There was nobody on the bottom floor, but she could hear movement in some of the back rooms. She tried to remember the layout from the night before – there was a large gathering room at the front, where they were in now. Beyond that she had seen a large dining room, which meant there had to be a kitchen, and both were separated from the gathering room by a narrow hallway that possibly let to more rooms. All the guest rooms had been on upper floors.

"How many of them do you think there are?" Lily whispered, crouching behind him when he dropped down next to the entrance to the dining room.

"Not many. Small group, maybe three or four. That's why only one guy was on the stairs. They're trying to scare us, trying to hold us here, till reinforcements arrive. Fucking idiots, I bet they weren't supposed to do anything, probably were just supposed to watch the house, but the temptation to bag such a large catch was too much. Too bad. I'm going to kill all of them and we're going to steal whatever car they came in, ditch that piece of shit we stole yesterday," Marc informed her.

"So only three shooters left?" she asked.

"If we're lucky. It's going to get harder. Two of them are down here, they won't hesitate like our friend upstairs. Stay behind me. Hit the floor if there's gun fire," he instructed.

"Or you could give me a gun and I could help!"

"No. You'll never have a gun while you're at my back. Now shut up, and -"

He never got to finish snapping at her. Bullets peppered the frame of the doorway where they were crouching. She clutched his backpack between her hands, praying for it to end. She'd never pictured it being so loud, so big. A gun fight. It felt like the whole house was shaking.

"Give us diamonds! No one get hurt!"

Marc ducked around the frame, fired five shots, rapid fire, then quickly moved back next to her. More shots were fired from the dining room. He seemed to hold his breath, waiting them out.

"One of them is in the kitchen, firing over a breakfast bar," he whispered when the bullets stopped.

"None others?"

"Not that I could see."

As if that had been a spoken cue, the front door to the house burst open. A screaming man came running in, two machine guns in his hands. Lily didn't even need instructions, she began scrambling backwards as the bullets started flying. Marc did the same, moving double time, shoving up between her legs as they fell into the hallway between the kitchen and gathering room. Marc laid down on top of her, forcing her flat, as he whipped out one of his other guns and began firing it in the direction of the living room.

"Go! Go! Look for a way out!" he was yelling at her.

She yanked herself out from underneath him just as the assailant from the dining room came rushing out. Two bullets to his chest dropped him, but Lily didn't think about that. She pressed her back against a wall and moved down the hall, just as Marc had done earlier.

*Two. That's two dead. If he's right, that means only two more. Man in the living room. Guy with the gun out back. Only two. We can do this. We **are** doing this.*

The machine guns from the living room erupted once again, but she didn't look back. There were three doors – one next to her, one in the opposite wall ahead of her, and one at the end of the hall. Two of them were closed and the one that lead into the kitchen was open. She gripped the door knob next to her, but found she was scared to open it. What if someone jumped out?

The chain was wrapped around her left arm, and she let it fall loose. She doled out about six feet worth, then doubled it, leaving three feet of excess hanging and making the chain seem twice as thick. She cast one glance back at Marc. He was pressed against the same wall as her, and he was reloading his gun. He looked back at her, flicked his eyes to her chain, then back to her face, and he nodded. She could almost hear his voice in her head.

Now or never, sweetheart.

She twisted the knob and shoved open the door. Nobody rushed out, so she dropped into a squat and peeked into the room. A couple heads were peeking back, looking over the top of a large metal desk. The family who owned the house, maybe some renters. One of them stood up, an old man, holding a gun that looked even older than him. Lily held up her hand. A peace offering. There was hesitation, then the man held up his hand as well, and he got back behind the desk. She stood back up, reached in and grabbed the door. As she swung it closed, gun shots started behind her again.

"I said look for a way out, sweetheart, not fucking make friends! *Move your fat ass!*" Marc started shouting.

Fat ass!?

Her success with the first door emboldened her, so Lily dashed to the end of the hall and repeated the act with that door. Broom closet. That just left the kitchen. That made her nervous, because it had open access to the dining room, which meant the living room. Also, the back door was in the kitchen, and it was open by the looks of it. All she had was her three feet of chain.

Fucking mercenary asshole.

There was no one in the kitchen, but the moment she stepped foot in it, the big gun outside started blazing. She hit the floor, dropping her chain and covering her ears. Fuck, it sounded like the gun was *in* the kitchen with her, it was so loud. Bullets ripped everything to shreds, blowing up appliances, taking cupboards off their hinges, hitting the door with such force it bounced shut, hitting her in the leg.

"Stop it!" she started screaming, not even realizing she was doing so. "*Stop it, stop it, stop it!*"

She didn't know if it was because of her pleas or not, but the burst of gun fire ceased. She breathed a sigh of relief, but then gun shots from the living room started. That was a much shorter burst. Footsteps came pounding down the hall and she scurried to get out of the way, crouching in front of shelves, trying to stay hidden. The door slammed open and she held her breath.

"Lily!?" Marc shouted, striding past her.

She grabbed the back of his pants and yanked him down, just as the gunman outside opened fire again. Marc scooted backwards, sitting back against the shelves next to her. He held up his gun.

"I'm out," was all he said. She patted down her legs, found one of the clips, and pulled it out. He slammed the gun down on it, then slapped it against his palm, locking the magazine into place. The shooting outside stopped.

"Man in the living room?" she asked, breathing hard.

"Doesn't exist anymore. What was in the room across the hall?"

"Office. Family who owns the place. No exits."

"Good job. Now to take out this nutter," Marc grumbled, pulling out his second gun from his back. Her Glock fell out of his pants and hit the floor, so she dove to grab it.

"Fucker! It's empty," she hissed, checking the clip. She tucked the useless gun into the back of her own pants.

"It's all yours, I guess," he began crawling towards the back door.

Lily went to move after him, but only got halfway across the floor when she was pulled to a stop. She looked back and saw that her doubled-up chain was caught under the door. She crawled back towards it and began yanking, but it wouldn't come free. It was lodged under the door in such a way that it wouldn't move, and the door wouldn't budge.

"I'm stuck!" she hissed, panic clawing at her chest. If she couldn't move, then she was a sitting duck. She sat back against her heels, pulling at the chain that was looped around her waist.

"I'll come back for you!" Marc snapped.

"No! No! Do not leave me here! You have no clue how many guys there could actually be!" Fuck whispering, Lily was practically yelling now.

"Shut the fuck up!" he yelled back, trying to look out the doorway without being seen.

She was about to respond with something witty and cutting, but she was interrupted by a crazy man that came running, screaming, into the kitchen. She shrieked and scooted backwards, moving herself up against the same shelves as before, watching while the guy leveled a sawed off shotgun on Marc. She didn't even think, she grabbed the closest thing to her and launched it at the shooter's head. A cast iron skillet hit him, causing him to howl in pain. He spun around, catching her in the side of the face with the butt of his gun. It was enough to stun her and send her to the ground. More gun shots were fired while her brain rattled around in her head.

I wonder if I got a concussion when Marc hit me that first day, and this has all been a coma dream?

There was a muffled sort of quiet. She could hear Marc shouting, she could see their new pal dropping to the tiled floor, his weapon clattering on the ground, but it was all sort of surreal. Fuzzy. Blood spread out from the dead gang member's head, spreading across the floor.

She glanced back towards the door, her hearing starting to clear up. She could detect footsteps racing towards them. Another person. She sat up, ignoring the dizziness that swept over her, and grabbed her chain, pulling it as taut as possible. It sprung up at an angle, hovering a couple inches above the floor.

When the man ran through the door, his foot caught on the chain, sending him sprawling to the ground. The force with which he tripped yanked her forward, towards him. He shouted angrily in another language, then saw the chain. He grabbed it and started reeling her into him.

Don't let him get you. Do something, Lily! **Do something!**

The shotgun was near her, so Lily grabbed it, swinging it in a wide arc. The barrel clipped him in the nose, causing him to shout in pain and drop the huge machete he'd been waving. He snatched the end of the gun, trying to pull it from her. Tug-o-war started, and she found herself once again being pulled towards him. So she did the only other thing she could think of – she pulled the trigger.

His hand turned into confetti, blood raining everywhere. The release of tension on the gun caused her to fall flat onto her back. The injured man fell to his side, as well, screaming in pain as he stared at where his hand used to be.

"*You fucking bitch! I kill you! I kill you, fucking bitch!*" he was screaming in English, as well as in his own language, while his remaining hand felt around for his machete.

Lily didn't give him the chance. While still laying flat, she swung the shot gun up, resting it on her chest and pointing it directly in his face. Then she turned her head away and pulled the trigger.

Just like that. No going back now.

She dropped the shot gun and laid still for a moment before opening her eyes. There was yelling outside, but she didn't listen to it. She pulled herself to her feet, still refusing to look down. She walked over to the kitchen door and tried to wiggle it. Nothing. She gave it a savage kick and it popped free, swinging shut. While she was picking up the chain, Marc came jogging back into the kitchen.

She hadn't even realized he'd left.

"Machine gunner outside is dead. What the fuck happened in here!?" he sounded shocked, staring down at the mess on the kitchen floor while he walked back towards her.

"You said four men. *Four men.* That's six, by my count," she said in a low voice, glancing at him.

"I said I was guessing. Did you really shoot that guy?" he asked, coming to stand next to her.

"Yes. Now *unchain me*," she growled, shaking the links in his face.

"I take it all back, princess, maybe you are cut out for this," he chuckled, then shocked her by yanking her close and bending her into a dip, kissing her hard.

She was stunned and she was appalled and she was angry and

she was *so tired*. She slapped at his arms, but didn't have the energy to actively shove him off. He put a lot of force into it, kissing her like it was the last kiss he would ever have in his life.

"Don't do that!" she snapped when he finally let her go.

"Why not!? Aren't you glad to be alive!? We fucking made it!" he actually sounded excited.

"I don't care if you just won the lottery. Don't fucking touch me," she warned him as she stomped across the kitchen.

"Baby, I don't know if you've forgotten, but my tongue has been in a lot more places on you than just your mouth," he reminded her.

"I *had* forgotten. You should've made it memorable when you had the chance. Now get this fucking chain off of me."

Marc chuckled, but didn't reply, and they went outside. There was a large machine gun mounted to the top of a truck. A man hung out the top along side it, a small garden spade sticking out of the side of his neck. Lily shuddered and looked away.

They found a pair of bolt cutters in the back of the truck and Marc set her free. He put the chain into his bag, threatening to lock her up again if she gave him any attitude.

There was a large walkie talkie also in the truck, and they listened to the chatter for a couple minutes, trying to glean some information. What sounded like a small army was headed their way. The gang in Liberia had called in a favor from a gang in Mali. A small group had been sent out immediately to find Marc and Lily – the group that was now bloody and laying all over the boarding house. They were supposed to keep Marc and Lily at their location until the larger group arrived, just like Marc had guessed.

Mission: Failed.

The truck would be stupid to take, the machine gun was bolted to the top. Marc was intent on figuring out how to take it off, but Lily couldn't stand to wait around and watch. She had to get out of there, *now*. Her skin was ready to crawl off her body and run away. She hacked her way through some bushes, and sure enough, another car was parked off to the side behind the truck.

It was an International Scout II, and it was actually in pretty good condition. Nice large tires, it would be perfect for off roading. And best of all, the keys were in the ignition. She climbed behind the wheel and turned the vehicle on, gunning the engine. Marc came out of the brush, his gun raised. She revved the engine again, lifting her hands in a sign of impatience.

"No way! Get the fuck out, I'm driving!" he yelled.

She put the car in reverse and started to back away.

He bitched about being in the passenger seat for the first couple miles, but Lily tuned him out. She had to keep moving, had to keep going forward. Couldn't stop. Couldn't look back. Just go forward.

Morocco. Have to get to Morocco. Don't think about the blood.

Marc produced a map at one point, told her where to turn, what direction to take. They were out of the savanna and heading into true desert. It should've been scary; if the car broke down, if they got lost, if just about anything happened, that was it. African desert in the summer? It wouldn't be pretty. It would be best to stop to get supplies. Stop to reevaluate her plan.

Don't think about the blood. So much blood. It was everywhere. All over the kitchen. All over you. His blood is on you. Blood. On you. Blood. On your face. Blood. On you.

Lily veered off the road, causing Marc to shout out in surprise. She didn't even cut the engine, just slammed on the emergency brake before opening the door and falling to the ground. She managed to crawl a couple feet away from the car before she started vomiting.

She hadn't wanted to kill anybody. Just Stankovski. She'd been stupid to think she could go all five years without hurting anyone else. She realized that, now. Even without Marc fucking everything up, she probably would've run into complications. She was carting around a shit ton of stolen blood diamonds. She was tooling around Africa alone. She was a single woman. Things could've been much worse, really.

Still.

I didn't want to hurt anybody.

"Not so easy, is it, sweetheart?" Marc's voice was soft as he came to stand next to her.

"God, just fuck off!" she yelled, then retched some more. He lowered into a squat and she was shocked when she felt his hand rubbing her back.

"It's okay. It's normal. Did you watch it happen?" he asked. She shook her head, wiping at her mouth with the back of her wrist. He handed her a bottle and she splashed water in her face, trying to wipe away the blood.

"No. Still."

"Yeah. I get it."

"You don't. You're awful."

"I am. But I still get it."

She cried, then. She hated to cry. She had cried at her sister's funeral. Cried when she was officially hired on for Stankovski's Bratva. Those were the only times, in five years.

And now, there she was, in the sand, on the side of the road in Africa, her head pressed to the ground, and she was sobbing.

I didn't want to hurt anybody.

She expected him to be mean. To make fun of her. To possibly leave her on the roadside. But he did none of the above. Marc eventually picked her up. Held her in his arms and walked her around the car. He slid her into the backseat, then went around and got behind the wheel. He sat there for a moment, and she tried to stop shaking.

"It gets easier," was all he said.

Then he started driving.

DAY THREE

Lily was surprised that Marc left her alone for the next couple hours. No smart ass remarks, no threats of violence, no name calling. She laid in the backseat for a while, her tank top pulled up and over her eyes to block out the sun.

Eventually the heat got to her. They hadn't eaten anything, and she hadn't had anything to drink all day. She dug a bottle of water out of his bag, then crawled between the seats to join him up front. She could tell he was looking at her, but she refused to return his stare. She just looked out the window, chugging water.

"Better?" was all he asked. She nodded.

"I just needed a minute."

"… or a couple hours."

"Shut up. Were you always this annoying!?"

"Probably. My good looks just blinded you to it."

She actually laughed. A real laugh, probably for the first time since he'd taken her hostage.

"Probably. Where are we?" she asked, pulling out the map from underneath her.

"Close to Mopti, still in Mali. We have a choice to make," he informed her, and she was shocked.

"You're giving me a say?" she double checked.

"The illusion of one. We can keep heading north, up into Algeria. More desert, more time, but safer. Or we can head west into Mauritania, head up towards the coast. Save time, get us to Tangier quicker, but more dangerous. They'll expect us to go that way," Marc explained. She scowled.

"How much time is '*more time*'?" she questioned.

"Algeria adds around fifteen hours, but either way, we're looking at about two full days. We should've driven through the night," he said. She rolled her eyes.

"You're the one who stopped."

"You needed the rest."

"I was fine."

"It's done," he snapped. "No point in fucking crying about it now."

She glowered for a moment.

"Two days, Marc. How are we supposed to do this?"

"Same plan as before. We'll get you there. You explain that you ran into hostile enemies and had to evade a psychotic mercenary," he said it all with a teasing tone of voice, but really, it was her only option.

"Okay. Okay, we'll have to do that. We have no choice. So let's plan out our next step," she said.

"What do you mean?"

"I need a plan. I can't fly by the seat of my pants. I need to know what we're doing, where we're going. *What's the plan,*" she stressed.

"Depends on which direction you want to go."

She rolled her eyes.

"North. We're already headed in that direction, so let's keep going."

"Okay. We've been on the road since around seven this morning. It's almost … two. That gives us about four more hours of sunlight," he told her.

"Should we be driving at night? Would it be better?" she wondered out loud.

"No, we'd look even more suspicious. We'll go as late as we can.

What's about six hours out from us?" he asked, glancing at the map. She unfolded it more, following different roads with her finger.

"Gossi is about six," she told him.

"Perfect. We'll stop there for the night. Boarding house was a bust. We'll stay in a five star hotel if they have one. Something gated, if we can," he said. She snorted.

"How are we supposed to pay for that? Did you bring your American Express card?"

"No. But you have a lot of money."

"In Moroccan dirhams. I have some West African francs, but not enough to cover a five star hotel," she explained.

"We'll trade in a bundle of those dirhams, that should do fine. Get some dinars, too, for Algeria," he suggested.

"I need this money to -"

"I wasn't asking, Lily. How much do you have?" he barked out.

"I don't know, I didn't ask how much the bribe was."

"Take it out and count it."

She grumbled, but decided to do as she was told. She pulled a roll of money out of a side pocket and counted it out – ten thousand dirhams. There were five bundles total, and she figured they would all be the same, but she grabbed the next bundle anyway, not wanting to hear him bitch. She peeled off the rubber band and unrolled the bills, and was surprised when something fell out of the roll.

"What is this?" she asked out loud, picking up a small electronic item that had a blinking red light.

Marc slammed on the brakes and she shrieked, bracing herself against the dashboard. The back end of the vehicle fish tailed a little, swinging around so when they came to a stop, they were straight across the middle of the road.

"Are you fucking kidding me!? You really are a stupid bitch," he growled, grabbing the item out of her hand and examining it. She gasped.

"Fuck you, you didn't know it was in there, either!" she called him out. He glared, but didn't say anything.

"They were tracking you through the money."

"And … what does that mean for us now?"

"That means at this point, they think we're heading north."

"So?"

"So now we're heading west," Marc grumbled, and he gunned the engine as they started moving again.

Actually, they kept heading north, to a small town called Tonka. Once there, Marc left the device in a tiny hotel.

After that, they hooked west, straight into the desert. In his bag, Marc had a beat up map of the area, much older than the one he'd taken from Lily's car. There was an old Jeep trail on the map, or maybe an old tracker trail, she couldn't tell. Just a dotted line that led through the sand. She was nervous, but trusted him as he drove them off into the night.

They went for hours, just headlights in the sand. She took off her boots and put her bare feet on the dash, sinking down in her seat. She chewed on the side of her thumb nail, then stopped, wondering how long it had been since she'd washed her hands. Since she'd taken a proper shower.

There was so much blood. Who knew the human head could hold so much blood?

"How old were you," she suddenly spoke out loud. Her voice was hoarse, after so many hours of silence.

"Huh?" he asked, looking at her like he'd forgotten she was there.

"How old were you, the first time you killed someone?" she asked in full, turning to look at him. It was dim in the car, but the dash lights cast a glow on his face and she watched as he clenched his jaw for a moment.

"Fifteen."

"Wow, so young."

"It wasn't a job," he filled in. "I wasn't … I wasn't what I am now."

"Then what were you?"

"Young and stupid."

She sighed.

"Tell me your story, Marc."

"Why?"

"Because we have a lot of time to kill, and maybe it'll make me hate you less," she offered, and it earned her a small smile.

"I was born in Haiti," he started, and she was shocked.

"Really? I never would've guessed!"

"My parents were American. They lived in a commune there with a bunch of other American do-gooder hippy types, taught English to local kids, taught people how to farm, how to irrigate, shit like that. We spent four months in Key West every summer, I wasn't exactly a 'local' in Haiti," he explained.

"Your parents were 'do-gooder hippy types' and you're a mercenary. How does something like that happen?" she asked.

"How does a loan officer from Cleveland become a transporter for a Russian Bratva?" he countered.

"Touché. And I wasn't a loan officer. I was in business accounts."

"There was a hurricane, a big one. We lived on the coast, it hit us hard. My parents were killed, along with most of the commune. I was badly injured. I was, *am*, American technically, so I should've been taken out by FEMA or Red Cross, or some shit. But I got carted off with a bunch of the local kids and left in a hospital, unconscious for about two weeks. Took me even longer to get my memory back after I woke up. By then, though, all the aide had pulled out. I didn't know what to do. I was eight, I didn't know anybody in the states, didn't have any family there. My family was dead. I was sent to live at a sort of orphanage. A weird kid who couldn't speak French wasn't high on their list of people to help," he told his story.

"But I've heard you speak French," she pointed out.

"*Oui*. I learned. Ran away from the orphanage when I was twelve. Joined a street gang, did some drug running. When I was fifteen I got mugged while on a run. I shoved a knife into his jugular. Didn't even think about it. He had a gun, I had a knife, I just knew I had to make it count.

"That made me realize I was better than running drugs. I had killed someone. Suddenly, I wasn't a scared little boy anymore. I was a commodity, someone unafraid of death. I stole what earnings there were from the drugs and I got the fuck out of Haiti. Stowed away on a boat to Jamaica, bought an identity while there, then hopped another boat to Puerto Rico. Flew to Miami, then started working my way through the crime circuit there. Honed my craft, you could say," he finished explaining.

"How does a guy go from Miami crime rings to Russian Bratvas?" she was curious. He shrugged.

"I got *really* good at what I do. Pulled off a couple big jobs, worked my way up the east coast. While I was in Jersey, the *Pshenichnikov Bratva* got in touch with me. Hired me for a hit. They liked my work, word spread to other Bratvas. I moved over to Europe and my reputation followed me. Lots of jobs in Armenia, Syria, Ukraine, that whole eastern area leading into Russia."

"How old were you then? When you first got involved with a Bratva?" she was fascinated. Five years had felt like a life time to her, and here was a man who had *literally* spent his whole life in crime.

"*Pshenichnikov*, I was … twenty-two? Twenty-three?" he guessed, rubbing his jaw.

"How old are you now?"

"Thirty."

"Wow."

"Why?"

"You look older."

"*Bitch.*"

She smiled anyway.

"Not too much. But you like it? You really like being this person?" she continued with her questions.

"Obviously. I make a fuck ton of money, I get to see the world, and I literally get to do whatever I want, whenever I want. Yeah, I fucking like it," he chuckled. She was quiet for a minute, mulling over his words.

"You're not doing whatever you want right now," she pointed

out, her voice soft as she went back to looking out the windshield.

"Yeah, well, every job has its moments."

She didn't respond, staring hard at something through the windshield.

"What is that?" she finally asked, leaning forward and trying to get a better look into the distance. Something was twinkling. He leaned forward as well, then barked out a laugh.

"*That* is a town. We're almost home, sweetheart."

Calling it a town was generous – Néma was more like a village. All rocks and sand and donkeys. A couple cars and a couple camels, as well. People stared as their vehicle tooled past. Marc scowled and kept going, and it took hardly any time before they were leaving the village behind them.

"Not stopping?" Lily asked, working to put her boots back on.

"Not in that town. If shit goes down, I don't want a bunch of locals getting shot up. We'll move on. Keep an eye out," he instructed.

Driving through the desert had been slow going, so Lily was happy to finally be on an actual road again. But then after about forty minutes, Marc spotted another dirt road and he immediately turned onto it.

"How do you know where it leads?" Lily asked, trying to unfold the map to see where in the hell they were going.

"I don't, but I know there's a lake around here. I bet there's houses," he told her, turning off the headlights. A half moon was out, lighting them up just enough to see where they were going. Lily struggled to read as they drove along for a while.

"Yeah, okay, there should be a lake."

"Look to your right."

She glanced out her window and sure enough, a body of water had appeared next to them. Moonlight shined across the surface.

"What is it? It just looks like a circle on the map, like a watering hole or something. '*Mahmouda*,'" she sounded out the name as she read it off the map.

"I don't care. There's a road, there's a body of water, and we're in the desert. *Someone* lives out here," Marc sounded positive.

He wasn't wrong. They finally came upon a decent sized home, and luck of all lucks, there was a generator alongside it. Marc drove past, went about a quarter of a mile, then ordered her to wait in the car while he checked out the house.

"*I want a gun.*"

Lily turned to stare at him as he opened his door. He glared back at her. She held her ground. She had earned a weapon, she thought. She'd had his back in that kitchen. She could've done nothing, could've not thrown the skillet, could've not tripped the second guy. She could have a clean conscience, could have lived with knowing she'd done nothing, that she hadn't actively pulled a trigger and ended someone's life.

But she'd done all those things, to save him. To save herself.

She was fully prepared to spew all those thoughts at him, but he capitulated. He yanked one of his guns out, put a fresh magazine in it, thumbed on the safety, and handed it to her. She went to take it, but he held fast.

"I'm trusting you," he said in a soft voice. She nodded.

"I know."

Then he was gone, jogging off into the night.

Lily got out of the car. Stretched her body. Then she climbed onto the hood of the car and knelt so she was leaning against the windshield. She braced her arms on top of the roof and she waited. If Marc had any trouble following him when he came back, she could help.

After about half an hour, a person appeared at the top of the hill. Lily froze, but as he got closer, she recognized it as Marc's form. He had a distinct way of walking, almost a swagger, like he was always carrying weight. Probably from years of wearing a flak jacket and gear and a billion guns on him everywhere he went.

"What did you find?" she whispered, sliding off the hood as he jogged up next to her.

"Exactly what I thought."

"Which is …?"

"*No people.*"

Lily was shocked and she hurried to get back in her seat.

"How did you know there wouldn't be any people?" she asked as he backed up the car, turning it around.

"Because *Eid al-Fitr* is tomorrow," he said, as if that explained anything to her.

"And that means?" she probed.

"It's a Muslim holiday – most of Mauritania, the country we're now in, is Muslim. Eid al-Fitr is the festival that marks the end of Ramadan. Huge celebrations, people break their month-long fasts. This house is so isolated, I figured the people who owned it had probably traveled elsewhere to celebrate with friends or family, like to Mali or Algeria," Marc explained as he pulled up to the house. He'd gotten the gate open during his little excursion and he drove right into the property.

"How do you know they won't come back?" Lily asked.

"I don't, but the festival is tomorrow, so I doubt they'll be coming back anytime soon. At least not until the day after," he guessed. He circled the car around and pointed it towards the gate, then backed up as close to the front door as he could get.

They got out and Lily watched while he ran back to the gate, pushing it closed. Then she leaned back into the car, grabbing his backpack. When she turned around, he was right in front of her, and he plucked the bag out of her hand.

"So much for trust," she snorted.

"I don't think you'll shoot me, but I have no doubt that you'd drive off with those diamonds in a heart beat, given half the chance."

She didn't deny the allegation and followed him up to the front of the house.

He'd picked the lock earlier and left the door open, so they walked right in. She was nervous, but he assured her that he'd "*swept the whole house*" – no one was home.

"Does that thing outside work?" she asked.

A few minutes later and he had the generator going, though he recommended not turning on any of the lights in the front of the house.

"Wanna know the best part?" his voice almost sounded teasing as he lead her down a hallway.

"What?" she asked, leery of nice-Marc. She'd gotten too used to surly-Marc.

"Two separate rooms. You don't have to sully yourself with my presence," he informed her as he pushed open a door and turned on a light.

Lily stayed quiet as she wandered into the room. It was nice, and it was clean. There was an actual bed, and it was made up. There was a window that faced out over the desert behind the house. And it was all hers, apparently.

The same time yesterday, she would've killed for a room of her own. For ten minutes away from him. But now … the idea of being alone felt like a weight. Like something to be dreaded. She didn't want to be alone and close her eyes.

All I see is blood.

"Nice," she managed to say, folding her arms in front of her chest.

"Gee, sweetheart, if I didn't know any better, I'd think you were sad at the idea of being away from me," he said, and this time his voice was definitely teasing. She turned to face him and rolled her eyes.

"What about food?"

They lit candles and tore the kitchen apart. Every non-perishable they could find, they stole, carrying it out to the car. They had saved all their empty water bottles and now refilled them, putting them in the car, as well. No one said it out loud, but she knew they were prepping the vehicle in case they had to leave in a hurry.

She didn't recognize a lot of the food in the house, but she made do with what she could find and scrounged together a dinner of sorts. They sat at a table, one candle between them, and ate together.

"We're leaving at sun up tomorrow," Marc informed her. She

nodded.

"Where to?"

"Boujdour is about a days drive. It's on the coast of Western Sahara. I figure if we drive in shifts, we can make it in one push. Then stay the night, then one more days push to Tangier," he told her. She nodded.

"How is Tangier going to go?" she asked.

"Didn't you have a plan?" he responded.

"Well, yeah, but in my plan, I'd be getting there tomorrow morning. Things are a little different now," she pointed out.

"Same plan, just two days late. You'll drop me off somewhere else, and I'll meet you at the boat. Do everything else the same."

"Don't you think that it's gonna seem kinda odd? I show up out of the blue, two days late, and act like everything is normal?" she questioned his plan.

"Well, yeah. You'll call Ivanov when we get to Tangier and explain to him that you had to shake me. Tell him you shot me, dumped my body in the desert, I don't care. Whatever. You'll be there, and your ferry guy can confirm that you have the diamonds, that's all he'll care about," Marc assured her. She nodded.

"What about you?" she continued. She couldn't stop with the questions, couldn't let the conversation drag. Couldn't let silence fall on her.

"What about me?" he asked around a full mouth as he shoveled in the last of his food.

"I give you the diamonds, then what? Poof? You disappear back into darkest Africa?" she guessed. He nodded.

"Something like that."

"What's your plan?"

"Jesus, is this twenty questions?" he snapped, finally looking at her. She stared at him for a second, at the way the candle light pooled in the bottom of his eyes.

"Just making conversation," she finally answered.

"Is this how you have a conversation? Goddamn, you're nosy," he grumbled, shoving his plate away.

"Well, how do you have a conversation? Grunting and shooting?" she snapped at him as she leaned back in her seat. He finally smiled.

"Sometimes. I don't know. Just talk. About shit. Anything. How old are you?" he asked, wiping a napkin across his lips before tossing it on the table.

"Twenty-seven."

"Huh, I was guessing younger."

"Thank you?"

"So what did you do, before all this?"

"I told you, I worked in a bank."

"I meant your life, Lily. Are you always this boring?" he asked. She threw a fork at him.

"No! I don't know, maybe. I went to college, but left because money at the bank was so good. I graduated from high school. I was a cheerleader, I was voted runner up for homecoming queen. I like old movies and I like reggae music. I like the beach, but I also like to ski. Anything else?" she prattled stuff off.

"Beaches, huh. Where's your favorite place to vacation?" he asked. She thought for a second.

"I don't know, haven't really been on many vacations. I actually like the Oregon coast a lot. Not crazy busy, miles of sand, wild ocean. Maybe like Cannon Beach," she was more thinking out loud than answering him, remembering vacations there from when she was little. Vacations with her family.

"Cannon Beach, I've been there. Good choice. There's this little island off the coast of Tanzania, called Pemba Island. I love it there," Marc sighed. Lily smiled.

"Never heard of it. It's nice?"

"Beautiful. If you like beaches, you'd love it. White sand. Peaceful."

"Sounds nice."

"Maybe," Marc started, running his finger across his plate to catch stray crumbs. "Maybe if we get out of this alive, we can go there."

She raised her eyebrows.

"'*We*'?" she questioned his use of the pronoun. He shrugged, running his crumb finger across his tongue.

"Yeah, why not. This has been a shit job, for both of us. I think we deserve a vacation," he told her. She smiled.

"The other day, you threatened to ... what did you say? '*Gut you like a fish*', I believe were your words. Now you wanna go on vacation with me?" she laughed.

"What can I say, we made a good team today. And I don't feel bad often, but I feel bad about this fucked up situation. A week on a beach in Pemba, on me," he said. She nodded.

"Alright, *Marcelle*. If you can get me through this alive, and you survive your own personal war with the Bratva and the Liberians, I will meet you on Pemba Island, your treat," she agreed.

"Only if you promise to never call me '*Marcelle*' again," he grumbled. She stood up and grabbed their plates, carrying them to a counter.

"Why? Is that not your real name?" she asked.

"No, it's my real name, I just don't care for it," he explained, standing as well.

"Really? I think it's kind of pretty."

"Exactly. Do I look like a '*pretty*' guy?" he asked.

Lily turned back around and leaned against the counter, letting her eyes wander over him. He was dirty, they hadn't had a chance to really clean up since their battle back in Bamako. His arm had started bleeding again, from where it had gotten cut on the window, during their fight back in Liberia. It really should get stitched up. He also had three deep scratches, like he'd gotten hit with shrapnel, just above his right eyebrow. He'd also been mean to her, threatened her, knocked her around, and almost gotten her killed, on several different occasions.

But all she could think about was his story from the car, the boy in Haiti. And the guy in Mali, picking her up from the side of the road and telling her it would get easier. The man from Liberia, making every cell in her body come back to life, after five years of dormancy.

"No," she agreed, her voice soft. "Pretty isn't a word I would use to describe you."

He gave her a tight smile.

"I'm beat. You gonna shower?" he asked, leaning over to blow out the candle.

"Yeah. Yeah, I probably should, I haven't since Liberia," she answered, wrapping her arms around herself and glancing out the window. The dark made her nervous now.

"Okay. I checked, the water tank is full, though I doubt there's hot water. I'll hop in when you're done. If you wake up before me in the morning, come get me, okay? Don't wander around outside. If you hear anything, stay in your room. Block the door. I'll come to you," he gave her instructions.

"Got it."

"See you in the morning."

And just like that, he strode out of the kitchen, leaving her all alone.

Lily scurried to the back of the house. Marc had his door shut. She didn't bother with her room, just went straight into the bathroom and turned on the shower. The room was in the back, as well, so she went ahead and turned on the lights. She didn't want to be in the dark anymore than was necessary.

You were planning on killing someone, anyway. What does it matter if you killed someone else? Someone who was going to kill you, first. No questions asked. It was nothing. It meant nothing.

Lily washed her body first, wincing at every new cut and bruise she found. Then she used soap to wash her hair as best as possible, scrubbing away any trace of blood from every inch of her being.

It meant nothing. It meant nothing. Two more days. Hold it together for two more days. Then you can cry all you want. Two more days.

The shower was basically a stall with no door, and it was built out of stout cement bricks. She sat on the floor and pressed her back against a wall, hugging her knees to her chest. She shoved her forehead against her kneecaps, praying for sleep. Praying to faint. But neither happened. Instead, she did what she hated most.

She cried.

Fake. Phony. All these years. You convinced yourself that you were something you're not. Marcelle De Sant is the real deal, he didn't even blink. But you, you're weak. Crying on a shower floor. How could you think you could do this? So weak.

She wasn't sure how long she was on the floor for; quite a while. Long enough to stop crying, but not long enough for the images of blood to leave her brain. She wanted them to be washed away. To not exist anymore.

"How long have you been like this?"

She lifted her head, startled to find Marc squatting down near her. She stayed hunched over her knees and lifted her hands, slicking her hair out of her face.

"Um, I don't know. I kind of drifted off, sorry. I'll get out, you can get in," she said, twisting away from him and standing up, moving back under the spray.

"Lily, you're no-"

"I can't hear you! Two minutes, can you wait outside? Thanks," she cut him off, raking her nails over her head.

There was silence, and she figured he'd left her alone, but then she heard a squeak and felt him moving right behind her. He grabbed her by the shoulders and forced her to turn around to face him. He was fully dressed, standing in the shower with her.

"Stop," he said simply. She folded her arms across her chest.

"Marc! Get the fuck out!" she snapped. He laughed.

"Babe, I hate to remind you, but I've already seen it," he teased. She shoved at his chest.

"I don't care! This is my space, my time! You had me chained to you for a fucking day, just give me some goddamn space!" she shouted at him.

"I don't think you want that," his voice was soft, and he moved his hands to push her hair over her shoulders.

"I do. I do want that. I just want to be alone," she breathed, letting her hands fall away from him as she dropped her head to his chest.

"What am I going to do with you, sweetheart?" he sighed, wrapping his arms around her.

"You're already done too much. Maybe cutting me a break would be a good idea," she mumbled. He snorted.

"Smart ass."

"I didn't want to kill him," Lily whispered. His fingers trailed up and down her spine.

"I know."

"I only wanted to kill one person. And it wasn't him."

"I know."

"He was going to kill me. He was going to kill you."

"I know."

"But still … I didn't want to kill him."

"*I know.*"

She gripped his t-shirt in her fists.

"Say it again. Tell me it gets easier," she begged. She felt him nod.

"*It gets easier*. You learn to shut it out. To not care. To recognize who deserves it, and who doesn't," he assured her.

"That's what you do? Only kill those who deserve it?" she asked.

"Who *I* think deserve it, yes," he told her. She shuddered.

"You said you would kill me."

"*I was bluffing.*"

When she lifted her head to see if he was joking, he kissed her. She was absolutely floored. She'd figured their night together had been somewhat of a scam. A way for him to figure her out, to learn more about her job, so he could steal the diamonds from her. Then when it had become obvious that he wasn't lying, that he really had been set up, things were too far gone. Everything was fucked. Sex was off limits. It would make everything even worse.

This was a bad idea. A huge, monumentally bad idea. Joking about vacationing together was one thing. Actually sleeping with the man who, a day ago, had threatened her with bodily harm multiple times, and actually hit her several times, was a bad, bad, *bad* idea. He wasn't exactly a guy she could take home to meet her parents.

You can either spend the next two days feeling alone and terrified, or maybe for tonight, you can feel that moment in heaven again. Your choice. Reality or oblivion.

Lily moaned and worked her hands under his wet shirt, dragging the heavy material up his body. He broke away long enough for it to go over his head, then his mouth was on hers again, and it wasn't gentle this time. He gripped her head between his hands, pushing her back against the shower wall, his tongue diving into her mouth.

"You know," he breathed, his mouth moving down to her chest, kissing the tops of her breasts, "the bruises actually look kind of sexy." She looked down, watching as his lips swept over a bruise in the middle of her sternum.

"Shut up. You put most of those there," she pointed out.

"You made me put most of them there, and I'm sure I have more," he retorted.

"You deserved them."

"Shut up."

While he cupped her breasts and nibbled on her nipples, she yanked his belt apart. She didn't even bother with his fly, just shoved her hand down his pants. They both moaned when she grabbed a hold of his hard on, her wet hand slick against his skin, sliding back and forth.

"You know this is a bad idea, right," she checked, her voice barely above a whisper as her hand pumped faster.

"All I know is that if you stop, I actually will kill you," he threatened, resting his forehead against her collarbone.

"This is just sex," she was reminding herself, more than saying it to him

"This is just *amazing* sex," he corrected her.

Before she could say anything else, his mouth was back on hers, and he was pushing his whole body against hers, forcing her into the wall again. She couldn't move her hand anymore, but it didn't matter, because he grabbed her wrist and pulled her free of his pants. Then his hands were on her hips, guiding her out of the shower.

They slipped on the wet floor, sliding into the wall in the hall-way. He wrapped his arms around her waist and picked her up, haul-ing her into her bedroom that way, her legs dangling. Then he put her on her bed before he started peeling off his pants.

"What if someone comes home?" she asked, leaning forward to help him tug at the wet material.

"I'll shoot them," he growled, fighting to get his foot free.

"I thought you only kill people who deserve it?"

"If someone interrupts this, then they deserve it."

He pushed her away, causing her to fall back against the mat-tress. He got his other leg free and he kicked the pants across the rooms, then he stared down at her.

"What?" she asked, propping herself up on her elbows.

"You're so fucking beautiful."

His voice was soft and simple, and it wasn't exactly poetry, but it caused a pain in her chest. The way he'd said it, so candidly. Like he wasn't used to seeing beautiful things.

Like she was a gift.

"*Come here.*"

He practically fell on her, his tongue in her mouth before his knees had even hit the mattress. One hand was on the back of her head, holding her in place, and she felt like he was stealing the air from her lungs.

They rolled around. She pinned him down, kissing his chest while her hand went back to his erection. He moaned, his hand mov-ing over her own, showing her how to touch him. How fast to move.

Then he shoved her away, forcing her onto her back, and he returned the favor. While his tongue learned the contours of her jaw, his hand trailed down her body. Scratched over her stomach. Slid through her wetness. He fluttered his fingers, playing her like a guitar, and she gasped, her hips jerking towards him. He listened to her body's demands and two fingers thrust inside of her, immediately pumping away.

"This is the second time I've had you wet and needy beneath me," he whispered in her ear.

"Count your blessings, it may not happen again," she countered.

He moved away, kissing her collar bone, then the tips of her breasts. Gentle, feathery kisses, all over her stomach. He took his fingers away and she groaned at the loss, then moaned in delight as he kissed her hip bone. Then the top of her bikini line. He forced her legs apart and she held her breath as he kissed the uppermost part of her thigh. But then he moved farther south, kissing and licking all the way to her knee. She began to pant and her hands went to his hair, trying to pull him back up her body.

"What are you trying to tell me," he breathed, moving to her other knee and sucking at the sensitive flesh behind it. She jerked away.

"Please, please, I need you," she panted. He lifted her leg, pointing it straight up, and he stood on his knees, dragging his teeth along her calf at the same time.

"Need me to what?"

He put her leg back down, as wide as it would go and bent at the knee.

"Please, Marc."

"Tell me."

He repeated the same action with her other leg and she was completely open to him.

"*Please.*"

"You're not saying anything."

She couldn't stand it. She felt like she was going to burst. She moved her fingers to her molten hot core, trying to relieve the pressure.

"Anything. I'll say anything, just please."

"Still waiting for the magic words."

She had two fingers inside of herself. Her other hand was cupping her breast. She could feel his hands on her ankles, squeezing for a moment, then he was scratching his way up to her knees. Then back down. Her thighs started to shake.

"God, Marc, *please,* please, just fuck me."

Apparently, those were the magic words. He grabbed her ankles and yanked hard, dragging her down the bed. She gasped, caught by surprise, and before she could even catch her breath, he was slamming inside of her. No pause necessary.

She screamed, clawing her nails down his back hard enough to break skin. He hissed, then clamped his teeth down where her neck met her shoulder.

They were both soaking wet, her in more ways than one, and their skin slid effortlessly against each other. She pressed her hands against either side of his face, kissing him the same way he kissed her, like he was an oxygen tank.

"Fuck, thank you for this. What a way to end a shitty fucking weekend," he groaned, pressing his forehead to hers.

"It's your fault it was shitty," she breathed, licking her lips. He growled and grabbed the back of her knee, roughly yanking her leg up so it was pressed against her chest.

"Shut the fuck up," he snapped, swiveling his hips, his pelvis slapping against her ass. She shrieked in time to his thrusts, turning her head away from him.

"Marc … Marc … I can't … I'm about to … please …," fully formed sentences were out of her reach.

"God, yes, please, I need to feel this again. Your pussy is *magic,*" he swore, lifting his head to look down between their bodies.

His words were too much. Knowing his eyes were on that most intimate part of them was too much. Just picturing him moving in and out of her was too much. She let out a sob, coming hard enough that she was sure her heart actually did stop. All of her muscles locked together in an orgasmic seizure, her body twisting away from him, away from the over stimulation as he continued to move his cock in and out of her.

"Please, please," she whimpered the word over and over again, though she wasn't even sure why.

"See? *Pure magic*," he sighed, kissing her temple.

He moved off of her, and she was too limp to care. He slowly moved her onto her stomach, and she didn't care about that, either. But when his fingers dug into her back, massaging her bruised and aching muscles, she moaned, stretching out underneath him. He moved his hands down to her ass, massaging it as well, then he leaned down, biting the supple flesh. She laughed, then held her breath again when he hiked her leg up to the side. Held herself still as he entered her from behind.

He took it slow, and she was thankful. Then, slowly but surely, her cells started to come to life again. She began to moan and move, working her ass back against his hips. He picked up on her subtle cues and began to thrust harder, faster. When she lifted her head to look over her shoulder, he reached out and grabbed a handful of hair, pulling gently.

"You feel so good to me," she moaned, meeting his eyes.

"Good," he grunted.

"I want you to feel good, too," she told him.

He groaned and pulled harder on her hair, slammed harder against her hips. She went crazy, began spouting off all kinds of filth, saying things she'd never said before; begging him to do things to her that no one else had ever done.

Before long, they were both completely drenched in sweat. He had moved her onto her knees properly, though keeping them wide apart. He put his hands flat on her shoulder blades, forcing her top half flat against the mattress, then he demanded that she touch herself. She complied, working her fingers around herself and him. His one hand moved to grip onto her ass, his fingers digging into her flesh in a way that she knew would leave marks. His other hand held onto her shoulder and he fucked her so hard, she wondered if she'd be able to walk in the morning. She screamed his name, her orgasm coming out of nowhere, it's size shocking her. Her pussy shut down, completely immobilizing him. He shouted as well and jerked forward, coming in the next instant, so hard she felt every burst.

"Fuck. I'm sorry, Lily, but … *fuck*," Mark panted.

"Don't be sorry for that," she breathed as he fell flat on top of her back.

"I couldn't stop," he kept going.

"I didn't want you to."

"You're too much for me."

"Likewise."

They laid that way for a while, and the same calm that had fallen over her the first time they'd had sex was back again. It was like after running a long race, then just laying in the grass. Every muscle, unwinding, pooling into lethargy beneath her skin. She'd been tired and run ragged for the last two days, so crazy sex shouldn't have been a good idea. Right then, though, it felt like the *best idea*.

Eventually, Marc rolled off of her. She moaned and pulled herself off the bed, dragging her feet as she went back into the shower. It was still running and she stepped under the spray, just to rinse off. But a minute later Marc joined her, saying he'd help wash her back.

I should be dead tired! How can he make me want him so bad!?

Despite falling in the shower, twice, they managed to come a couple more times before calling a truce. They seemed to be working out their demons by diving into each others skin, and she was fine with that – it seemed to be working. But she also needed to lay down and get the feeling back in her legs.

"Where do you get all your energy!?" she asked, pulling on one of his t-shirts before she collapsed into bed. He came into her room, carrying a bowl with one hand while hiking up a pair of pants with the other. He left them undone and laid on the bed next to her.

"Just blessed that way," he sighed, holding the bowl out to her. It was full of dates, so she took one.

"I could sleep for days," she told him.

"Too bad. You get six hours."

"Slave driver."

"You love it."

She cleared her throat, toying with her date.

"What does this mean, now?" she asked.

"What do *you* mean?"

"Yesterday, we were ready to kill each other. Tonight, we just had sex for two hours straight. What's tomorrow? Pistols at dawn?" she joked.

"No way," he started laughing. "I've seen you with a gun, you'd win."

"Probably."

"It doesn't mean anything, Lily. It's just sex. I like to fuck. You're amazing. We both feel like shit – this made us feel better. Like I said earlier, we're a good team. We particularly excel in this department," he informed her.

She couldn't deny it.

"Okay. As long as that's all it is – we can't do this again," she stated.

"That's all it can be, and if you say so."

"I do. It'll just make things worse. I only have one plan," she started reminding him. "I have to get there, Marc. I have to kill -"

"You really think you can pull that off?" Marc asked, looking back at her. He was lower on the bed, his head near her thigh.

"Yes."

"You didn't handle earlier so well," he pointed out. She kneed him in the shoulder.

"I handled earlier *just fine*, it was the after I didn't handle so well. During is all that matters. As long as I can get through it, which I already proved that I can, then I'm good," she babbled, trying to convince herself more than anything else.

They were silent for a couple minutes, Marc munching away at the dates. She fiddled with the hem of his shirt, staring at the ceiling.

"You have to change your way of thinking," his gruff voice cut through the silence.

"What do you mean?"

"You're upset that you killed that guy." It was a statement, and she nodded.

"Yes."

"Because you think he didn't deserve it. Because he was just doing a job. Because he was acting under orders. Because it's a human life and that's sacred," Marc filled in. She was surprised; he'd captured her thoughts perfectly.

"Yeah, all of that," she agreed.

"And that's all true, but if you think of it that way, it'll drive you crazy."

"I figured that much out, but it doesn't stop it from being true."

"No, but think of it this way. How many people had that man killed? How many women had he raped? How many drugs had he sold? How many lives had he helped to ruin?" Marc prattled off questions.

"But you don't know if any of that's true," she pointed out. He burst out laughing.

"You really are fucking stupid. Do you know what the gangs are like over here? Didn't you listen when I told you what I saw in Liberia? There's no law out here, sweetheart. If he's in a gang, he's done bad shit. Where do you think your diamonds came from?" he asked, glancing up at her again.

"My … what?" she was caught off guard.

"Those diamonds. Your precious passport to Moscow. So intent on avenging the unjust murder of your sister," Marc said in a comically serious voice. "How many people do you think died for those stones? Those are the clearest diamonds to ever come out of the Ivory Coast, do you think they were taken willingly? No. They were taken from another outfit, who got them from somewhere else, leading all the way back to a mine. Who do you think works that mine? Happy little elves? Whistling away? Try kids. Sick people. Indentured slaves. And it's not exactly fun work," Marc enlightened her. She furrowed her brow.

"That's not my battle. I came here for one reason, not to save the world," she snapped. He chuckled and tossed a date into the air, catching it in his mouth.

"Now you're talking like a mercenary."

She didn't know whether that made her happy or sad.

"That's the goal, I suppose."

"So now that you're on this road to a heartless act of violence, do you think you can go back to your old life?" he repeated his question from the other day. She sighed, rubbing her hands down her face.

"I don't know. I thought I could. After today … I don't know. I can't unsee all that. How am I supposed to go back to working in a bank?" she asked, spearing her hands through her hair. He moved and she heard the bowl clatter on the floor.

"You don't," he said it as if it was simple.

"Then what do I do?"

"This."

"What?"

"*This.*"

It actually took her a second to catch on.

"Keep doing what I've been doing?" she checked. His arm moved and he laid it between her legs, gripping her right foot in his hand and massaging her arch.

"Why not? You're good at it, obviously. You're going through hell, and when you come out the other side, you'll be even better. You can get paid a lot of money for the things you'll be able to do," he explained.

"But do I want to do those things?" she whispered.

"You don't have to kill. You can keep transporting. Keep laundering. Keep moving," he suggested.

"Hmmm," was all she said in response. He cleared his throat, squeezing her foot.

"How long have we known each other now?" he asked. She was thrown for a second and had to think.

"I don't know, like five weeks?" she tried to think back over the days.

"That long? Jesus, think of all the naked time we missed out on. I should've fucked you on the first day."

"Shoulda, coulda, woulda."

"Know what the first thing I thought was, when I saw you?" he switched again. She smiled.

"I'm almost scared to ask."

"I thought you were an escort."

She kneed his shoulder again.

"Shut up."

"No, really. You were so clean, and so gorgeous. What the fuck was someone like you doing at a Bratva safe house, in Africa of all places? All that creamy skin, that dark red hair. Naughty accountant, that was my other thought," he told her.

"Pretty close. Naughty banker," she corrected him, laughing.

"What I'm trying to say is 'badass bitch who will shoot first and ask questions later' does not come to mind when someone looks at you. That's good. You're unassuming looking. You can go a lot of places a guy like me can't," he explained. She nodded.

"I hadn't thought of it that way. You *do* look like a badass bitch who will shoot first," she agreed. His fingers dug into the bottom of her foot and she yelped, yanking away. Both of them laughed and he rubbed away the sting.

"Exactly. Think of the damage we could do *together*."

Lily went completely still, soaking in his words.

"What are you saying?" she asked in a low voice.

"I told you – we make a great team," he repeated.

She sat up, looking down at him.

"Are you serious? Are you asking me to, like, be your partner in crime?" she was shocked. He shrugged.

"Sort of. I can help you, I can make you better. You can take jobs.

If I need your help on something, I can call you. You need my help, you can call me," he broke it down.

Lily was beyond shocked. She laid back down, trying to focus on the ceiling.

Five years. After Stankovski was dead, the plan had been to go back home. See her parents for the first time in two years. See her friends, if she still had any. Try to go back to some form of normalcy.

But now, when she really tried to picture it, she couldn't. What, she was going to blow a man's head off, then go sit down to Thanksgiving dinner? Work nine-to-five in some bank, after days and years of traveling the world? Going where she wanted, when she wanted, because she knew she had the weight of something bigger than herself to back her up.

What had Marc said earlier? *Lawless.* That's what she was now. Could she go back to living within the law? It was like asking a wolf to go back and live as a house dog. She'd run wild for too long. Maybe she wasn't fit to live in society anymore.

"I don't know, Marc," she whispered. "I don't know what I want anymore."

He shifted around on the mattress, then he was crawling over her. He pushed the shirt up as he went, running his tongue along her breast bone. She let him push and yank the material over her head and free of her arms.

"It's not like you have to make a decision now, Lily. Get to Morocco first, get on that ferry. If you can do it, if you can kill him, then maybe you'll know what you want," he suggested, laying his full weight on her and kissing the side of her neck. She sighed and wrapped her arms around his shoulders.

"*If* I can, huh. A lot of faith you have in me," she pointed out his phrasing. He held still for a moment, then his lips moved down to her shoulder.

"You don't have to do it," he whispered.

"What?"

"You don't have to do this," he repeated himself. "You don't have to do any of it."

"Wait," she was almost more shocked than when he'd offered her a partnership. She pushed at his shoulders, forcing him to lean away from her. "What are you saying!?"

"I'm saying, you don't have to do this. Remember what you told me, back before the boarding house? I could just walk away," he started to explain, his fingers drawing lazy circles around one of her nipples. She grabbed his hand.

"Walking away?"

"Those diamonds, Lily. Do you have any idea how much they're worth?" he asked. She shook her head.

"No. I mean, a lot, obviously, I understand that, but not the exact amount," she explained.

"Millions. So many millions of dollars. We could turn into something else. No one would ever know. Lily and Marc wouldn't exist anymore," he told her.

"Wait. Wait, wait, wait. You're suggesting we … run away together? Keep the diamonds, sell them ourselves?" she checked.

"Basically."

"*You* want to run away *with me?*" She was officially beyond shocked.

"Jesus, I'm not asking you to get married. We could leave, split up the diamonds, and never speak again. Or we could go off and fuck for the next three years. I'm just trying to say, *we don't need to be these people anymore*," he stressed.

She finally looked straight up at him and he was glaring back down at her. She couldn't believe what she was hearing. How had they gotten to this point?

He had described the first time he'd seen her; she tried to remember the first time she'd seen him. It had only been her second day in Africa, and she'd been taking a tour of the safe house. The compound had a large backyard that wrapped around the side of the house, which was where her car had been kept. While being walked to it, she had seen him.

Of course he caught her eye. He was a commanding presence, even when he wasn't moving or saying anything. But when he was moving, when he was in action, he was impossible not to notice. He'd been carrying a large bag across the yard, laughing loudly with one of the bodyguards. He'd glanced at Lily and their eyes had caught for a moment. Just a moment. He hadn't been able to guess what her job was, but she'd known immediately what purpose he was serving for the Bratva.

He's so strong. He could do it. He could just take it all and leave everything behind. Even take me with him. Take everything.

"I can't," she choked out, then cleared her throat. "I just can't. Five years. I made promises to yesterday. I can't start giving away my tomorrows."

Marc nodded and looked away from her, staring at the wall for a second. Then over her head, around the room. Then he nodded again and looked back down at her.

"Okay then. We'll get you to Moscow," he said, his voice strong and clear. She let out a breath that she hadn't realized she'd been holding.

"Thank you, Marc."

"And technically, since we've already had sex tonight, and it's *still* tonight," his voice lowered to a growl and he laid back down on her, his teeth on her collar bone, "then the '*no sex*' thing doesn't start back up till tomorrow."

She laughed and scratched her nails across his shoulder blades.

"Only because you said it so nicely."

DAY FOUR

Lily sat up in bed, hugging the blanket to her chest. She shoved her hair out of her face and looked around. The room was empty.

She went to call out for Marc, but then thought better of it and stood up, shuffling across the room. They'd washed their clothes the night before, scrubbing them in the shower. Marc had stressed the importance of keeping their clothes as clean as possible – neither of them had anything else to wear, and they couldn't afford to get infections in any of the multiple wounds they both had peppered across their bodies.

She cursed at herself for not asking Marc for a weapon the night before; all she had was her Glock, which was empty. She tucked it into her belt anyway, figuring loaded or not loaded, it was at least scary looking.

She crept into the hallway, staying silent and listening to the house. There was no noise, so she kept moving. She went through every room with her gun out, but she was alone in the building. She stood in the bathroom, her hands on her hips, wondering where the fuck he'd gone.

He wouldn't …

She ran back into his room, shoving through the door. It was empty, the bed made up. Of course it was, he hadn't slept in it. He'd spent the whole night with her. But there was nothing else in the room. No weapons, no clothing, and not his stupid backpack.

He didn't!

She ran through the house, not even worrying if anyone was outside. Somewhere in the back of her mind, she already knew what was waiting out there.

He couldn't.

Lily burst into the front yard, skidding on the pebbles and loose rocks. She bent forward, her hands on her thighs, breathing hard. Her gun fell to the ground. Then she followed suit, dropping to her knees. She shoved her hands into her hair, pulling at the roots.

"He did," she sighed, staring at the empty driveway.

No car.

No Marc.

No anything.

Lily sighed, sipping at the coffee she'd managed to make. She wedged the cup behind her foot, then adjusted the white sheet she had draped over her. It was helping to keep the sun at bay.

She was sitting on the roof of the house. It was the best vantage point, she figured. The house was at the top of a small hill. She could see for miles in every direction, so she would know a car was coming before they'd know she was at the house.

The owners had to turn up at some point. And if they didn't, maybe she'd luck out and another car would drive past. The dirt road they were on seemed to circle back around to the main road, and further down the way, she saw another house.

Someone *had* to go by at some point.

She wanted to be angry at Marc, but she wasn't. She was angry at herself. She'd fallen for it *again*. A nice body and good dick, good god, Lily. She expected better from herself. He'd lulled her right back into that secure feeling, all those touches, all those words.

"… we don't need to be these people anymore …"

The man was good. She'd completely fallen for it. She'd believed him, every word. Such an awful day. Such a wonderful night. Her soul had been begging to hear someone talk to her that way.

What would he have done if she'd taken him up on it?

He was gone. He'd taken the car and the diamonds. All the weapons. Everything. He was probably in a whole different country already, probably back in Mali. Meanwhile, she was alone in a house in a strange country, with no means of communications. No way to defend herself. Almost no food left, as well.

Whenever the home owners returned, she would have to steal their car. Have to pray that her empty Glock would be enough to scare them. She felt bad, leaving them carless, but she had to get out of there. Had to get anywhere else, she still had all the money in her pants, and then make a plan. Figure out what she could do next. What options were left to her.

She went to take another sip of coffee, then nearly dropped the mug. There was a dust trail way off in the distance, and it was heading her way. She'd been out there for two hours and nothing in the desert had moved. It could only be one thing.

Lily scrambled to the back of the roof, then cursed. She'd found a wooden ladder on the side of the house and had used it to climb to her perch. It had gotten knocked over somehow and was now resting on the ground.

She chucked the sheet down first, then sat down, her legs dangling over the side of the house. Praying that all those hours in the gym had really paid off, she gripped the edge of the roof and slowly twisted, careful as she lowered herself.

Her arms did her proud and she was able to lower herself till she was dangling. It was only a one story, so she dropped to the ground. She kept swearing under her breath, wondering how long that little jaunt had taken her. Then she climbed through the window into her bedroom, fighting with the curtains.

Just as she broke free of the fabric, she heard the front door open. She cursed. Some "*badass*" she was turning out to be; she was useless without Marc. Her plan was falling to shit. Keeping her footsteps light, she dashed across the room, pressing her back against the wall by the door. She held the Glock up by her head and she tried to catch her breath. Tried to slow her heart beat.

You can do this. **You can do this.** *You killed a gang member yesterday. You can take some family hostage. You got this.*

Heavy footsteps moved through the house. Slowly, almost like the person was looking for something. Maybe it wasn't the homeowner. Maybe it was a Bratva member, someone who'd tracked her down.

It didn't matter. She widened her stance, ready to pivot forward, all her weight on her right leg. She locked her arms into place, ready to snap the gun out. She wouldn't go down without a fight. She wouldn't let herself be taken.

The footsteps were in the hall, outside the other bedroom. Pause. Then they moved, drawing nearer. Paused outside her door. Lily held her breath, stared at the ceiling for a second. Said a small prayer. Then she heard it.

The knob started to turn.

She spun around as the door fell open and she shoved her gun forward, holding it up at an angle. It pushed up underneath a chin and she made a big show of racking the slide. Everything froze.

"If I didn't know any better, I'd say you missed me, *sweetheart.*"

Marc was smiling, but Lily kept the gun in place.

"You left me," she hissed.

"That gun isn't loaded."

Five years of training with that specific gun hadn't gone to waste. Almost faster than either of them could blink, she yanked the gun away, ripped off the slide, and shoved the frame into the side of his neck. She braced her free hand behind it, her palm flat against the back of the gun. One sharp shove and an arterial spray would redecorate the walls of the room.

"Still a weapon. Where the fuck did you go!?" she demanded. He blinked down at her, standing completely still.

"You were snoring like a fucking pig, I decided to go do some recon," he explained. She glared.

"I don't snore. Why didn't you wake me up?"

"Princess, I -"

She jerked against the frame, causing him to choke on his words.

"*My fucking name is Lily!*"

"Alright, *Lily*, I went to go search the other houses to see if I could find a phone. I drove back to Néma to see if I could get some ammo, some more guns," he explained, his voice soft as he raised his hands, holding them up like he was under arrest.

"Why didn't you take me with you?" she asked.

"You were asleep."

"Fucking liar."

"It's the truth."

"You should've woken me up," she told him. He smiled at her.

"I'm realizing that now."

She hesitated. Should never hesitate. But she wasn't sure whether or not she should believe him. His story sounded legit – he'd come back, after all. And in that moment of trying to decide, he saw her hesitance, and he acted.

And that's why he's better than you.

He grabbed her wrist, twisting the gun away from his throat. She was forced to move with her arm, and in another instant she was bent over in front of him, her wrists secured behind her back.

"Jesus, I'm impressed, sweetheart! Talk about getting the drop on me. I thought this was going to become a permanent part of my anatomy," Marc chuckled, and she saw the gun frame get tossed onto the bed.

"Obviously wasn't good enough," she snapped, struggling against his hold. He jerked harder on her arms, forcing her head even lower. She couldn't maintain her balance, she was almost completely bent in half. If he let her go, she would fall on her face.

"I don't know. This is working out pretty good for me," he said, and she felt his hand move across her ass. She tried to jerk away.

"*Cut it out!*"

He finally let her go, helping her to stand upright. She pulled away from him, made a production of straightening out her clothing.

"I was serious," he said, heading back into the living room. Lily followed and watched as he picked up a large bag. "That was good, using the gun was good. If I was a stranger, you would've scared the shit out of me."

"I still don't understand why you didn't wake me up," she grumbled, standing next to him when he dropped the bag on a table.

"Because you look adorable when you sleep."

"Fuck off."

He opened the bag, and Lily's eyes bulged as she took in the array of weapons and ammo that were inside. He tossed a box to her and she caught it, looking it over. Bullets that would fit in her Glock.

"I also got us some jugs, we can fill them up with water and gas, I saw some drums out back. I'll get started on that while you sort this shit out," Marc told her.

It was a huge gesture. He'd just barely trusted her with a loaded gun the night before – now he was leaving her with a whole bag full of weapons. He went to head back towards the front door and Lily grabbed his shirt, stopping him before he could get past her.

"I thought you left me," she stated it simply, but hoped her voice conveyed how upset she really was. His brows furrowed together.

"I only went -" he started, but she shook her head.

"You took everything. The car. The guns. *The diamonds.* Everything. I thought you had lied, and I thought you had left me. *Don't do it again,*" she instructed him. He stared at her for a second.

"I wouldn't leave you, Lily. Not now," he kept his voice soft. She nodded and let go of his t-shirt.

"*Good.*"

She went to turn away and he slapped her on the ass, then grabbed her belt, pulling her back into him.

"Not now that I know how accommodating you can be," he

growled in her ear, but his tone was teasing and he wrapped an arm around her waist, holding her close.

"Get off of me, no more of that," she snapped, pushing his hands way.

Lily took inventory of the weapons while Marc loaded up the jugs. She sat in the doorway, the guns spread out on the ground in front of her. She looked up every now and then, watching Marc move around the yard. The heat was stifling, and he took off his t-shirt at one point, wrapping it around his head. She tried not to stare.

What were you thinking!? Last time you slept with him, **everything** *got ruined. What'll happen this time!? Never again, Liliana. Never again.*

But as she watched him hoist himself up on top of the large car, watched the different batches of muscles stretch and constrict, she could feel her mouth start to water and her resolve start to slip.

"*Stop undressing me with your eyes, let's get out of here!*"

She prattled off their weaponry, discarding two guns that wouldn't work – turned out he'd bought the bag as a sort of take-it-as-is bundle. While she loaded her Glock, he explained that he'd taken some of the bribe money from her pants in order to pay for everything.

"You what!?" she exclaimed, climbing into the passenger seat of the Scout.

"We needed it," he said simply, tossing the bag-o-guns behind her seat before walking around and getting behind the wheel.

"I need that money, Marc, it has a specific purpose."

"We needed it for this, too."

He turned the ignition, but she reached over and grabbed his arm before the car could move.

"I want to see the diamonds."

They were silent for a second, staring at each other. He glared at her.

"Are you serious? After last night?" he asked. She swallowed thickly and nodded.

"Yes. You left me. You didn't say anything, just left me. I want to see the diamonds," she repeated her request.

He grumbled, but he dug around behind his seat. He produced the backpack that never seemed to be far from him and dropped it in her lap. Then he gunned the engine, peeling out of the driveway.

Lily yanked the gallon baggie free from the pack. She hadn't seen the diamonds since Liberia, and even then, she hadn't gotten a very good look at them. Not in their entirety. She spun the bag around in her hand, watching the light bounce off all the little stones.

"Happy!?" he snapped.

"So much trouble, for a bunch of rocks," she sighed, digging her fingers into the sides of the bag.

"A bunch of rocks worth *a lot* of money," Marc added, glancing at her.

"I never cared about the money," she said, then began tucking the bag back into the bottom of his pack.

"How much did you get paid for this transport job?" he asked.

"How much did *you* get paid to steal the diamonds?" she counter asked.

"Why is everything a fucking battle with you? I feel like I need to constantly be kicking your ass just to get anything I want," he complained. She smiled.

"Technically, you have yet to kick my ass," she corrected him.

"Um, I knocked you on your ass in Liberia."

"Sucker punch, I wasn't even looking. What kind of man sucker punches a girl!?"

"The next morning, when you pulled your swallowing trick."

"You've yet to see my '*swallowing trick*', and again, you took me when I wasn't on guard *and* when I was chained to you. *Pussy,*" she taunted him.

"When you freaked the fuck out and thought I was selling you."

"Oh, c'mon!" she burst out. "That was a pretty even fight, and you may have won, but only because of the gun. You definitely got your ass kicked *way* harder!"

"I wouldn't say '*way*.'"

"You spit out a tooth."

"It was a crown."

"That's almost worse."

"It was already loose."

"Jesus! I kicked your ass, seven different ways to Sunday, and if you can't admit that a girl kicked your ass, then it's fine, but that doesn't make it not true, because I definitely -"

She was sitting on her knees in her seat, turned to face him. She was picking at her nail, not paying attention, so she wasn't prepared at all when he grabbed her by the back of the neck and yanked her forward. She squealed in the second before his lips covered her own, his hand moving around to cup her jaw. Again, that feeling of her breath being sucked away. Tossed into the wind. Right along with her cares.

"I'm almost beginning to like your feistiness," he sighed, then his fingers dug into her cheeks. "*But don't fucking push it.*"

She knocked his hand away.

"You're going to miss my '*feistiness*' when I'm gone, admit it," she laughed, falling back into her seat.

"No, I won't."

"Is '*feistiness*' even a word?"

"Lily, shut up."

"I'm just asking if -"

An explosion rang through the air, causing both of them to duck and Lily to shriek. Marc swerved a little, trying to look in the rear view mirror. She scrambled to turn around in her seat.

"What the fuck was that!?" he demanded.

"I'm checking," she was already climbing between the seats as she answered him.

She knew there was a small pair of binoculars in Marc's bag, so she fished them out before leaning over the back seat. She could see a black cloud rising up from behind a hill they'd just gone over, and she concentrated on that when she lifted the binoculars.

"What do you see?" Marc asked.

"I see … a cloud. Maybe flames. Something blew up."

"No shit. What was it?"

"I can't be sure, but it looks like it came from the direction of the house," she said slowly.

"*Shit*. Are you sure?"

Lily adjusted the focus, did calculations in her mind. She couldn't be positive, but …

"Yeah, I'm pretty sure. I think someone just blew up that house," she told him.

"Fuck."

"It gets worse."

"Worse!?"

"There's a car coming."

"*Fuck*."

An SUV came over the hill behind them. It was quite a ways off, but it was really hauling ass.

"What did you do on your little jaunt this morning!?" Lily snapped, sliding back into the front.

"Nothing! I fucking searched the only other house on that road, then I drove back to that dust bowl of a village, found someone to buy guns off of!" he snapped back.

"Well, clearly, that was a bad fucking idea! Someone spotted you!" she yelled. He took a deep breath.

"Maybe," he agreed, and she was shocked into silence. "They must have lost me when I left, then found that road."

"You fucking idiot!" Lily swore, rubbing her forehead.

"*Hey!* No use fucking crying about it now, so suck it the fuck up, sweetheart, and get your big girl panties on. We're about to deal with a lot of fire and I would appreciate not having to listen to you bitch the whole time," he informed her.

"Maybe they're not after us. Maybe it's someone else entirely," Lily mumbled, staring into the side view.

"Please don't say stupid things right now. Switch seats with me," he replied.

"Huh?"

"*Move.*"

It always looked so easy in the movies, but switching seats while doing eighty miles per hour was no easy task. Marc was a big guy, Lily had to maneuver over him, meanwhile both of them had to work around the gear shift. Their speed dropped about in half, then they almost went off the road when she hit the brake instead of the clutch.

"Sorry! Sorry," she said quickly, before he could yell at her. He glared for a second, then reached behind the seat.

"Where are they?" he asked as he picked up the bag of guns. She glanced in the rear view mirror.

"Maybe five hundred feet and closing," she guesstimated. He propped up a pump action shotgun between them, then put the bag on the floor under his feet.

"Okay. Be ready. It could be simple. Maybe they're just tailing us. They most likely want us alive, in case we -"

There was the sound of a gun shot and the back window exploded.

"Still think they want us alive!?" Lily shouted.

"Fuck off, worry about the driving!" he snapped back.

More shots were fired, riddling the back end of their car with bullets. Lily ducked down as far as she could, hugging the door. The car they were driving was an older model SUV type, and while it was a nice enough car, it wasn't exactly in perfect condition. It was old. It was beat up. They were pushing maximum speed. Their pursuers were driving a black suburban, so shiny new that it looked out of place. It was able to speed up and ram into their bumper. Lily cursed, and when Marc leaned over his seat and began firing back, she covered her right ear with her hand.

"One down!" he shouted, leaning back to grab another fully loaded clip.

"Really!?"

Lily was surprised, but as she looked in the rear view, she could see the passenger door on the suburban open up. A moment later, and a body was pushed out and onto the road. Then the car sped up again, ramming their bumper one more time.

"I think there's six of them! Well, five now. Do not let them get in front of us," Marc instructed.

"I'll do my best," she answered.

"Your '*best*'!? You're a fucking transporter, so *do your job*," was all he said before going back to shooting.

Lily had done all her training on smaller cars. She'd taken multiple courses in stunt driving and race car driving, so she felt comfortable behind just about any wheel. But the majority of her time had been spent driving BMWs and Audis. Little fast cars.

With bullets whizzing past her head, Lily watched her mirrors as best she could, shadowing the larger car's movement. He wanted to get around her, so she drove down the center lane, taking up the whole road as best she could. It was murder on her speed, but it kept her in front.

"If you could hit the driver, that would be swell!" she shouted over the wind that was rushing through the car.

"You wanna come over here and try, princess!?" he yelled back, picking up another gun.

"*Shit!*"

They were going around a curve and on the other side, a broken down vehicle took up the whole right lane of the road, with a group of people standing on the center line.

Lily yanked the wheel to the left, causing Marc to slam into her side. They rode along with two tires off the pavement, threatening to slide down a small embankment. She glanced to the side and saw that the suburban had split right, and was now jumping and cruising over shrubs and bushes.

Don't let them get ahead. Don't let them get ahead.

She fought to get the car back on the road and cranked the wheel hard to the right. The suburban pulled the same move and they slammed into each other. Metal was grinding on metal, making a deafening roar.

The back seat of the suburban was even with their front seats, and as a tinted window began to roll down, Marc grabbed the shotgun. He jammed it through the gap, and before their guests could roll their window back up, he pulled the trigger. The other driver must have hit the brakes, because the larger car fell behind, the shotgun and the sounds of yelling going with it.

"I think there's only two left now," Marc said, sitting in his seat and digging through the guns at his feet. "We're all over the place, I can't get any clean shots."

"Oh, I'm sorry, would you like me to pull over?" Lily asked.

"I'd like you to have less fucking attitude and fucking figure something out."

Lily thought for a second, then felt a light bulb go off over her head.

"Take off the top!" she called out.

"Excuse me!?"

"The top, over the back! It's removable! Take it off," she instructed.

She was surprised that he didn't ask anymore questions. Most of the snaps that held the top down were broken off, so getting it loose wasn't a problem. A couple flips, a couple pounds from his fist, and the wind did the rest, ripping the top off and blowing it away behind them.

As soon as it happened, Lily downshifted, yanked the wheel, and pressed down on the emergency brake. The back end of the car spun around in a 180, and before it could fully come to a stop, she slammed the gearshift into reverse and hit the gas at the same time as popping the brake. White smoke curled around them as the tires screamed and sought for purchase on the hot asphalt.

"Thank you!" Marc shouted, moving back to stand on his seat, leaning against the roll bar.

"Make it count, I don't want to get shot today," she replied, looking behind them while holding onto his belt.

While she steered as best she could, she listened as his bullets pinged off of metal. Penetrated through glass. She kept waiting for him to announce that everyone was dead, that he had once again saved the day, but it didn't happen.

"Goddamn gun is jammed!" Marc yelled.

"Figure it out, I'm about to burn out our transmission!" Lily shouted back, glancing at the dials on the dashboard.

"Hand me something else!"

Grumbling, Lily leaned as best she could to the side while maintaining an eye on the road. She rifled through the bag, then her hand came across something. It felt like a handgun, only bigger. Almost cartoonish. It took her a second, then she got it. She gasped, getting another idea.

"Sit down!" she urged, pulling the weapon free of the bag and juggling it around so it was pointing out her window.

"Why? And are you slowing down!?" he sounded beyond shocked.

"*Trust me.*"

Marc sat down just as the suburban pulled up even with them. A window slowly rolled down and the driver smiled at her, several gold teeth winking in the sun. Lily smiled back, then she pulled the trigger.

A flare gun seemed like a silly choice, and how it had gotten mixed up with all the other weapons, she didn't know. But as a burning flare shot into the other car, she was glad it had found its way to them.

The reaction was instantaneous. There were shouts and screams, smoke billowing out of the windows. The car jerked back and forth, then began to swerve away. Lily let out a sigh of relief at first, but then the other vehicle swerved back, almost completely cutting across the lanes. Lily had time to yell one good swear word before the suburban rammed into the front panel of their car.

They didn't flip, thank god, but they did spin around in several circles. The back end lost control, leading the mutiny, and eventually it dragged them into the ditch that ran along side the road. Lily was wearing her seat belt, but she still slammed her head against the steering wheel. No air bag deployed for her, though about a minute after the crash, a passenger air bag went off.

Awesome safety features. I'm so tired of getting hit in the head.

"Fuck. *Princess,*" Marc grumbled, and she could hear him moving around. She moaned, wondering what the wailing sound was that seemed to be surrounding her. As she felt his hand slithering between her chest and the wheel, she realized she was leaning against the horn.

"I just want to pass out, just for like a minute," she whispered as he pushed her back. He was gentle, supporting the back of her head while he moved her. He got up onto his knees, leaning over to inspect her.

"Just a scratch. Look at me," he ordered, and she trained her eyes on his. "Good. I don't think there's a concussion."

"Are you sure? This *really* hurts," she complained, and it got him to laugh. He picked up the hem of his t-shirt and pressed it to the top right side of her forehead. When he pulled away, she saw there was blood on the material.

"You did good. I'm gonna go see if those scumbags are alive," Marc told her, then he all but leapt out of the car.

Lily was not as enthusiastic about going after their attackers. She gingerly climbed out of the car, then groaned when she saw all the damage. A back rear wheel had been completely shredded and ripped off the rim. On the other side, where the suburban had rammed into them, the metal was completely concave, pinning the tire inside the wheel well.

There goes another vehicle. How many is that now?

"*Fuck,*" she whispered, wiping sweat off her forehead. When she rubbed her hand on her tank top, a rusty red color smeared down the white front. She frowned. *Not sweat, blood.* She was still bleeding. Probably not a good sign.

There was shouting coming from somewhere, so she climbed

out of the ditch and winced. The suburban was dead on the road, facing the opposite direction. The driver's side corner in the front had been completely crunched in, the fender hanging at an awkward angle. The passenger seat seemed to be on fire and all the windows were shot out, the windshield one massive spiderweb of cracks.

Pressing the heel of her hand to her head wound, she braced one arm against the crumpled up hood and walked around the vehicle. There was a dead guy on the ground – the gold-toothed driver who'd smiled at her. Marc had another man pinned against the side of the car, a gun pressed to the guy's forehead.

"How did you find us!?" Marc demanded.

The man spit in his face and Lily grimaced. That hadn't worked out so well for her, when she'd done it to Marc. He cracked his gun across the man's nose, then went back to pointing the barrel at him.

"I do not answer to you," the man answered, a Russian accent very evident in his voice.

"Maybe not me, but I've got nine bullets in here that think you'll talk to them," Marc replied.

The man said something in another language, and it didn't sound pleasant. He was given another hit across the nose.

Lily didn't want to watch any more. She felt dizzy, and she couldn't care less who sent them. It was Ivanov, or someone above him. Maybe even big boss Stankovski. All she cared about was how involved she looked – did Stankovski know that she and Marc were trying to steal his diamonds?

"Jesus, can we just get out of here!?" she shouted.

"Not until he tells me -"

Marc didn't get to finish his statement. Lily gave a strangled yell as an arm wrapped around her throat. She went to swing her arm back at whoever was holding her, but a gun was suddenly pressed into the side of her head. She froze, holding up her hands.

"Alright! Give us the diamonds!"

Lily paused for a moment, a little surprised – the man holding her hostage had a thick cockney accent.

"This doesn't need to get messy," Marc started in a slow voice. "Let her go. I let him go."

"I don't give two shits about him, or this bitch! You tell me where those fuckin' diamonds are, or the last thing you'll see is me putting a bullet through your girlfriend's head!"

Marc narrowed his eyes.

"Let her go, or the last thing *you'll* see is me putting a bullet through *your friend's* head," Marc counter threatened.

The guy holding her jerked to the side, and for a second, Lily thought she was dead. But the gun was pulled away from her head and pointed straight out. Marc dove backwards and Lily screamed before biting down on the arm that was restraining her. Her assailant let out a growl, but didn't let go of her. Instead, he pulled the trigger, shooting his partner in the back of the head. Then he slammed the butt of the gun against the side of her skull. Her reality spun around in a circle and she stopped biting down, almost going limp in his grasp.

"Not a problem anymore, now is it!? *Get me those fuckin' stones!*" he was shouting so loud he was spitting as he talked, spraying against Lily's shoulder. She didn't care. It was taking all her energy and focus just to stay standing. She tried to keep her eyes on Marc, but there seemed to be two of him getting up off the ground.

"Alright, alright," he sighed, dusting himself off. "You want the stones. I have the stones. Let her go, she's not part of this. I've just been holding her hostage, she doesn't mean anything."

"Do I fucking look stupid!?"

"Is that a real question?"

"I changed my mind, mate. The last thing you'll see – after I shoot you in both your knee caps – is me fucking your girlfriend's face. You'd like that, wouldn't you, sweetheart?" her new friend growled in her ear. She took a deep breath.

"Whatever ends this quicker, sure," she managed to say, though it felt like it took all her energy just to push the words out.

"Oi! My kind of woman! Now, before I have to make good on

my word, be a love and tell me where those diamonds are," he asked. Lily nodded again, her eyes falling shut.

"Hey! Princess, look at me!" Marc snapped. Her eye lids fluttered open and again, it took a moment before three of him turned into just one. "Keep those pretty green eyes on me, okay?"

"I can't make any promises," she mumbled.

"This isn't the family fuckin' feud! You think I came all the way to Africa to have a fuckin' chat!? The diamonds, friend! Get me Stankovski's diamonds!"

"Did I ever tell you that, Lily?" Marc asked, standing casually with his hands clasped behind his back.

"Tell me what?" she asked back. The arm around her neck got tighter, the man behind her angrier, screaming out slang curse words that she didn't understand. She ignored him, just concentrated on Marc, just like he'd asked her.

"That you have the absolutely most gorgeous eyes I've ever seen," Marc answered. She smiled.

"Really?"

"Really. Don't ever stop looking at me, okay?"

"Okay."

It happened so fast. She didn't blink. Didn't look away. While the angry Brit was spitting and swearing, Marc whipped his right arm forward. A fraction of a second, and he pulled the trigger. A fraction of an inch, and Lily would've been shot. A fraction of a heartbeat, and the man behind her was dead. He fell backwards, the gun sliding out of his hand, his arm around her neck pulling tight. She almost went down with him, but she staggered backwards and grabbed the ruined hood of the suburban, managing to shrug him off.

"Are you okay?" Marc was suddenly at her side.

"What? Yeah. Fine. Okay. Nice shot," she mumbled, rubbing the side of her head.

"Fuck, there went any leads. I can't believe he shot his friend," Marc said, cupping her face in his hands and tilting it up towards him.

"He was kind of a dick," Lily agreed, letting her eyes roll up so she could stare at the sky.

"Maybe I was wrong, maybe you do have a concussion," Marc mumbled, putting his thumbs under her eyes and pulling down on her skin. She finally looked at him.

"Do you really think I have gorgeous eyes?" she asked. He smiled at her.

"Sweetheart, you have *beautiful* eyes. Like emeralds."

"Always jewels with you."

"What can I say, princess, I always did like emeralds more than diamonds."

"I hate that," she sighed. "My name is Lily. Why can't you just call me Lily?"

"Because saying your name feels too comfortable, sweetheart. And I'm the kind of man who can't afford to get too comfortable," he explained. She laughed.

"You've said my name lots. I think you're already too comfortable," she teased. He frowned.

"I think I am, too."

She wanted to examine that statement. To pull it apart and understand him. Understand such a dangerous, complicated man. Wanted him to be comfortable. Wanted him to curl up in her soul and make her understand her own dangers, her own complications. Wanted him to change her. To change *for* her. To change *everything*.

… want him to catch me before I hit the ground …

That was her last thought as her eyes rolled back in her head and she passed out.

DAY FOUR

Marc grimaced, rubbing a hand across his jaw. He hadn't shaved in four days, not since the morning of the heist. He would kill for a razor and some soap.

And just a break. A goddamn fucking break, for five fucking minutes.

There was a noise behind him and he glanced away from the road, into the backseat. Lily was stretched out on the seat, mostly hidden underneath a blanket. Only her arm had worked its way out and into view, stretching towards the door. He smiled and went back to watching the road.

She'd been unconscious for hours, ever since she'd passed out after their car chase. It had been eleven hours, he'd started to get worried, but there wasn't a whole lot he could do – it wasn't like there was a hospital every couple miles, and even if there had been, stopping wasn't necessarily in their best interest. Mauritania had a strong terrorist presence, particularly in its border regions. Terrorists that delighted in kidnapping westerners. Marc was confident in his ability to give off a *"just try and kidnap me"* vibe, but Lily was like a beacon, just begging to be captured. Tall, redhead, fair skin, and about as All-American as a person could come; all she needed to complete the look was an apple pie in one hand.

No, stopping for a CAT scan was out of the question.

"Where the fuck am I?"

Marc chuckled and looked back again. She was struggling to push the blanket away from her face as she attempted to sit up.

"Take it easy there, sweetheart. I put you in the back seat so you could stretch out," Marc explained. She brushed her messy out of her face, then winced. Her fingers must have rubbed against the cut on her forehead. It was up near her hair line, almost unnoticeable with her hair down.

"Where are we? Didn't we crash our car?" she asked, her voice scratchy.

"Yeah. I took the other car, but I'm not sure how long it's going to last. Here," he said, passing a water bottle back to her.

"*Yes*, thank god," she groaned, lifting it to her lips. She guzzled it down, the liquid spilling over her chin and down her front.

"Careful, don't make yourself sick," he warned her. She waved him away and polished off the whole bottle.

"Okay. First, I need food. I'm starving," she stressed, tossing the blanket aside before crawling between the front seats and sitting next to him.

"I figured you would be," he replied, moving a bag out from under her feet and dropping it in her lap. "Mostly dried fruits, some bread. We can find you something more substantial when we pick up another car. We're right outside of Nouakchott."

The capital city of the entire country, it sat right on the Atlantic ocean and was just a few miles south of Western Sahara. If Lily hadn't woken up, he would've gotten them a hotel for the night. But she'd slept clean through the day – she'd be good to drive all night. They could make it all the way to the border of Morocco without stopping, then just one more day till they could reach Tangier. Till it would be over and he could have his diamonds. Clear his name.

Because that's what's important still. Right. Do you actually buy that?

"Wow, you drove all that way? In this piece of shit?" she asked, her eyes wandering over the hood while she dug food out of the bag.

The Scout they'd been driving had been useless. Marc had loaded everything up into the suburban, then drove off, hoping for the best. The windshield had been so badly cracked that he had just kicked it out. They had no windows, at all. It made a god awful squealing sound, and white smoke was constantly belching out from underneath the hood, and when he hit fifty miles per hour, it felt like it was going to shake apart. But it kept running, and that was all that mattered.

"Yup. How's your head? What all do you remember?" he asked, cupping her chin and moving her head so she faced him.

"Eh, kinda hurts. I remember crashing. I remember … getting out of the Scout. I remember … you, and a guy. Shooting? You talking to me. Something," her voice trailed off as she searched her memory.

"Close enough," he figured it might be better that she didn't remember everything.

It had been a bold move, to shoot a man who was holding a gun to her head. Risky. Marc was a good shot, but so many things could have gone wrong. Just one wrong breath, and Lily would've gotten shot. By him, or by the hired gunman.

Never. I would never let that happen.

Sometime between leaving the boarding house in Mali and their car chase earlier that day, things had changed. At first, Lily had been a chew toy. Something to play with, something to tie in knots. Then she had been an adversary. An enemy. An agent of betrayal, sent to ruin his career at best, and end his life at worst. Later on still, a nuisance. Swallowing the diamonds. Arguing with him. Punching him in the face. Trying to shoot him.

But she had also proven her worth. Originally unarmed, she had stopped two assailants at that boarding house, and killed one. She had never been scared of him, not once. And she'd also almost kicked his ass, on several occasions. He almost admired her. Was definitely amused by her.

Undeniably attracted to her.

Seeing her helpless, though, had trumped any and all of those thoughts. Wanted or not, she had become more than just his partner in their little adventure. Her body had belonged to him on two separate occasions, and apparently that was more than enough for him to take complete possession of it, in his mind. Seeing the other man leer at her, threatening to sexually assault her ... shooting wasn't good enough. It made Marc long for his knife kit. He'd wanted to *eviscerate* the other man. Remove his intestines while he was still alive. Make him regret even noticing that Lily existed, let alone threatening her. Touching her.

Motherfucker.

Bad, bad, bad. Marc loved women because he liked to fuck – that was it. Lily was a good fuck and a hell of a fighter. That was all it could *ever* be, nothing else. She was going to Moscow on some stupid suicide mission to kill the Pakhan of the Bratva. Marc was returning to prove his innocence and to kill Ivanov. They were destined for two very different paths.

Maybe not so different ...

He shook his head. A redhead with big green eyes was not going to derail his life. He just had to keep his head straight. No more thinking about that red hair *or* those green eyes. No more sex. Get to Tangier. Get the diamonds. Get to Liberia. Get the fuck out of Africa. Get the fuck back to work. There would be plenty of time for sex with lots of other women, if he could just finish this one job.

But none of those other women will be like her.

"We're going to die of carbon monoxide poisoning before we get anywhere," Lily's voice interrupted his thoughts. She coughed and waved her hand in front of her face.

"We're fine, we have plenty of ventilation."

"You didn't see any other cars along the way?"

"Excuse me if I didn't have time to go traipsing around Africa with your dead weight slung over my shoulder, searching for a stretch limo for you," he snapped, his anger at their attraction bubbling over onto her.

"Want me to drive?" she suddenly asked.

"Why?"

"Because you're bitching like a cranky five year old. I think you need a nap," she informed him, and he burst out laughing.

"Shut up. Not only did I not want to waste time since this car was still running, but this area is super fucked up. Terrorists, gangs, land mines. I didn't really feel like wandering off the beaten path," he explained. She grimaced.

"God, I hate this place," she grumbled.

"You volunteered for the job," he reminded her. She sighed and nodded.

"Means to an end. I always remind myself of that."

They drove in silence for a while. The more she ate, the more her color and general attitude improved. She almost seemed chipper. It probably also helped that she'd gotten the most sleep either of them had seen since Liberia, *before* the heist. She almost seemed like the woman he had first met back at the Bratva's safe house.

Five weeks ago.

A million years ago.

When they entered the center of the city of Nouakchott, Marc hooked south and drove till he came upon the district of El Mina. He'd been there before, when he'd been a lot younger. Him and a friend, visiting the city's "secret" red light district – El Mina was known for prostitution. The neighborhood was rough, dangerous, but perfect for what he needed to do. Mauritania was an Islamic country and Nouakchott had very strict rules and laws pertaining to its governing religion. A foreigner stealing a car would not go over well. Being in El Mina was risky, but he decided it was less than the risk that would come from stealing where cops would be likely to catch him.

"Do you think this is a good idea?" Lily asked, peering out her side of the car as they came to a stop. She was hunched low in her seat, with the blanket curled around her head and draped across her front.

"No. But I think it's the best option we've got," he replied, re-loading his gun before tucking it into the waist of his pants. What he wouldn't give for one of his holsters.

"I read this article," Lily started, her voice barely above a whisper, "about how carjacking is such an issue in South Africa that people do crazy things to protect their cars. Rig it so if their doors are opened from the outside, shit like lye and mace or even explosions will go off in the carjacker's face."

Marc snorted and leaned over the wheel, watching the traffic in front of them. There were a few people out and about, but they were all men. Not one single woman. Every now and then, a beat up car rolled past, or a truck. Once a donkey pulling a cart.

"Good thing we're not in South Africa. Once I get the car, follow me. If you see anything happen, just drive," Marc instructed as he opened his door and got out of the car.

"I'm not just gonna leave -"

"*Drive*," he snapped, slamming the door shut before leaning in the open window. "Find the nicest hotel in town and wait there. I'll find you."

"This is stupid."

"Shut up, Lily, and just wish me luck."

"Good luck."

Marc jogged away from the car, hurrying to the side of a building and hugging the wall. There didn't seem to be any people anywhere near, and he poked his head around the corner, looking up and down the street. A couple men at the end of the block. Another young man sitting on a stoop at the other end of the street.

Perfect.

Marc took his gun out of his pants and flicked off the safety, resting his finger alongside the trigger. He didn't think he'd have to use it, but a person could never be too careful. He expected it to be a quick in and out. Scare the driver, yank him out of his seat, then take the car. Circle back so Lily could follow him. Easy, peezy, lemon squeezy. He hurried out into the road, pointing the gun at the car coming towards him.

A Kalashnikov rifle jutted out the window and Marc ducked as bullets laced the ground in front of him, a staccato beat in the night air. He crab walked backwards, shuffling behind an abandoned vehicle. A few more shots were fired, then the other car sped off. Marc stayed down, holding his gun up, ready to fire back.

There was a familiar squealing sound and suddenly the suburban pulled up next to where he was hiding. He glared as he ran around and hopped in the car. Lily didn't say anything, just sped off down the street.

"Not a fucking word," he swore.

"*I told you so.*"

"Fuck you."

"What the fuck did you think would happen!? We're in the fucking '*hood*' of one of the countries that has a permanent spot on the '*don't fucking go there*' list from the U.N.! Did you think they were really just going to give up their car!?" she snapped.

"Enough! I don't hear any bright fucking ideas coming out of your mouth!" he shouted at her. She glared at him for a moment, her eyes just a flash of green as they drove under a lone street light.

"You know what? Yeah, I *do* have an idea."

They drove for about twenty minutes, getting lost at one point. Eventually, though, she found the way to a busy street that was lined with large, important looking buildings. He narrowed his eyes as he watched sign after sign go past.

"Is this a joke?" he asked, turning towards her.

"No."

"Lily. We have millions of dollars worth of conflict diamonds, not to mention a shit ton of illegal weapons, no passports, and no visas. I don't think driving down *embassy row* is such a smart fucking idea," he growled.

"How about you shut up and just trust me for once!?"

She found a nice hotel near the French embassy and parked down the street. Marc couldn't figure it out – she was going to seek help from the French? But she didn't get out of the car. She climbed into the back seat, discarding the blanket as she went. Marc turned and watched as she took off her boots.

"What are you doing?" he questioned. She held out her hand.

"Give me a knife."

He dug one out of their weapons bag and handed it to her, then watched in surprise as she used it to rip a hole near the top of one pant leg. She dragged the knife through the material, lifting her hips so she could get underneath her thigh. When it was almost a complete circle, she dropped the knife and just ripped the pant leg away.

"What the fuck are you doing!?" he repeated the question as she did the same to her other pant leg. The sensible cargo pants she'd been wearing during their entire time together were now a pair of incredibly short shorts. She handed the knife back to him.

"Coming up with a plan that will actually work *and* won't get anyone killed," she said, scooting to the edge of the seat. She scrunched up the bottom of her tank top, then gathered it at her back, pulling it tight and knotting it, creating a mid-riff shirt that ended just below her breasts. Then she yanked on the neck line, pulling on it till it showed well past the top of her bra.

"While this is a lovely show, I have no fucking clue what you're doing," he told her. She moved to the floor of the car, standing on her knees while she rearranged her auburn locks, piling them into a messy bun on top of her head.

"How do I look?" she asked, reaching into the front of the car and tilting the rear view mirror so she could see her reflection.

"Hot. Your legs look amazing, but not as good as your tits," he answered honestly. She rubbed at her neck, at the fading marks.

"What about the bruises? Too much?" she mumbled to him as she put her boots back on.

"Too much for what? You look like you had a rough day, but not crazy," he answered, his eyes sweeping over her form. The bruise on her chest was buried in her cleavage, her bra aiding in hiding it. Most of her other bruises were high up on her rib cage, still hidden by her shirt. There was nothing she could do about her neck, but luckily her legs had gotten away unscathed. He let his eyes wander over every inch of creamy skin.

Focus!

"Oh, well. Doesn't matter," she mumbled, then pushed open the door and hopped out.

"Hey! What are you doing?" he asked for the third time, beginning to get annoyed as he climbed out of the car right behind her. She pushed past him and leaned across the passenger seat. He stared at her ass, which her shorts didn't quite cover anymore.

"So here's the plan," she started, turning around, holding his map in her hands. "Do not let me out of your sight, but don't say a fucking word. We are going to wait out here. When the richest, stupidest looking guy pulls up, I'm going to follow him. I'm going to make '*friends*' with him. I'm going to get him to take me back to his car. Then you can come in all guns-a-blazing, got it? Good. Let's go."

She started walking away, and Marc was almost stunned enough to let her go. But he reached out and grabbed her arm, roughly yanking her to him.

"Let me get this straight – you're gonna fuck some guy to get us a car?" he clarified. He didn't know what was more shocking; the plan that she'd come up with, or how angry he was at the idea of her sleeping with someone else.

"*No!* Are you kidding!? Jesus, I'm going to *pretend* to be a hooker, I'm not actually going to fuck anybody!" she hissed, slapping him in the chest.

"You think this will really fucking work?" he snapped. She glared and folded her arms in front of her chest.

"Listen, *Marcelle*. I spent a month in Liberia planning for this trip, figuring out back up plans, researching the different cities I'd be going through. One thing I learned? If you're in Africa and you want a high end prostitute, if you want a westerner, *if you want to pay to fuck a white woman*, you find them in expensive, posh hotels that cater to westerners. If I had a sexy dress, I'd put it on. But this is all I got. Slutty tourist. Let's pray it works."

"I don't like this plan," he stated.

"I don't care. You think I want to do this? You think I like look-ing like this? Like you said, it's not a good idea – it's just the best we've got. Now *get back in the car.*"

Marc sat in the passenger seat, staring in the side view. Lily leaned against the back of the car, the map unfolded in front of her. She looked like she was lost. Just a silly American girl, in desperate need of help.

Such a bad fucking plan.

Several men came and left from the hotel, but she didn't move. Not until a dark green Ford Explorer pulled up. The hotel was gated with a security stand in the front. People had to stop to give their name and room number before they could be allowed on the prem-ises. There were two cars ahead of the Explorer. Lily jogged up to the SUV and Marc leaned close to his window so he could listen.

"*Excuse me!*" her voice was soft. "I'm so sorry. I'm so lost! Could you help me?"

She giggled. Marc was pretty sure he'd never heard that sound come out of her before – it was like finding out a bobcat could giggle. Bizarre.

She stood on her toes, leaning into the man's window. Marc could see his face, could watch as the man directed all his answers to Lily's chest. There was some more chatting, some more giggling, and some light touching; the stranger ran his finger up and down Lily's arm. Marc had been fiddling with a pencil during the whole interaction, and now snapped it in half. He was annoyed, but he also recognized that Lily was pretty much in with the man, so Marc leaned back and grabbed the pack that held the diamonds and his gear, strapping it across his back.

An agreement seemed to have been made because Lily jumped up and down a couple times, then began to scurry around the other man's vehicle. Marc didn't waste any time and he hopped out of the suburban, keeping his eyes on the security stand. The guards were busy, having some difficulty with a guest in the first car. Marc jogged to the back end of the Explorer and he effortlessly crawled underneath it. He rolled onto his back and was able to latch onto some of the fittings between the front tires and he held on tight as the large vehicle began to move.

He gritted his teeth as they drove through security, then went in a circle around what could only be a roundabout. The car stopped, but the engine didn't die, and he watched as Lily's feet hit the ground and began walking towards a pair of doors, escorted by a man's feet. Then the car started moving forward again.

Valet.

It was dark out and he couldn't see any other cars or people, so Marc took a chance and lowered himself to the ground, letting the vehicle pass over him. He was next to a hedge and he immediately rolled into it, hiding himself before he scanned the area.

He was in the front of the hotel, right before an entrance to a basement garage. The entrance to the hotel was maybe a hundred feet away. Several bell hops and other hotel staff lingered out front, waiting for more guests. Across from the entrance was a circular fountain, the thing they must have driven around, and across from it was another building, though what purpose it served, Marc had no clue. All he knew was that he had to get the guys away from the door.

The drive was lined entirely with decorative pebbles, and he picked one up. He eyed a window across the way, then stood up quickly and launched the rock. He ducked back down as a window shattered.

It had the desired effect. The staff all turned towards the sound, then eventually sauntered off to investigate. Mark stepped out of the hedges and made a beeline for the doors. He didn't run – he didn't want to look suspicious, but he didn't want to get caught, either.

He made it inside without incident and let out a deep breath when he saw Lily's red hair. She was sitting on a sofa in a lounge area, across from the reception desk. Smart girl, she had waited for him. A man sat next to her and she was cuddled up close to him, her chest pressed against his arm while she giggled in his ear.

Fucking giggling. I'm going to puke.

Marc grabbed a newspaper off a table, then made a big production of sitting on a couch that backed up to the one Lily and her guest were occupying. He rustled the paper and cleared his throat. A moment later he felt a sharp nail scratch across the back of his neck. His presence was known.

"… can't believe a girl like you is here, doing work like this," the man was saying in a French accent.

"Work? I would never call what I do '*work*', it's too much fun," Lily laughed.

"I think we could have a lot of *fun* together," her mark agreed.

"Mmmm, me, too," all the giggling was gone from her voice, replaced by a sexy, husky tone that Marc knew very well. The edges of the paper crinkled in his grip as he clenched his fists.

"I have a wonderful room, king sized bed. But if I pay, you must do whatever I want," the man informed her.

"Of course."

"I have very specific tastes that must be met, or I will not pay."

"I completely understand. But I have one demand, myself," she began to warn him.

"A hooker making a demand?"

"I *love* having sex in cars," she told him.

"Cars!?"

"Mmmm hmmm. So hot. Knowing anyone could catch us. Being so naughty," she explained.

"You want to have sex with me in my car?" the French man double checked. Lily leaned close and Marc could feel her warmth against the back of his neck.

"I want you to *fuck me* in your car," she whispered in such a sexy, breathy voice that even Marc got a little hot.

No more discussion was needed after that, the man jumped up and bustled her to the lift. She didn't give one look to Marc, just laughed and pushed herself against the stranger, her breasts almost spilling out of her top.

He gave them about a minute head start, then Marc folded up

his paper and got up off the couch. Went over to the same elevator they had taken and pressed the down button, just like they had pushed. The hotel only had four levels – ground, two room levels, and garage. So down he went.

It wasn't a big garage, the hotel didn't accommodate that many people. He could hear Lily's stupid giggling and he followed it. The lovebirds were on the other side of the garage, stumbling towards the Explorer, the man pawing at her, grabbing her ass, working his hand underneath the leg of her shorts. She laughed louder, wrapping her arm around his shoulders as they fell against the vehicle. Marc crept along, dodging in between cars, staying out of site.

"Please, come on, take everything off," the guy was begging. Marc got behind the trunk of the car next to them and peered over the top.

"But I want you to turn it on," Lily was whining, grabbing his lapels and squeezing her arms together, forcing her breasts higher.

"Why do you want this?"

"Because it turns *me* on, that *big* engine, just *pumping* away," she sighed. Marc rolled his eyes.

Good god, is he really going to fall for this bullshit!?

When Lily leaned forward, placing a slow lick up the side of the man's neck while rubbing at the front of his crotch, Marc realized her bullshit would *definitely* work. She could start prattling off the ABCs and any man would do just about anything she wanted.

Frenchie fumbled with his keys and dropped them, but as he bent down to grab them, temptation became too much. He dove head first into her cleavage, almost knocking her off balance. She fell against the car, staring down at him. Marc stood up and glared at her.

"*End this now,*" he mouthed, dragging his thumb across his neck in a kill sign. She raised her arms in a "*whatever*" gesture, then began pushing at the man who was mauling her breasts.

"No, no, no, baby, you wanted a show, right? Let me give you a show," she said, managing to finally get him off of her.

"Yes, yes, a show. I like a show. Take it all off, *slowly.*"

Marc was completely floored when she seemed to com, stepped back and unbuttoned her shorts, then worked dow zipper. Slowly peeled the material over her curvy hips, then turn and bent at the waist, her perfect, round ass pointing straight at the stranger. She was almost completely in half, working her shorts to her ankles and carefully stepping out of them.

When the man slapped her on the ass, Marc couldn't take it any-more. He was going to kill him, he didn't care. But as he started to stand up again, he saw what she was doing. While the pervert was massaging her ass, Lily was trying her damnedest to get the keys, which had fallen behind the wheel. Before Marc could take a step forward, she had them. She hooked them into her hand, then imme-diately stood up, spinning around.

"I changed my mind," she stated in a loud voice, stepping out of arm's reach of the guy.

"*Excusez-moi?*" the man was so caught off guard, he didn't know what language to speak.

"I said, I changed my mind. I'm not going to fuck you. But I am going to take your car, I'm very sorry," she said simply.

The man was a large guy, heavy set. He had gray hair and was balding, and was wearing a cheap suit. Very unassuming. So Marc figured it was safe to say that they were all a little shocked when the man leapt forward and wrapped his hands around Lily's neck, all while screaming obscenities in French.

She screamed and Marc jumped to her rescue, but he should've known better. Before he could even reach her, she had kicked the guy in the nuts and then the face, laying him out flat. By the time Marc got to her side, it was over. She was coughing and rubbing at her neck.

"I did not see that coming," she said, clearing her throat.

"Me, neither. But did you have to get half fucking naked!?" he asked, glaring down at her peach colored panties.

"Hey! I would like it noted that in my plan, no one got shot at *and* we got the car! Now shut the fuck up and drive!" she snapped, snatching her shorts off the ground and stomping around the car.

"Don't you fucking get lippy with me! He was about to eat one of your tits, and you would've let him! You could've just knocked him out and taken his keys!" Marc pointed out when they were both in the car. She threw the keys at him.

"Violence isn't always necessary, Mr. Caveman!"

"Judging by the fact that the asshole is now unconscious on the ground, I'd say it is. You just fucking liked it, didn't you?" Marc called her out. She threw her head back and laughed.

"For fuck's sake, you're jealous! Of some fat guy in cheap polyester! Oh yeah, you're totally right, I loved it. If only you weren't here, I could be happily boinking my brains out right now," Lily taunted him.

"You are the most annoying woman I've ever met."

"Yeah? Well the feeling is entirely *mutual.*"

Marc was about to respond when he clued into the fact that they weren't the only ones talking. He blinked at her for a second, then twisted around, looking out the door. The French man was on the ground, barking into a cell phone as he scooted backwards away from the Explorer. Marc groaned and slammed his door shut.

"Nothing is ever easy with you," he growled, jamming the keys in the ignition and firing up the engine.

"Only because it's *you* who slows us down," she dished right back to him.

The tires squealed as he tore up the ramp out of the garage. Several guards were running down the ramp, and they dove out of the way. The front gate was opening up, letting several guard cars race into the hotel's grounds. Marc went around the fountain once, then zipped out past the gate.

"*Fuck,*" he swore, watching in the mirrors as several cars followed them down the streets, lights blazing.

"This would have been the perfect plan," Lily grumbled as she climbed onto her knees, watching their pursuers over the back of her seat. He glanced at her, did a double take at her mostly bare ass, then went back to the road.

"Can you stop bitching for a moment and use that big bra. yours to get us out of this situation? Seeing as how you're *so* good it," he reminded her. She smacked him in the arm.

"Shut up. I left the map in the hotel, I have no clue where to go. Do you have any guns?" she asked.

"One."

"Then I guess we'd better make it count. Give it to me," she said, and he handed it over.

"Don't do anything crazy. If we break this car, you can fucking walk to Morocco."

"Whatever, just slow down."

She rolled down her window as he dropped speed. She pulled herself out of the car so she was sitting on the door and Marc automatically grabbed her leg, holding her behind her knee, in case she fell.

"Go for a tire!" he shouted over the wind. "These streets are so narrow, if the car flips, it'll block all the rest from getting through!"

"Got it!"

There was silence. No gun shots. Marc watched as the security cars got closer and closer. He glanced at her, then glanced at the mirrors. Then back to her. Back to the mirrors. The closest car was right behind them, almost touching their bumper. He lost his patience.

"What the fuck are you waiting for!?"

BAM.

One gun shot, and he watched as the car behind them swerved dramatically back and forth before ramming into a post. One of the cars following behind it didn't have time to stop and rammed into it, flipping it on its side, completely blocking the road. Two more cars added to the mess, and it was soon obvious that no one would be following them.

Admit it, she's good. Better than you even thought possible.

Marc punched the gas pedal and cranked the wheel, taking a sharp right down a narrow street. Lily managed to slowly slide back inside as he took four more turns, trying to put as much distance between them and the hotel, as quickly as possible, but without getting so far away that he couldn't find his way back without the map.

"That was amazing!" Lily shouted when they screeched to a stop behind a dumpster, out of sight of the road.

"I can't believe you made that shot!" he exclaimed, leaning forward to press his head against the wheel.

"I can't, either! Did you see it!?" she sounded amazed, and she got back onto her knees, looking out the back of the car. He sat up again.

"Of course I fucking saw it. It was an amazing shot," he agreed.

"It was an amazing plan! We pulled something off, *as planned*, finally!" she laughed, turning towards him.

"About fucking time," he agreed, smiling back at her.

They stared at each other for a minute, and then it was like someone hit a bell.

Ding! Round One: Marc vs. Lily

They crashed into each other, barely meeting at the mouths. Her tongue swept across the front of his teeth as his hands dove into the back of her underwear, forcing her closer. She tried to crawl over the console between them, but his seat was too close to the wheel and her ass set off the horn for a moment. He wrapped his arm around her waist and leaned them backwards, forcing them between the seats.

They wiggled and moved and stretched, falling into the back seat all while still groping each other. He managed to sit upright and she was on him immediately, straddling his lap. She pulled his t-shirt off and while her nails scratched across his chest, he shoved his hand into her underwear, finding her burning hot and ready for him.

"You should shoot out tires more often if it gets you this wet," he said as she panted in his ear.

"Good idea. Maybe I should also hit on other men more often, since it seems to have gotten *you* so hot," she replied. He knotted his free hand in the hair on the back of her head and yanked.

"Not fucking funny. No more plans like that," he informed her.

"No more."

Then her hand was down his pants, squeezing the base of his dick, and it was a different kind of battle. He had the advantage; with his hand underneath her, he could manipulate multiple fingers in multiple different ways. She was only able to stroke him a couple times before she wasn't able to control her movements.

"Not yet," he whispered, pulling his hand away. She let out a frustrated cry, but he swallowed it with his mouth, kissing her hard while he worked his pants down his hips.

She pulled her tank top off while he pushed the crotch of her panties to the side. She was working on taking her bra off, but he couldn't wait. He held his dick with one hand, then wrapped his arm around her waist and forced her down on top of him. All over him. She shuddered and groaned, her hands dropping to his shoulders, nails digging into his skin.

"God, this always feels so good," she whispered. He nodded, moving his hands to her waist.

"*You* always feel so good."

She rocked her hips slowly at first, her head rolling back on her shoulders. Marc cupped her breast in one hand, sucking on her nipple through the material of her bra. Then she picked up speed, using her legs to lift up and down, all while still rocking her hips to meet his with every thrust.

"*Marc*," she cried out his name, and he loved the way it sounded on her lips.

"Yes," he responded, not caring what he was saying. She leaned away, bracing one hand against the seat back behind her, which enabled her to thrust even harder. He groaned and reached around to hold onto her ass.

"Please," she panted, her other hand pressing flat against his chest. "*Please*."

He slid one of his hands around to where their pelvises were meeting. He twisted his thumb in the lace of her panties, then used the material against her, used the friction against her sensitivity. She shrieked, almost jumping off of him, her whole body shaking for a moment.

"Whoa now, you're not going anywhere, sweetheart," he growled, yanking her back down on top of him. Impaling her on him.

"I'm ... I'm ... I'm ...," she chanted, both her hands moving to hold onto the back of his neck.

"You're gonna come. Please, please, *please,* come for me, Lily," he begged, moving his thumb faster, pumping his hips harder.

He could feel it start. He wasn't a small guy, and she was a tight girl – he could feel every muscle twitch and spasm. Her cries got louder, her shuddering grew more intense, and even in the flickering street light, he could see her pale chest turning an almost crimson red. Her bouncing grew erratic and she closed her eyes, shoving her forehead against his own.

A woman's orgasm was such a strange thing to him. It was like an explosion, the screaming, the gasping, the shaking. Yet everything constricted at the same time, her arms coiling around him, her leg muscles freezing, her pussy locking him into place, almost making him come at the same time as her.

*Such an **amazing** thing.*

"I can't ... I can't even," she breathed after a solid minute had passed. He chuckled.

"I was beginning to wonder if you were still alive."

He laid her down flat on the seat and worked above her. No gentle thrusting after such a big orgasm – he immediately pounded into her, eliciting more shrieks. He groaned and worked his hand underneath her bra, clenching his fingers around her breast. He wanted all of her, every inch of her, right now, five minutes ago, *yesterday.*

He was well aware that they were on a street, in a car, fucking in public, in a city where women weren't even supposed to be outside after dark. But he didn't care. The only thing he could think about was coming until she was overflowing.

He was being greedy, he knew that; only thinking about his own pleasure in that moment. So when she came for a second time, it completely caught him off guard. He had worked her bra up her chest and he had her nipple in his mouth when it happened, and he groaned, biting down on the edge of her areola. It had an obvious effect on her and she screamed, her back arching off the seat as her orgasm intensified. He couldn't take it and he came with a shout, wrapping his arms tightly around her waist as his hips kept jerking involuntarily, till there was no more of him to give.

Ding ding! Round one over! Marc: One. Lily: Two.

"This was a bad decision," she panted. He collapsed on top of her, all of his weight flattening her on the seat.

"Horrible. Terrible. I'm ashamed of myself. Give me fifteen minutes, and we'll make an even worse decision," he replied.

"Fifteen minutes, huh."

He laughed, and then she laughed. She combed her fingers through his hair. He pulled on her hair. She sighed his name. His bit down on her bottom lip. She managed to work her bra off. He ripped her underwear off.

Fifteen minutes was an over estimation – he only needed ten.

DAY FIVE

They spent the rest of the night, and most of the next morning, driving to Dakhla – a coastal city, about a third of the way into Western Sahara. Marc drove them across the border. Apparently, his comment about land mines hadn't been a joke. The area was riddled with them, and he wanted to take it slow and easy.

After finally wearing each other out in the back seat, they'd gotten dressed and headed back towards the French embassy. As they drove along, Lily flung her ruined underwear out a window, earning a smirk from Marc. She shimmied back into her shorts, regretting not having any other clothing. She did, however, untie her tank top and return it to normal.

They went back for their gear. Marc hopped out a couple streets down, with a promise to meet her on the outskirts of town. Lily had parked at their designated meeting spot, then she sat and chewed on her fingernails, ducking down in her seat. Worried that he wouldn't show up. Worried that someone would investigate her car. Worried the cops would pop up and question her.

None of those things happened, and after twenty minutes, Marc pulled up in the beat up suburban. They transferred everything to the stolen Explorer, then hit the road, driving off into the night.

When the sun began to rise, they switched places, and as they approached Dakhla, Marc suggested that they stop and take a breather.

"For how long?" Lily asked, glancing around the desert on either side of them. Western Sahara wasn't exactly an ideal vacation spot. There were three different countries, *and* inside factions, that were constantly fighting over ownership of the tiny country. The northern area had been claimed by Morocco, and Lily wanted to get up there as quickly as possible.

"Just for a night. I'm beat, you're beat, and I don't want one of us driving off the road here. Getting blown up probably isn't as fun as it sounds," he told her.

"You slept most of the way to the border," she pointed out.

"Shut up. You'll love it here."

Apparently, it wasn't so much a suggestion as a statement. They were stopping, and that was it.

Lily was shocked when they finally made their way into the small city. Dakhla was actually very pretty. Palm trees lined the dusty streets, and to their left, blue-green water lined an expansive strip of beach. It was really quite picturesque.

But sometimes nasty things can come in pretty packages. Lily herself was proof of that. She cleared her throat as Marc looked around for a hotel.

"Every time we've stopped," she started, keeping her voice even so she wouldn't come off as bratty or condescending, "something bad has happened. The boarding house in Mali, the home in Mauritania. It seems like whenever we stop to catch our breath, trouble catches up to us. I think this is a *really* bad idea."

"Maybe so, and maybe it will catch up to us, but sweetheart, we still need to catch our breath. This is a new car, so it's not possible that it would be bugged. No one would think to look for us here, since we had to get off the main road. They would assume we drove straight on into the city of Laayoune, or even into Morocco proper. We have to stop, Lily. I need to breathe," he said simply.

It struck Lily that Marc didn't like being in the car. It hadn't oc-curred to her before, but it kind of made sense. He did most of his work on his feet, creeping around in shadows. He was movement personified. Sitting still for hours on end must have been hard on him.

"Alright. But we *have* to move on, first thing in the morning," she stressed.

"Yes, mistress, anything you say, mistress."

"I like that. Keep calling me that."

They splurged and stopped at what seemed to be the nicest hotel in the small city. It sat *on* the beach, and had a quaint feel to it that had Lily remembering vacations in Mexico. A surreal quality that had her forgetting the here and now, the why and the what for of their situation.

"I hope you don't mind sharing a bed," Marc commented, barely holding the door open long enough for her to make it through into the room. She snorted at him.

"I guess I can deal with it, if you make it worth my while."

Denying their attraction to each other was stupid and pointless. They obviously couldn't keep their hands off each other, so they'd decided to just go with it. Sex relieved tension, and tension had become a way of life.

"We can just get dinner here, lay low," Marc called out as she wandered around the space and into the bathroom. She gasped.

"Oh my god, a bath tub," she moaned, falling against the door frame. There were footsteps, then Marc was right behind her.

"You take a bath," he suggested, "and I'll go out and scrounge up some more supplies. We barely have any food left, and it's like a fifteen hour drive to Tangier."

Lily frowned. Tangier, Morocco. Where she would get on a ferry to go to Barcelona, Spain. Where she would head off to end a very ugly chapter in her life. Where she would leave behind a very worthy opponent.

A very worthy friend.

Marc left and Lily turned on the water. Then she blockaded the front door to the room. If she was going to get any sort of rest, she would need to feel secure and like she could actually relax. So she jammed a chair under the door handle, and even shoved a huge dresser in front of the entrance, as well.

She left a trail of clothing across the floor as she dragged herself back into the bathroom. The water was almost scalding hot, but she didn't even care. She couldn't remember the last time she'd felt warm water on her body. *Hot* water. She groaned, scooting as much of herself under the water as she could and dunking her whole head.

After cleaning every inch of her skin with a rough sponge, she laid her head back against a towel and just relaxed, letting her mind wander.

What are you doing, Liliana?

It was a question she'd been asking herself since their night together at the house they'd broken into, though it had been on non-stop repeat since the night before, since their night in the back seat of the Explorer.

For five years, she hadn't been able to see beyond her one goal. Beyond getting close enough to Stankovski to kill him. She'd slept with plenty of guys in that time period. Guys she was attracted to, guys she was just using to get ahead in the underworld. None of them mattered, none of them stuck. When she'd had sex with Marc back in Liberia, it had been with the intention that he would just be another one of the many. Nothing special.

Which it wasn't ... was it?

They were like magnets, fighting against each other one minute, then stuck together the next. Whatever it was, it was tangible, and powerful, and very real, and very present. He was the first person to ever make her question her plan. To ever make her wonder if maybe revenge wasn't the answer.

"... we don't have to be these people anymore ..."

Who was she, anyway?

And more importantly, whoever she was, did she even want to be that person without him? Maybe it would be easier to be someone else *with* him. Maybe, just maybe, revenge wasn't the answer. Her revenge plan had almost gotten them both killed, several different times. Was it worth it? And Marc was right, killing Stankovski wouldn't bring Kaylee back – her sister would still be dead. Killing him wouldn't change anything, except Lily's perception of herself. And did she want to be that person?

Who am I, anyway?

Lily woke up with a start, jerking away at the sound of something hitting the ground. She sat up, splashing water in her face. She'd fallen asleep in the tub. She rubbed at her eyes and blinked around.

"You blocked the door."

She looked up and took in Marc, standing in the bathroom doorway.

"I wanted to relax," she yawned, gathering her wet hair in one hand and wringing out the ends.

"I had to pick the lock on the sliding glass entry. You didn't block that door," he pointed out. She shrugged and turned the hot water faucet on.

"Was too tired to remember. What time is it?"

"Like two or so. I got you some things," he said, bending down to dig in the bag he'd dropped at his feet. He pulled out some things for himself, then kicked the bag to the side of the tub.

"Like what?" she asked, picking through the items. She was happy to see a pair of pants and a shirt, and shocked to find a bathing suit.

"Essentials. Your hooker shorts are too much, we'll get shot if you keep walking around in them," he told her.

"Essentials, huh. Underwear should've made the list over a bikini," she replied, chucking the bottoms at him. He was standing in front of the mirror, spreading a shaving cream over his scruffy beard.

"Pffft, maybe on *your* list. Underwear didn't even make it onto my list. What's the point of them, anyway. They just get in my way," he replied. She laughed and settled back into the water.

"I don't think there's much that gets in your way, *Marcelle*," she teased him.

"Damn straight."

They were quiet for a while. Marc shaved while she turned off her hot water and tried to pretend that she wasn't ridiculously happy to see him. Every time he left her, she had a small fear that he wouldn't come back. That the ultimate betrayal was yet to happen, and it was only a matter of time before he stole the diamonds and left her in nowheres-ville, Africa. But he always came back for her, and she was beginning to think that maybe he always would.

"Scoot over."

She lifted her head to find him standing next to her, pulling his t-shirt off. She scooted forward while he dropped his pants, then he climbed into the water behind her, stretching his legs out on either side of her. It took some adjusting, but eventually they were situated with her stretched out on his legs, her back to his chest, his arms around her waist.

"This is nice," she whispered, leaning her head back so it rested on his shoulder.

"God. I think I'd actually forgotten what hot water feels like," he moaned, echoing her thoughts from when she'd first gotten in the bath. She turned her head, glancing at his face.

"I'd forgotten what you look like without shit all over your face," she replied, and he laughed as she ran her fingers down his cheek.

"'*Shit all over your face*'. You are a wordsmith, sweetheart," he sighed.

"Damn straight."

They chatted for a while, about nonsense. It was almost like old times, like back in the Bratva safe house. Only more nudity. But then their pauses got longer and longer, Marc's voice got heavier and heavier. Eventually he didn't respond to a question, and Lily looked up to find he'd fallen asleep.

I'd forgotten what he looks like without all that scruff. Forgotten that he's so good looking.

Scruff or no scruff, Marc was sexy. But without it, he looked sharper. Less crazy, more cunning. His brows were knitted together in his sleep, and his jaw was clenched. She wondered what he was dreaming about, what was making him so tense, even in his sleep.

She twisted around in the bathtub, laying against him, pressing her breasts against his abdomen. She hugged him close, managing to slide her hands around his back.

"Tell me what do, Marc," she breathed against his skin. "I've been making decisions for too long. Have they all been wrong? *Tell me what do.*"

Ridiculously, she felt teary eyed. She took that as a sign that they'd been in the water too long, and she climbed out, waking him up in the process. She put the bikini on, then found an ancient blow dryer in a bottom drawer of the vanity. A luxury. She blew out her hair, using a comb to tame the locks.

"My god, you almost look nice," Marc commented, looking over her reflection as he walked up behind her. She elbowed him in the stomach.

"Shut up."

While he got dressed, she headed out of the room. They had a glass door that led out to a small, fenced in patio. Lily stopped, glanced around, then simply hiked a leg over the wrought iron fencing. One more step, and she was at the side of the hotel's pool. Beyond that, a beach stretched out in front of her, disappearing in a haze where it met the ocean. She headed across the sand.

She couldn't get over it. In front of her was one of the most gorgeous sights she'd ever seen. Behind her was one of the most terrifying places she'd ever been. *Everywhere* they'd been was "*the most terrifying*"; going into the job, she'd known western Africa was dangerous. But a person couldn't really grasp the breadth of something like that till it was right in front of them. All around them.

Wow, talk about an analogy for this whole fucked up situation …

"What the fuck are you doing!?"

She heard Marc shouting from behind her, and she turned around, shielding her eyes from the sun. She had gone right up to the water and he looked tiny, standing in front of their hotel room.

"Come join me!" she yelled back, waving him forward.

"Get in here, right now!"

"What!? No, it's gorgeous out here! Just come here!"

"You fuckhead, it's not safe out there! Get in here, *NOW!*"

When she flipped him the bird, he started coming after her. She turned her back to him and continued watching the water as it lapped at her feet.

"We've been moving, non stop, for the last four days, I just want -" she began when she heard him right behind her.

"I know, believe me. But it's not safe to be outside. Anyone could see us," he informed her. He didn't come around to her front, or even to her side. He stayed directly behind her.

"What do you mean? Like who? A bell boy? A local? Oh no, god forbid they see us!" she laughed.

"I'm fucking serious."

"Me, too. I'm so pale, I might blind someone if they look directly at me," she joked, looking down the length of her body. She still thought they were teasing, but there was nothing funny in the way Marc grabbed her and spun her around.

"Do you want to get fucking shot? Standing out here, half naked, that red fucking hair everywhere. Want a sign that says '*shoot me*'?" he demanded, his fingers squeezing her biceps painfully.

"You're hurting me!" she snapped. He gave one more sharp squeeze, then let her go.

"*Good.* There's people out there that would do a lot worse than anything I've done to you. I'm just trying to protect you," he explained.

"Well, thank you very much, Mr. De Sant, but I think I've shown that I'm very capable of taking care of myself," she reminded him.

"No, you *think* you're '*very capable*', which is worse than knowing you're not," he snapped.

Lily's first reaction was to get mad, to tell him to go fuck himself. But she paused for a second and stared up at him. He was upset, irrationally so. It had been his idea to stop and take a breather – what was better for taking a breath than the seaside? She was on a beach, at a beach side hotel, in her bathing suit. There were other people scattered about the beach, also in bathing suits. There were black people and white people and tan people, all sorts of different colors. She didn't stand out *that* much, he was completely overreacting.

And Marc didn't overreact.

"What's going on?" she asked, cocking her head to the side.

"Huh?"

"You're freaking out. What's the big deal? Did something happen when you were out and about?" she continued.

He glared down at her for another moment, then sighed and looked away, scanning the horizon behind her.

"No," he answered. "It's been a long weekend, sweetheart. I've invested a lot energy in this mission. It would be a shame if we got this close to the end, only for you to get shot or kidnapped."

He's worried about me!?

"That's almost sweet, Marc, but I'm fine out here. If this is wearing you out so much, you don't have to continue, you know. You could still just leave," she pointed out, though once it was out of her mouth, she was nervous. She didn't want him to go.

"Not getting rid of me that easily, I'm getting those diamonds, we had a deal," he said quickly. She smiled, though she almost felt worse than before; it wasn't exactly a proclamation of love and devotion, a sonnet dedicated to how he felt a burning need to be in her presence.

Not that I want those things from him …

"Alright, then. I promise not to get shot or kidnapped, at least not anytime soon. Can we get something to eat now, or is that too dangerous?" she asked, her tone mocking.

He wrapped an arm around her shoulders and guided her back towards the hotel. He hugged her close to his side, babbling about some shop he'd been in while on his jaunt about town. But when she looked up at him, he wasn't looking at her. Wasn't looking ahead of them. His eyes seemed to be scanning the top floor the hotel. She followed his gaze, searching the windows for any sign of movement.

"… maybe we can have them deliver lunch to our rooms," Marc was finishing as they walked around the edge of the pool.

"Marc," she started, before climbing over the railing to their patio area. "Is there someone following you?"

"Why would you ask me that?"

"Because you're all twitchy and you were staring at the top floor."

"I wasn't staring, and I'm not twitchy."

"You're very twitchy."

"Shut up, Lily."

"Look at you, you're all nervous, and -"

He grabbed her arm again and pulled her close, catching her off guard. She stumbled into him and he immediately kissed her, walking her backwards through the sliding glass door. She moaned and pressed her hands against his face, standing on her toes to kiss him back.

"You talk too much," he breathed when he finally pulled away, slamming the glass door closed and locking it.

"You have the worst game of any man I've ever met. You're always insulting me. You must never get ass on your own," she pointed out. He wrapped an arm around her waist, pulling her towards the bathroom.

"I got *you*."

"Lack of options. You were the only man in Liberia worth fucking."

"I take what I can get."

Once in the room, he pushed her up against a wall, shoved his tongue down her throat. Worked his leg between hers, forcing her to straddle his thigh. Every time she moved, it caused sensitive areas to rub and move and come alive.

"Why'd you get me a bathing suit if you didn't want me on the beach?" she struggled to breathe while his teeth worked at the outline of her clavicle.

"There's that talking problem again," he mumbled, untying the bikini strap from behind her neck.

"Did you only want to rent a hotel room to do this?" she questioned. She'd always thought his request to stop had been strange – had he done it for nookie?

"Beats the back seat of a car."

"Yeah, but at least in the car, we wouldn't need to stop for a whole -"

"Seriously, Lily. Shut your mouth, or I'm going to find something more useful for it."

"Big talk."

When he grabbed her hair and forced her to her knees, it didn't seem like such big talk anymore.

Maybe stopping for the night isn't such a bad idea.

Lily twitched and rubbed at her nose, still half asleep. She was laying on her stomach, the sheets yanked away from her body and twisted around her legs. She yawned and stretched out her left arm, feeling around for Marc. But the bed next to her was empty. She twisted her head to the side and cracked open an eyelid.

"Marc?" she croaked out, then cleared her throat.

She hadn't so much fallen asleep, it was more like passing out. Marc's energy was never ending, and he had hard ons to match. They went through lunch, fooled around in the shower, then he bent her over the bed and didn't let up till she literally begged him to stop. And even then, as she was almost asleep, his fingers were back between her thighs, and before she could say yay or nay, his head had replaced his fingers, and well, a girl simply couldn't say no to that, not when a man was so good with his tongue.

Lily rolled over onto her back and propped herself up on her elbows, glaring around the room. She wasn't sure how long she'd been asleep. The last thing she remembered was going to the bathroom and putting her t-shirt and bikini bottoms back on, with the intention of staying awake. But then she'd laid down, just for a second, and that was it. Lights out. It had to have been an hour since then, at least.

It was dark in the room, the sun had set, and she was starving – they had never gotten around to eating anything. She tried to look out the glass doors of the room, to see if he was sitting on their terrace, and wondered why he hadn't woken her up. Then she looked out the window, which offered a view of the pool, and wondered why he'd let her sleep for so long. Then she turned her head to the other side of the room.

Oh, and I definitely wonder why there's a strange man in the room with me.

She immediately started scrambling sideways across the bed, but he was quick, leaping forward and grabbing her arm. He was also strong – one good yank, and she was pulled off the mattress, landing in a heap on the floor. As he tugged her to her feet, she swung her free arm, directing her elbow towards his head, but he managed to duck, and grabbed that arm, as well. Both her wrists were pinned behind her back and his free hand gripped onto her shoulder, squeezing painfully.

"Let's not make this difficult, shall we?"

Whoever he was, he had a very posh British accent. Very cultured sounding, very refined. She growled and yanked around, trying to pull free.

"*Fuck you.*"

"Lovely, a charmer. Let's go, darling."

He pressed her wrists hard into her spine, forcing her back to arch, and his fingers pulled on her shoulder, pulling her into an awkward back bend of sorts. She had to walk on her toes as she was pushed around the bed.

"Wait, wait, wait," she breathed, refusing to move.

"No waiting."

"Please. You don't understand. I know why you're here," she tried to kill time, hoping Marc would show up. Or was Marc already dead?

Or did he leave you? He was acting so strange. Maybe he saw this coming. Maybe he left you and took the diamonds.

"I don't think you know anything. Please, keep walking," the man instructed.

"I'm not stealing the diamonds. I'm still going to Morocco. I'm still doing the job," she insisted.

"Really? Didn't look like you were on the job this afternoon," he called her out. She scowled.

"Oh, a hitman *and* a peeping tom. Versatile," she didn't hide the disdain in her voice.

"When a show is that good, darling, you don't look away. You were very impressive. Very flexible," his voice was almost teasing. She pressed back into him, sticking her butt out as much as was possible in her position, pushing directly into his crotch.

"You have no idea how *flexible* I can be," she whispered.

"Don't fall for it, she'll fuck you up."

Marc's voice startled her and she immediately started looking for him. Her captor twisted them around, pointing them back towards the glass doors. One of them was open, and they turned just in time to see Marc drop to the ground. He'd been hiding in the trellis that extended beyond their little patio area. As he walked forward, she saw light from the pool area glinting off the barrel of the gun he had pointed at them.

"You say that, but how do I know you're not just keeping the goods to yourself?" their intruder commented. It threw Lily off. There was a familiarity in the way he talked to Marc.

"I am doing that, but I'm also not lying. That wildcat you're holding has kicked my ass on several different occasions. She'll say anything you want to hear and then she'll hand you your nuts," he explained.

"She didn't look so threatening earlier – you handled her pretty well."

"I have a magic touch. Subdues her like nothing else."

"Hey!" she finally yelled. "I am *actually* in the room! Is this a kidnapping or not!? Because if not, I'd really love it if you could take your *fucking hands off of me!*"

There was silence for a second, then she was abruptly shoved forward. She fell to her knees, catching herself with her hands. When she looked up, the man had used the distraction to pull out a firearm of his own. Marc was fully in the room and the two men glared at each other, guns pointed and ready to fire.

"I can't believe it," Marc was growling. "How much is the bounty, huh? Must be pretty fucking big to get you here."

"That hurts. When I saw your name come across the board, I didn't even look at the price. An opportunity to take out *the* Marcelle De Sant? Couldn't resist, mate," the man commented.

"Pity you wasted the opportunity. Whatever happened to being friends, huh?" Marc asked.

"Whatever happened to honor? I know you're a thief, De Sant, but stealing from the hand that feeds you? Tsk tsk," the guy clucked his tongue. Marc glared.

"Easy to do when the hand that was feeding me turned around and tried to set me up and have me killed, *after* I completed the job," he countered.

"Is that the truth?"

"Do you really think I'd lie about this?"

There was a long pause. The way they were staring at each other was intense. Lily held still, sitting on the floor in front of the British man. They clearly knew each other some how. A hit had been taken out on Marc, obviously from the Bratva. The stranger had taken the job. And he was a friend of Marc's. Or colleague? Something.

What an asshole.

Lily was sitting at an angle, on her left hip, her legs bent at her side. The two men were distracted by angrily glaring at each other, so she decided to act fast. Pushing off the ground with her hands, she jabbed her right leg out, slamming her foot into the other man's knee. He let out a surprised shout, bending forward, and she swept her leg behind his ankles, sending him to his ass.

She was on him in a second, grabbing him by the hair and slamming his head into the ground. He dropped his gun and his hands went to her hips, holding her tight against his waist. She still had her hands in his hair when he surged forward, rolling them backwards. Suddenly, he was on top, with her legs wrapped around his waist.

"Christ, where did you find this woman!?" he shouted. She pulled his head towards her and bit down on his ear, earning her a strangled cry.

"Told you she'd kick your ass!" Marc shouted from above them.

Why isn't he doing anything!?

The intruder pulled away, his ear bleeding. Lily dug her fingers into the sensitive underside of his arm, trying to pinch skin through his knit sweater, but before she could get a good grip, his hands went around her neck. He wasn't fucking around – her wind pipe felt like it was pinched in half.

"You were right, De Sant. *A wildcat.* She's practically feral. Best to put her down," the guy said through gritted teeth, his fingers squeezing harder.

I did not live through Bratvas and Liberian gangs and darkest Africa and Marcelle De fucking Sant, just to get strangled to death in a posh hotel room. How embarrassing.

There was the sound of a slide being racked and everything froze. Lily and her attacker both looked up at the same time. Marc was standing over them, the barrel of the gun pressed up against the back of the man's head.

"Maybe so, but you see, that's *my* wildcat, and I'd really appreciate it if you got the fuck off of her, *now.*"

The guy let go of her throat and she hacked and coughed, sucking in air. He slowly climbed off her, his hands raised in the air. She rolled to her side, trying to catch her breath.

"Now De Sant, you know I could've killed her. I didn't," the man pointed out. Marc kept the gun at the back of his head.

"What do you think, sweetheart? Shoot him or no?" Marc called out. She got onto her hands and knees, still coughing.

"Shoot him," she croaked out.

"Since when do you take orders from a woman?" the assassin asked. Marc snorted.

"I don't. She makes horrible fucking decisions," he replied, then he dropped his gun.

Lily was shocked, but was doubly so when the British man turned around and held out his arms, hugging Marc. The two men laughed and clapped each other on the back.

Maybe he choked me unconscious and I'm hallucinating.

"I really thought you came here to kill me," Marc was chuckling as he pulled away.

"I'm crushed, De Sant. You think I'd kill a brother? When I found out they were looking for someone to take you out, I decided to immediately fly out here. Figured if I could get here first, maybe you'd actually have a chance at pulling off whatever it is you're trying to do," the man explained, taking a few steps back and pulling off the black gloves he was wearing.

"We were pulling it off just fine before you, thanks, but help is always appreciated," Marc told him.

"Go on, tell me how glad you are that I'm here."

"Well, I don't like to lie."

"Since when?"

"Excuse me!" Lily interrupted, climbing to her feet. "But when you two gentlemen are done *blowing each other*, could you explain to me what the fuck is going on!?"

"Lily, this is a friend of mine, of sorts," Marc said. The man took off the black bulletproof vest he was wearing and let it drop to the floor before he leaned towards her, holding his hand out.

"Cheers, darling, a pleasure to meet you," he said. She refused to shake his hand.

"Sorry I can't say the same," she hissed.

"Don't worry, you'll learn to love me"

"Doubtful."

"All the ladies do."

"I think I'm going to vomit. Can you get him out of here?" she asked Marc.

"No. Law is the kind of person you want on your side," he replied quickly.

"Excuse me? What law?" she was confused. The man finally took her hand into his own, raising the back of it to his lips.

"*My* law, darling. Kingsley Law, at your service," he introduced himself. She yanked her hand away.

"Now I *definitely* know I'm going to vomit."

Lily didn't want to like Kingsley, she really didn't. She didn't like new people, in general. She didn't like having a whole new wrench thrown into her plan. She didn't like someone who had watched her have sex, then broke into her hotel room, attempted to abduct her, choked her, then proved to have a closer relationship with Marc than she could ever hope to have. She wanted to hate him.

But he'd been telling the truth – he was impossible to dislike.

He was charming and he was funny, but even more than that, he was ridiculously good looking. He was also all the things his voice had hinted at; cultured, refined, intelligent.

Marc was all rough sexiness, five o'clock shadow and gritted teeth, his presence filling a room like a bomb blast.

Kingsley was smoothness personified, with gel in his hair, and a suit under all his black gear. He was well groomed and had stormy blue eyes and fair skin, a sharp jaw and broad shoulders, complimented by perfect pearly teeth and a perfect pearly smile. His presence was sharp, like a knife.

They probably make one hell of a team.

"That's why you were freaking out on the beach," Lily put it all together.

"I knew I was being tailed in town," Marc explained. "He's good enough to stay out of sight, but not good enough to go unnoticed."

"Oi, watch it. I wanted to be noticed," Kingsley cut in.

"Sure. Whatever you say."

"Why didn't you tell me!?" Lily snapped, punching Marc in the arm.

"Well, we were a little busy. '*Hey, we might have an assassin following us*', seems an awkward thing to say when I'm inside of you. Didn't want to kill the mood."

They went to dinner and spent a few hours introducing Lily and Kingsley, explaining their back stories to each other, or as much as they were willing to share, and then going over the previous five days. They had dinner in the hotel's restaurant, sitting outside on a large cement patio. It was the most relaxing thing Lily had done since she'd arrived in Africa. Probably in the last five years. They ate, they drank, they chatted. Like a normal group of friends, on a normal vacation.

"As fun as this is," Kingsley sighed, leaning forward to pour more wine in his glass, "what about tomorrow, folks?"

"The plan was to push on through to Tangier, Lily has to get on the ferry there," Marc explained, sipping at a beer.

"That's good. Best to move on. How're you going to handle the exchange?" he pressed.

"Marc won't be there for that," Lily filled in. "He's going to get a ticket and get on the ferry before me. I'm going to call Ivanov, the guy who orchestrated all this, the night before and set it up. I should be able to show the diamonds and just get on. Then hand the diamonds off to Marc."

"Who then just … comes back?" Kingsley finished.

"Yeah," Lily and Marc said in unison.

"Right," he sighed, then pulled a pack of fancy looking cigarettes out of the inside pocket of his jacket. A heaviness fell over the conversation.

"Well," Lily stood up from her seat, "I'll leave you two lovebirds alone. Kingsley, it *really* was a pleasure. Sorry I tried to break your knee cap and bite off your ear. Will I see you in the morning?"

"Darling, I wouldn't dream of leaving without saying goodbye, and you can nibble on my ear anytime," Kingsley offered, taking her hand and pulling her close. Lily laughed and Marc glared.

"I don't know about that, we'll see how tomorrow goes," she joked, sliding her hand free of his.

"If it would help you decide, I could spend the night. I give a beautiful full body, deep tissue massage. You must be fully naked, of course, but it's for medicinal purposes, only," he assured her.

"That would get really awkward since I plan on being in that bed naked as well," Marc piped up.

"That does put a damper on things."

A couple more jokes and Lily finally made her escape. It was almost midnight, they were the only people left in the restaurant. She also still wanted to leave early in the morning. It was going to be a long drive, a full day and night, and she wanted to make sure they got to Tangier during the day time.

She walked along the sand, skirting the pool area on the way back to their room. Her mind was wandering. The day before, she'd been a pretend prostitute, helping Marc to steal a car. Now, it felt like she was on holiday with two gorgeous male friends, one of which she was sleeping with.

One of which felt like more than a friend.

"*... we don't have to be these people anymore ...*"

She wondered what he'd meant by that, if he'd been serious. Would he run away with her? They'd only known each other for a little over a month, and the past week had been a little extreme. Outside of Africa, what would it be like? Lily was wondering if she was truly built for a life of crime, and she got the feeling Marc wouldn't be willing to wait around while she figured out the ropes.

Or would he?

When she got in the room, she stripped naked – *after* closing all the curtains – and climbed between the sheets. She stared at the ceiling for a while, trying to clear her mind. Trying to think of what it was she wanted in life, what she *really* wanted.

I don't know anymore.

DAY FIVE

Lily had barely walked out of view when Kingsley spoke up.

"She's bloody gorgeous. Cheers," he commented, toasting his wine glass up.

"Yeah, she's pretty sexy," Marc agreed.

"How long have you two been together?" his friend asked, tapping a cigarette against the table before lighting it.

"I think it's been five days. The day after the heist," Marc explained, finishing off the last of his meal.

"No, I meant *together*," Kingsley stressed, blowing a stream of smoke into the breeze. Marc shook his head.

"I don't get what you mean. We were never together before then, we stayed at separate places, only saw each other at the safe house."

"Either you're avoiding answering me, or you're incredibly stupid."

Marc sighed.

"We slept together after the heist, the night before she left. I didn't think anything of it, we'd been dancing around each other all month, we weren't supposed to ever see each other again. You've seen her, I couldn't walk away without a taste," he answered honestly.

"Ah. So this whole time, you've -"

"No. I thought she set me up, I almost killed her. I wasn't joking back in the room, that woman will fuck your world up. She looks like a pin up, fucks like a porn star, and fights like Tyson," he described her. Kingsley laughed and rubbed the ear she'd chewed on.

"I certainly got that impression, and I won't deny the rest. Yet you didn't kill her," he pointed out.

"No. She wouldn't let me, and she really hadn't known about the set up. And then we were in Mali, and she held her own in a gun fight, might have even saved me a time or two. I owe her. I told her I'd help her, so I am," he finished.

"Doesn't sound like the De Sant I know. You sure you're only helping her because you *owe her*?" Kingsley checked.

"Why else would I be?"

"Seems very obvious to me that you like the girl."

"I like the girl plenty, most of all when she's naked."

"I don't think that's it."

"Enlighten me."

"Look, why are you even doing this, anyway? Why not just sell the diamonds and make a run for it?" Kingsley asked.

"Tried that angle. Told her we could split them, we could sell them together. She's got her own agenda that she won't let go of, she's gotta get to Moscow," Marc answered.

"What's in Moscow?"

"Big boss Stankovski. She's got some plan to put a bullet between his eyes."

"Oh my. She *is* a wildcat."

"You have no idea."

"So why aren't you going with her?"

"Why in the fuck would I go with her!?"

"Stankovski will kill her. She's good, but she's raw, Marc. Her temper is going to be the death of her. She needs your help," Kingsley stressed. Marc glared.

"She's done pretty goddamn fine all on her own. She got to Africa, didn't she?"

"Not the same."

"No one held our hands, when you and I were making names

for ourselves."

"*Not the same*. She's not trying to make a name. She's trying to find closure, and she thinks it'll come from a gun," Kingsley stressed.

"I've explained all this to her. She's got a thick head, and that's not my problem. I get her to Tangier, I get her on that ferry. That was the deal. She wasn't interested in any other plans, and frankly, neither am I," Marc stated.

"That's a bloody lie if I ever heard one," Kingsley called him out. Marc scowled.

"What would you suggest I do, Law? Mr. Ladies Man? Throw her over my shoulder and walk off into the sunset?" he was snide.

"Yes. You like her. She clearly likes you, though for the life of me I can't figure out why, especially now that she's met me," his friend smiled at him.

"Shut up."

"The chemistry between you is so thick, I'm surprised the table didn't catch on fire. Would it be so bad to hang up your guns and retire? From what I was told, those diamonds would fetch a pretty price," Kingsley pointed out.

"Retire from a job that I love, a life that I love, for a woman I just met, that I can barely stand, that has tried to kill me several times, all because I like how she fucks?" Mark double checked the stupidity of Kingsley's statement.

"If that helps you sleep at night, then keep telling yourself all of that. We'll see how you feel when you're waving goodbye to that ferry, watching that red hair get farther and farther away," Kingsley sighed.

"Since when do you pop up out of nowhere and dole out relationship advice? How the fuck did you find us, anyway?" Marc demanded.

"You seem to forget, I know you. Recognize your touch," Kingsley teased.

"Answer the question."

"Reports were coming out of Nouakchott. Someone had stolen

a car that belonged to the cousin of an attaché of the French ambassador. A spectacular incident, apparently the thief was a prostitute operating with a surly pimp, luring the man away from the hotel. There was a car chase and allegedly tires were shot out causing a huge crash. Lots of damage. The moment I heard the word '*surly*', I knew it could only be one person causing all that trouble," he laughed.

"Fuck off. How'd you know we'd be in Dakhla?"

"I've been following you since Guerguerat, mate. Just inside the border. I was actually heading down towards Nouakchott and we passed each other. Can you believe it? Lily was driving. I turned around, and when you stopped to steal some gas, I planted a tracker on your bumper," he explained.

"Damn. I'm getting lax in my old age," Marc chuckled, though he didn't feel like laughing.

"I'd say it's more like you were distracted," Kingsley suggested.

"Shut up."

"Understandably so."

"So even more reason why it has to be goodbye in Tangier."

"Or you could get better at your job."

"I *am* good at my job, that's why I have to leave her."

"We're talking in circles," Kingsley sighed. "Fine. Say goodbye. But I think you're passing up a golden opportunity to train someone who could become like your right hand. And if you're not willing to take advantage of that, than I am."

"No, you're not," Marc informed him.

"I'm not?"

"If you ever make a move on her, now or in the future, I'll shove your head so far up your ass, you'll be able to lick your own stomach lining," Marc threatened.

"Oh, I see how it is – you don't want her, but no one else can have her. Selfish, De Sant," Kingsley scolded him.

"I can live with that."

"You're impossible."

The other man abruptly stood up.

"Where are you going?" Marc asked, a little startled.

"I have an aversion to spending time with stupid people, and you're being very stupid. So good night, and I'll see you in the morning. Maybe you'll have come to your senses by then," he said, stubbing out his cigarette.

"Fuck you."

Kingsley was already walking away, waving goodbye without looking.

Marc paid their bill and finally headed back to their room. Lily had only had about a thirty minute lead on him, but when he got to the room, she was already out cold. She tended to stretch out on her stomach, as he now knew, her arms spread out to her sides. He'd woken up earlier with a hand in his face.

While she slept, he sat in a chair and pulled up a night table, systematically going through their weapons. He cast aside the guns that no longer had any ammo. Then he began breaking down the remaining ones, cleaning them.

It was unnecessary; they hadn't used the guns since Mauritania, when Lily had shot out the tire. If things kept going the way they were, they wouldn't need them at all anymore. Just her precious Glock. But cleaning them helped clear his mind. Helped him think. Helped him pretend like he wasn't thinking about her.

He glanced at her while he worked. Her head was facing him, some strands of hair laying across her face. She pouted her lips in her sleep, almost like she was about to blow him a kiss. He smiled to himself.

What have I gotten myself into?

Kingsley was completely right. Marc did like Lily. *A lot.* He thought they were a hell of a team, and it didn't hurt that he liked the way she looked, liked the way she talked. Liked everything about her.

But what could he offer her? A life that was roughly the same as the last five days. Small moments of calm with random outbursts of violence. She'd already mentioned several times that she couldn't wait to get out of Africa, couldn't wait to get out of the life she'd been living for the last five years. How could he ask her to stay in it?

And tough as she was, there was a tender girl under that hard facade. A million self defense classes couldn't hide that fact from him. She could threaten and kick and fight, but when she'd actually pulled the trigger, actually killed someone, it had wrecked her. Disgusted her.

Marc had no problem pulling the trigger. How could she be with someone like him? And if she did stay with him, it wouldn't be long before he changed that part of her. Made her as cold and cynical as himself. *Ruined* that part of her.

He moved to sit on the bed next to her. The sheet had fallen down to her waist, exposing her bare back. He lightly touched his fingertips to her skin, drawing them down to the edge of the blanket. Then he moved them back up to her shoulders and repeated the motion. He loved her skin, it felt like the softest satin he'd ever touched. The finest silk.

Much too rich for me. I could never afford this.

"*Marcelle*," she mumbled in her sleep. He smiled at the use of his full name, and wondered what she was dreaming about.

"*Liliana*," he returned the favor. "In spite of everything, it's been a fun ride."

She shuddered and scooted closer to him, tucking her arms under her chest. As she moved, he saw a large bruise on the side of her rib cage, and he frowned. His eyes moved to another bruise. Then another. Red marks around her throat.

In Monrovia, the first time they'd slept together, there had been no marks on her body. Just smooth expanses of milky white skin that blushed red in the wake of his fingertips. Now, she was riddled with bruises. She'd been banged up, and while it didn't detract from her looks at all, it compounded his guilt. She wouldn't have them, if it weren't for him. If he'd just left Africa, like she'd suggested. He'd gotten away from the gang in Monrovia, saving his reputation hadn't really been necessary. If he'd just fled the continent, she would've already made it to Tangier. She would've gotten to Barcelona. She would've already accomplished her goal.

She'd probably be dead.

"Your plan is a bad one, but staying with me? That's worse," he sighed, putting his elbows on his knees and his head in his hands.

I've been doing wrong for so many years. How do I know what's right?

DAY SIX

Lily woke up with the sunrise, relishing in the feel of not having to bolt the moment she opened her eyes. She laid in one spot for a while, watching the beach through the glass door. When it was fully light out, she turned on her side, wondering if Marc was awake. He was a light sleeper, he always seemed to be awake before her. She hoped he was, it would be their last time alone for a while. Last time to play with each other without any threats looming over them, or fears of being attacked.

But when she rolled over, Marc was on the extreme opposite side of the king sized bed. He was fully clothed, on top of the covers, with his back to her. If that wasn't body language that screamed *"don't fucking touch me"*, then Lily didn't know what was. She decided to heed it, and she slipped out of bed. She pulled the black bikini back on, slipped on her shirt, then headed out onto the patio.

"Morning, darling."

Lily looked to her right. Kingsley was sitting in one of their chairs, reading a Spanish newspaper. He was wearing a pair of silk pajama pants and no shirt, showing a lean torso that was outlined in tone muscles. He also had a pair of old fashioned sunglasses perched on his nose, and he glanced over them when she sat across from him.

"Good morning," she yawned, pouring herself a cup of coffee from the pitcher he had sitting on the table.

"And where's Mr. De Sant?"

"Inside, sleeping."

"Lazy."

She laughed.

"Not a word I ever would've used to describe him. Though he didn't even bother changing out of the clothes he wore yesterday," she commented.

"Really. *Interesting*," was all Kingsley said.

"So how long have you and Marc known each other?" she questioned. She knew Marc wouldn't allow her to ask questions, but Kingsley seemed more open. The other man smiled and folded up his newspaper.

"Ah, how long, how long. Feels like forever! We met in New York, maybe ... six years ago? Seven? He was young. I had been hired to assassinate a diplomat from Uzbekistan. I had it all set up, long range shot from a building, to be made while the mark was jogging. I was all set to pull the trigger when this tiny puppy dog of a man ran into the shot. Some jogger, in sweats and a beat up hoodie, ran smack into my target, almost knocking him down.

"I thought it was just some clumsy idiot, barreling through the park. But when he ran off, my target was on the ground. Turned out the bastard had cut the man's brachial artery clean in half – that's the major blood vessel in the upper arm. He died in about four minutes. It didn't have any sense of style, and he could've been caught, but it was simple. It got the job done, and it was quick. I was impressed. I went back to the people who I took the job from, managed to find out who had claimed the bounty. Tracked Marc down to an abandoned building in Queens. We've been friends ever since," Kingsley finished the story.

Lily wasn't sure how to feel about it. She'd seen Marc kill people, but it had always been in self defense. She'd never seen him do it for profit, or for sport. Knowing he'd done it before, and hearing a detailed description of it actually happening, were two very different things. She leaned back in her chair.

"Do you guys work together, like partners?" she asked, staring out at the ocean.

"Sometimes. We have our strengths, we help each other out when we can. Marc isn't as good at stealth as I am, and no one can crack a safe as quickly as me. But he's got a sort of brutish way about him that can come in handy, and his knowledge of weapons and human anatomy have saved me a time or two. That man could've been a surgeon," he told her.

"Oh god. I can already picture his bedside manner."

"Seems to me you've already experienced his bedside manner."

She finally looked at him again.

"You mention that quite a bit," she pointed out. "Does it bother you?"

"No. I'm jealous," he answered honestly, taking a sip of his coffee.

"Jealous!?"

"I don't know if anyone's ever told you this, darling, but you're a very attractive woman. You also aren't bothered by our profession. In other words, a rarity. And on top of that, I did get to see you in action the other day, in more ways than one. When you get tired of Marc, I do hope you'll give me a call," he said, picking something up from the table and handing it to her. It was a card.

"You can't be serious," she actually laughed as she looked the item over. At first she thought it was just solid black, and she didn't get the point, but then as she tilted it, she realized there was debossing on one side. "*LAW.*", in large capital letters, took up the middle of the card. When she flipped it over, she saw that a bunch of tiny numbers marched across the bottom of the card, also debossed. It was all very classy, very chic. Very him.

"Dead serious, love. Marc may not know a good thing when he's got it, but I certainly do," he assured her. She nodded and set the card in her lap.

"Well ... um ... thank you?" she searched for what to say. She felt like she was being propositioned. Like she should point out that she was with his best friend, and what he was doing was inappropriate. But she wasn't really *with* Marc, and what counted as proper when dealing with mercenaries?

"Don't seem so shocked," Kingsley laughed, then leaned forward and grabbed her right ankle. He put her foot in his lap and began massaging it. "I'd like to say it's you making me this way, but I am a firm believer in honesty, and to be frank, most anything with tits makes me act this way."

She burst out laughing.

"That actually makes me feel better, thank you."

"So, Lily, right? Tell me what your plan is," Kingsley told her, rotating her foot at the ankle, stretching it towards her calf. She winced, but it felt good.

"What plan?" she asked, then groaned as he stretched her foot the other way, curling her toes downwards.

"After this, your plan. Marc makes it sound like you're both going to skip down the yellow brick road, walk a red carpet onto some boat, then waltz through Moscow, shooting one of the most powerful men in the underworld. I'm curious as to how you're going to pull this off," he explained.

"We don't think it's going to be easy. Nothing about this trip has been easy. It's been war this whole time. I don't expect that to stop. But I fought my way this far, so I'm not giving up," she stressed.

"Wishes and intentions are very noble, but don't get the job done. *What is your plan.*"

She told him what she and Marc had previously come up with - about getting from Barcelona to Moscow. Then her own personal plan, to claim she was delivering the diamonds. That she would only place them in Stankovski's hands, and his alone. Use that to get into his house, into his space. Then she would blow his brains out.

"And you honestly think that will work?"

"Yes. It has to."

"Ah, of course. It has to, so clearly it will."

"Do you have a better plan?"

"No. I just think there's more to it. What if Ivanov doesn't believe you? What if he's laying in wait for you, in Tangier? What if Stankovski has already sent someone else to collect the diamonds from you in Barcelona?" Kingsley prattled off questions, all while his fingers dug into the bottom of her foot.

"What if, what if, what if. What if we get blown up tomorrow? What if thirty Liberians burst into this hotel right now? What it Bratva members parachute out of the sky? I can only plan for what I know, and hope to roll with whatever punches may come," she replied. He smiled widely at her.

"Wonderful answer, darling. You know, I think you have a lot to learn, but I also think you have real potential," he told her.

"Potential for what?"

"Potential to be very good in this profession. Women are in high demand, and one who looks like you, who will be able to say she fought her way across Africa? You could charge any price you wanted for your services."

She was completely thrown off guard.

"You think so?"

"I know so."

She picked up his card, looking over it again. She tapped her finger against the edge.

"I don't know if I want to lead that kind of life," she said in a soft voice.

"Darling, I hate to tell you this, but based on what I've heard thus far, you already *do* lead that kind of life," he replied. She nodded.

"Yes. But how? All my connections are with this Bratva, and a different one in New York. I'm pretty sure those recommendations will die with Stankovski," she told him.

"If you pull this off, love, that'll be all the recommendation you need. But you'll also have people like Marc and myself willing to recommend you, which will speak leagues," he added.

"I've trained to transport. I got my start in money laundering. Is that enough? I don't think I want to kill people," she said the last part quickly.

"You don't have to do anything you don't want to, love, that's the beauty of our profession. You take the jobs you want. Stick with transporting, or learn how to hack computers, crack safes, kidnap, whatever you'd like," he listed off different aspects of his job. She thought for a second.

"Do you think Marc would teach me those things?"

"*No.*"

The voice came from behind her, and she tilted her head backwards to watch the object of her question come walking through the door. He glanced at Kingsley, then did a double take at the foot massage that was happening. He glared and snatched the card out from between Lily's fingers.

"We were just -" she started, then gasped as he ripped the card up and scattered the pieces on the table.

"I know what's going on, and *you* can fuck right off," Marc said, pointing at Kingsley before knocking Lily's foot out of his lap.

"Just having a conversation, mate."

"Fuck you."

"Someone woke up on the wrong side of the bed," Lily accused him.

"Fuck you, too."

Kingsley kept smiling, even as he drank his coffee.

"Sooooo …," Lily let her voice trail off when she and Marc finally went back into their room.

"So what?" he snapped, scratching his fingers through his hair as he walked into the bathroom. She followed him and leaned against the door frame.

"So what's your problem?" she asked.

"I don't have a problem."

"Really? Cause you're acting like you have a *big* problem," she pointed out.

"Well, I don't."

"I think you do."

"I don't care."

"I think you do."

"*Lily.*"

"I thought you and Kingsley were friends," she said, watching as he grabbed their toiletry items and began throwing them into the duffle bag.

"That's stretching it," he replied.

"If you're going to keep acting like a dick, then I'm going back outside," she warned him.

"Go ahead, I'm sure you'd enjoy it."

"You're acting like a jealous bitch," she called him out. He turned to look at her, and his face had murder written on it.

"You're out there, parading around in your goddamn underwear, your feet in his crotch – how the fuck am I supposed to react?" Marc demanded. She laughed again, actually flattered.

"Ooohhh, just think, if you'd come out five minutes later, you could've caught me giving one of my world famous '*foot jobs*'!" she teased.

"*Fuck you.*"

He was really angry, and she suddenly clued into the fact that it probably had very little to do with Kingsley.

"Hey," she said, grabbing the front of his t-shirt and turning his body towards her. "We were just talking. What's going on with you?"

"Nothing, we gotta get out of here," he grumbled, trying to push past her. She moved with him, blocking him from leaving the bathroom.

"Not until you explain to me why you're being such an asshole," she stated.

"I don't have to explain shit to you."

He hadn't talked to her that way in a while, not since Liberia. He cussed all the time, and snapped at her, and they argued like cats and dogs, but he didn't talk down to her. Not until that moment. She frowned while he struggled with her, trying to bodily move her out of the way.

Do something.

Normally she would've smacked him, or kicked him in the nuts. Knock some sense into him, literally. But she decided to take a page out of his book and she grabbed him by the back of the neck, yanking him down to her height and kissing him.

She figured he would shove her away, but he didn't. In fact, he dove into the kiss with such zeal that they lost their balance, tripping across the bathroom and slamming into the door. She gasped and his tongue plunged into her mouth, almost choking her. His hands were in her hair, holding her in place, and his hips started grinding against hers.

"If that's what you wanted, all you had to do was say something," she whispered when he finally pulled away.

"Hard to say anything when you're always talking," he breathed, leaning back.

"Shut up, Marc."

"Just had a bad night, that's all. I like Law, I really do, I just … don't like people sometimes," he tried to explain.

"Want me to leave you alone?"

"You're an exception."

She felt a warmth spread across her chest.

"I am?"

He glared at her for a second, then walked out of the bathroom.

"Get dressed. We're leaving in ten minutes."

Did he become bipolar over night!?

Marc had bought her the bikini, a sleeveless shirt, and a pair of thick, black leggings. She put everything on, chucking her shorts and old tank top into the trash, along with her bra. Then she finished loading up the duffle bag with all their weapons while Marc took everything out of his pack and rearranged. Just as he was lifting up the bag with the diamonds, Kingsley walked into the room.

"Oh my, my, my, there's a pretty sight," he sighed, dropping a bag of his own on the floor and walking towards the glistening stones. Marc glared and buried them in his pack before zipping it shut and throwing it onto his back.

"Let's go," Lily said, standing up quickly, trying to stop any sort of fighting before it could start.

They loaded up the Explorer and took off. Lily opted to sit in the back seat, while Marc drove and Kingsley navigated. Marc seemed to loosen up, slipping into an easy banter with his friend, and it made her smile. If anything happened, she felt like she couldn't be in better company to handle it. She felt comfortable with these men. Secure.

After about six hours, they shifted around. Marc hadn't been lying about not sleeping well – the minute he stretched out in the back seat, he passed out. Lily made herself comfortable, sticking one leg out the passenger window. Then she and Kingsley talked for an hour or so, chit chatting about nonsense. Things that didn't pertain to their situation. Then as they fell quiet, she started thinking about what he'd said back at the hotel.

"Hey," she suddenly realized something. "You asked about ours, but what's your plan?"

"Hmmm?"

"Your plan. What are you doing with us? You came here to assassinate Marc, but really to warn him. Mission accomplished. Now what?" she asked.

"Now I'll try to make myself useful, for as long as possible. I don't have any other jobs lined up, and I'll have to lay low for a while after this one, so better make it count," he replied.

"Are you going to get in trouble, for not killing him?"

"'In trouble'? Darling, this isn't primary school. I don't have a boss I answer to. Yes, Stankovski won't be happy, but his power is not all-reaching. He has enemies, just like everyone else, and as a free agent, I can work for them – which I have done before, and will continue to do, regardless. Besides, none of that will matter, if you stick to *your* plan and actually kill him," Kingsley explained.

"Then your welcome, in advance."

"And afterwards ... have you thought about that all?" he continued.

"Yes ... maybe. I don't know," she replied. He nodded.

"Well, love, whatever you decide, keep this old chap in mind, alright? And if De Sant back there won't help you out, know that you should never be above asking the Law for help," he informed her. She burst out laughing.

"I hope you know how much of a tool bag you sound like," she wheezed and snorted.

"Yes, but it works for me, doesn't it?"

"It kinda does."

"But I'm very serious. If Marc is too adverse to the idea, then I would be more than happy to help assist you in honing your craft," Kingsley added.

Before she could say anything, there was a growl from the back seat.

"He'd like to assist you in honing *something*. Where the fuck are we?" Marc grumbled, sitting up. Lily glanced at him.

"We just passed Laayoune about an hour ago," she answered. "We're maybe three hours outside of Tantan, Morocco."

"Are we driving Ms. Daisy around? How about we pick up the pace," Marc snapped.

"Would you like to drive, darling?" Kingsley asked, glancing in the rear view mirror. Lily tried not to laugh.

"Yes, cause then we'd get somewhere."

"I could have killed you in Dakhla, you know that. There's still a price on your head, so please stop annoying me," Kingsley warned him.

"You couldn't have killed shit, I knew where you were every step of the way."

"Delusion is a very sad thing, De Sant."

"Shut up, Law."

"How about *EVERYONE* shut up?" Lily offered.

"*Shut up,*" they both snapped in unison at her.

"Maybe I should -"

It felt like there was a small explosion and Lily's sentence was cut off as she shrieked. She was thrown against the side of the door as Kingsley fought to get control of the vehicle. It zigged and zagged across the lanes before he was finally able to bring it to a stop.

"What happened? Were we shot!?" Marc yelled, crouching low as he looked out all their windows.

"Tire blew," Kingsley replied through gritted teeth.

"Yeah, but *how!?*" Marc demanded.

"Do I look like a mechanic? Am I currently outside the vehicle?" the other man asked, turning in his seat.

"Don't give me fucking attitude, you don't know what this trip has been like – every time we get a car, something fucked up happens," Marc tried to explain.

"If I'm giving you attitude, darling, it's because *you've* had attitude all day."

"Call me '*darling*' one more time."

While the men argued, Lily turned in her seat and surveyed the area. They had ocean to their left, and pretty much flat land to their right. If someone had shot them, they were either long gone, or very good at hiding. Besides, they had chosen to take the coastal route, instead of the more popular – and quicker – main road that would lead straight into Morocco proper. Would someone really have guessed that, and then waited all day in the blistering sun, just in case they drove by?

I doubt it.

Tired of listening to them bicker, she took a chance and swung her door open. Both men immediately yelled at her, but she hopped out onto the ground, slamming the door shut in their faces. She surveyed the horizon and didn't see any movement, so she moved around to the back of the car and saw what had caused the problem.

"Just a regular flat!" she called out, squatting down next to the rear driver's side tire. A chunk of wood was attached to the side of it, and she yanked it free. It looked like a part from some sort of cart, maybe a piece of side railing, and a long nail was sticking out of it. They must have rolled right over it, puncturing the tire.

"That was really stupid, Lily," Marc was grumbling as he walked up behind her.

"Geez, *Marcelle*, if I didn't know any better, I'd think you were worried about me," she snorted at him. He shoved her in the back of the head as she began to stand up.

"Alright, so we change it out. Simple," Kingsley said, walking up next to them.

Only it wasn't simple. Not only was the spare for the Explorer also flat, but the entire tire kit was missing from the vehicle. They could have a perfect spare, and without a tire iron or jack, they wouldn't be changing anything.

"We're cursed," Marc groaned, letting his head fall back.

"Yes," Lily agreed.

"I think you've always been a little cursed, mate," Kingsley teased.

"You know what? Get fucked. Until you showed up, we'd been having the smoothest ride of our trip, so seems to me, this is your fault," Marc snapped.

"*My* fault? How!?"

"Who was driving?"

"Clever monkey, De Sant! I left that bit of wood on the road side on purpose! Planted it yesterday, cause I thought it would be fun to be stuck out here with an arsehole!" Kingsley finally started to lose the cool he always seemed to be permanently relaxing in.

"Boys, boys, boys! This isn't going to help anything!" Lily yelled. She was ignored.

"No one invited you! No one said you had to tag along!" Marc snapped. Kingsley pushed past Lily, causing her to stumble a few feet away.

"Yeah, well, my conscience did because if I left it up to you, you'd both be dead in the next eighteen hours, and while I could live with not having to deal with *you* ever again, I wouldn't be able to live with myself if something happened to *her* because of your stupidity," he hissed.

Uh oh.

"Guys, c'mon," Lily urged, grabbing Marc's arm and pulling him backwards. Kingsley followed, unbuttoning his jacket.

"My stupidity? Well, my stupidity has kept her alive so far!" Marc replied, shaking free of her.

Did a flat tire just turn into a fight over me? Is this actually happening?

"Yes, it has! You're both very big, very strong capable men! Okay!? So just stop!" she shouted, trying to get between them. Both of them shoved her out of the way and they continued circling each other, moving farther down the road.

"Your stupidity has gotten me into trouble more times than I can count, and here I am again! Just like Rio, all over again! Remember that!?" Kingsley yelled, shrugging out of his jacket and letting it fall to the pavement.

"All I remember is dragging you out of a burning building! Should've left you to fucking die!" Marc shouted back, taking off his backpack and chucking it to the ground.

"This is the stupidest fucking thing I've ever witnessed! *Stop it!*" Lily was almost shrieking.

"And I remember being caught in that burning building because of *someone's* shitty intel!"

"Shitty intel!?"

Lily was ready to start throwing things at them, when she heard something behind her. She turned around and was shocked to see the car rolling away from them, down a small embankment. It had come to a stop at a downward angle, and Kingsley must have left it in neutral.

"Guys!" she shouted, turning towards them.

"*Shut up!*"

"Um, I just thought you'd like to know," she started jogging back towards the car as it picked up speed, making a beeline for the beach, "*the fucking car is escaping!*"

When she glanced over her shoulder, both men were sprinting after her, so she slowed her pace. It wasn't like she could do much; if she grabbed the bumper, it would just drag her with it, and the way

Marc was running, he would beat her to the car, anyway.

"*Stop!*" he was yelling.

"I am! But do you see where bitching like little girls gets you!? Now we'll have to -"

There was an explosion. Lily was knocked backwards, and luckily Marc was right behind her. He wrapped an arm around her waist, hugging her to him as he curled their bodies down and away from the blast, his other arm going around her head to protect it. They stayed on the ground, his body almost completely covering her own.

Debris fell around them, and she assumed it was pieces of the car. When he finally let up a little, she glanced around. Kingsley was flat on the ground, lifting his head up, as well. She turned to look over her shoulder, and the Explorer was stopped dead. Pieces of it were everywhere. A door had gotten blown off and laid halfway between the shell of the vehicle and themselves.

"Bomb?" she breathed. Marc shook his head and got off of her.

"Land mine. Are you okay?" he asked, hauling her to her feet and examining her face and her head.

"I'm fine," she assured him, but his hands continued on a path down her body, as if he was determined to check for himself that she was in one piece.

"The border area is riddled with them," Kingsley was saying as he walked back to where his jacket was, scooping it up and dusting it off. "Probably not a good idea to take a stroll down to the water."

"I should've warned you," Marc was grumbling.

"I know. All our guns, all our supplies," she sighed.

"Are you shitting me? Lily, I don't give a fuck about those things. A couple more steps, and you would've been off the road. *You* could be in pieces right now," he pointed out.

"But I didn't, and I'm not," she replied.

He shocked her by pulling her into a hug. Outside of the random crazy sex they had, they hardly ever touched. She racked her brain, trying to remember if he'd ever hugged her. If she'd ever hugged him. He was really upset. She smoothed her hands up his back, hooking onto the tops of his shoulders.

"It's dangerous out here," he whispered in her ear.

"I know that, Marc. I'm a dangerous person," she whispered back. He shook his head.

"Not as much as you'd like to think."

When they pulled apart, Kingsley was standing a discreet distance away, his back to them. They walked over to him and Marc picked his pack up off the ground, pulling the straps across his chest.

"At least we have the diamonds," Lily tried to find a silver lining. Marc frowned.

"Yeah. Let's start walking."

It was hot out – much hotter than was usual for the area. The day before had been in the low eighties, nice. But as they walked down the road, Lily felt like her skin was burning off.

"What's the temperature?" she asked. Kingsley pulled a gadget out of his pocket, hit a couple buttons.

"Thirty four Celsius," he answered. She did the math in her head. Around ninety-three degrees, Fahrenheit. In direct sun. *Fuck.*

Marc surprised her by producing a light weight wind breaker from the bottom of his magical Mary Poppins bag. It was huge on her, hanging to her mid-thighs, but it shielded her from the sun a little, so she took it and was grateful.

If felt like they walked forever. No cars came, which she wasn't sure if that was a blessing, or more of their vehicular curse at play. Marc produced a canteen, and they all took turns sipping at the warm water. Then he pulled out an old map, the one she hadn't seen since Mali.

"Best I can figure," Marc started, tracing his finger along a line. "We're about twenty-four kilometers from the town of Tarfaya."

Fifteen miles … in this heat … fuck.

"Is that the closest place?" Lily double checked.

"Yes. We could head back the way we came, but the nearest town is thirty-three kilometers," his eyes wandered over the map.

"*Fuck,*" she swore out loud.

"I concur," Kingsley added.

"If we can average a twenty minute mile, we should be in Tarfaya around seven, just after night fall. We can stay the night, then steal a car," Marc suggested before tucking the map back into his bag.

"Another night," she sighed, lacing her fingers together on top of her head.

"You'll get there," Marc assured her, then picked up their pace.

Lily wasn't weak, she knew that, but five hours in the African sun was a lot for anybody. Water rations were low, they weren't allowed to drink at leisure. She and Kingsley chatted for a while, but after two hours they all stayed silent. Another hour and she felt like she was going to drop. She kept pushing, though. If the boys could do it, she sure as hell could do it, too.

Then randomly, Marc took off his pack and handed it to her. She was shocked that he was letting her hold it, and then more shocked that he was asking her to carry it. Big strong mercenary Marc couldn't handle his own stupid pack!?

But then he stepped in front of her. Didn't say a word, just blocked her path, forcing her to stop. He hunched down a little, and it took her a second to realize what he was doing. She quickly put on the pack, then hopped onto Marc's back, wrapping her arms around his shoulders.

He carried her for so long, she actually fell asleep, her cheek against his shoulder. She only woke up when he started to sit her down. She found her footing and let go of him so he could stand upright again.

"Where are we?" she yawned. He turned her around and dug in the pack.

"About a half an hour outside of Tarfaya," he replied, and she could hear the map crinkling in his hands. She looked up at the sky. The sun had set and the stars were shining everywhere.

"Half an hour, good," she sighed, unclipping his pack and pulling off the windbreaker as well.

"You good to walk?" he double checked, coming around to

stand in front of her.

"Yeah, you didn't have to carry me for so long," she told him, feeling guilty while she shoved the coat into the bag.

"I didn't mind."

They kept moving. The rest from Marc's piggyback had actually made things worse – her feet had gotten a chance to rest and tighten up and swell. She gritted through the pain and moved along at the same pace as the men.

When they first saw the outskirts of Tarfaya, she wanted to weep. It was like an oasis rising out of the sand. But they still had quite a ways to walk. Even once inside the town, they still had to find somewhere to stay. They stuck close to the oceanside, dragging their feet as they looked for a hotel. A *cheap* hotel; most of Kingsley's money, and all of Lily's, had gotten blown up in the Explorer.

Finally, around nine o'clock, almost six hours after they'd started walking, they stumbled upon some cabins on the beach. More like shanties, they were one room, with single army cots and a tiny table in each of them. A foot around the top, beneath the roofing, was all mosquito netting - it was the only form of air conditioning.

Marc and Lily were all for just breaking into one, but Kingsley pointed out their presence was already noticed within the small town. If they were caught breaking and entering, it wouldn't be pretty. He was able to barter with the owner of the shacks, trading Marc's expensive diving watch for one night in the shacks. Marc grumbled and complained, but handed the watch over.

"You owe me one," Marc said.

"You could be sleeping with the sand and the scorpions, De Sant. I didn't need to ask for two. Care to share a room, Lily?" Kingsley asked, smiling broadly at her. His hair was disheveled, and his suit was dusty, but his charm was untarnished.

"Fuck off, Law," Marc said, shoving her towards one of the beach shacks.

It was late, but just having somewhere to sit for a moment did wonders. While Marc collapsed on the cot, Lily took off her leggings and made her way down to the water. She was suddenly thankful that Marc had bought her the bikini instead of underwear, and she sat down on the wet sand. The beach was fairly well lit, and several groups of people were wandering around on it. As she relaxed, a couple stumbled up to her.

"Excuse me," the man asked. "American?"

"Sure," Lily grunted, rubbing the balls of her feet.

"Us, too!" the woman laughed.

"We just got here, today. We're with the Red Cross, but we decided to have a little vacation before we head into Algeria," the man explained.

"Wonderful," was all Lily said, praying that they'd go away.

"We never imagined it would be so beautiful here! Isn't Africa *beautiful*?" the girl sighed, looking around the beach. Lily let go of her feet and looked up at them.

"Beautiful? Yeah, sure. Beautiful like a shark. Good luck in Algeria, you'll need it," she warned them, then turned to stare out over the ocean, hoping that would be enough of a hint that she wanted to be alone.

"What are you doing here?" the girl asked, squatting down next to her.

Why me?

"Not working with the Red Cross, that's for sure."

"Are you like a travel blogger?"

Is this for real?

"No."

"Here with the embassy?"

"*No.*"

"Chuck and I always wanted to come to Africa for our honeymoon – are you here with your husband?" the girl guessed.

"No."

"Then why are you in Africa?"

She finally turned back to them, leaning over a little.

"To steal something and to kill someone, *that's* why I'm in Africa, now *fuck off,*" Lily snapped.

The couple gasped, then hustled away, the girl glaring at her. Lily didn't care. She had felt completely disconnected from them. Like they were speaking different languages, were from different countries. *Different planets.* It was like a cheetah sitting down and having tea with two lambs. No thank you.

"See, darling? Going back to '*real life*' is going to be quite difficult," a soft, accented voice said from behind her. She let her head drop back, staring at Kingsley from upside down. He was keeping his distance, not allowing his shoes to get wet. In the distance, she could see Marc heading towards them, as well.

"I'm seeing that, now. That was bizarre. Is that what it's like for you?" she asked. He shook his head.

"No, but I've always been a people person. That's why you'll find that while Marc is requested for jobs like this, I'm requested for ones that tend to have a public slant. Corporate espionage, things of that nature," he explained.

"You don't do brute force, huh."

"I can be as brute as you'd like me to be, darling."

"Let's go find something to eat," Marc called out. Lily finally got up, groaning as her leg muscles screamed in protest. She wiped the sand off her butt and followed the men back to shore.

After swapping her bikini bottoms out for the leggings, they went in search of food. There was a hotel nearby, and though it was late, the restaurant was still serving food. The American couple from the beach were sitting inside, and they got nervous when Lily walked in, their eyes bouncing between everyone in her group. She smiled back, wiggling her fingers at them.

"No one likes a bitch, sweetheart," Marc said under his breath, grabbing her hand. She smiled – it was the first time he'd used a pet name for her since Kingsley had shown up. Maybe some of his good humor was returning.

"*You* do."

"I tolerate one, there's a difference."

They ordered whatever was cheapest and had the most servings, guzzling down water along with the food. Kingsley babbled away as they ate, it seemed to be in his nature to always be talking. Always be saying something. Marc grunted out responses around his food. Lily stayed quiet, just trying to stay awake.

"So what's your plan after this, De Sant? Say it all goes according to plan, you return the diamonds to the Liberians and send them after the dirty dealing Bratva. Then what?" Kingsley asked.

"God, then it's time for a fucking vacation," he groaned, stretching backwards over his chair.

"Sounds lovely. Have anywhere in mind?"

Lily expected him to say Pemba Island, the place they had discussed during their night together in the commandeered house. It had been rattling around in the back of her brain, during their walk that day. If she could just get through everything. She wouldn't think about the future, until she lived through the present. If she could manage to stay alive, then maybe she could actually give him some of her tomorrows. Maybe even give some to herself.

"Not sure. Maybe Thailand. Maybe Greece," Marc said quickly.

What the huh!?

Lily glanced at him, but he wasn't looking at her. He was glaring across the restaurant, looking outside. Kingsley's eyes were bouncing back and forth between them, and that smirky smile of his spread across his face. Like he knew exactly what each of them were thinking.

Maybe he doesn't want Kingsley to know. Maybe it's a secret.

"And what about you, Lily? If you survive your little revenge plan, what's afterwards? Short term, of course," the British man asked her. She shrugged.

"Don't know. A vacation does sound like a good idea. Somewhere relaxing," she sighed.

"Mmmm, I know just the place," Kingsley pushed his empty plate out of the way and leaned towards her. "I have an amazing estate, just outside of Phuket. Isolated, calm, beaches for days, including my own private one. I would love for you to visit."

"You don't even know me, Kingsley. You may want to kill me after one week in my presence," she teased. Marc cleared his throat.

"I can attest to that being exactly what will happen."

"I very much doubt that. I think you and I are kindred spirits, actually. Get you in some decent clothing, and together we could bring a bit of style to this business," Kingsley pointed out.

"I thought you said vacation, not work," she pointed out.

"Well, a man can be hopeful. A partner would be nice to have."

"I thought Marc was like a partner to you."

"A partner who looks good in a dress."

"I look fucking fabulous in a dress," Marc interrupted.

"I'm sure you do," Lily nodded her head.

"De Sant in a dress is one of the most horrifying memories I have, and on that note, I'm going to go be sick, then go to bed. Cheers, darlings," Kingsley said, standing up. He nodded at Marc, winked at Lily, then walked away without another word, paying their tab on his way out. Lily smiled after him, watching him disappear into the darkness of the beach.

"Would you actually go there?" Marc interrupted her thoughts as he stood up.

"Excuse me?"

"Would you go there? To Phuket?"

She got up and followed him out of the restaurant.

"I don't know. I do like him. A lot. Maybe I would. If I didn't have a better offer to go anywhere else."

He stayed silent.

They didn't immediately go back to their cabin. Despite walking for most of the day, Marc seemed restless. So they walked back down to the water, throwing shells and rocks into the ocean.

"So the plan for tomorrow -" Lily started.

"Leave the car to me. Law and I will go out early, get something lined up," he interrupted her.

"Okay. I feel like I'm getting kicked out of the band," she joked, dropping the rest of her rocks into the water.

"Sweetheart, this band existed long before you showed up. It's more like a reunion tour," he teased. She glared at him.

"You know what I mean."

"When we started, all you wanted was to get rid of me," Marc pointed out, turning towards her. She shrugged, not looking back at him.

"You grew on me," was all she said in response.

"Why, Liliana! If I didn't know any better, I'd think you like me," his voice was teasing again, and he got close enough for his chest to press against her arm. She finally looked up at him.

"I do like you, Marc. I've always liked you. I mean, maybe for a minute there I wanted you dead, and I kind of want to kick your ass on a regular basis, and I hate that you fucked everything up for me. But I liked you in Liberia. You're a likable guy. I like you now. I will miss you," she was honest with him.

"I'll miss you, too, Lily. It's been an adventure. Pretty awful, but pretty amazing," he told her.

We still have fifteen hours till Tangier. 800 miles. Why does this feel like goodbye?

"The plan tomorrow," Lily started again. "We get to Tangier. I call Ivanov. I get on the ferry the next day, meeting you there. I give you the diamonds."

"The diamonds," Marc sighed, turning to look out over the water. "A bag of rocks. All our problems. So many problems. Over a bag of stupid fucking rocks."

"*A lot* of stupid fucking rocks," Lily pointed out.

"*Expensive* fucking rocks."

"*Dangerous* fucking rocks."

"Come here," Marc suddenly grabbed her arm, pulling her around so she was in front of him.

"What?" she asked, holding still as he held her at arm's length.

"You are gorgeous, I'll give you that," he started, and she beamed at him. But he didn't stop there. "But you're fucking temperamental.

You think of the now, not the after. Getting those diamonds to Moscow, brilliant fucking plan. Did you ever once consider what would happen if it didn't go according to plan? Cause it clearly fucking didn't."

"No. Because it had to work. I don't think of things failing because I won't allow them to. Like this plan – maybe it hasn't gone exactly according *to* plan, but even the best laid plans can fall apart. You just keep going. Failure isn't an option. *Failure* isn't part of my plan," she stressed.

"Your '*Pollyanna*' attitude is real fucking cute, but it's going to get you killed," he warned her. She glared at him.

"Would it kill you, just once, to say '*good job*'!? To admit that I've handled myself just as well as you on this fucked up trip, if not better sometimes!?" she demanded.

"I would, but I hate to lie."

"It wouldn't be a lie, I've been just as good as you."

"I can't for the life of me figure out what you're referring to. Unless you're talking about fucking, then I'll freely admit that's one thing you're actually very good at."

She slapped him.

"That's for being a dick," she informed him.

"A slap? Really? Kind of a pussy move, coming from you," he chuckled.

She pulled her arm back, ready to punch him in the throat, but he grabbed her wrist and yanked her forward. He twisted her arm behind her back, holding it against her spine.

"'*Pussy move*', being scared of a girl," Lily mocked him.

Sometimes she wondered if fighting was like foreplay to Marc. Or maybe just being aggressive, in general. He seemed to like to pick fights with her, or just pick on her. Either way, it worked for him, so she wasn't too shocked when he leaned down and kissed her.

"You are a pretty scary girl," he agreed, letting go of her arm and working his hands into her hair.

"I take that as a compliment," she assured him.

"I meant it as one."

They stood still, pressing against each other, the waves coming in around their feet, soaking through her boots. She gripped onto his t-shirt, pulling hard on the material, wanting to be closer to him. Always close to him.

Why does this feel like goodbye? And why didn't I plan for this? I never thought about what goodbye would feel like ...

"So after tonight," she breathed out, and he groaned, moving his lips down her neck.

"Seriously with the talking. Like two seconds of you not talking would be fucking amazing," he told her.

"After all this," she ignored him, then gasped as his hands dove into her leggings and gripped her ass. "After Liberia and Moscow and the diamonds ..."

"Lily, if you say one word in the next three hours, I swear to god, I will drown you in this fucking ocean."

Maybe fighting is like foreplay to me, too.

He picked her up, and she loved that sensation. She wasn't a tiny girl, five-foot-seven, with lots of tits and ass, curves and lanky limbs, but Marc was always able to handle her like she weighed nothing at all. She wrapped her legs around his waist, coiled her arms around his neck, forced her tongue into his mouth.

He carried her across the sand, falling into the side of their cabin. He leaned his weight into her, pinning her in place against the wall. She pulled his t-shirt up in between them, working it over his head.

"Three hours isn't that long. It's not even ... midnight ...," she panted as one of his hands worked its way under her own shirt.

"You can fill out a complaint form when I'm done."

The door was a simple screen, and it banged shut behind them as Marc carried her inside. They fell across the room, crashing into the table. He sat her down on it, ripping her shirt over her head, then dove back in, kissing her hard, stealing all her air once again.

When she felt dizzy, she pushed him away and hopped off the

table. While she fought to take off her boots, he dropped his pants. Once he'd stepped free of them, he grabbed her by the hips and whirled her around, slamming her down on the table top.

"Someone's in a hurry," she breathed, a little surprised by his force. He got her leggings off of her with one yank, dropping to the floor with them.

He kissed her calf, then the back of her knee, then the top of her ass cheek. Dragged his tongue up the center of her spine. Then he was pressed up against her, his mouth on her neck.

"Always in a hurry to be inside you," he responded, then bit down on her shoulder.

While his teeth were still leaving imprints in her skin, his erection was pressing into her from behind. She gripped the edge of the table and gritted her teeth as it all happened in one go, his hips meeting her ass in one push.

"Jesus, Marc, you really are," she gasped.

"*You have no idea.*"

He started pumping into her, one hand curling into a fist in her hair, yanking her up. She cried out, pushing back from the table. Pushing back against him. His free hand gripped her hip, hanging onto her. Grounding her. She needed it. He was fucking her into higher orbit, making it hard to remember what it was like down on earth.

"*Oh my god!*" she shrieked, unable to handle how deep he was striking. Loving how deep he was striking.

"You know there's no real door, right," he panted.

"Right, right," she agreed, though she had no clue what he was asking. She would've said anything at that point, as long as he kept touching her.

"The whole top half is basically a screen," he kept going, letting go of her. She fell down flat on the table top, and a moment later his t-shirt was thrown against the wall, landing next to her.

"Mmmm hmmm," she moaned low in her throat.

"Everyone can hear you," he warned her.

"I don't care. I hope they can, I hope they hear *everything*," she replied.

"God, you're an amazing woman."

He paused for a moment, then slammed back inside of her, so abrupt and so hard that it shocked her.

"Oh ... my ... god ... yes ... please," she couldn't unclench her teeth.

"Lily," he growled her name, his hand going to the back of her neck. He held her down and used the leverage to thrust harder.

"*Yes! Yes!*" she shrieked.

"When you're in Tangier," he started, running his other hand down the side of her body.

"Please, Marc, faster," she begged, and he complied.

"And when you're in Moscow," he continued.

"I'm so close," she whined, then felt his free hand moving between her and the table.

"When you're in those places, if you fuck anyone else," he started, pulling her back towards him, his hand flat against her stomach and pulling her up onto her toes.

"No one else," she told him, and it caused him to moan again.

"Never forget who made you feel this way," he whispered, his hand slipping lower and lower down her body.

"I could never," she assured him.

"*Good.*"

He jackhammered his hips against her, and she screamed. His hand on her neck moved to her shoulder, actually yanking her back against him. Pushing her down harder on his cock. She started to come, and in true Marc fashion, he just fucked her harder. Her whole body went into seizure mode, shaking and shuddering, all while one of his fingers tapped along with her ticking muscles.

I wonder if I could ever pass out from sensory overload.

She went completely limp, and didn't even care. They'd had enough sex for her to know that he didn't particularly care, either. His hands on her shoulder gripped harder, painfully so, and she moaned.

"God, I'm gonna miss this."

She hadn't meant to say it out loud. She could feel that they were both thinking it, could still feel that "*goodbye*" hanging in the air, but she hadn't wanted to ruin the moment. Still, he sucked it right out of her, just like he always did with all her oxygen.

"Come here, move."

She actually didn't have to move. Marc simply backed away, dragging her with him, then shoved her onto the bed. She'd barely turned over when he was on top of her, forcing her flat as he crawled between her legs. Then he slid his hands under her back, holding on while he laid his chest on top of hers. They were just about as physically close as two people could ever be, in that moment.

"Hi," she laughed, staring at him as his face hovered inches above her own.

"I meant what I said, you know," he said, his voice soft. She was confused.

"When?"

"Your eyes," he continued, as if that cleared anything up.

"What about them?"

"They are the most beautiful thing I've ever seen," he sighed.

"Really?"

"I'm going to remember them for a long time," he assured her.

"I hope so."

"I know so. At night, when I'm alone, in some kind of trouble that I've no doubt gotten myself into," he started, and they both chuckled, "I'll picture your eyes. Your smile, your body, your voice. But most of all your eyes. I could look into them forever. I'll miss them. Will miss seeing you look at me."

No one had ever spoken to her like that before, she almost wanted to cry. Then he started rocking his hips against her, but gently, and she did tear up. She wrapped her arms around his shoulders, pulling him completely flush against her and hooking her ankles together behind his back.

"I'll miss you, too," she breathed.

He whispered more words in her ear, words she'd never heard before, in a voice she *always* wanted to hear. He was gentle with her, in a way he'd never been before, with a touch she could learn to live for. And as he breathed life into her veins and new thoughts into her mind and different feelings into her soul, there was just one phrase repeating itself in her head.

"*... we don't have to be these people anymore ...*"

DAY SEVEN

"**A**lright?"

Marc was pulling a t-shirt into place as he walked up to Kingsley's cabin. The British man was out on his steps, smoking a cigarette. He didn't look away from the ocean, just repeated his question.

"Yeah, sure," Marc replied, moving up so he was sitting next to the other man.

"You do realize that these shacks aren't exactly *insulated* – not that it would matter if they were, I'm pretty sure they heard you all the way on the coast of Spain," Kingsley assured him.

"Good. Something that amazing deserves an audience."

They both laughed for a second before falling quiet.

"You're making a mistake," Kingsley's voice was soft.

"I haven't done anything."

"But you're thinking about it."

"Look," Marc rubbed a hand down his face, "let's go over tomorrow. You and I are gonna go get some cars. I'll come back and get her. And then …"

"C'mon, big boy, say it," Kingsley urged.

"Then we'll send her on her way."

"Does she know about this plan?"

"She doesn't have a say in this plan."

"It involves her, so I think she should -"

"No one asked you," Marc interrupted.

"You like her." Kingsley made a statement. Pointed out a fact.

"Yes," Marc didn't deny it. Kingsley shook his head.

"So why are you going to make her do all this alone?" he asked.

"I got her through the hard part. Fuck, I *am* the hard part. I fucked everything up for her. I just made it worse. Today, when she was running for that car, all I could think was '*holy shit, I'm about to watch her get blown up*'. And I was scared to death. I've never been scared like that before, ever. If we hadn't been fighting, if we hadn't taken that road, if I hadn't fucking gotten in her car back in Liberia … I can't handle the thought of something happening to her, because of me. If I'm with her in Morocco, and Ivanov shows up, it's game over. He kills us both. If I'm in Liberia, it's just me," Marc tried to explain where he was coming from.

"And you think that'll make her feel safe and warm and fuzzy?" Kingsley questioned.

"I don't care. It'll keep her alive, and that's all that matters to me."

"You genuinely believe she has a better chance finishing this without you than she does with you?" Kingsley sounded amazed.

"Finishing it *alive*, yes."

"Then you're an idiot."

"This shouldn't be shocking to you."

"De Sant," the other man sighed. "I'm speaking to you as a mate, now. A partner. *Do not do this.* Women like the one asleep over there do not come along very often – don't throw her back to the wolves. She needs you. And whether you want to admit it or not, you need her. This is the most human I've seen you, since I met you. You've let this job ruin you. *Let her fix you.*"

"And ruin her in the process? No thanks. I'd rather be alone and a wreck than be together and destroy her," Marc replied.

"Stupid, De Sant. Very stupid. Your new-found conscience is going to get the both of you killed, and I, for one, will not stand around and watch it happen," Kingsley snapped as he climbed to his feet.

"What? You're leaving? Go for it."

"Oh no, I'm not leaving. I'm going to be with you every single minute, from here on out, reminding you every step of the way of exactly how fucking ridiculous you're being," Kingsley broke it down, then he stomped into his cabin and slammed the door shut.

"You know it's just a screen, right!? Kind of defeats the purpose of slamming it in my face!" Marc hollered.

"*Piss off!*"

"See you in the morning!"

"Not if I smother you in your sleep!"

Marc made his way back to his own cabin, dragging his feet through the sand. He was surprised at Kingsley's outburst. He'd figured the seasoned mercenary would agree with him. Women were nothing but trouble, that was usually Kingsley's opinion. It was obvious he and Lily liked each other – *too much,* in Marc's opinion – but it didn't quite explain why he wanted Marc and Lily to be together so badly.

He walked into their cabin, shutting the screen carefully behind him. Lily was asleep on the cot. It had cooled off to around seventy degrees outside, and before she'd fallen asleep, he'd given her one of his t-shirts to wear. She was laying on her side, her knees tucked up towards her chest, her hands underneath her cheek. It made her look young and vulnerable.

"Oh, Lily, what am I going to do with you," he sighed, sitting down next to her. She didn't respond, just mumbled in her sleep.

He smoothed his hand down her thigh, savoring the smoothness of her skin. Then he worked his hand up and under the shirt, memorizing the curve of her hip. Not that he could ever forget. He would never be able to forget Lily. Never forget their time together.

It occurred to him that he'd probably spent more time alone with her than anyone else in his life. At least since he'd been a teenager. He was always on the go, always on the move, and if he did work with people, he usually worked in teams. Hell, the most time he'd ever spent alone with Kingsley had been four days, and he was pretty sure he'd been unconscious for one of them.

A week in Africa with Lily. A new record. A new friend.

So much more than a friend …

"Lily," he whispered, stretching out next to her. The cot was tiny, barely big enough for them to both lay on their sides. His nose was inches from her own, and he smiled as she yawned. "Say something. Say anything. Tell me what's right. Tell me that wanting you is okay. Tell me that being with you is okay."

Of course she didn't answer. He was pretty sure he knew what she'd say, anyway, and it certainly wouldn't have been what was right.

Then she rolled away from him, stretching in her sleep before turning her back to him. The shirt had ridden up to her waist, and her bare ass pressed against his crotch as she cuddled back against him. He stared down for a minute, then began working the shirt up higher.

Talking is too dangerous. The decision has been made. Might as well spend our last hours having fun.

Lily knotted the top lace on her boots, then stood up. She glanced around the little shack, but of course there was nothing in it. It hadn't come with any extra frills, not even a blanket, and she didn't have anything other than the clothes she was wearing. Marc had taken his pack with him, so there was nothing left behind.

She'd woken up in the middle of the night to him already working his fingers inside of her. Then he hadn't let her sleep for the next two hours. The gentle, sweet man from earlier was long gone – he was all hard muscle and forceful hands. Her ass felt sore from all the spankings, her legs felt like jelly from all the stretching, and she was pretty sure he had effectively ruined her sex drive for all other men. Despite the fact that she felt like she could sleep for ten years, when she'd watched him get dressed in the morning, it had only been him scrambling to meet Kingsley that had stopped her from taking his clothing back off.

Crazy to think that a week ago I hated him. A month ago, I didn't even know him. And now, I always want to be with him.

She'd been given strict instructions to stay in the cabin, but Lily hated being told what to do, and hated being confined. She sat on the front steps, stretching out her legs and grabbing her toes, making her muscles pull tight. She hissed, relishing the ache and strain, and held on for a solid fifteen seconds.

"*I told you to wait inside.*"

Lily actually shrieked, leaping sideways out of her seat. She fell off the stairs, landing in a heap on the sand. Marc had come from behind the cabin, melting out of the shrubs and bushes, materializing next to her.

"You almost gave me a fucking heart attack!" she yelled at him, throwing a rock at his head. He ducked out of the way.

"Well, you should've waited inside. C'mon, we gotta move," he replied, holding a hand out. She grabbed it and he yanked her to her feet.

The cabins they'd stayed in were at the edge of the city – they'd essentially walked through the whole town to get to them. Now they backtracked, heading towards where they'd entered the town. They didn't quite sneak around, but they did hurry through the streets.

It didn't take very long, Tarfaya was a small town. Pretty soon they were hurrying along the edge of a highway, Lily almost having to jog to keep up with Marc's stride. When they got to a large warehouse, Marc veered off course, cutting across the sand. Lily hesitated for a second, remembering the moment yesterday, when she'd almost been introduced to a field of land mines. But Marc wouldn't blindly stride across hostile ground, so she followed in his foot steps.

When they came around the building, she was surprised to see two vehicles. One was a 1980s Buick, and the other was a shiny new looking Toyota Rav. Kingsley stood between them, adjusting his tie, not noticing their approach. She smiled to herself. It was the same suit he'd been wearing since the day before, the suit he'd walked in for hours on end, but it looked crisp and clean and sharp. Just like him.

"Why did you get two cars? Is Kingsley heading back?" Lily asked. Hearing his name, the other man looked up and smiled, making his way towards them.

"Looking good, darling. As always," he told her, leaning close and kissing her on the cheek.

"Liar," she laughed, smoothing her hands over her dusty leggings.

"I haven't known you long, Ms. Lily, but I have a feeling I will miss you a great deal," he sighed.

"You could come with us," she suggested.

"Us?" he seemed confused.

"Yeah. Whatever Marc said, it's a lie, you should come with us," she figured Marc's rude attitude had scared the British man away. Kingsley started scowling.

"You didn't tell her? All that time," he growled.

Wait ... what?

"Jesus, Law," Marc growled right back.

"Tell me what?" Lily demanded.

Both men were silent and still for a minute, and that just about scared her more than anything. Kingsley was always running his mouth, and Marc was always moving. Something bad had been decided.

"Darling," Kingsley finally sighed, stepping forward. "It has been a pleasure spending these last couple days with you. Sorry for strangling you a bit, though I must admit, I kind of enjoyed it. Maybe we can do it again sometime. But for now, De Sant here has decided it's best if we go our separate ways."

Lily turned towards Marc, narrowing her eyes.

"I was going to tell you," he offered.

"Oh? When? After we were in separate cars?"

"No, just till you were out of hitting range. And kicking."

"Really manly, Marc," she made her voice snide. "After everything we've been through, you didn't even have the balls to just say *'hey, I'm out'*!?"

This moment was going to happen sooner or later, Lily knew that, but it still hurt. And the way he'd gone about it hurt even more. Wanted or not, she had forged a bond with this man. A connection. Something that was tangible and real to her, as if that chain was still around her waist, linking her to him. Binding her to him.

And there he was, just able to walk away, with barely an explanation. Barely a goodbye.

Fuck that. You don't get off that easy, De Sant.

"I wasn't just going to leave you in the desert, Lily, calm down. I just didn't want to start the morning with, *'you're on your own'*, alright?" he snapped.

"You owe me more than this, and you know it," Lily said in a low, even voice. He snorted at her.

"I don't owe you shit."

"*Asshole.*"

Without even thinking, Lily snapped her hand out, slapping him across the face.

"You hit like a girl," he taunted her.

Her fist was closed for the next hit.

"Why'd you have to make it like this!?" she yelled at him. "It didn't have to be like this! You could've just said goodbye!"

"How would you rather this go, Lily!? Two days from now, in Tangier? Would that make it easier!?" he was yelling back, a vein throbbing in the side of his neck as he glared down at her.

"No. I don't know. But I guess I always figured that whenever it was gonna happen, you would've handled it like a man. My mistake, I forgot I was dealing with a *bitch*," she called him out.

"Well, sweetheart, as they say, it takes one to know one, and you are by far the biggest bitch I have ever met."

She hit him again.

"Keep calling me names, *Marcelle*," she threatened.

"This doesn't have to be like this," he stated.

"*You* made it like this. You could've just said goodbye. After everything. *Everything.* And you had to wait for Kingsley to say it. You're not a man. You're a *coward*. You think being a mercenary makes you a man? Killing people makes you a man? No. You hide behind those things because you're not brave enough to walk with real people. *A fucking coward,*" she hissed.

Marc's hand was suddenly around her throat, and for a moment, she was completely stunned. He was able to back her up against the Buick while her mind reeled. He hadn't touched her in an aggressive manner since before the boarding house, in Mali. She'd almost forgotten that he could be rough with her.

"*Watch your fucking mouth,*" he growled, leaning down close to her. "You think I'm a coward? I have *carried* you this far. I *killed people* for you. I *saved your life* on multiple occasions. Does all that sound cowardly?"

"*Carried me!?*" she practically squealed. "Okay, FIRST OF ALL, I wouldn't be in this situation if it wasn't for you. Second of all, you didn't need to kill anyone '*for me*', you brought that all on yourself. And third of all, I didn't ask you to save my life. I don't need you to save my life. I don't want you *in my life.*"

Liar.

"Do you honestly mean that?" he asked, his voice steely as his fingers squeezed tighter. She had her hands wrapped around his wrist, and she tugged at it.

"Did I fucking stutter? There is nothing you've done for me that I couldn't have done for myself, all you do is fuck things up, for everyone. For everything. Drag me out here. Dragged Kingsley into it. How many other people are going to have to die for your fuck ups, De Sant!?" she yelled at him.

"Possibly just one more," he threatened, glaring down at her.

"You don't have the balls."

"Oh, I'm sure I do."

"And you sure as shit don't have the talent."

"Question my abilities one more fucking time, Lily, and I -"

Enough.

Lily shot her arm out, driving the heel of her palm straight into his nose. He was completely caught off guard and let out a shout, backing away from her as his hands flew to his face. She took the opportunity to elbow him in the stomach, and when he bent over, she kicked him in the hip, sending him to the ground. From behind her, Kingsley started clapping.

"Does that count as questioning you!?" she shrieked at him.

Suddenly, her legs were kicked out from under her and she went straight down on her back. She didn't hesitate, she immediately rolled to the side and began scrambling to get under the Rav. But Marc grabbed a hold of her legs and with one sharp yank, he pulled her to him, flipping her over at the same time.

"Calm the fuck down!" he was shouting at her as he straddled her hips.

"*You* calm down! Everything we've fucking been through, and you were just gonna shove me in a car and that was it!? *Get fucked, De Sant!*" she screamed at him. He fought to get a hold of her wrists, pinning them to sand by her head.

"That's not it!" he roared, and she finally stopped yelling, though she did continue to try to break free from him. "You think this is fucking easy for me!? It's fucking not. But I know it's for the best, I know it's what's safest for you, and I know it's the *right* thing to do. So if that makes me a fucking coward, then fine, I'm a fucking coward. But I also know when it's *time to do something right.*"

It was hard to argue with that logic. She wouldn't have thought it possible for Marc to say something so sweet. Well, *almost* sweet. She laid still, staring at the blue sky over his shoulder. Fought to get control of her breathing.

"It doesn't feel right," she whispered. He sighed.

"I know, sweetheart. I know. But it is. Look, this had to end some time. We're not on vacation here. I don't want to prolong the inevitable, and I don't want to make things worse for you," he explained in a soft voice.

"Wish you would've made that decision a week ago," she even managed to laugh, but still refused to look at him.

"Me, too."

That just made her feel worse.

"So you're just sending me out to the wolves?" she asked.

"No, I left you something," he replied, leaning away from her and gesturing to the Buick. "I left you my pack. It has all our water, some money, the diamonds, even your precious Glock."

"You remembered," she whispered again, smiling.

"I remembered."

He backed off her then, dusting his pants off as he stood. She glanced over to see Kingsley leaning in the backseat of the Rav, very clearly pretending not to notice the heavy moment that was occurring. Then Marc grabbed her arm, hauling her to her feet and dusting her off, as well.

"So this is it," she sighed, finally looking at him again. If she hadn't known any better, she would've thought that he looked upset. Maybe even pained.

"Take care of yourself," his voice suddenly turned serious, and he stepped up close, his shadow falling over her.

"Always do," she assured him.

"I'm serious. You hesitate – don't. You overthink – go with your gut. Say whatever you have to, do whatever you can, to convince Ivanov that you're telling the truth. And when you get to Moscow, *pull the trigger.*"

She decided to take his advice and she didn't think about it, just pressed her hand flat against his chest. Right over his heart. His own hand covered hers, squeezing her fingers, and he glared down at her. She'd forgotten how blue his eyes looked, set against his tan skin. How intense they looked, staring into her soul.

"I will," she whispered.

He stared at her for a second longer, squeezed her fingers even harder, then he nodded and walked away. Just dropped her hand and turned around.

"Is that it!?" Kingsley exclaimed, watching as Marc got into the driver's seat of the Rav.

"Let's go! The lady's on a deadline!" he yelled back.

"Bloody hell. Fuck that, that's no way to say goodbye," Kingsley grumbled, then slammed the back door shut. Lily laughed as he walked towards her.

"I'll miss you, too, Mr. Law, even if -"

She was cut off as he grabbed her around the waist and dipped her, pressing his lips against her own. It was actually very chaste, no tongue, but his arms squeezed her tight and held her flush against him. She squealed and laughed against his mouth, pushing at his shoulders till he let her up.

"*Let's go!*" Marc was shouting, banging on the roof of his car.

"Couldn't resist, darling," Kingsley said, giving her a wink before pulling her into a much more platonic embrace. She wrapped her arms around his shoulders.

"I know we don't know each other well, but I'll miss you, too," she was honest. He held her tighter and she felt his breath hot against her neck.

"*Anytime you need anything, I'm here.*"

Before she could question what he meant, or even how he expected her to be able to get a hold of him, he pulled away. Straightened out his jacket as he climbed into the Rav.

And then there was one.

"Take care of each other!" she called out, watching as their car started to roll forward. Marc stared at her for a second, then looked away as he turned the wheel.

*Don't panic. Don't cry. Don't say anything. You were alone seven days ago. You were alone for five years. You've always been alone. You can do this. You don't need him. He obviously doesn't care that much about you. You don't care about him. **You don't need him**.*

Lily took a deep breath. She couldn't bear to watch them drive away, so she turned to the Buick and opened the back door. Leaned in and grabbed Marc's pack, unzipping it and digging through the items. She took the Glock out and put it in the front seat. Took another deep breath. Grabbed a bottle of water and set it next to the Glock. Took a shakier breath and grabbed the bag of diamonds. Before she could pull them out, though, there was a noise behind her that caused her to pause. Someone grabbed her arm and yanked her around, and before she could say anything, Marc was kissing her, pressing her against the car.

Thank god.

His hands cupped either side of her neck and she moaned, scratching her nails down his biceps before holding onto his forearms. His kiss was just like the man behind it; blunt, forceful, and breathtaking. *All* her breaths, *all* her air.

"He's right, that was a shitty goodbye," Marc panted when he finally pulled his lips away. His hands stayed on her neck, his thumbs pointing underneath her chin, forcing her to look up at him.

"It really was," she agreed. He kissed her again, and she gasped around his tongue. Moved her hands to the front of his waist, gripping onto his belt and holding him tight against her.

"I don't want to go," he told her, pressing his forehead against hers. "But it's for the best, I promise."

She could've wept. Listening to him say things she needed to hear. It was so much. It was everything.

"I want you to stay," she said back, though she knew it was useless.

"You hated me a week ago," he read her thoughts from earlier.

"You were awful a week ago. You're nicer now," she joked, though her voice was shaky.

"No, I'm just better at hiding it from you," he assured her.

"You're a lot better in bed now," she switched tactics. He burst out laughing.

"I was fucking amazing that first time," he argued. She laughed as well, but it felt too much like crying, so she stopped.

"You really were. I would've killed you a long time ago, if it hadn't been for your amazing prowess in the bedroom," she told him.

"Not the first time I've heard that."

"When did we turn into this?" Lily whispered. He sighed.

"I don't know. I certainly didn't plan on this happening," he whispered back.

They kissed one more time. Said goodbyes. Kissed again. He told her again to take care of herself. Then another kiss.

"I meant every word I said to you. I'll miss these eyes," he told her, brushing his thumb down her cheek as he finally stepped away. She snorted.

"I give you one week before you're saying that same thing to some blue eyed beauty," she called him out. He shook his head.

"No. Only you. Only your eyes."

She swallowed past the lump in her throat.

"I learned a lot from you Marc. Thank you, really. For everything," she was completely honest.

"Same here, sweetheart. Thank you."

This time he didn't get in his car. Just stood back and waited while she got in her car. She turned the engine and stared at the dash for a minute. Then stared at him. Finally, she hit the gas, blowing a kiss as she peeled out of the sandy lot where they were parked. She roared off down the road, heading back towards Tarfaya at a break neck pace.

And she didn't look back. Not even once.

Liliana Brewster doesn't look back. Only forward.

DAY SEVEN

She could've made it to Tangier in one long push, it was only about fifteen hours away. But she stopped short, deciding to stay in Casablanca. She'd been racing for Tangier the whole time, and now that it was right in front of her, she was hesitating.

Never hesitate.

Lily made the call to Ivanov. She stole an old cell phone, and after finding the necessary cables in a tiny pawn shop, she was able to patch the phone through a call box behind an old house on the outskirts of the city. She didn't mind if he knew she was in Casablanca, but she didn't need him knowing her *exact* location.

She told him the story Marc had fed her. The one she had rehearsed for the entire eleven hour drive to Casablanca. Marc had kidnapped her. Marc had kept her hostage. Marc had dragged her across Africa, looking for a buyer for the diamonds. It was only through her own cunning that she had managed to escape him and made her way to Morocco with all the diamonds in tow.

"De Sant is dead?"

Again, she hesitated. Marc's new plan was to just vanish. Leave Africa, and never look back. He never had to work with that particular Bratva again, or any others for that matter. He was freelance, he could do whatever he wanted. Become whoever he wanted.

But still … she worried about revenge. About retribution.

"*Yes*," she answered. Explained that an assassin had shown up in Dakhla. Had killed Marc while she'd been making her escape with the stones.

She didn't know if Ivanov necessarily believed her, but he didn't really have a choice. She had millions of dollars worth of his diamonds. *Stankovski's* diamonds. It was too big a risk. He gave her the name of a hotel in Tangier and told her to stay there for three days while he sent her new bribe money and arranged for her to catch another ferry.

Days, days, days. My life is one long string of days, connected by sand and bad memories.

She checked into a hotel in Casablanca. It was cheap and had no air conditioning. She checked the floor to make sure no one was watching, no one was peeking out windows, then she locked herself in her room and blocked the door with a heavy dresser. Checked all the windows and made sure they were locked and the blinds tightly drawn.

Then she knelt at the foot of the bed and took the baggie of diamonds out of the pack. She let the stones spill across the bedspread. She spread them out, making a flat layer, then she leaned forward, lacing her fingers together and resting her hands on the bed, her chin on top of them.

So much trouble. So many rocks. Such *little* rocks. She'd never seen them all out before, spread out like they were. They didn't seem quite as impressive. No weight, no heft. Just individual stones, tiny and insignificant.

Just individual days, tiny and insignificant.

They looked so pure, so clear, that to think of what they represented was such a contrast. Illegal mines. Indentured slaves. Gang wars. Bratvas. Mafias. Corporations. Murders. Theft. Her life. Marc's life. Her precious five year plan.

What did it all mean?

She was getting revenge for her sister. For Kaylee. But how often did she even think about that anymore? How much of it was purely for revenge, and how much of it was because she *enjoyed* what she did now?

Kingsley had told her she was good at what she did; even Marc had admitted it. Both had warned her that revenge would not help her. That it would most likely get her killed. Both had warned her that she wasn't ready for something so drastic. Both had told her that she had other options. Her life didn't have to be about this plan. It could be so much bigger.

"*… we don't have to be these people anymore …*"

She buried her hands in the diamonds, clenching her fingers together. Squeezing so tight, she could feel some of the bigger rocks cutting into her skin. Drawing blood.

I don't. I don't want to be this person anymore.

She knew what she had to do.

DAY SEVEN

He could've made it back to Nouakchott in one long push, it was only about sixteen hours away. But Marc was stopped short, what with Kingsley asking to be dropped off in Dakhla.

"What?" Marc asked, not sure he'd heard right. He'd been daydreaming. Thinking about red hair and green eyes.

"Stop here, mate. I left most of my gear here," Kingsley explained.

"Okay, we can grab it, then get some lunch."

"Let's eat first."

They found a restaurant and made themselves comfortable. Kingsley ordered tea and Marc ordered food, then they sat and waited. Avoided talking about the person they were both thinking about.

"I'm heading down to Nouakchott, and I'm gonna try to get some documents while I'm there, try to fly out. Are you gonna fly with with me?" Marc started. Kingsley shrugged.

"Not sure. Do you think that's a good idea?" he asked.

"Why wouldn't it be?"

"What if you fly out and then she calls you, needing your help," Kingsley suggested. Marc scowled.

"That won't happen. Besides, I don't think she'd call me. She's too pig headed, she thinks she can do it all on her own."

"Sounds familiar."

"Fuck you."

Kingsley sighed.

"Look. I like you, mate," he started. Marc groaned.

"Don't fucking start. I already feel like shit."

"I know. But I still have to say this. You're making a mistake. I genuinely thought we'd make it a couple kilometers before you'd realize what an idiot you're being, and you'd turn back," Kingsley explained.

"Well, I guess you thought wrong."

"No. I just had higher expectations of you. Now I'm going to be completely straight with you. I don't want to hear any bullshit. Not a word. Just hear the truth from me, and we'll be done with it," Kingsley offered.

"Alright, but then it's *done*," Marc stressed.

"You are making a mistake," Kingsley stated, for what felt like the millionth time. A waiter came with their orders, and as soon as he left, Kingsley started in again. "You care for that woman, and there is nothing wrong with that. It does not make you weak. It does not take away from all you've accomplished. If anything, I'd say it makes you better, having a little humanity. And that woman cares for you, as anyone with eyes could tell you. She is also very lost, and needs help. *Your* help.

"You think you are helping her by staying away? You are sending her into a situation she is completely unprepared for, and completely unable to properly handle on her own. *You* are doing that. You could've asked her to come with us – I bet she would've said yes. You could've asked her to run away with you – she would've gone for it, this time. Yet you did none of those things. You are either scared, or stupid. Neither is complimentary."

It was a lot of information to unload, and Kingsley did it all in almost one breath, his posh British accent taking on a hard edge. He was stabbing at the table top with his finger, pounding out his points. Marc leaned back in his chair.

"You've known her for a grand total of what, two days? Maybe three? You haven't seen her in action the way I have, Law. A couple days ago, she stripped to her underwear and pretended to be a pros-titute in order to steal us a car, after which she hung out of said car and shot out the tires of a pursuit vehicle, all while half naked. And the day before that? While doing sixty miles an hour and driving backwards, she fired a flare into a car full of hired thugs. The woman has no problem handling herself," Marc assured him. Assured him-self.

That has to be true. I almost got her blown up. She has to be better without me.

"I've said my piece. You sent her off with a bag full of perfect stones, but you really had a diamond in the rough in your own hands. And you let it go. I think she is going to get to Tangier. I think the Bratva will show up. I think they will show her what this lifestyle truly looks like. And I think they will kill her."

At the words "*kill her*", Marc felt a sharp, stabbing, burning pain in his stomach. He scowled and looked away, wondering where the nearest bottle of Maalox was.

In one week, the bitch managed to give me an ulcer.

"I think you're wrong. I think she'll get there, they'll show up, and those diamonds will be her bargaining tool. She won't show them unless she's guaranteed safe passage – the girl is smart, Law. They care more about their investment. I don't think she'll pull the trigger in Moscow, but I'm glad about that. She'll be fine," Marc stressed. Kingsley abruptly stood up, stubbing out his cigarette as he did so.

"I've said my piece. I told you, I didn't want to hear any bullshit. I'm going to go stay at the same hotel we left behind yesterday. If you bother me, I'll shoot you in the leg," he warned him.

"Fuck off with your condescending bullshit, Law. You forget I know you, know that you don't have the fucking right to lecture me about anything, least of all how I should or shouldn't be treating a woman," Marc called after him, but Kingsley was already on his way out of the restaurant. He didn't even look back.

Marc finished his food, glaring at the table like it had been the one to offend him. When he was finished, he pushed away abruptly, his chair scraping loudly against the floor. Several people turned to look at him, but didn't say anything.

Fuck Kingsley Law. What did he know about Lily? He'd only known her for two fucking days! A couple meals, and he was acting like a lovesick puppy dog, trying to do everything he could to get "*mom and dad*" back together.

Why can't he see that I'm doing this for her? She didn't stop me. She didn't beg me to go with her. She drove away first …

… because it was the right thing to do.

DAY EIGHT

Marc was dreaming. He was in the water, and the harder he swam, the deeper he sank. There were sunbeams breaking through the surface, but he kept getting farther and farther away. Everything was getting darker. Before he completely faded into blackness, he could've sworn he saw a flash of red …

He sat up abruptly, yanking his gun out from underneath his pillow. The door to his hotel room burst open, and he put two bullets in the wall next to the head of the person barging in on him.

"Get up!" Kingsley shouted, not even phased by the gun shots. He threw a bag onto the foot of the bed.

"What the fuck do you think you're doing!?" Marc demanded. They hadn't spoken since Kingsley had walked out of the restaurant.

"I just got a call, we need to move," the other man was breathing hard as he grabbed Marc's duffle and put it on the bed as well.

"What call? What are you talking about? Why?" Marc asked as he jumped out of the bed. He grabbed his pants and yanked them on at the same time as he pulled his other t-shirt out of his duffle bag.

"You know that hit on you?" Kingsley reminded him.

"Yeah. What, another guy decided to take a shot at me?" Marc groaned, though he was surprised at Kingsley's concern. Marc could more than handle himself with some greedy hit-hungry assassin.

"No, not you."

"What does that mean?"

"The bounty has been removed from your head."

"Is this a joke? That's a good thing, it means I can go back to bed," Marc groaned, stopping his frantic rush to pull on his shoes.

"Now there's one on Lily."

Marc jammed his foot into his shoe.

"What!? Why!? How did you learn this!?"

"My guy out of Brooklyn, he called me. Told me not to bother with you anymore, and that her bounty is twice what yours was. De Sant, people are going to be all over this. A lot of these blokes are already in Africa, looking for your ass. With her, they already have a location. I was told the target was known to be arriving in Tangier today," Kingsley broke it down.

"Fuck. *Fuck.* Why would they do this!? It's fucking stupid! If one of these quick-draw playroom assassins finds out she has a bag full of fucking diamonds, they'll shoot her and just take them," Marc said, heading out the door. The other man followed close behind.

"No mention of the stones. All that was said was dead or alive, though if the target could be acquired alive, there would be a bonus," Kingsley explained, jogging up to their car and throwing his gear in the back seat.

"Fuck. How far are we from Tangier!? Goddammit, how did this fucking happen," Marc was cursing.

They peeled out of the parking lot, leaving burning rubber in their wake. Marc did the math in his head. They were about a day's drive from Tangier. They had left Lily in Tarfaya the day before, which was only about 15 hours from Tangier. She should've gotten there the night before, but the bounty instructions had said she would be arriving in Tangier today. She must have stopped somewhere for the night.

Good girl.

A day was a long time. How far was she from Tangier? Casablanca was a major city between Tarfaya and Tangier, as was Marrakesh. It was a safe bet that she'd stopped in one of those places, which meant she was only a couple hours from Tangier, six at most. He was twenty.

FUCK.

"We can't do anything if you get us killed before we can even get there," Kingsley pointed out, gripping the side of his door as Marc passed dangerously close to a horse-and-cart.

"Let me worry about the driving. Is there anyone here that would help us out?" Marc questioned. Assassins and mercenaries didn't exactly have club meetings, or a union, but they did run into each other from time to time. Friendships and bonds were formed. There weren't many people Marc claimed as friends, less than he could count on one hand. But there were some.

"No. The Swede is in Bangkok, and no one's heard from Advay in about a month," Kingsley answered.

"Shit."

"We're on our own. What's the plan?"

"We have to get to her before one of these other guys do. She's good one-on-one, but her situational awareness is non-existent. She won't know she's being tailed till she's got a bullet in her. We also need gear. I don't have anything, just what I'm wearing and two handguns. Make some calls, find somewhere in Tangier or Casablanca that we can just dip in and out of," Marc prattled off. Kingsley took out his notepad and began jotting things down.

"Okay, what am I looking for."

"Vest. Leg holsters, shoulder holster. Crowbar. Two way radios, a throat mic set. Two Colt .45s and a shotgun – shorty. Did you bring the big girl?" he questioned.

"I don't leave home without her," Kingsley chuckled.

"Make the call. I wanna make this drive in fifteen hours," Marc explained, then pressed harder on the gas.

"Jesus. Just don't crash."

"I won't. We're getting there. We *have* to get there."

Marc wasn't sure if he was making a statement, or a prayer.

We have to get there.

DAY NINE

Being in Tangier made Lily nervous.

 She went to the hotel Ivanov had instructed her to stay in, and she checked into the room he had booked for her, then went to a restaurant down the street and ate lunch. Hours later, she came back to the hotel and checked into a new room. Under a whole other name. Lily was still booked into Ivanov's suite. *Kaylee* was staying in one of the cheapest rooms in the building, on the second floor.

 What if Ivanov doesn't believe anything you say? What if he says he wants to take the diamonds himself?

 She shook away the bad thoughts and made her way to the roof of the hotel. She stared out over the city of Tangier, paying attention to the streets around the hotel. She looked for anything out of the ordinary. A motorcade in front of the hotel. Or maybe an out-of-place car, parked within surveillance distance of the hotel. Anything that might indicate that people were following her. But everything looked normal, as far as she could tell.

 Still. She didn't want to be caught off guard by anything.

 I just want this to end. For one plan to work without a hitch. Marc, if this can reach you, come back for me. You came back every single other time. Come back this time.

 After the sun rose, she headed back downstairs. Crept through service corridors, took emergency stairwells. The hotel was quiet and she didn't run into anyone, not even a wayward maid.

Once in her room, Lily peeled off her leggings. There was a full length mirror, and she frowned at her reflection. She'd showered at the hotel in Casablanca and washed the bikini, but she still would've killed for some new clothing. Some nice clothing. Some *normal* clothing.

What's normal?

She peeled back the scratchy comforter and laid on top of cool sheets, staring at the ceiling. Her eyes slowly fell shut, but she didn't want to sleep. She wanted to sweep the hotel in half an hour, just as a safety precaution, so she tried to think of something that would keep her awake.

She thought of Marc.

They'd only known each other within their roles in Africa. A mercenary and a transporter in Liberia. Captor and captive in Mali. Allies in Mauritania. And … friends, through everything else. What would they be like if they met outside of Africa? Would he still like her? She thought back to the last time she'd seen him. Their last kiss.

She bent her legs at the knees, putting her feet flat on the mattress. Then she took a deep breath and put her hands behind her head. She imagined his sexy smile and his mean glare. The scar on the side of his chin, that made him look hard and dangerous. His large hands, that he knew exactly how to use. The way his teeth would skim along the edge of his bottom lip when he was looking at something he *really* wanted.

Her hand was in her bikini bottoms before she even realized it. She moaned, her toes curling into the blanket as she remembered their last night together. Remembered all their nights together. The time in the house, when he'd lost it from her talking dirty to him. She gasped, moving her fingers lower. The time in the car, when it had been more like an explosion than sex. Unable to stop, unable to think, unable to keep away. Her head tossed back and forth, one finger sliding in and out of herself. The first time, in Liberia, in his room. Doing it like it was something they'd practiced before, like it was something they'd done a hundred times together. Two fingers now, running a race with her heart to see which would make her explode first. Her free hand was under her shirt, moving from breast to breast.

God, I wish he was here. I wish he could see this. He would love this.

The orgasm wasn't as good as the ones Marc had given her, but it wasn't anything to scoff at, either. She stretched completely out, her hands reaching above her head, and she smiled to herself. He wasn't even in the same city, and he could still make her come.

He'd love that.

The moment was slightly ruined, however, when someone broke down the door to her hotel room.

DAY NINE

"Jesus, cart, left side!"

Marc yanked the wheel, narrowly missing a cart full of fabric, which was being pulled across the street.

"Thanks."

"Do you have a death wish!? Slow the fuck down!" Kingsley yelled, one hand braced against the dash as they took a sharp right turn.

"I have a bad feeling," Marc grumbled.

They'd been driving at a break neck pace all night. He'd been hoping to make it to Tangier in 15 hours, but it took them closer to eighteen hours. They'd had to stop in Casablanca to pick up Marc's list of stuff, and that had been its own adventure which had ended with the black market gun trader being tied up and left in his own basement.

Then they'd continued on their journey, and they'd watched the sun rise as they entered the outskirts of Tangier. But the closer they got to the city center, the worse the pain in his stomach got; something was most definitely wrong.

"Well, then even more reason not to get us killed! We're of no use if we're roadkill," Kingsley pointed out.

"Shut up. What was the name of the hotel?"

Kingsley's contact in Brooklyn had come through with more information. Lily's bounty was all over the network, information was flowing everywhere. It hadn't taken long to figure out what hotel she was staying at, even which room. Ivanov had booked it, himself.

"You realize all of this wouldn't be necessary, if you'd just stayed with her in the first place," Kingsley pointed out.

"Shut the fuck up."

They parked a couple blocks away from the hotel and suited up. Every piece of gear Marc had listed off was eventually attached to his body in some way; even the shotgun was resting against the length of his spine, the crowbar right next to it. He pulled on the final strap of his new flak jacket, tightening it as much as possible.

"So, how do you want to do this? Set up a standard stakeout? Case the hotel, sweep for other -" Kingsley started while they walked down the street.

"Let's just worry about getting to her before anyone else does, okay? Once we do that, we can talk about the plan," Marc said.

"Right."

They came around a corner, exiting an alley and coming out onto a main road. Lily's hotel was across the street and a couple doors down. They'd only walked a few feet when something caught Marc's eyes. He swung out his arm, slapping his hand against Kingsley's chest, stopping him. He stared for a second longer, then grabbed the other man's tie and yanked on it, dropping them both to the ground.

"What the fuck is that!?" he hissed, crouching down and scurrying to the front of a parked car.

"I can't see anything, move," Kingsley said, shoving at his shoulder. Marc let the Brit get ahead of him, and watched as he pulled a small pair of binoculars out of his pocket.

"Tell me everything," Marc instructed.

"Looks like four Escalades. Tinted windows. Diplomatic flags. Small contingency of body guards – seven … no, eight," Kingsley listed off.

"*Byki*," Marc whispered. Bratva bodyguards. He yanked the binoculars away and looked through them. He recognized some of the men on the other side of the street, he'd spent time with them in Liberia.

"*The doors!*" Kingsley snapped.

Marc shifted his gaze, watching the front of the hotel. One door had opened, then a second was pushed open as well. A man in a black suit came out – another bodyguard. Then another. Then the pig himself, Ivanov. Marc clenched his jaw, preparing himself for what he knew was coming.

She looked pissed, and she wasn't wearing any pants, but Lily was in one piece, and that's what mattered the most to him. She had her wrists pinned behind her back and the men on either side of her were holding her arms, almost carrying her down the steps. Her toes barely brushed the ground. She wasn't struggling, smart girl, but her mouth was moving double time, and if he hadn't felt like puking, Marc would have smiled as he imagined the things she was saying.

"Go get the car," he stated.

"Huh?"

"Go get the fucking car. *Now!*"

While Kingsley took off back down the alley, Marc watched the scene unfold. Ivanov was saying something to Lily, holding her face between his hands. She was scowling and trying to pull free. He laughed at whatever she said, then moved his hands, cupping her breasts. Marc's vision turned red.

He dies first.

She spit in Ivanov's face, and when he went to rub the saliva way, she kicked him in the balls, sending him to his knees. One of the bodyguards grabbed her by the back of the head, yanking her back by her hair. Marc could hear her shriek all the way from his hiding place, and he grimaced.

Ivanov eventually stood up. She got slapped across the face, twice, then everyone was instructed to load up. Marc balanced on his toes, ready to sprint if necessary. If Kingsley didn't show up soon, Marc was going to try to take over one of the cars. Or hitch on beneath one. Anything. He couldn't lose them. Couldn't lose her.

The cars began filling up with people, with Ivanov and Lily in the third car. Then car one started to pull away. Then car two. Marc stood up and started walking forward as car three began to roll, but then a car squealed to a stop next to him. He turned to see Kingsley leaning across the seat, pushing the passenger door open. Marc dove into the vehicle.

"They've got her," he breathed, buckling himself in. "Ivanov is with her. She looks pissed."

"Doesn't sound good."

"No, they've never seen her pissed. I'm almost scared for them."

They wove their way through Tangier, keeping three cars between them and Ivanov's entourage at all times. Kingsley got on his phone, started barking out questions to any informants he knew, trying to figure out where she was being taken. No one seemed to know anything – Ivanov's presence in Tangier was a surprise. Why would he be there, if he'd taken a hit out on Lily?

Maybe he didn't take out the hit. Boss man Stankovski ...

They followed them to the outer reaches of the city, putting more and more distance between them. Marc put on his radio, strapping the apparatus around his neck. He set the channels, then tossed the other radio into Kingsley's lap.

Get ready.

The small motorcade pulled in behind what looked like an abandoned medical center, in a sketchy neighborhood. No one was on the streets, and the apartment buildings surrounding them also looked to be mostly abandoned. Kingsley cruised by, with Marc laying back in his seat, invisible from the outside. They went down the street, took two lefts, then headed up the small street that ran parallel to the one they'd just come down.

They parked in front of a squatty apartment building and Marc hopped out before the car even stopped rolling. He got into the backseat and began hauling out the rest of their gear. He watched as Kingsley took off his suit jacket and began putting his "work" clothes back on – black knit sweater. Black flak jacket over it. Black slacks. Black gloves. Then he put on his radio.

"You hear this?" Marc checked, pushing down on the device that rested against this throat.

"Good to go," Kingsley's voice whispered through the ear piece.

"Okay, once I get across the street, leave the mics on. I'm just gonna find an entrance and go. You set up, get a view. See if you can find what room they're in, help me out. You see shit go down, start shooting, okay? Don't worry about me, just take out anyone standing in her way," Marc instructed.

"No problem. You sure about this?"

Marc stopped for a second. He'd never gone into a job so unprepared, before; well, not counting the whole last week. Usually, when he was going for an extraction, or a heist, he knew the property backwards and forwards. He knew most of the individuals who would be on the property. He had a route mapped out, multiple entrance points, and multiple exit points. *He had a plan.*

He knew nothing of the building he was about to enter, he had no clue how many men would actually be inside, and he had no idea what kind of condition Lily would be in once he found her.

He had no plan.

"Positive. Let's go get that wildcat," he sighed. The two men nodded to each other, then Marc took off jogging.

Hold on, Lily. Don't say anything that'll get you shot. I'm coming. Just hold on.

DAY NINE

Well, if this ain't a *bitch* ...

Lily sighed, resting her forehead against her bicep. She shifted her weight from foot to foot, trying to alleviate the pressure in her legs. She had an itch between her shoulder blades that was threatening to drive her insane, but she couldn't reach it.

Her wrists were handcuffed together and hooked to a chain, which was hanging from the ceiling.

It was fitting. Her week had begun with her being chained up. Now it was ending that way. Possibly ending permanently. She leaned her head back, looking to see where the chain was attached. A heavy metal plate with a ring in it was bolted to the cement ceiling, with the chain running through the ring. She furrowed her brow, examining the metal plate.

Hmmm.

Ivanov was pissed. At the hotel, he'd tossed both the fake room and the room she'd booked for herself, and he hadn't been able to find the diamonds. She'd had multiple guns shoved into various parts of her anatomy, and she'd been smacked around plenty, but she hadn't said a word. Not one word since they'd left the hotel. It drove the other men insane, earned her more hits, but still she kept her mouth shut.

Lily used the time to think. How was she going to get herself free. She was wearing her bikini and the sleeveless shirt, that was it. Not even shoes. She had no firearms. She was chained up. Once again, just like the beginning of her week, the only weapon she had was the diamonds. She was the only person who knew their where-abouts.

I have to get out of here. But how? God, this would be easier if Marc was here.

She kept staring at the metal plate, then her eyes followed the chain, all the way to the handcuffs she was wearing. Then back up again. She licked her lips and glanced around. She was alone in a room on the third floor of a building, the windows all facing an apartment building. No one could see her. She took several quick, sharp breaths, then let her legs go completely limp, forcing her wrists to catch all her weight.

"*Fuck!*" she hissed, biting into her bottom lip as she got her feet back underneath herself.

She looked up again and smiled. It had hurt like a bitch, the metal from the cuffs cutting into her skin, but it had worked. Sever-al small cracks had formed in the rock around the plate. She stood upright on her toes, gripped the chain between her hands this time, then dropped herself again. She winced, the cuffs still scraping, but it wasn't as bad as before, and there were definitely more cracks.

This could work.

After several more drops, her left wrist was bleeding, the crim-son liquid trailing down her raised arm. Either she was going to rip the plate out of the ceiling, or she was going to be able to slip free of the cuff, dislocating her thumb and ripping off a layer of skin in the process. She wasn't sure which would happen first, and she didn't really care. As long as she was free.

"*Liliana!*"

The door burst open and Lily got back onto her feet. She lifted her arms up as high as they would go, trying to relieve some of the pain in her wrists. Ivanov waddled into the room, and several large men filed in after him.

"Did you bring breakfast? I'm starving," Lily sighed. Ivanov chortled and laughed as he dragged a chair across the room so he could sit in front of her.

"Were you always this funny, Ms. Lily? I wish we would have talked more," he snickered.

"Eh, I don't think you'd get my sense of humor."

"True."

"What is this about? I mean, I enjoy a bit of kink as much as the next girl," Lily joked, shaking her chains for emphasis, "but this is a bit extreme."

"Liliana, you cannot disappear with my diamonds and not expect me to be a little upset," he replied.

"Disappear? I told you what happened, you *know* what happened. I did the best I could, he had me chained to him! I still finished the job. I still made it here, I can still make it to Moscow," Lily snapped, her teeth clenched together.

"That will be unnecessary."

"Why? I don't understand. I got away from him, I kept them safe," she stressed.

"Yes, that is what you say. But where are diamonds?" he asked.

She swallowed thickly.

"Safe."

"We searched your room and the other room. And entire hotel. No stones. I would very much like to see them," he told her. She took a deep breath.

Plan. Plan. Stick to the plan.

"Let me go," she said.

"Impossible."

"I'm the only one who knows where they are, I hid them somewhere," she told him.

"And why would you do that? If you are innocent like you claim."

"Because I knew you probably wouldn't believe me, and I am not going to die in this country. Not for those stones. Not at your hands," Lily swore.

"We shall see about that. *Alexei*," Ivanov snapped his fingers at one of the men in the room, gesturing for him to come forward. The young man stepped towards her and without hesitating, he wrapped his hands around Lily's neck and squeezed.

"You'll never find them! *You'll never find them!*" she managed to shriek before her air supply could be cut off. The choking stopped, but he didn't remove his hands. Lily stayed on her toes, staring at Ivanov out of the corner of her eye.

"Tell us where they are, Liliana. Our reach is very far. You wouldn't like to see your family hurt," he threatened. She just barely stopped herself from laughing.

"You don't even know what my last name really is," she hissed.

"*Alexei.*"

The young man in front of her squeezed her neck so hard, her blood immediately began to rush to her ears. She shook her body back and forth, trying to break free, but he was like a tree trunk. Unwavering. So she hiked back her leg and kicked him in the nuts, as hard as she could. Like she was trying to make a 300 yard field goal. He let out a string of Russian words that could only be curses, then fell to his knees. Lily hacked and coughed, sucking in air.

"Let me go … and I'll take you … take you to the stones …," she gasped.

"Tell us where stones are, and then maybe I let you go!" Ivanov yelled back.

"No. I'm not dying here. I *will not* die here," she breathed.

"You *will* die, and it will be very slow, and it will be very painful, I assure you," he threatened. The young man managed to get to his knees, his face beet red, his own breathing haggard.

"Why the theatrics, Ivanov? You barely ever left the safe house in Liberia. Now you're flying all the way to Morocco? Threatening me, when if you'd just let me go, the diamonds would be yours. Why?" Lily asked.

Before Ivanov could answer, the man he'd called Alexei got to his feet and slapped Lily, with the full force of his arm. She flew to the side, her legs going out from underneath her, and she howled in pain. Not from the hit, but from the handcuffs biting into her already bruised and bleeding wrists. She struggled to stand upright.

"You do not question me, girl! I came here for stones, and only for stones! *Stankovski's* stones!" Ivanov was yelling, his face turning red. She glanced up, noticing that the metal plate was even looser than before, wiggling in place above her as she moved around.

"And I want to give you the stones! So let me go!" she yelled back.

"No. I have other ways of making you talk, stupid girl. Do you like your toes? Because you are about to lose some of them. They will make excellent additions to my collection," he informed her.

"Please," she moaned, reduced to begging. "Please. This doesn't have to be like this – we were partners in Liberia. We still are. Same team. You don't have to do this, I will give you the stones. You can come with me."

"We are not on same team. We are not even on same field. You will tell me where the stones are, and then you and stones will be given to Stankovski as gift," he informed her. She frowned. Something seemed off.

"Why would he want me? Even as a gift? I'm not his type."

"As apology, for delay in getting stones."

"But surely even he would understand – De Sant is dead, that's what he wanted, right? He got his revenge. Why would he need an apology from you?" Lily asked.

"It does not matter! That he became involved is worthy of apology!" Ivanov yelled.

"Became involved … wasn't Stankovski always involved?" she was confused.

"No no no! Now is not time for talking!"

Something clicked in Lily's brain. She went still for a second, then stared very directly at Ivanov.

"He didn't know," she breathed. Ivanov frowned.

"What?"

"He didn't know. You told the Liberian gang that Marc stole their diamonds, that Marc was trying to sell them for himself. You must have told Stankovski the same thing. But somehow … somehow he found out. Found out that wasn't true, that Marc had me and we still had the diamonds. You lied to him, didn't you?" the pieces fell into place in Lily's brain.

"You shut your mouth!" Ivanov yelled, leaping out of his chair. His anger only confirmed her theory.

"You were going to keep them for yourself! Tell everyone that Marc stole them, then count on someone killing him, solving that little problem for you. But you didn't count on Marc being smarter than you. Stronger than you. Stronger than anything you could throw at him!" Lily was yelling back.

"I will kill you, you whore! You ruined everything!" Ivanov shouted through clenched teeth. Lily chuckled.

"Oh, you stupid, stupid man. I can't wait to see who kills you first. Stankovski or Marc," she sighed, gripping the chain between her hands. Her fingers were starting to go numb.

"You said De Sant was dead," Ivanov remind her. Her chuckling turned to laughter and she pulled on the chain, spinning herself in a lazy circle.

"I lied. He's not dead. He's alive. Someday, he'll find you. And then, he's going to kill you," she laughed and laughed, twirling around.

"Shut your mouth!" Ivanov was almost shrieking.

"He's going to kill you. *Kill you*. I can't wait," she kept laughing.

"Shut up!"

Ivanov leapt forward, surprisingly nimble for such a heavy man. He grabbed her by her ponytail and yanked her head back. As she was forced into a back bend, he brought around a large knife and pressed the blade hard against her jaw bone.

"You'll never find them!" she screamed, gritting her teeth as the serrated edge scratched her skin, drawing blood.

"You tell me, or I cut off your head!" he was screaming back.

"Fuck you! I'm not telling you *shit!*" Lily kept her eyes squeezed shut. If she was going to die by having her neck sliced open, she didn't want Oleg Ivanov to be the last image she was going to see.

"I will do it! I will kill you!"

"*Then fucking do it!*"

She could feel the blade, could already feel a trickle of blood running down her neck. He moved the knife, placing it heavily against the side of her throat, right over the throbbing vein there, and she held her breath. Tried to think of something pleasant. Anything. Anything to make dying slightly more bearable. A voice began whispering in the back of her brain, and she almost smiled.

"*... we don't have to be these people anymore ...*"

DAY NINE

Getting past the guard in the back of the building was easy – Marc got him in a choke hold till he passed out. Left him halfway under a car, sleeping it off.

"*De Sant,*" a voice hissed in his ear.

"A little busy," he growled. He was scurrying up a metal ladder that ran the length of the outer wall.

"*Third floor. Street facing room. I count four doors down, on your left,*" Kingsley's voice was low.

"Can you see her!?" Marc demanded.

"*I can see her.*"

"Is she alive?"

"*Yes.*"

"Condition?" Marc asked.

"*She seems okay. They've got her chained to the ceiling. She's alone, and she - wait. Movement,*" Kingsley spoke in hushed tones.

"What's going on!?" Marc snapped.

He stopped climbing at the fourth floor and worked his way onto the ledge outside of a window. No one was in the room, so he broke out a pane of glass, undid the latch, and opened the window. He dropped into the room, crouching low and moving fast as he made his way to the door.

"*There's bodyguards. Ivanov. And her. He's sitting. They're talking,*"

Kingsley described.

"Find out what they're saying!"

Kingsley always carried a Long Distance Listening Device, it was a standard part of his gear. Marc listened to the hiss and pop of the radio static, then there was a shuffling noise and the line opened up again.

"*He's asking where the diamonds are. She's saying that she hid them,*" the other man filled him in. Marc closed his eyes for a second.

Thank god. Smart girl.

"Is there anyone on my floor?"

"*You're clear. The building appears to be abandoned. I only see a couple guards on the bottom floor, then everyone else in the room with Lily.*"

Marc dashed into the hall, his gun pointed straight ahead. There was a staircase at one end of the hall, but he ignored it and went the other way. He located an ancient looking pair of elevator doors and, using the crowbar, pulled the doors apart.

"Going in the elevator shaft. Anything happening?" he asked, grabbing the closest cable and sliding down it slowly.

"*Still talking. Arguing. He wants to know where the diamonds are, he's threatened to - **one of the guards is choking her!**"*

Marc lost his grip and shot down the rest of the cable, landing hard on top of the stopped elevator.

"What!? Is she okay!? Shoot that mother -" Marc started growling, scrambling to locate the maintenance hatch.

"*It's over. She laid the guy out, one kick between the legs. Scary woman,*" Kingsley interrupted him. Marc let out the breath he'd been holding.

"You have no idea."

The maintenance hatch gave way under the crowbar and Marc dropped into the elevator. He was now on the third floor. He was four doors down from her. Four doors away from saving her.

Four doors away from losing her.

"*They're talking about something. Wait. What? She seems to have figured something out. She … she's accusing Ivanov of setting everyone up. Getting you to take the fall, so he could keep the diamonds. Screw Stankovski over,"* Kingsley filled him in. Marc was crouching on the floor, pulling apart the electrical panel, and he paused.

"Smart. Such a clever girl. I never even thought of that," he mumbled, talking to himself.

"She must have something because Ivanov is losing his shit. Threatening to cut off her toes, blah blah," Kingsley described. Marc yanked a couple wires out, cut them, twisted other wires together. Then he cut two more and pulled them out as far as the wires would allow, before laying them on the ground, making sure they didn't touch.

"Get ready, I'm gonna drop the lift. How's she doing?" Marc grunted out as he worked to pull the doors open manually.

"She's … laughing."

"Laughing!?" Marc double checked. He wedged the end of the crowbar under one of the doors, forcing them to stay open. He was glad to see that the door across the hall was open, it would make his plan that much easier. Then he risked peeking down the hall. It was empty, but he could hear raised voices from the other end of the building.

"She was telling him that you were alive – apparently she led them to believe you were dead. She's telling him that you're going to kill him."

Now Marc was laughing.

"God, I might actually be in love with this girl," he sighed, creeping into the hallway, holding the two wires in his hands.

*"Heads up! He's moving on her. He's got her hair. **Shit**,"* Kingsley hissed.

"What!?" Marc snapped, stopping in the middle of the hallway.

"Marc. He's got a knife on her throat. He's threatening to use it."

"And what's she got to say about that?"

*"I believe her response was, '**just fucking do it**', or something to that effect."*

Marc closed his eyes. Took a deep breath.

"Law," he whispered.

"*De Sant.*"

"Whatever happens. It's been good knowing you. Good times."

"*Don't get mushy on me now, darling. You can give us a big kiss when you come out of there alive.*"

"Sounds good. You ready?"

"*Always.*"

"Bring the fire."

Marc twisted the wires together, causing the elevator to drop. As he tucked and rolled into the empty room across the hall, heavy artillery shots were fired on the outside of the building. Specifically on a section about four doors down. Just as Marc came to a stop behind a door, the elevator met the bottom floor in a spectacular sounding crash, causing the old building to shake.

The reaction was pretty much as desired. As Marc slid into a standing position, his gun at the ready, he could hear feet charging down the hall. People screaming. The foot steps ran past him, down a stairwell. Then there was the sound of a sprinkler system kicking on, and someone weeping. He strained his ears, trying to place if it was a woman or a man.

"*One down. Ivanov's hit. Two ran out of the room,*" Kingsley's voice was whispering, but it sounded loud in Marc's ear.

"And ...?" he dared to ask.

"*She seems fine, she's standing on her own.*"

"So that's it? Just Ivanov is in the room?" Marc checked.

"*Far as I can tell, yes. She's struggling with her chain. Ivanov is on the ground, I can only see his feet. I clipped his shoulder.*"

"Good. I want to be the one to end him. Going in. Watch the bottom floor, pick off anyone who tries to leave," Marc instructed.

"*Already on it.*"

Despite wanting to run in there, guns blazing, Marc took his time. He kept himself tight to the wall and jogged down the hallway. He took short, quick breaths, wanting to stay sharp. Alert. He paused outside of the door to her room, tried to think back. Something wasn't right. How many bodyguards had come out of the hotel? How many were downstairs?

But then Lily screamed, and caution and logic and reasoning flew out the window.

One more second, sweetheart, and we'll be free, one way or another.

DAY NINE

What the fuck was that!?

Lily's ears were ringing. Whoever was shooting had to be across the street, but still. The sounds in the room had been deafening for a moment. Gun shots, screaming, the sprinklers going off. A body guard hit the ground. A bullet had ripped through him with such force that most of his heart was no longer inside his chest.

What kind of gun does that? I want one next time I do one of these stupid jobs.

She tucked herself down as small as she could, dangling from her chain, and just prayed that whoever was shooting would magically miss her. She watched Ivanov get shot, his shoulder almost taken clean off. He howled and fell to the ground, rolling to just beneath the windows. Then in between gun shots, there was a small explosion, from somewhere underneath them. The other two bodyguards, notoriously fearless *byki,* who were supposed to let no one and nothing get close to their boss, turned tail and ran like scared little girls.

Once the bullets stopped, Lily dared to stand upright. She looked around, taking in the damage. Ivanov was moaning on the ground, mumbling in Russian. The last remaining bodyguard was pressed against the wall next to the windows, breathing hard, looking like he couldn't decide whether he should've joined his friends or not.

"Hey!" Lily snapped, getting the guard's attention. "Hey! Get these fucking chains off of me! If I die, those diamonds will never be found."

He didn't move. On the ground, Ivanov began to wail, crying loudly and theatrically as he rolled further into the room. She rolled her eyes and looked back up at the ceiling. The metal plate, which was keeping her in place, was still stuck there. She gritted her teeth and began yanking and shaking the chain, trying to pull it free.

"No. No, you stop," the remaining bodyguard finally said something.

Lily ignored him. Just a couple more yanks, and she'd be free. She didn't care that she was handcuffed, she was getting the fuck out of there. God only knew who was shooting at them. Would a Liberian gang follow the Bratva all the way to Morocco!? Or maybe they had connections there, had called in a favor. Maybe it was someone else all together. The Mafia. Al-Qaeda. Anyone. Anyone at all. Anyone …

She was so lost in thought, so busy trying to pull herself free, she didn't notice Ivanov worming his way across the floor. He grabbed her left foot, shocking her, then he bit down, *hard*, breaking the skin immediately. She screamed and kicked him in the face, trying to shake him off.

There was another commotion and when she looked up, she had to blink to make sure she wasn't seeing things. Shake her head to clear the water out of her eyes. Someone was striding through the door, a gun held at the ready. She couldn't believe it.

I knew he'd come back.

"Behind you!" she shrieked, at the same time the bodyguard pounced on Marc, grabbing his wrist. Two bullets were fired into the wall, then the two men were dancing around. The bodyguard caught an elbow to the throat, but he didn't lose his grip. Marc got a foot hooked around his ankle and they both went down.

Lily lurched forward, then cried out as the her chains stopped her. She went to kick, hoping it would do something, when another high powered bullet crashed into the room. She shrieked again, jumping back as the projectile blew a small crater in the wooden floor boards. She turned to look out the windows, staring at the building across from them. The sun glinted off something on the roof. Something small and shiny. *A scope.*

Kingsley!?

Hands grabbed her by the hips, and she grunted as Ivanov pulled himself up her length. She tried to shimmy away from him, but he was too heavy. Soon enough, he was standing upright, one arm wrapped around her shoulders, forcing her to face the windows. He stood behind her, ducked down, making it impossible for someone to shoot him without shooting her.

Please, god, let that be Kingsley out there.

"Enough!" Ivanov roared, and the knife he'd had earlier was now digging into Lily's throat, right below her chin.

Everything stopped. Marc and the bodyguard were on their knees, both of them gripping Marc's gun. They paused, then the gun was ripped out of Marc's hands. He sighed and held up his hands.

"This didn't have to be like this," he said, his voice as calm as if they were discussing the stock market. Lily smiled.

I missed his voice.

"You are supposed to be dead!" Ivanov shouted, jerking on Lily's shoulder. She hissed as pain burned through her wrists. The water from the sprinklers mixed with her blood, turning her limbs pink.

"I'm not so good at dying," Marc explained. "But I'm here now. I fucked everything up. Let her go, and you can have me."

"No!" Lily shouted.

"Let her go, and I'll take you to where we hid the diamonds," he offered.

"He's lying! He doesn't know!" she kept going. What was he doing!? Of all the times for Marc to become a stand up guy, it had to be right then.

"I do know. Your scheme was a good one, Ivanov. I figured if I was going to get blamed for stealing them, might as well actually take them. She didn't have anything to do with it," he bluffed even more.

"I let her go, and you tell me where diamonds are?" Ivanov

checked.

"*Please,*" Lily moaned. They would both be dead. They would kill Marc, then kill her before she could get two steps, and all for nothing. She had to stop this, she had to do something.

Ivanov was still holding onto her, still had the knife at her throat, but it wasn't as sharp as before – he was using his bad arm to hold it up, it must have been painful. Marc was on his knees, his hands raised, the bodyguard behind him still holding the gun. What could she do? What could she do!?

Kingsley.

He could see them, obviously. But she was also pretty sure he could hear them. How else would Marc have known what floor she was on? What room she was in? That she had claimed to have hidden the diamonds? Marc was wearing a mic set around his throat, and she was willing to bet it was set to always be on.

Big gamble.

"Shoot!" she suddenly yelled. Everyone glanced at her for a second.

"You want me to shoot him?" Ivanov asked. She ignored him and stared out the window. Stared directly at the shiny object on the top of the roof across the street. Her hands were gripping the chain above her head, both her index fingers pointing straight up.

Straight up to where her chain connected to the ceiling.

"Look at me and shoot!" she shrieked, hopping on the balls of her feet.

"You want me to shoot you!?" Ivanov sounded incredulous.

"Shut the fuck up, Lily!" Marc yelled.

"*JUST FUCKING SHOOT!*"

A roar. Glass shattering. She turned her head away, and thanked god that Kingsley wasn't as stupid as Marc. The metal plate was ripped off the ceiling, bringing down a large chunk of cement with it. A chunk that landed directly on Ivanov's head. He groaned and slumped to the floor, dragging her with him. The knife fell out of his hands.

She had trusted that Marc would know what to do, and he didn't fail her. He grabbed the bodyguard's wrist and drove his fist into the other man's solar plexus. Lily scrambled around on the ground, pulling her chain out from underneath Ivanov.

Goddamn chains. Started in chains. Ending in chains. Fuck chains.

The fat man rolled around, moaning as he brought his hands to his head. She wasted no time and jumped on his back, coiling the metal links around his neck and yanking them tight. Ivanov was an obese man, she never would've expected him to be able to put up a fight. But he was actually very tenacious, and he reached over his shoulder and grabbed a hand full of her hair. She shrieked as she was pulled over him and slammed onto the ground.

She rolled onto her stomach and was about to jump to her feet when her eyes locked onto Marc. He had gotten to his feet, but the bodyguard still hadn't relinquished the gun. Marc stepped into him, elbowed him in the throat, pulled the gun free, then shoved the barrel under the other guy's chin. Then the trigger was pulled. No hesitation.

Just like he told you to do – so why are you hesitating right now?

"Stupid bitch!"

Lily let out a scream as searing pain washed over her body. Ivanov had just shoved his huge fucking K Bar right though her arm. The blade went right between her the bones of her forearm, straight through flesh, and lodged into the wood underneath her arm. She went to grab the handle of the knife when there was an all too familiar sound, right next to her ear.

The slide being pulled back on a Glock. *Her* Glock.

That gun is cursed.

"You stop now," Ivanov sighed, climbing to his knees, all the while holding Lily's own gun against her head.

"You stop," Marc replied, training his own firearm on Ivanov's forehead.

"I do not think so. You shoot me, I still have time to shoot her."

"You sure about that? That's a pretty big gun outside – he could kill you at any moment," Marc pointed out.

"Not if he can't see me," Ivanov retaliated.

He was right. Where Lily was laying, Ivanov was just outside of the view through the window. He was also on his knees, making him even less visible. She gritted her teeth, sliding her arm up and down on the blade a little. It made her want to puke, and there wasn't much give. She would have to yank hard to get the knife dislodged, and she didn't want to do that while a gun was pressed to the side of her head. She lifted her head to look at Marc.

"Quite a pickle, sweetheart. I think you're bad luck," he joked, winking at her. She scowled.

"I think *you're* bad luck," she snapped back. He tossed his gun to the ground, then put his hands together on the back of his head.

"You didn't think that a couple nights ago. In fact, I think you were feeling *very* lucky."

Is he flirting with me!? Now, of all times!? I know we're gonna die in two seconds, but goddamn, Marc!

"We're in a bit of trouble here, De Sant, could you shut the fuck up for two seconds!?" she yelled.

"Both of you, shut up!" Ivanov yelled.

"Did I ever tell you something, Lily?" Marc randomly asked.

"Tell me what?" she was lost.

"That you have the absolutely most gorgeous eyes, I've ever seen."

She was hurled back in time. To when they'd been in a car chase, after they'd stayed in the empty house. The crazy cockney mercenary, holding her hostage, while she'd been half conscious. Marc prattling away to her, distracting her. Distracting her captor.

Clever man.

"You may have said it, but it bears repeating," she told him.

"I said shut up!" Ivanov kept shouting.

"I dream about those eyes."

"Good, I'm glad. Maybe next time, don't leave me, and you won't have to dream about them."

"Sounds like a plan."

"That's it!" Ivanov was full on shrieking as he whipped the gun up, pointing it at Marc's chest. "I kill you and make your girlfriend watch it happen!"

Now free from his gun, Lily yanked her arm up as hard as she could. The pain that ripped through her nervous system was intense, unlike anything she'd ever experienced. But she pushed it down, way down into her psyche, where most of her feelings were sent to die. The blade was stuck in her flesh, the handle resting against the top of her arm, the jagged point sticking out the other side. She twisted to her side, and with a shout, shoved the exposed blade right into Ivanov's stomach. She pressed forward, using her chest to jam the knife into place.

He let out a strangled yell and fired off three rounds, right into Marc's chest. Lily shrieked as she watched him go down, flat on his back. Ivanov growled and rolled forward, towards her. She leaned away, pulling the knife free. Blood gushed from his wound, but he didn't stop moving. He grabbed one of her legs, trying to hold her in place and crawl up her length.

"Stop it! Stop it! No!" she shouted, trying to kick and wiggle as best she could. The knife finally slid free from her arm, clattering across the floor. Ivanov ignored it, just kept on crawling.

"You. For you, quick death is too good. I am going to rape your mouth, and then I am going to allow every many in Tangier to do the same. I will send video to your mother. And then when you are all used up, dirty and disgusting, I will put a bullet in you, just like De Sant," Ivanov was threatening, struggling to crawl with only one good arm, his weight pinning her legs in place.

"Like I give two fucks! You're never getting those diamonds. And you wanna know why!? *Cause I threw them in the goddamn ocean!*" she screamed. The look on Ivanov's face. Shock mixed with absolute terror. He paused his movements.

"You lie!"

"Like hell I am! Why do you think I stopped in Casablanca!?

Why it took me so long to drive here!? Because I made a special little detour, drove all the way to the beach, rented a boat, and I threw those cursed fucking stones into the darkest part of the ocean. You thought I brought them here!? So fucking stupid. No one will ever have those diamonds. Not you, and sure as shit not Stankovski!" she swore.

"How could you do something so stupid!? So much money! I will kill you! You are dead!" he started shouting.

"And Stankovski will kill *you!* The only one getting raped around here will be *you*," she threw back at him, then spit in his face. He cried out and stopped moving, wiping the saliva away.

"Stupid girl! You must want to die!" he proclaimed.

"*Not quite yet.*"

Lily had been able to draw her legs up, getting her knees in between his chest and her body. She braced her feet against the tops of his thighs, then she pushed. The motion caused him to stumble up into a standing position. Lily immediately scooted backwards, pressing herself up against the windows behind her. Ivanov made a face and went to step forward.

"*Princess.*"

Both of them whipped their heads to the side, just in time to see Marc sitting upright and pulling a shotgun from behind his back. Ivanov barely had to time to gasp before the trigger was pulled. Lead pellets ripped through his torso, causing him to spin around. Then another blast from outside, and a bullet zipped through the room.

One minute, Oleg Ivanov was the Brigadier for the Stankovski Bratva, second only to the Pakhan himself, Anatoly Stankovski.

The next minute, his head was a water balloon that had been popped, and Oleg Ivanov was nobody.

Lily slumped back, letting her eyes flutter shut. Letting the water run over her body, easing the sting in her cut. In her head. In her soul.

"Baby! Stay with me!" Marc was shouting, suddenly kneeling at her side.

"I'm not unconscious, you idiot, I'm just tired," she groaned, opening her eyes as he picked up her arm.

"I just saved your life, a little gratitude would be nice!" he yelled at her, but he was smiling. He ripped off the bottom edge of his t-shirt and wrapped it tightly around her forearm, over where she'd been stabbed. She hissed, then frowned at the amount of blood that was pooled on the floor next to her.

"That hurt like a *bitch*," she hissed, pulling her arm free from him.

"Oh yeah? Try getting shot in the chest three times. Kevlar ain't as strong as it used to be, I swear."

"Shut up, Marc."

"God, I thought you were dead," his voice got lower and his hands went to her face. Brushing her wet hair out of the way. Cupping her cheeks.

"Yeah, there were a couple moments there that had me nervous. I didn't … I just … thought that you …," she couldn't find the words.

"I came back for you," he breathed, then he leaned in and kissed her. Not his usual kiss – there was no roughness. No hard edge. No strict boundaries. It was soft and it was warm and it was gentle.

And it still stole every breath she'd ever had.

"I didn't think you would," she whispered when he pulled away.

"I never should've let you go."

She grabbed his vest and pulled him close. His hands slid around to her back, yanking her up against him. His tongue plunged into her mouth, sweeping along her teeth.

"I can't believe you came back," she breathed in between kisses.

"I had to. I had to save you. I've never wanted to protect anything in my life, but I always want to protect you. I was ready to burn this city down," he told her.

"When I got rid of the diamonds, I kept praying you'd come find me. I didn't know where you'd gone, didn't know how to get a hold of you," she realized tears were mixing with the sprinkler water on her face. "I was so scared that I'd never see you again."

"Never be scared. I never want you to be scared, ever again," he whispered, kissing along the side of her jaw.

Such beautiful words from such a rough man.

Lily shifted around onto her knees, trying to get closer to him. *Needing* to be closer to him. But without the proper use of her hands, she became unbalanced and started to fall to the side.

"Get these off of me," she growled, moving away from him and yanking at her handcuffs. The heavy moment between them broke, and they both remembered exactly where it was they were.

"Yeah. Yeah, let's get the fuck out of here," he said, then grabbed her arm and pulled her to her feet.

Marc searched Ivanov's corpse, but didn't find any keys. The dead bodyguard didn't have any, either. Marc helped her to wrap the chain around her torso, then led her down the hallway. She'd taken her Glock back from Ivanov's dead fingers – maybe it wasn't cursed. None of its bullets had ever killed anybody. Maybe it was her guardian angel.

They slowly made their way downstairs. The second floor was clear, but on the landing to the first floor, they heard shouting, and before they could retreat, a man in a suit came running up the stairs. Lily got right behind Marc and he backed them into a corner, shielding her body with his own, his back flattening her against the wall.

"You shoot I shoot!" the other man was yelling.

"No one fucking shoots! Just walk away!" Marc yelled back.

"You no shoot! You, down! You gun down!" the man yelled in broken English. Lily pressed her forehead to Marc's shoulders, beginning to shiver, which was strange, considering how warm it was in the building.

"I'm not fucking around, back the fuck up!" Marc's voice was aggressive, almost unhinged sounding. It had been a long morning.

"You back fuck up!"

A gun shot rang out, causing both Lily and Marc to flinch and duck. The bodyguard howled in pain and dropped to the ground, gripping his leg. Blood began to pour out of a bullet wound in his calf.

"Are we having our afternoon tea? I would really enjoy it if we could get the fuck out of here."

Lily smiled as the soft, posh British accent filled her ears. She peeked over Marc's shoulder and watched as Kingsley de-armed the man on the floor. Once all the guns were pulled away, Marc moved forward again, reaching back to grab one of her hands.

"Took you long enough," Marc growled as they hurried through the bottom floor.

"Excuse me? Did I, or did I not, just save the both of you?" Kingsley asked as they flanked the front door. Lily looked around and grimaced. The floor and walls were riddled with bullets, and several men were lying on the ground, dead and shredded by bullets.

"What!? *I* shot Ivanov at point blank range with a shotgun! He was dead before you even pulled your trigger!" Marc snapped. Both men turned in unison and went through the front door, making sure the street was clear. Then Marc reached back through the door, grabbed her handcuffs, and pulled Lily along behind him.

"Is that so? Who shot Lily loose? If I hadn't done that, you both would've been as good as dead," Kingsley pointed out as they crossed the street and slipped down an alley.

"I had the drop on him, you know I could've made that shot," Marc replied.

"Can you both shut the fuck up!?" Lily snapped. "If I hadn't stalled, and I hadn't gotten you to shoot the chain, and I hadn't stabbed that asshole, *none of it* would've worked out, so really, *I* did all the saving. *I'm* the badass here."

They stopped at the end of the alley and the two men glanced at each other. Looked back at her. She glared back at them. Marc was soaking wet, but otherwise looked none the worse for wear. Kingsley was in his all-black assassin gear, making him look devastatingly handsome and chillingly dangerous.

Lily was wearing a black bikini, a sleeveless orange shirt, was bleeding from multiple points on her body, and had multiple bruises and contusions.

"She has a point," Kingsley admitted. Marc snorted.

"Shut up."

They loaded up into the same car Marc had been driving when she'd left them in Tarfaya. She pulled herself into the backseat, hissing in pain, feeling every wound. She held her arm against her stomach and glanced into the large back end of the car. A huge gun was laying on its side.

"Is that what you were shooting!?" Lily exclaimed. Kingsley slid into the passenger seat and looked back at her.

"Ah, Sheila. I don't leave home without her."

"What is it?"

"*She* is a Barrett M82A1, fifty caliber. Make you shit bricks or eat lead, good for any situation," Kingsley answered.

"Except for close range," Marc added, then burned rubber as he drove out of the neighborhood.

"Either way, I'm glad you brought it. *Her*," Lily sighed, leaning back in her seat.

"Hey!" Marc shouted, snapping his fingers. "Hey, don't fall asleep back there, sweetheart."

"Are you joking!? I'm tired in a way I didn't even know was possible," she moaned, settling her head back on the seat and closing her eyes.

"You've lost a lot of blood. Stay with us," Marc instructed.

"You know what I want?" she asked through a yawn. "Pants. I would love some pants." She could feel goosebumps break out across her skin and her teeth started to chatter.

"Hello, darling," Kingsley grunted as he crawled between the seats and sat down next to her. "Let's take a look, shall we?"

He peeled back Marc's makeshift bandage on her arm, examining her wound. She didn't look at the cut, but watched as Kingsley grimaced. He leaned over the seat and reached into the back end, pulling a black bag up.

"Is it bad?" she asked.

"I've seen worse. You'll be fine. Just want to stop the bleeding," he assured her, taking a first aid kit out of the bag, as well as a lock picking kit.

"Got any pants in there?" she asked, glancing at the bag.

"You know, I just might," he replied, then pulled out a black pair of dress slacks.

"I think my ass will be too fat for them," she joked.

"Pity. Guess you'll have to keep walking around in your knickers," he sighed, getting to work on opening her handcuffs. Lily laughed.

"You would like that. Can I sleep now?" she asked, yawning again.

"No, I think Marc's right. I think staying awake would be a very good idea," he urged. She shook her head.

"Marc's never right," she mumbled.

"I heard that! Lily! *Lily!?*" Marc yelled from he front seat.

But she was too tired to answer. She slipped into unconsciousness, grateful for the blankness.

In one version, Ivanov shot Marc in the head, not the chest.

In another version, he stabbed Lily in the back, not her arm.

In yet another version, the bodyguard shot Marc in the neck.

And still another version, Ivanov slit her throat, and while she watched, he shot Marc in the temple.

NO!

Lily jerked upright, gasping for air, still halfway caught in her nightmares. She was being bound to something and she struggled, pulling away from her restraints.

"Stop. Stop it, you're safe. *You're safe,*" Marc's voice filtered into her brain, and she felt hands on her arms. She stopped moving and looked around. Found his blue eyes.

"I was dreaming," she panted.

"I know. You kept talking. But I'm not dead. You're not dead. We're fine. We made it."

She didn't quite believe him, but she nodded and glanced around. She was in some sort of medical center, or possibly a field hospital. She had an IV drip going into her arm, and when she turned her head, she saw ugly looking stitches trotting across her other forearm. She frowned.

"That's going to leave such a scar," she complained.

"I think scars are sexy," he told her.

"You would."

She laid back down and Marc explained that she had passed out in the car, due to blood loss and shock. Kingsley had done his best to slow the bleeding, then they'd driven around, looking for a hospital. Only, they couldn't go to just any major hospital. Ivanov still had allies in the city. They needed somewhere no one would think to look for them; after forty minutes of driving, Marc had found a Globa-Doc field hospital.

Ironic.

"How long have I been out?" Lily asked.

"Most of the day. Kingsley's actually asleep in the bed next to us," Marc explained, moving his chair to sit right next to her.

"Are you okay?" she asked, her eyes wandering over him.

"Oh yeah, just a few bruises. Breathing kind of hurts – that flak jacket wasn't exactly top of the line, but I can't complain," he assured her.

"Good."

"Tell me something," he started, leaning onto her mattress. "Did you mean what you said?"

"When?" she asked.

"Back in that room, to Ivanov. You kept saying you hid the diamonds, but then at the end, you said you threw them away. Did you really?" he asked. Lily was instantly suspicious.

"Is this why you came back?" she demanded. "For some fucking diamonds!? Well, good luck finding them, I hope you can hold your breath for a really long time."

"Shut up," he snapped. "I came back for *you*. I don't give two fucks about those diamonds. But if you're lying and if they are somewhere out there, hidden away, they can help you a lot. Help *us* a lot."

She cleared her throat.

"Us?"

"Yeah, sweetheart. *Us*," he sighed, then took her hand into his own, linking their fingers.

"We make a pretty good team," she whispered. He nodded, kissing the back of her hand.

"We make the *best* team."

"I was so scared," she whispered. He nodded.

"I know, but you didn't show it. That was very good."

"You weren't scared at all."

"I was."

"You didn't show it, either."

"I push it away. You'll learn to do that, too," he told her.

"I will?"

"Yes."

"I don't know if I can."

"I *know* you can. You're the strongest person I know. *Stronger than me.*"

Who would've thought over a month ago, when she'd watched the rough and tumble mercenary walk across a yard, that they'd be a team. An unstoppable duo. She wondered what that meant for the future. For her. For them.

"Marc?" her voice was shaky, and she cursed herself.

"Hmmm?" was all he said in response, his thumb tracing the edge of her jaw.

"I'm really glad you came back."

He moved then, and crawled onto the bed with her. He was careful of her IV drips and her banged up arm, and he spooned up next to her. Buried his face in her hair and sighed.

"*Me, too.*"

DAY TEN

The next morning, they managed to slip out of the hospital unnoticed. She kept the hospital gown and wore it over the pants Kingsley had given her. They didn't stop for anything, just drove out of the city without looking back.

"Darling," Kingsley called out. They had all the windows down, the air rushing through the car.

"Yes?" she called back, scooting to the edge of the back seat and sticking her arm out the window.

"You're sure you threw those diamonds away? *All* of them?" he double checked. She glanced at him, then in the rear view mirror, just in time to catch Marc staring at her. He looked away quickly.

"If I didn't know any better, I'd think you only came back to get the stones," she replied. Marc kept his eyes trained on the road, so obvious in his attempt to be un-obvious. She narrowed her eyes.

"Never, darling! Never entered my mind. I was just thinking if you'd held back a few, it would do wonders in getting us out of here."

Lily cleared her throat and looked away. Stared at her arm as she slowly waved it in the breeze. Let her eyes wander over the ace bandage, which covered her wound.

"No, I didn't hold anything back," she whispered.

"Pity."

They drove back to Casablanca, figuring if anyone went looking for them, they wouldn't think to look somewhere so close, since it was only about four hours away from Tangier. They didn't talk about what they were doing or why they were going there. Marc just drove. They stopped at one point, and Lily wandered through a market, picking out clothing. Using money they'd lifted from Ivanov's wallet, she bought herself underwear and shorts and two t-shirts, and a good pair of hiking boots. As she got dressed in the backseat of the car, she began to feel almost human again.

Almost ...

"You okay?" Marc asked as they stood in the lobby of a cheap hotel. She nodded, rubbing her fingertips across her forehead. Kingsley was at the front desk, smooth talking the lady clerk into a good deal.

"Yeah, just ... got some images that'll be burned into my brain forever," she joked. He frowned at her.

"We don't have to stay here," he assured her. "We can go straight to the airport, put you on a plane to wherever you want to go."

You ... you ... so singular. What happened to "us"?

"No, I want to take a shower. Just ... is it really safe?" she asked for the millionth time, glancing around them. She felt jittery, on edge. Her mind knew the worst was behind them. Her body was still on high alert. It was having a weird polarizing effect on her brain.

"Safer than we were on the drive over here," he joked. She glared at him and he cleared his throat. "I honestly don't know. Stankovski took out the hit on you, not Ivanov – that's why Ivanov came rushing to Tangier. He wanted to get to you, get to those diamonds, before anyone else. I think that was Stankovski's ploy all along, I think he'd figured out Ivanov's little scheme and he wanted to draw the man out. By now, Stankovski probably knows that Ivanov's dead. No one knows where we are, but I'm sure he'd like to know where his diamonds are, so ... you're as safe as you can be, in this situation."

Not. Helpful.

If anything, Lily felt worse.

Those diamonds are the only thing anyone wants – saving me was just a side note.

"Shower. I just want to shower."

Marc got them a room together and she didn't argue. Just stripped as she walked across the suite, then filled up the bath as high as she could, shloshing water over the sides as she climbed into the tub. Then she stayed in there for two hours, her bandaged arm hanging over the side.

"You gonna sleep in there!?" Marc called out, banging on the door. Lily let her head roll to the side, looking across the room.

"Thinking about it!" she yelled back before picking up a sponge.

"We're starving, let's go eat!"

"You guys go ahead!"

"You have ten minutes, then I'm coming in to get you."

"*Alright!*"

It was tough, washing her hair without getting her bandage wet. Eventually she took it off, cringing as the hot water stung against her stitches. Then she finished scrubbing every inch of her body, moaning and groaning with each new bruise she found.

"*You washing up in there, or having sex!?*"

Lily rolled her eyes and climbed out of the tub. She put her clothes back on, then towel dried her hair. She was attempting to put her bandage back on when Marc finally burst into the room.

"Jesus, it's been twenty minutes since I told you to get out!" he snapped, stomping over to her.

"Sorry," she mumbled, fighting with the material. He yanked her arm towards himself, then deftly wrapped the bandage tightly around her wound. He secured it in place, then let her go.

"Are you mad about something?" he asked in a blunt voice.

"What do you mean?"

"You seem upset. Almost … angry at me. I did my best, I don't know what more you want," he stated. She laughed.

"God, you're pigheaded. No, it's not about any of that. I'm glad you showed up, really. I'd be dead right now if you hadn't."

"Then what's the problem? Dead guys? I told you, you can't

think -"

"Ivanov deserved to die. I would've done it myself, if my hands hadn't been cuffed," she snapped. "And as for everyone else, it was them or us. I choose us. I'm pissed off because I still get the feeling that the only reason you two came back was for a baggie full of rocks."

Marc laughed, long and loud. She continued to glare at him, even as he placed his hands on either side of her face.

"You are too much, sweetheart," he chuckled, backing her up so she was pressed against the sink.

"*You're* too much."

"Entirely. It's what you love about me."

"Don't flatter yourself."

"I came back," he started, his voice taking on a serious note. "Because I felt miserable leaving you. I hated it. I worried about you, every minute. Every second. Not because I don't think you can handle yourself, but because I want to handle everything *for you*. The thought of someone hurting you, makes me want to commit murder. Double homicide. *Genocide*. But the worst thing of all? The *worst* thought? Was that I might never see you again. That a goodbye kiss in some dusty parking lot would be our last moment together. And *that* I just could not handle. Everything else was secondary, just an excuse. I would've come back. Even if you'd pulled your plan off without a problem and Ivanov took the diamonds. *I would've come back for you*."

Lily laughed at him. In five years, she had cried a handful of times.

Once, at her sister's funeral.

Another time, when she'd done her first kill.

And now again, when the infamous mercenary Marcelle De Sant told her that he couldn't bear the thought of never seeing her again.

Who needs diamonds when you have such precious words?

Before things could get any heavier, Kingsley pounded on their door before letting himself into the room. Marc smiled at her, wiped away her tears, then strode into the main room, laughing at the British man. Lily quickly cleaned up her face, fanning her eyes to make the redness go away.

"I look crazy, like I got dragged behind a car," she commented when she finally came out of the room. She still had fading bruises from her journey with Marc, and now she had added a bandage covering almost her whole forearm, and various other cuts and marks. Thankfully, her face had escaped the majority of it, but still. She didn't exactly look like a top model.

"But a very sexy kind of crazy, I assure you," Kingsley teased, before grabbing her hand and kissing it.

They went to a nice, open air restaurant. Kingsley's treat – he'd managed to steal a wallet earlier in the day, and it turned out the mark had been rather well off. He even got them a bottle of champagne.

"Is this normal?" Lily asked, flinching as the cork flew past her.

"What do you mean?" Marc asked.

"Well, like a day ago, we were practically blowing up a building and killing a shit ton of people. Now we're sitting down to champagne and pan seared scallops?" she pointed out. Kingsley laughed.

"Yes. You get kind of used to it. All in a day's work. Granted, this was slightly more stressful. I don't think I've ever pulled off such a last minute mission," he commented. Marc shook his head.

"Me, neither."

"But we can't dwell on it. What's done is done, always move forward!" Kingsley proclaimed.

"So that's what your life is like? Just … surviving, one job to the next?" she summarized it.

"Darling, isn't that all anyone is doing? A liquor store clerk gets up in the morning, does his best to make it through the day, then goes home at night, where maybe he gets to have a celebratory cocktail, all before doing it again the next day. There is nothing different in what we're doing now," he broke it down.

"Dwelling on it would negate the whole purpose of the job,"

Marc added. She glanced at him. "Why do something you hate? This is an entirely voluntary job. No one becomes a mercenary or a hitman just to pay the bills. You have to seek it out. What would be the point, if I went home and cried every night? I do it because I enjoy it, and I like the payout. So yeah, after killing a bunch of people, I come home, I have a nice meal, and I'm thankful I'm alive."

The logic still seemed wrong to her, but so was the whole situation, so Lily toasted her champagne glass, and they all drank.

During the car ride to Casablanca, they'd spent a lot of time talking about what had happened. Piecing together Ivanov and Stankovski's plans. Going over what had happened in the building. Loosely discussing their next steps.

By an unspoken agreement, no one talked about those things at dinner. Kingsley talked about what it had been like to go to an all boys Catholic school in England. Lily talked about the first transport gig she'd ever done, hauling a van full of stolen furs from the Bronx to Newark. Marc recited, in French, entire portions of Edgar Allen Poe's "The Raven". Lily had never heard him speak French at length before; it was pretty hot.

"I should've eaten more," Lily sighed. Marc burst out laughing.

"I'm pretty sure you ate the restaurant out of shrimp," he pointed out, gesturing to the array of plates in front of her.

"Yeah, but I'm really feeling that champagne," she chuckled. Now it was Kingsley's turn to snort.

"Oh, really? And maybe also the four beers you decided to chase it down with?" he questioned.

"Hey. It's been a stressful week."

"Whatever you say, love."

They paid their tab and made their way back out onto the street. Kingsley wandered a little ways ahead of them, smoking one of his cigarettes. He was walking leisurely enough, but he kept peering down alleyways, as if he was looking for someone or something.

"What is he doing?" Lily finally asked.

"Just watch. You drank to unwind. I babbled poetry. Now you

get to see Law's method," Marc told her.

They went for a couple more blocks, then Kingsley stopped and stared down an alley. Smiled and stubbed out his cigarette, then called out in French.

"What is he saying?" Lily whispered. Marc frowned.

"Nothing polite."

"I just stabbed a guy in the stomach – I can handle whatever he's saying," she snapped.

"He's asking if her pussy is as good as her tits," Marc translated.

"Wow. Classy guy."

"Told you. In case you wanted to know, she said yes, and that's she's wet and ready for him to -"

"Sometimes I'm not sure why I talk to you."

"Righty-o," Kingsley turned towards them. "I'm off! I'll meet you in the morning. You know how to reach me if anything goes wrong?"

"Yeah. If shit goes down and we need to bail, meet up in Dakhla," Marc added.

"Ah, Dakhla. Beginning to feel like a second home. How depressing. Cheers," he said as a farewell before charging off down the alley.

"So, sweetheart, can I ply you with more alcohol? Or are you ready to go to bed?" Marc asked.

"No, no more alcohol, I feel spinny enough as it is. Hotel, please," she replied. He laughed, and she was shocked when she felt his hand curl around hers, his fingers lacing with her own.

"Spinny. I like it. C'mon, let's go home."

Home.

He held her hand the whole way, and between that and the alcohol, she could feel her temperature going through the roof. Her cheeks were hot, and no doubt red, and she was glad that it was dark out. Nothing like blushing over hand holding to make a woman feel all of thirteen.

*You just helped kill a bajillion people. You're gonna blush over **hand holding**!?*

"Maybe I should chop all my hair off," Lily blurted out the first thought in her head as soon as they entered their room.

"Excuse me!?" Marc exclaimed, turning to face her.

"My hair," she reiterated as she stumbled around, pulling off her shoes. "You pulled it. Kingsley pulled it. Ivanov pulled it. Great big handfuls. That shit hurts, I'd almost rather get stabbed again. Maybe I should just cut it off."

Marc was in her face in a second, backing her into a wall. His eyes wandered over the top of her head, his hand raising to finger the end of her ponytail.

"If you *ever* cut your hair off, I will shoot first and ask questions later," he informed her. She laughed at him.

"Stop. I could be bald and you probably wouldn't care," she snickered, pushing at his chest. He refused to budge.

"Are you joking? The first thing I ever noticed about you was your hair. It's the first thing I look for when I lose sight of you. The hair stays," he stated.

"Alright. If you feel so strongly about it, alright," she replied.

He didn't move, just kept glaring down at her. She stared back at him, holding her breath. She'd never been scared of Marc, not really. She'd tracked him down the first time they'd slept together. The second time, in the house they'd broken into, she certainly hadn't resisted him. And even right after they'd stolen the Explorer, it had definitely been a mutual thing. Sex was easy and natural between them. Like a playing a game, and she had always felt like his equal.

But now, for some reason, she was nervous. *Scared*, and she couldn't place why. Not necessarily *of him*, but of what he represented. A future she wasn't sure she was ready for. A man she was positive she wanted. A beginning she couldn't see an ending to.

His mouth crashed into hers, and if she hadn't known any better, she would've thought he was a little scared, too. He kissed her like he was afraid she was going to disappear. Like he'd move his lips for a moment, and she'd get taken away.

I'm not going anywhere.

She started pulling at his t-shirt and he grabbed her by the wrists, pinning her arms above her head. She hissed at the pain; her left arm was tender. But she ignored it, and so did he, his free hand moving to press against her chest, then slipping over her breasts.

"You were incredible, you know that, right?" he asked, his lips sliding across her cheek.

"No. I was scared. I thought I was all alone. I thought I was going to die," she panted, straining her hips towards him.

"You're never alone," he whispered. "I'd never let you die."

He let go of her wrists finally and both their hands flew to her shorts, yanking them open and pulling them down. While she kicked them free of her feet, he pulled apart his own belt and worked his pants down. Then he was back against her, forcing her flat again.

His hands went to the back of her thighs and he gripped her there, lifting her off the ground. She wrapped her legs around his waist and braced her arms on top of his shoulders.

"Why does this feel different?" she moaned, barely aware that she was talking out loud.

"Because *we're* different," he surprised her by answering.

His hand was sliding between their bodies, pulling at the side of her underwear, following the seam between her legs. She gasped when his warm hand was flat against her, the heel of his palm pressing down, two of his fingers sliding inside of her. She rocked her hips forward, seeking more from him, wanting more from him.

He'd always been able to read her body language like it had been written in a code just for him, and he pulled his hand free. It was a bit of a struggle, working the crotch of her panties to the side while also holding her up *and* pushing his hard on inside of her, but they both refused to slow down and step away. Marc was nothing if not determined, and soon enough she was groaning as she slid into place over him.

"Please, please," she started whispering. He moaned and she felt his fingers tightening on her hips.

"Fuck, I don't think I can be gentle. I've been dying for this," he whispered back. She actually laughed at him.

"Is this a joke? No one asked you to be gentle," she teased, trying to wiggle her body against him.

"I don't want to hurt you," his voice sounded strained.

"Gee, I wish you'd felt that way a week ago, when you gave me a concussion."

"You were being a bitch then."

"Should I be a bitch now?"

"*Lily*," he growled her in name in warning. She started panting as she shifted around in his arms; he was so hard, so large inside of her, that it was beginning to make breathing difficult.

"You can't hurt me. I just survived hell. I want you to make me feel good. Please, Marc. *Make me feel good*," she begged.

Begging was always his undoing, and he finally pulled back and thrust into her. She gasped, then shrieked as he started pumping away. She scrambled to keep her arms around his neck, her legs around his waist, all his while his hips slammed her into the wall.

"Fuck, this never stops feeling like the best thing ever," he groaned, one of his hands moving to cup the underside of her ass.

"Mmmm hmmm," she agreed, lacing her fingers together behind his neck and pulling his head forward so she could kiss him. His other hand gripped the top her thigh, painfully so, then actually moved between her thigh and his hip. With the hand under her ass, he jerked her forward sharply, and then his free hand was under her leg. He hooked his arm under her knee and yanked her leg up, giving him even deeper access.

"Goddamn, where did you come from," he hissed, breaking free of the hold on his neck and leaning away so he could look down the length of her torso.

"I don't know," she managed to respond, holding onto his shoulders as she slid down the wall a little, her hips jutting out. He pounded harder.

"How did I find you? How did I get so fucking lucky?" he kept asking, stretching her leg away from their bodies.

"*Marc!* Marc …," she cried out his name.

He came back to her, dropping her leg as he kissed her hard. Using the hand under her ass, he kept her against him and he turned them around, carrying her across the room to the bed, stepping out of his pants as he went. He dropped her on the mattress, then knelt between her legs. When he leaned away to pull off his t-shirt, she copied his actions, yanking her own tank top off. As she went to toss it across the room, she felt his hands sliding around her rib cage, making their way slowly to her spine, where they unhooked her bra. While she worked the straps down her arm, he tugged and pulled at her underwear, working the material out from under her butt and dragging them down her legs.

"Your skin is always so soft," he sighed, his hands gliding over the tops of her thighs as he worked his way back up her body. She laid down flat and stretched her arms out.

"Your hands are always so rough," she replied. As if to confirm that fact, his fingernails scratched at the sides of her breasts before he cupped them in his palms.

"You like rough," he whispered, his mouth moving to a nipple.

"I like *you* rough."

Teeth met sensitive skin and she jumped, forcing more of her breast into his mouth. He chuckled and pulled back, letting his tongue skim all the way up to her neck. Then he left her and it was like someone took all her heat away. She reached for him, but her fingertips barely brushed against his chest before he was gone.

"Come here," he breathed, grabbing her by the waist and dragging her towards him. Her eyes rolled back in her head and she bit down on her lip, relishing in the feeling of being full with him again. Then he was moving them again, holding her hips up to meet him as he stood on his knees. Her back arched, leaving just her shoulder blades flat against the mattress.

"God! Yes, Marc, yes … just … like … that," she panted in time to his thrusts. He was pounding into her, drilling her into the mattress.

"Tell me you love this," he grunted, one of his hands slipping through the sheen of sweat that was covering her body and gripping onto her breast.

"I love this. God, I love this so much," she concurred.

"No one's ever made you feel this way," he kept going.

"No one. Never," her voice reached a pitch she'd never heard before as his hips started moving at a breakneck pace.

"You want me. You want this with me."

"So much. All the time."

"Always?"

"*Always.*"

If he asked anymore questions, Lily couldn't hear him. She'd lost control of her mouth, was moaning and shrieking. The headboard was slamming against the wall, causing a decorative painting to fall. His hand let go of her breast, and she replaced it with her own, kneading and pinching. His fingers dragged against her skin, scratching a path to where his pelvis was trying its hardest to turn her inside out. When his fingers pinched and kneaded at the same time as hers, she couldn't handle it anymore.

I was never able to handle him.

She screamed when she came, her hands flying to the mattress, gripping the blanket in her fists. She sobbed and begged him to stop moving, unable to handle the electricity that was coursing through her body alongside his cock moving in out of her.

He didn't stop, just like usual, but he did let go of her hips. Moved with her and laid flat on top of her. While she shuddered and convulsed underneath him, he wiggled an arm under her back, moving his hand up her spine till he gripped her shoulder. She kept shuddering as he twisted his hips against her. Her orgasm had lessened, but hadn't stopped. It felt like a cattle prod kept zapping her, low in her belly, and she jerked and moved, unable to reciprocate any of his movements.

His other arm encircled her waist, and they were in complete contact. One entity, every inch of skin touching from hips to chest.

The electrical jolts grew stronger, the orgasm gaining traction again. She was whimpering incoherently, and she almost missed it when he pressed his lips to her ear and whispered something. Something she would've hated to miss.

"*Always.*"

Her orgasm came into full bloom at the same time as his erupted. His whole body flexed, his arms holding her so tightly she had trouble breathing. His hips twitched and jerk for what felt like forever, but she didn't mind. She would lay like that forever, if he'd let her.

Always.

She would've passed out if he would've left her alone, but of course he didn't. He dragged her off the bed and into the shower. She complained, but as she stood under the hot water, she realized it was a good idea. *All* of her muscles were sore, and now that she wasn't caught in a sexual fog, she could feel that her arm was *aching*.

Marc washed her body for her, massaging her muscles as he worked over her skin. Then he helped her wash her hair, and she laughed at him, explaining that she had never imaged him to be a good caregiver. Or good at anything gentle for that matter.

She got smacked in the face with a washcloth.

"How often do you do that?" Lily groaned, crawling across the bed and getting under the sheet.

"Do what?" Marc asked, sitting down next to her. He grabbed her injured arm and held it across his legs.

"Fuck women till they can't think straight."

He chuckled while he wrapped her arm back up in the ace bandage.

"As often as possible, sweetheart," was his response.

"When was the last time you had a girlfriend?" Lily decided to be forward. He glanced down at her.

"Why? You applying for the job?" he asked a question of his own.

"That's probably exactly what it would be like – a job," she joked.

"This lifestyle and relationships don't exactly go hand in hand," he finally answered. "I know a couple people who manage it, lead double lives, only take select jobs. Most opt for Law's lifestyle, though."

"What's '*Law's lifestyle*'?" she asked. He moved under the sheet, then slid down so he was laying flat next to her.

"Fucking anything that moves. I'm surprised he hasn't gotten you into bed yet. If that man didn't get sex regularly, I'm pretty sure his brain would melt down. He needs it to function," Marc explained.

"I wonder why?"

"It's a long story. Take my advice – *never ask*."

"And what about you, Mr. De Sant? Do you need it to function?" she asked, rolling onto her side to face him. He smiled as he stared up at the ceiling.

"No. I only sleep with sexy redheads who like to beat the shit out of me," he replied.

She laughed and went to smack him in the arm, but she froze mid swing. There was a sound coming from the room next to him. She lifted her head while Marc propped himself up on his elbows. They listened in silence for a moment, but then she caught onto what it was and her hand flew to her mouth.

"Oh my god," she whispered. "Is that *Kingsley*!?"

There was no mistaking the accent as the voice in the other room got louder. Lily stared at Marc while she listened to the things coming out of the other man's mouth. She didn't even know some of the swear words he was yelling. A woman was in the room with him, but she wasn't saying words. Well, that wasn't necessarily true. She kept screaming yes, over and over again, in several different languages. There was the sound of something being slapped, repeatedly, and her screams increased in volume. His dirty talk got even louder.

"Yeah, yeah sounds like him. I didn't realize he was in the room next to us," Marc commented.

"Are we going to have to listen to this all night?" Lily moaned, laying back down.

"Probably."

"*God.*"

"It's okay, cause you know what?" Marc asked, rolling onto his side as well and wrapping his arm around her waist.

"What?"

"If you can't beat 'em, join 'em. Let's give him a run for his money," Marc suggested, rolling back over and pulling her with him. She smiled and moved so she was straddling his waist.

"Finally, a plan I can get behind."

DAY ELEVEN

"**M**orning, darling!"

Marc glanced over his shoulder, watching as Kingsley approached. The Brit looked out of place, walking across the sand while wearing an almost shiny gunmetal suit, tailored to fit.

"Morning," Marc replied, returning his attention to the shore-line.

"Sounds like you had a bang up night last night. I swear, there is nothing like a little bit of rough sex to get rid of those post-job jitters," Kingsley sighed as he plopped down in the sand.

"Very true, I should try it more often."

"Well, that should be easy from now on."

"Not really."

"Based on the noises I heard coming out of your room last night, it should be *beyond* easy. In fact, I have very serious doubts that you'll even be able to keep up with her," Kingsley teased, and gestured with his head at the object of their discussion.

Marc smiled, watching as Lily waded around in thigh deep water. She was quite a distance away, wearing the black bikini he'd bought for her only a couple days ago.

So little time together. So much time together.

"Yeah, yeah I have those same doubts, too. Listen, I have some bad news ...," Marc let his voice trail off.

After their second or third round on the bed, Marc had gotten up to go to the bathroom. Washed his face, then decided to brush his teeth. When he'd come back into the room, Lily had already been asleep, lying flat on her stomach once again

He watched her for a long time. It had sort of become a habit, he realized. Shocking. Marc had never been around anyone long enough to form any habits with them. But he liked it. Her presence soothed him, eased the world weary ache that had settled into his bones. Into his *soul*.

But there was no rest for the wicked. That's why Marc hardly ever slept. While Lily dreamed away, he got busy. He'd taken a laptop out of Kingsley's gear and set it up on a table in the corner of the room. Hacking into it wasn't difficult, and soon enough, Marc was surfing on the world wide web.

In his line of work, Marc stuck strictly to organized crime rings. In his experience, they were more trustworthy, at least in the sense that they always paid, and rarely double crossed – current circumstances notwithstanding. He'd worked with branches of La Cosa Nostra, Mexican drug rings, the Jewish Mob, and of course, many Russian Bratvas. Marc was a freelancer, working only for himself, and had different ways he could be contacted. Burner phones, secure e-mail addresses, and a call service out of Thailand.

But there were a lot of people who preferred to have someone else handle the technicalities of the business, like Kingsley. The British mercenary had a contractor out of Brooklyn, a man by the name of Carl, who would deal with the lowlifes, and call Kingsley with the job offers. The people paying Kingsley never knew his actual identity. The contractor negotiated the price, and got a cut of the fee. Kingsley's anonymity was protected. Carl had been trying to get Marc to work with him for years, so getting a hold of him wasn't hard, and getting news out of him was even easier.

"Oh jesus, do I even want to know? I haven't even had breakfast, I -" Kingsley started to complain, but Marc held up his hand. Two men were walking down the beach, right at the shoreline. Marc watched them, his other hand resting on the butt of his gun. But luckily all they did was stare at Lily, catcalled her a little, while still walking past. She flipped them off and Marc smiled.

"Stankovski's taken out hits on us," Marc said. Kingsley snorted.

"Add it to the list. No one's gotten me yet. How many is that for you?"

"I don't know, a few. The price tags aren't even that big."

"Then what's the big deal? You're scared?"

"He also kept the hit on her," Marc went on.

"Oh. Well, so? We've both had prices on our heads for years, and we've survived quite nicely."

"One million."

"I beg your pardon?"

"*One million.* One million dollars for her head," Marc repeated himself.

Kingsley made a choking noise, inhaling too sharply and gagging on air. He turned his head back towards the ocean.

"You're telling me that Anatoly Stankovski is offering one million dollars for Lily's death!?" he exclaimed. Marc nodded.

"That's exactly what I'm saying. Apparently, he'd really like his diamonds back."

"But she said she threw them away!"

"And now you see the problem."

"I can't believe it. One million dollars," Kingsley mumbled. Marc turned and saw that the other man was staring at Lily.

"Hey. Don't get any fucking ideas, alright? Or I'll be collecting on *your* bounty," Marc threatened. Kingsley rolled his eyes.

"You would never. And for that matter, neither would I. It's obvious why you've grown so attached. She's a very special girl," he commented.

"She's a pain in the ass," Marc snapped, then turned back so he could watch her.

"Ah, but she's *your* pain."

Marc continued to glare, taking deep breaths through his nose.

"She was so upset yesterday," he started talking in a soft voice. "Kind of all over the place before dinner. She was freaked out. Jumpy. *Scared*. Then she told me that she thought the only reason we'd gone back for her was to get the diamonds. She was upset."

"All normal reactions for a person, I'd say," Kingsley pointed out.

"Yeah, for a *normal* person. We're not normal people, Law. This is not a normal lifestyle. She was only doing it to get revenge. She wasn't meant to be this person. I don't want her to be this person. I don't want …," Marc's voice died out.

*I don't want to be the one to turn her into **that** person.*

"I don't think any of that's really your business. She's a grown woman who got into this business all on her own, by herself, which in itself is a feat. She's obviously also very good at it. So, regardless of whether or not you want her to be 'this person', it's her choice, and you need to let her make it, " Kingsley double checked.

"I don't know if I can do that."

"Why?"

"Because … I care about her too much."

"Jesus, De Sant," Kingsley sighed. "You go all out, don't you? Find a woman who can actually keep up with you, in every sense of the word, and you're worried she'll get hurt. I wasn't even aware you were capable of worrying about *anybody*."

"Shut up."

"So when are you going to tell her about the hit?" Kingsley asked.

"I'm not."

"Why not!?"

"Because it'll just freak her out. I'm going to take care of all this. I'll sort it out."

"This is stupid, De Sant. Even for you."

"Maybe. But I'm willing to be stupid, if it means protecting her."

"*Talk to her*. She seems quite capable of taking care of herself. You need to start thinking of her as a partner, not as a delicate doll."

"I don't think of her as a doll. I think of her as something … *important*. Something that needs to be kept safe."

Kingsley heaved a deep sigh.

"Of all the fucking times to find nobility, De Sant."

"Right? Just in time."

DAY ELEVEN

"**Y**ou can't be serious."

Lily stood in the hallway of the hotel, watching as Kingsley dragged his rucksack out of his room.

"It's a funny thing, darling," he sighed as he pulled on a suit jacket. "I love De Sant like a brother, which also means after too much time together, I want to kill him. He's coming perilously close to getting a bullet in the head from me, so I must be off."

Lily wasn't sure what had happened in her absence. She'd spent most of the morning on the beach, soaking in the sun and surf. When she'd come back to their room, Marc had been gone. Kingsley had been gone. But all their stuff was still there, so she hadn't worried about it too much. Got herself lunch in the hotel's restaurant, then went back upstairs and took a nap, stretching across the whole bed. Marc woke her up a couple hours later, informing her that Kingsley was leaving.

"Just stay another night," Lily begged, sad to see him ago. She enjoyed Kingsley's company, his wit and his banter. The easiness they had with each other. She didn't find that often with other people, and wanted to cling to it. Cling to a little bit of normalcy.

"What's one more night going to do, aside from make tomorrow even harder?" he asked. She frowned.

"I just thought it would be nice …," her voice trailed off. What could she say? Nice to stay together? What, the three of them ride off in the sunset together? Buy a duplex in suburban Cleveland and live side by side? Marc could get a job managing a grocery store, Kingsley could work in advertising, Lily could go back to banking.

You're so out of your league with these men. Time to decide if you want to jump into the deep end, or hang back in the kiddie pool.

"Me, too. I'm very easy to get attached to, I understand," he joked, smiling down at her. He had to crane his neck a little, he was so much taller than her. A tall, lanky man, so handsome in his designer suits.

"I'm going to miss you," she said simply.

"And I, you. But we'll see each other again," he assured her.

"We will?"

"Oh, I'm sure of that. Something tells me you won't be able to stay out of trouble long, and then good ol' Law will have to come in and save the day again," he teased, pinching her chin between his fingers and waggling her head.

"Again? You held me down and choked me!"

"And wasn't it fun? I already can't wait for the next time."

Before she could respond, he leaned down and hugged her, wrapping his arms around her tightly. Lily went onto her tip toes and hugged him back, as tight as she could. He'd done so much for her. She'd done so little for him. It didn't feel right.

"Thank you, for everything," she whispered.

"You're very welcome, darling," he whispered back.

The moment was incredibly heavy, so it was doubly shocking when he squeezed her ass before spanking her sharply. She laughed and pulled away from him. He gave her another wink and a smile, then shouldered his pack before striding off down the hall. She sighed as she watched him go, all the way till he disappeared into the elevator.

"Jesus, that was dramatic. I kept waiting for you to shove your tongue in his mouth."

Lily rolled her eyes and turned around, finding Marc standing in their doorway.

"I was going to, but I could feel your beady little eyes on us. I can't believe you didn't even say goodbye," she grumbled, pushing past him and walking into the room.

"I've said goodbye to him plenty of times. Never helps, he keeps coming back," Marc joked.

"That could be the last time you ever see him, you know. What if he gets killed on his next job? What if someone finally collects on the hit on him?" Lily asked, sitting on the foot of the bed.

"Then I will tell his mother and I will go to his funeral. But until that day actually happens, he's alive, and I'll treat him like that. Have to keep moving, sweetheart. Can't dwell on ifs or buts," he informed her.

"Easier said than done," she complained.

Marc took a deep breath, then squatted down in front of her. He placed his palms on her thighs, patting out a rhythm at first, then sliding up to the hem of her shorts. He dug his fingers into her flesh and clawed his way back down to her knees.

"I've been thinking," he started, and she was instantly on guard.

"That's never a good thing."

"What's next for us?" he asked.

They hadn't really discussed it. Lily was almost scared to broach the subject because not only was she not sure of exactly what she wanted, but she had *no clue* what he wanted. Rejection was almost scarier than having a gun to her head, as she was now acutely aware.

"What do you want to be next?" she countered, not willing to crack first.

He looked away from her, his gaze staring out the window. He was silent for a long time, then a smile began to play across his lips.

"Pemba."

Her heart skipped a beat.

"What?"

"Remember that house? That night? I told you about that place, off the coast – Pemba Island," he explained. Of course she remembered. How could she have forgotten?

"What about it?" she asked cautiously.

"We could still go there. Maybe take a vacation. You like the beach."

He remembers, too.

"I would love to take a vacation with you," she whispered. He nodded.

"Alright. But there's some things we need to clear up."

His voice went back to its usual loud, commanding tone, and he stood up, pacing around the room.

"Like what?" Lily asked.

"You don't hardly exist in this world, but I'm a big player. Stankovski isn't just going to let me walk away from this, not now that the diamonds are gone. I need to go back to Liberia, take care of loose ends there. And then I need to disappear. Pull all the assets I have, make sure all my contacts know that I've gone dark. I need to make us as safe as possible. I need to become invisible," he explained.

"Okay, I get that, but does that have to happen *right now*?" she questioned.

"Yes. I have no doubt that he's already taking steps to freeze any accounts I have, cut me off from my money. I have a large chunk buried somewhere, I need to go get that, if we want to survive. I need to do this now, as quickly as possible. If I don't, we could be dead before we start," Marc warned her. Her chest warmed at his use of the plural, "*we*", "*us*".

Hardened criminal transporter, and you still get giddy when a boy holds your hand and implies that you're together.

"I understand. So we go to Liberia, and -"

"Not you. Just me."

"Why can't I go!?" Lily demanded.

"Because you've done enough, sweetheart, and I'm sorry to say it, but I'll move faster without you," he told her. She felt her blood start to boil, but before she could let loose on him, he kept going. "In ten days, we'll meet there. Ten days, to get rid of all the skeletons in my closets. Ten days, and we can become new people," he told her.

"New people," she echoed, longing for the idea so much that it was almost physically painful. So much that it blocked out her concerns.

"New people, *together*."

Sold.

In Lily's mind, she'd always kept the idea of them "*being together*" at bay. He was a ruthless mercenary, she'd watched him kill multiple people, he couldn't possibly want to be with her. He'd never once mentioned anything about feeling any type of way about her. Only that he liked sleeping with her, that was it. She was a greenhorn, someone tiptoeing around in his natural habitat. As badass as she thought she was, she still felt like she didn't quite live up to him. Why would he want to be with someone he didn't consider an equal?

But maybe none of that mattered. Maybe he was ready to change his lifestyle; maybe he was ready to take a chance on something else.

On her.

"I wouldn't slow you down," she said cautiously. He shook his head.

"You would. And even if you didn't, I wouldn't want you with me."

"Why not?"

"Because seeing Ivanov almost kill you was the worst thing I've ever experienced in my life. I can't handle that happening again, and there's a chance it could if you're running around with me. I just can't, Lily. If anything happened to you ... I would go insane."

Forget blushing, Lily's whole body caught on fire, and she looked up at him. Into those blue eyes that were staring back at her so hard.

"You'll come back for me," she whispered.

"I never want to be away from you," he whispered, dropping to his knees in front of her. "But I *have* to do this."

"I don't want you to go."

"I know."

"Okay," she sighed. "So. You said ten days? We'll meet in ten days?"

"Yes. There's a resort, I'm going to book us a villa. Private, on the beach. You'll go there ahead of me, relax. Call your parents. Wash away the last five years. Then when I've got all my ducks in a row, I'll meet you there."

"Promise?" she asked.

He hesitated, his gaze so intense that she felt like he was reading her mind. Was hearing just how badly she wanted this from him. How badly she wanted *him*.

"*I promise*," he replied. She smiled.

"Okay. So sometime within ten days, you'll show up. We'll be together. And then …?"

"And then," Marc smiled as well and put his hands on either side of her hips, forcing her to lay down. "I'm going to defile you in ways you never thought possible."

"Okay, and after that fifteen minutes is up, then what?"

He burst out laughing.

"You're awfully obsessed with our future together. I think you have a crush on me, Lily," he joked in a soft voice. She snorted.

"I have a massive crush on your body. You, on the other hand, I want to kill most of the time."

"Pity, cause most of the time, I just want to devour you," he whispered, lowering his mouth to her neck.

"Ten days," she breathed, stretching out her arms.

"Ten days."

"And then we'll be together. We'll be different people."

"Different people."

That's all I ever wanted, to be someone else. Someone who could hurt. Someone who could kill. Who do I want to be now?

DAY TWENTY-THREE

Lily paced across a hotel room.
　　Looked out a window.
　　Paced back.
　　Looked at the satellite phone she had.
　　Paced back.
　　Where the fuck is he!?

Once she'd arrived at the resort, Lily had thought she'd be able to relax. But she couldn't really. Staying in Africa made her nervous. It gave her anxiety. Tanzania and Zanzibar were very different from western Africa, they were huge tourist destinations, but still. She kept looking over her shoulder, and she paid for everything in cash, even her flights.

　　Marc had left her well provided for – he'd managed to get some of his money transferred to an international bank in Casablanca. Dangerous and completely traceable, but he'd said since they wouldn't be staying there long, it didn't really matter. He gave almost all of it to her, then went out and found her new documentation, a new passport, new ID. She was a whole new person, in less than a day.

Saying goodbye had been hard. A lot harder than she would've thought. Ten days wasn't that long, and they'd only been together for about the same amount of time. She tried to be strong at the airport, tried to show no emotion. But when he'd kissed her in a way that had made her heart hurt, she couldn't help it. She'd shed a tear or two for him. For them.

She was booked into a seafront villa – the resort was stunning and expansive, all inclusive and exclusive. Marc had really spared no expense. But she was still nervous, so when she got to her villa, she thoroughly checked it out. She even crawled under the wooden walkway, looking for signs that someone had been there, maybe planted a bomb under the building. But she found nothing. The room seemed untouched.

It had been hard, at first, to be alone. It took her a while to get back into the swing of normality. Getting up every day, and having nothing truly important to do. She didn't like it. Before, she'd had a specific purpose every day. A job to prepare for, training to do, a trip to make. Now, her biggest concern was whether or not to have fruit or oatmeal for breakfast.

She kind of hated it.

The only thing that made it bearable was Marc. He had given her an untraceable satellite phone, and he'd called her on their first day apart. Then he called the next day. And the next. Some conversations were only five minutes, just him checking in with her. Some lasted hours, going deep into the night while she listened to his voice. The voice that said all the words she'd been dying to hear.

But after a particularly long, sweet, phone call, they'd stopped coming. From the eighth day on, she didn't hear from him. She had no clue why. Didn't know if he was okay. He had warned her that he might have to drop out of communication at some point, so she hadn't been shocked, at first. She figured he would call or turn up when he was able to.

Then the tenth day came. She sat in the villa all day, waiting for him. Sat through the evening. Sat clear through the entire night. In the morning, there was still no Marc. No word from him. No nothing.

It was now the twelfth day, and still no sign of him. It chilled her. Marc was invincible in her mind, but she knew in reality he was very human. Very mortal. She worried that he'd been captured, or hurt, or worse.

That can't happen. He wouldn't let it. He promised. He's coming back.

She didn't know what to do. The phone number stored in her sat phone, the one that Marc had been calling from, no longer worked. She felt like she had been cast adrift into the ocean. No bearing, no oars, no knowledge of sailing.

What in the fuck is going on!?

It was driving her batty. She'd spent five years virtually alone without any problems. One week with Marc and suddenly being alone was a big fucking problem. She spent the day pacing around the villa, not sure what to do with herself. Then she looked outside. Realized she couldn't just stand around, doing nothing. She would go insane. So she went into the bedroom and started digging in her luggage. Well, it couldn't really be called luggage.

It was the backpack that Marc had given her. The one he'd never been without. The one physical piece of him she had with her.

She was shocked to find she was almost nostalgic for their time together. It had been scary and dangerous and constant movement. Fighting and yelling and constantly trying to beat each other. He had challenged her, and ultimately, she had liked it.

Rolling with the nostalgia, she pulled out the shorts she'd bought when they'd been fleeing Tangier, on their way to Casablanca. She smiled at the memories. Kingsley teasing her. Marc touching her.

She pulled her clothing off and was slipping on the shorts when there was a sharp knock at the door. It snapped her out of her memories and she whirled around. It was six o'clock at night. She didn't know anyone. Who could be visiting?

Marc!?

She wasn't stupid, though, so she made her way to the front door with her Glock out in front of her. She tip toed up and looked out the peep hole. A man stood outside, dressed in the hotel's uniform. He held a silver tray, with something on it. Something white, like a folded piece of paper. Lily narrowed her eyes, then yanked the door open, pointing the gun in his face.

"What do you want!?" she demanded.

He was a young man, and he was visibly frightened of her gun. Probably her whole appearance – she hadn't bothered with putting on a shirt and was only wearing the shorts and a bra. She took another step forward and watched as he shuddered.

"You … you have a letter, ma'am … letter for you," he stuttered, holding the tray up. It was an envelope that was on it, and Lily snatched it.

"Get the fuck out of here!" she snapped, then slammed the door in his face.

She watched out the peephole while he ran away, then she scurried back into the bedroom. The envelope had a watermark on it, the logo of the hotel in Casablanca, and her fake name was scrawled across the front in big letters. She tore it open and pulled out a piece of paper. It also bore the hotel's emblem. Whoever had written the letter, they'd done it while she'd been in Casablanca. Done it while they'd been in that hotel. Not a good sign. She sat on the edge of the bed as she unfolded it.

Sweetheart …

She smiled, tracing her fingers over the word. She hated being called by pet names, had hated it when he wouldn't use her real name. Now, she would've killed to hear him whispering it to her.

I told you it was beautiful, didn't I? I bet you didn't believe me. Such a bitch.

She laughed out loud.

I wish I was there with you now. I wish we were sitting in the sand. Laughing. Arguing. Anything, as long as it was with you.
But that's not happening.
And it isn't going to.

Lily held her breath.

You are very good at what you do, sweetheart, but you have a long ways to go, and this life just isn't suited for you. Too temperamental, too naive, too easy to trick – this letter is a prime example of how easy you are to manipulate. Not a good thing, in my world. Beyond that, you have a goodness, at your core, and if I allowed that to become tainted, if I ruined that, I'd never be able to forgive myself. You deserve better than me. Someone who has real feelings and a real life. Someone who can grow with you and move with you and change with you. Someone who won't put your life in danger, simply by being in a room with you.

It was incredibly sweet. Touching, really. But still.
She wanted to find him and punch him in the throat.

No one will ever be able to hurt you. I'm going after Stankovski. I'll get him for you. I can do it faster than you could have, anyway. I can actually accomplish your goal. It's better this way. No more jobs. No more doing something for no reason. I will make him pay, for everything he did to us. Everything he did to you. To your sister Kaylee. I promise. I don't care if it takes me years, I don't care if it costs me my life; you'll never have to worry about him again. He's no longer your problem.
I miss you. I miss your body. I miss being inside you. I miss your eyes. I miss you telling me what to do. I miss you making me laugh. And god help me, I miss being in a car with you. Any car with you.
I think I'll always miss you.

Go home. Go home to your parents. Go home to your friends. Go home to your life. Please believe me when I say this is right. Please have faith in me that I will get your revenge for you. Go. Live. Be alive. Enjoy it.

Forget this life. Forget this man. Forget Africa.

Always,
Marcelle De Sant

Lily folded up the letter and calmly put it back into the envelope. She sat for a minute, staring at her hands. Then she got up. Put on a shirt. She stopped long enough to grab a cup of tea out of the kitchen, then made her way down to the shore. To the beach.

Her favorite place.

He'd tricked her. Fed her the dream of Pemba, the dream of them actually being together, in order to get her to do what he wanted. He'd led her to believe that they were in this together. That he was doing everything to be with her, though he'd never had *any* intention of being with her.

He didn't think she was good enough to compete in his lifestyle, after all she'd done. After everything they'd gone through, she still wasn't "*good enough*" for him. He would get Stankovski "*for her*", would be "*faster than her*", he claimed. Discounting all the work they'd done *together*.

He didn't think she was cut out for his lifestyle. "*Go home*", he'd said. Where the fuck was home? Ohio!? How? How, after everything she'd been through? Five years of her life, and for what? A working knowledge of crime rings that couldn't be applied to every day life, and a wicked punch combo that wouldn't help her back in suburbia.

And for what!? She had nothing to show for it. No illustrious career. No revenge. Not even Marc. Nothing. She got lied to, and she got abandoned.

She got *dumped*.

Five years of her life, wasted. One week of her life, to screw everything up. A few conversations with a man, to manipulate her into letting him go. And one lie, that left her alone on a beach, with a slightly broken heart.

I really believed him. I really wanted this. I really liked him.

"*That motherfucker,*" she growled, throwing her mug into the ocean.

She stood up and brushed the sand off her legs. The tears out of her eyes. Wondered what her next move was; the villa was paid up through the next week, and she had plenty of money to go anywhere she wanted. But where to go? What to do? The only thing she could think of right then, was tracking Marc down and making him physically hurt as much as she was emotionally hurting.

He didn't believe in me. I believed in him, and he didn't believe in me. Didn't believe in **us**.

She stared out over the ocean, her mind wandering over the days. So many days. So much sand. Sand and roads and highways and rocks. Stones. *Diamonds.* She remembered him asking her about the diamonds, if she had really thrown them into the ocean. Remembered Kingsley asking her about the diamonds. Remembered Marc watching her.

Had that been it? Lily had told them she'd thrown them into the ocean – not getting them back, so what was the point in being with her anymore? Maybe she wasn't worth anything to Marc, without those diamonds. Without the promise of a payout. Without the promise of something big.

God, this hurts. I think I'd rather get stabbed again.

As she headed up the beach, she dug into her back pocket, searching for her room key. When she pulled it out, though, something else came out, and she watched as what looked like a scrap of paper fell to the ground. When she picked it up, though, she could feel that it was a heavy card stock. And it was strange, all black. Both sides.

Wait a minute.

She recognized it, of course, and seeing the word, the name,

"*Law.*", debossed on the front confirmed it. Kingsley's card. The last time she'd seen one, Marc had been ripping it up. How'd this one get into her back pocket?

Lily remembered her goodbyes with Kingsley. The tight embrace. Him whispering in her ear. Then him smacking her ass. Grabbing it playfully. It must have been then.

He knew. He knew Marc was going to leave me. That's why he left so abruptly. He knew, and he left me this card so I could find him.

She stared at the card, gripping it between her fingertips. So little detail, so much potential.

Kingsley wanted her to find him.

Marc didn't want her to find him.

Kingsley had never lied to her, as far as she could tell.

Marc had spun the biggest lie, just when they'd been the closest.

Marc hadn't believed in her ability to take care of herself, and thus obviously wasn't willing to help her or train her.

But Kingsley was.

Lily strode up the walk towards her villa, almost jogging.

Finally, a purpose.

Finally, a *job*.

*Alright, Marc. You think I can't do this? You think I need you to fight my battles? You think I'm not tough enough to be this person? You think you're better, faster, without me? You don't want to be with me? Fine. That's totally fine. I'll just find someone better than **you**. Faster than you. Someone who **does** want to be with me.*

Just you wait, Marcelle De Sant. I'll be the best anyone in this business has ever seen. Just you fucking wait.

To Be Continued …

Read to the end for scenes from the conclusion.

ACKNOWLEDGEMENTS

This book started out as something completely different. A friend asked if I would ever do a captor/captive story. I wanted something in the desert, so I started writing a book that took place in Mexico, which I didn't like from the get go – so many "dark" books take place there. I also didn't want it to be about sex trafficking and/or drugs, as there are also quite a few of those about, and I wasn't sure I could compete, so somehow I came up with "diamond thief". But I didn't like how it was going. So I shelved it. Didn't think about it again for a while.

Then I got to talking with another friend about books, and I don't remember exactly how it started, maybe assassin books, and I said I didn't like that idea, there are so many books about hitmen/assassins. Then we thought what else could an anti-hero do? What other kind of book would I like to write? I mentioned my diamond-thief-in-the-desert book and she asked why didn't I finish it and I explained my reasons, so we got to talking about it. I thought, if I want desert and diamonds, why not Africa? Where so many diamonds come from? She figured why a kidnapper or an assassin? Why not all of the above? I wanted the heroine to be badass, my friend wanted the hero to be French-ish (I don't know enough about French culture to make a character from there, so I made him American but raised part time in Haiti, so he speaks French and is exotic. Cheating!).

Thus, Marc and Lily were born. A complete and total 180 from the story I had started maybe a year before. I absolutely live for action movies, "Die Hard" is one of my all-time favorite movies, and I just about died for "Mad Max: Fury Road" this summer, so I poured all of that into this book. I wrote it 100% for me, the action movie I would like to see, just in book form.

I have always been a "pantster", meaning I don't use outlines, I type it as it comes to me. Sometimes I strike gold – Degradation, My Time in the Affair. Most of the time, I strike out – the fifteen other unfinished documents on my computer. I started coming to a wall with Marc and Lily's story and I could feel it, the dreaded shelving-of-a-project. Things *never* come off the shelf.

Ratula Roy asked me, "what's the problem? What's stopping you?" So I told her. Writing is a very linear thing for me. Once I start along a plot line, I can't see past it. I can't think outside of the box I've created. She was able to see it in 3D, and threw out suggestions, things I never would have thought of on my own. I was able to go back and change the course of the plot in such a way that it got rid of my wall and I was able to keep writing. Something I'd never been able to do before. She also did in such a way that the story remained organic to myself and my own thoughts. She changed the way I look at my own writing, something I've been doing for a very long time, and that alone is amazing. These characters belong to her almost as much as they do to me, and her effort on this story was almost as great as my own. Enough thanks cannot be said.

Angie D. – the way you look at a story and dissect it, your attention to detail, your work ethic, your tireless effort, your amazing teasers, so much. I don't know how to thank you, and pray that you will always be able to read for me. I feel very lucky that you found me.

To my beta readers: Sunny, Lheanne, Rebecca, Beatriz, Jo, Letty, Shannon, Sue, thanks for all your feedback and for taking the time to read for me, even when it's unedited drivel.

To Rebeka, for all you do for me, and the eight million e-mails I make you send, and for waiting a billion years for me to mail your stuff.

To Shh Mom's Reading for handling all of my releases and reveals, and handling it all so well.

To Najla Qamber Designs for ALL of my amazing covers, I love each one more than the last, which is hard to even imagine since I love each one more than anything ever.

To Champagne Formats for the amazing paperback editions! You've now done all of my books, and I love each and every single one.

And to Bruce Willis and Tom Hardy. To Colin Firth in "Kingsman", and Tom Cruise in "Mission: Impossible". To "The Matrix" and "Kung Fu Hustle". "Mr. & Mrs. Smith", "Romancing the Stone", "The Protector", and "Taken". And especially to Angelina Jolie, Maggie Q., Michelle Yeoh, Sonja Blade, Chun-Li, Storm, and all those ladies who kicked more ass than their male counterparts ever did.

To the readers, the new ones just discovering this story, and the ones who have been there since Jameson's first *"shut the fuck up"*. A year ago, no one but family and close friends had ever written anything I'd put down on paper, so it's still amazing that this book can find it's way to you. I hope you enjoyed it. I hope you enjoy the others. I hope you enjoy what's next to come. Thank you for reading, always.

And as always, thanks to my husband. Doing this is not easy. I work a full-time job. Then I come home, and I plug into a send full-time job. One that takes all my concentration. For me, a book takes about three-four months to create, from conception to publish. The actual writing process and the editing are the worse – I virtually don't speak to anyone during those two. As I'm writing this, I can't remember the last time I sat down and watched a movie the whole way through. A month ago? And he suffers through all of this in the most under-standing way, tries to make things more comfortable for me, takes care of me, and most importantly, lets me be me. From the bottom of my heart, thank you, Mr. F.

OUT OF PLANS

THE MERCENARIES #2

DAY TWO HUNDRED AND SIX

Liliana Brewster used one hand to hold the roll bar above her head. Her other arm was out the side of the car, holding against the door. She used her grip to stabilize her body as the Jeep she was riding in crashed through the jungle, roaring through puddles and leaping off of downed trees.

"You see!?" the man driving the vehicle shouted, pointing through the windshield. She squinted her eyes, trying to see what was out there, but dirt was splattered all over the glass, and a mist had started to come down on them, making visibility low.

"No!" she shouted back.

"Hold on, we are almost to the part where -"

The Jeep began to skid as he pumped the brakes, the tires losing traction in the mud and causing the back end to swing around a little. When they came to a stop, Lily looked over to find they were on the ledge of a very steep embankment. She stood up on her seat and leaned her hips against the windshield.

"Where did you see it?" she asked, bringing a pair of large binoculars to her eyes.

"Over there, to the right," her guide said, motioning to the same place as before, leaning over his wheel.

Lily turned, straining her eyes. The weather was shit. Low cloud cover hung over the jungle, threatening to dump on them at any moment – the mist was just a warning. She wanted to get to her destination before that happened. She wiped her damp hair off her forehead and kept looking.

"*There!*" she shouted.

A couple miles in the distance, rising out of the thick canopy, was a spindly little plume of smoke. Light gray and barely noticeable, it couldn't have been anything more than a campfire. A *small* campfire. Suitable for one or two people, max. She dropped the binoculars into the back seat, then tracked the smoke with her bare eyes. She began to smile.

"Ms. Lily," her guide started. "Why do you search so badly for this man?"

"What man?" she asked, trying to guesstimate how long it would take for them to drive to the smoke.

"I heard you last night, you said you are searching for a man," he explained. Her smile turned to a frown.

"*Marcelle De Sant,*" she said softly.

"Yes. Why do you want to find this … this De Sant person so badly?"

"Because," she finally looked down at her guide.

"Because why?"

"*I'm going to kill him.*"

The Kane Trilogy

degradation

Available Now

If you haven't met Jameson Kane yet, read below for a sneak peek …

Prologue

SHE HAD COME OVER TO their apartment just to drop off some boxes of stuff for her sister, Eloise - *Ellie*. Tatum had just turned eighteen and was moving to her own apartment in downtown Boston. She had been in a dorm room for her first semester at Harvard, but her parents didn't "*approve*" of her roommate, so her father had rented her an apartment off campus. When Tate's father said jump, all she was ever allowed to say was "*how high?*", so, she was moving.

Her sister Ellie was four years older, and they had never gotten along very well. About two years ago, Ellie had started dating Jameson Kane – *Kane*, as just about everyone called him. The relationship was strange to Tate; Ellie and Jameson seemed more like acquaintances than people who slept with each other, but who was she to judge? She didn't even really like her own boyfriend.

Tate didn't really know what to make of Jameson. He was so good looking, it was probably illegal. She worried if she looked at him too long, she'd go blind. He was also *very* smart – he had graduated early from Yale with an MBA, and was taking some time off to review his job prospects. He came from old money, his father was some sort of big wig on Wall Street, and the talk was that Jameson would follow in his footsteps.

In the two years he had been dating her sister, Jameson hadn't seemed to take much notice of Tate. He ignored her, treated her with indifference. When he had to deal with her, it was almost like an after thought, like he had forgotten she existed. He was tall, and handsome, and experienced, and smart. Tate was a brainy, naive, clueless girl, fresh out of high school, no real experience with the world or worldly people. He intimidated her.

It felt weird, showing up at Ellie's apartment without her being there. Jameson had let Tate in, and then pretty much ignored her. *Such a gentleman.* Tate had to haul several heavy boxes from the parking lot to the building, and then down a long hall to their apartment, all by herself. When she got to the last box, she dropped it by their bed, huffing and puffing.

"Did you want me to help?" Jameson asked, appearing in the doorway. Tate whirled around, startled.

"No, that was the last box," she replied, straightening out her cardigan. He always made her feel nervous. His eyes wandered over her face.

"You look really red. Want something to drink?" he asked. She felt herself turn even redder than she apparently already was; she was never prepared for his blunt manners.

"If you have any tea, that would be great," she replied, then followed him to the kitchen. She thought he was going to pour it for her, but he just gestured to the fridge.

"I don't know what Ellie has in there, lots of health food shit. Dig around," he offered. She made a face at his back.

"Water is fine," she told him, then just filled a glass from the tap.

"So. New apartment, all alone in a big city. You ready?" he asked. She nodded and turned to face him. His piercing blue eyes were wandering over her face and she resisted the urge to wipe at her skin. Was she dribbling water down her chin?

"As I'll ever be, I guess. I'm pretty self-reliant, so I think I'm ready," she replied, taking delicate sips of her drink. He chuckled.

"C'mon, you look like you're dying. Let's sit down, you can chug it," he offered, leading her to a table. He even shocked her by pulling out a chair for her.

"Thanks," Tate said, before following his instructions and downing the water in a few gulps. Without asking, he pulled the glass from her hands and refilled it before sitting down across from her.

"Don't you have like a boyfriend, or something? Is he in Boston?" Jameson asked, sliding her glass back across the table. She shook her head.

"No, Drew stayed in state," she replied.

"You guys have been going out for a while – how is it, being in a long distance relationship?" he asked. She was surprised at the question. Jameson never cared about anything she did.

"We've been together three years, but I don't know how long it's gonna last. He didn't want me to go to Harvard, wanted me to just follow him to Penn State. We argued about it a lot. He wants to try to work it out, but I think it's just time to get over it. Move on. We're in college now, I don't have time for that kind of crap," she let it all spill out. Jameson raised an eyebrow.

"Wow, very mature approach. How old are you again?" he asked. Tate rolled her eyes.

"You've known me for two years, Jameson, and you can't even remember my age?" she responded with a question. He shrugged.

"I don't think I even know Ellie's age. How old?" he pressed.

"I just turned eighteen, two weeks ago. How could you not know Ellie's age? You've been together for so long," Tate pointed out. He shrugged again.

"I don't pay attention to things like that. So what are you going to school for?" he asked. Tate had to stop herself from pointing out, *again*, that he should already know these things – it had been discussed, many times, in front of him. She had never realized it before, but he was kind of self centered. Arrogant.

"Political science," she said.

"We'll see how long that lasts. Go into economics, more money," he told her. She narrowed her eyes.

"I'm not doing it for money," she replied.

"Then you're stupid."

"You're kind of a dick," she blurted out, shocking herself. She wasn't prone to foul language most of the time, or being rude. She had just done both. He didn't seem bothered, though; he burst out laughing.

"You're just now realizing that?"

Tate smiled. He had a nice laugh, and a sexy smile. She could feel herself blushing. She could remember the first time Ellie had brought him home. Tate had developed a crush on him the instant she'd seen him – tall, dark hair, bright blue eyes, killer smile; what girl wouldn't fall head over heels in love with him at first sight? But it had never gone beyond that, she knew Jameson was so far out of her league, she wasn't even visible to him. She didn't waste too much time fantasizing about him.

But now, sitting across the table from him, she felt herself getting hot under her sweater.

"Well, yeah, you never talk to me," she pointed out.

"I talk to you."

"When?"

"Excuse me?"

"When do you talk to me? When was the last time you talked to me?" Tate asked. He thought for a second, looking up at the ceiling.

"I asked if you were okay, after your dog died," he replied, smiling at her.

"That was *last year*," she told him. Jameson started laughing again.

"Hey, at least I remembered," he pointed out. She found herself laughing as well.

"I guess that's something. Doesn't matter anyway, I'll be gone – no more awkward, silent family dinners to go to, thank god. You and Ellie will be on your own," she warned him.

"Well, you'll have to come back sometimes."

"No," she shook her head, "I won't. I've decided, I'm not coming back till I'm done with school, if then. I'm trying to get through a masters program in four years, or less."

"Wow. Hell of a challenge, baby girl. You think you're up for that?" he asked. She shivered at his use of "*baby girl*", he had never called her that before – never called her *anything*. She cleared her throat.

"I think I'm up for anything I set my mind to," she responded. He smiled.

"Good answer. Would you like a drink? Ellie should be home any minute, we could crack something open and have it ready for her," he suddenly asked, getting out of his chair. Tate held up her glass.

"I have water right here," she pointed out. He laughed as he pulled a bottle out of a cupboard.

"I meant a *real* drink, Tate. Seeing as how I've apparently '*never*' talked to you, I guess now is a good time to give you some congratulations. I'm assuming I never did that, right?" he asked, holding a bottle of champagne in his hand. She laughed.

"No, you weren't even at my graduation. And maybe just one glass," she replied, pushing the water she'd been drinking out of the way.

Having been too busy with school and all her extra classes, Tate had never been a party girl. No crazy parties and almost no experience with alcohol. Some champagne at Christmas with Granny O'Shea at the O'Shea farm in the Hamptons was about it. But she didn't want Jameson to know that – she wanted to seem mature, like a girl who had champagne all the time. It was silly, but she couldn't help it.

They polished off the first bottle, discussing politics and the current economic situation in the country. He disagreed vehemently with most of her views, but he never got heated or upset. He managed to get under her skin, though, and she found herself arguing just to get a rise out of him, but he was impossible to rile up. The champagne loosened her up a little, and she was a lot bolder with her opinions; or at least, more so than usual.

"No more after this, baby girl needs to be presentable for her family tomorrow," Jameson said, taking out a second bottle. She made a face at him.

They drank and chatted some more. Ellie texted him that she would be late. She was a paralegal, and her hours were all over the place. Tate was fine with that, she never felt comfortable around her sister. Ellie was tall and beautiful, with dark blonde hair that was *always* done up in *just* the perfect style. She was *always* wearing *the most* stylish clothing.

Tate was average height, with dark hair, almost black, and she had never paid attention to what was stylish, just wore what her mother bought for her. She was intimidated by Ellie, plain and simple. That's why she was going into an accelerated program at Harvard – to beat Ellie. Ellie was the golden child, the favorite child. Tate had always had to work ten times harder, just to always fall slightly behind.

She wound up blabbering all that to Jameson. Then went onto tell him all about her boyfriend Drew, whom he couldn't remember ever having met, even though he had – *several times*. How boring Drew was, how he always wanted to tell her what to do, but he never wanted to do *anything*. Jameson nodded and listened to her prattle, sliding the champagne out of her reach.

"You're pretty funny, Tate. I never knew," he chuckled. She rolled her eyes, shrugging out of her cardigan.

"*Shocking*. No one ever notices me, not when Ellie's around," she snorted, pulling her hair into a ponytail. He raised an eyebrow.

"I wouldn't say that, Ellie's not as great as you make her out to be," he told her.

"*Pffft*. She looks like what would happen if Cindy Crawford and Christy Turlington had a baby," Tate pointed out.

"You're pretty, too."

"You have to say that, you're her boyfriend. You have to be nice to me."

"No I don't. I'm hardly ever nice, and I almost never lie. You're an attractive girl, you just have bad self esteem, and worse taste in men," he informed her. She shrugged.

"Maybe, but that doesn't change the fact that Ellie is still better in most peoples eyes," she replied, fiddling with the stem of her champagne glass. Jameson leaned back in his chair, folding his arms across his chest.

"I wouldn't say that. From a technical stand point, if we're being completely honest, I would have to say that you're *much* sexier than your sister," he told her.

She didn't breathe for a moment. Did Jameson Kane really just say that to her? Or was it the champagne? She glanced at him, and he was staring right back at her, a small smile playing on his lips. She shook her head and shook off her nerves. No. He was just being nice. That had to be it – what kind of a guy would tell his *girlfriend's sister* that she was the sexier of the two? Not a very good guy, that's for sure.

"Whatever. It'll all be behind me in a couple weeks. It'll be like a new Tate, that's what I'm going for; Ellie can suck it," Tate proclaimed, then abruptly hiccuped. Jameson burst out laughing.

"See, now *that's* funny. Your sister sucking something – would never happen," he joked. Tate could feel her cheeks turning bright red.

"Gross," she blurted out.

"Too much? I guess we're not that good of buddies yet," he sighed.

"You shouldn't talk that way about your girlfriend, it's not very nice," Tate told him. He shrugged.

"Sometimes she's not a very nice girlfriend," he replied. Tate's eyes got wide as she had a realization.

"Are you going to dump my sister?"

"Now, why would you ask that?" Jameson responded, his smile gone as his eyes stared into her own.

"I don't know. Your voice, your attitude. Are you?" she pressed. He sighed, rubbing a hand over his face.

"I shouldn't have given you champagne. I didn't know you'd turn into Nancy Drew," he commented.

"Oh my god. You're gonna dump Ellie. You've been together for two years. She thinks you're gonna propose. She's gonna die," Tate gushed, pressing a hand to her chest. His eyes narrowed.

"We haven't even talked about marriage, why would she think that? And I don't know what's going to happen with Ellie and I, we've got a lot to talk about; *do not* talk to her about this," Jameson commanded, pointing a finger at Tate. She raised her hands.

"I go out of my way to not talk to her, I won't breathe a word. But can I ask why?" she pressed, reaching out for the champagne. Jameson didn't even notice, he was so lost in thought, so she poured herself another glass.

"I don't know. It's ... boring. Not exciting. Like you were saying about Drew. She wants this pre-programmed life, has everything decided for us. She knows what she's having for dinner next Tuesday, where we're going for the fourth of July, what we'll name our first child. She goes to bed at ten, gets up at six – I'm not allowed to touch her between those hours, I'm not even joking. I don't like being told what to do," his voice got quiet towards the end. Tate nodded, taking a large swig of her champagne.

"Sounds like Ellie. Did you know, one time when she was mad at me, to get back at me, she got into my room and organized my closet? That was her idea of revenge," she told him.

He burst out laughing, and that set Tate off. They both bent over, unable to breathe for how much they were laughing. It was hilarious, and it was totally true. Ellie was like OCD Barbie. Very pretty, and a little crazy.

"Oh my god, that sounds like her," he chuckled. Tate nodded.

"I know! I've got a hundred more, she -" Tate started, but she was gesturing with her glass, and champagne sloshed all over her front.

"Oh god, I knew this was going to happen," Jameson shook his head, but he was laughing. Tate snorted, holding her wet shirt away from her chest.

"Then you shouldn't have given it to me," she replied. He stood up.

"I tried to take it away. C'mon, I'm sure Ellie has something you can wear," he said, gesturing for her to follow him. She got out of her chair.

"Oh no, she'll kill me, I'm not allowed to wear her stuff," Tate told him, following him across the living room and back into the bedroom.

"Who cares? She owns so much shit, she'll never know. Just grab something, her stuff is in there," he explained, pointing to a section of the wardrobe before walking back out of the room.

Tate stared into the wardrobe for a while, letting her eyes wander over the clothes. Everything Ellie owned was expensive; from a designer. From a young age, Tate had been taught not to touch. Jameson had just given her free reign. She snorted and dove in, yanking back the hangers. She laughed and pulled down a silk blouse – it looked *ridiculously* expensive.

Perfect.

She spun around and threw the shirt on the bed, stumbling as she did so. She didn't think she was drunk, but she was feeling a little light. *Spinny.* She laughed to herself, curling her fingers around the hem of her shirt and pulling the wet material up. She went to yank it over her head, but something happened. The shirt's tag got caught in a string of pearls she was wearing, which then got tangled in her hair, and she was stuck with her arms in the air, struggling to pull the shirt one way or the other.

"*Oh my god,*" Tate laughed at herself, stepping back and forth.

She lost her footing and stumbled clear across the room. She rammed into something, a dresser, and moved so her butt was against it. She was really laughing now, struggling not to hyperventilate with the shirt covering her mouth. Her elbows were pinned above her head and she tried to reach the base of her neck with her fingers, arching her back. Her fingernails were just brushing the top of her spine when she heard something.

"What are you doing?"

She went stock still, her laughter dying. Jameson was in the room, and pretty close to her, judging by the sound of his voice. With her shirt up over her head, she was standing there in just her bra and khaki skirt.

Oh my god, oh my god, oh my god.

"Um, I got stuck," Tate offered in a small voice. He chuckled, and he was even closer than before – right in front of her.

"Obviously. Help?" he asked. She managed to shake her head.

"No, I think I -" she started, but then felt his fingers at the neck of the shirt. He pushed it up, exposing her mouth and nose, but then left it there. She took deep breaths.

"Are you drunk, Tate?" he asked, talking slowly. She shook her head again.

"No. I mean, I don't think so. I'm just stuck," she replied. He gave a small chuckle and she felt him pulling at the neck of the shirt again. A couple tugs, and the strand of pearls broke. She could feel them running down her body, some catching in her bra while the rest clattered to the floor. The shirt came free from her head and Jameson pulled it away, holding it in his right hand. He was staring down at her. She struggled to control her breathing.

"You're very different from Ellie," he told her in a quiet voice. She rubbed her lips together and nodded.

"I know," she replied.

Tate knew she should move, should grab her shirt, do something to cover herself. Run for the bathroom. She should not be standing in front of her sister's boyfriend, only wearing a black lace bra. He dropped her shirt as his eyes wandered down her body, and she found that she was frozen to the spot, unable to move a single muscle.

"Family heirloom?" he asked, then he reached out, tracing a finger down her chest. He ran it down her cleavage and she thought she might faint. But then he held his hand up, and he had a pearl pinched between his fingers.

"Present. From Drew," her voice was just above a whisper. He examined the pearl.

"He's cheap. It's not real," he commented. She almost laughed.

"What?"

Jameson let the pearl drop and his attention went back to her. Tate still couldn't move. Had even stopped breathing. He was looking at her like she was dinner. She couldn't believe it. Twenty-three year old Jameson Kane was looking at her, *really seeing her*, for the first time ever. It was wrong, so wrong. She tried to think of Ellie, but couldn't make herself. She could only see his eyes.

"You should leave this room," Jameson told her, his hands gliding onto her hips. Her skin jumped at his touch and she could feel an electrical current pass between them. She gave a full body shiver and nodded.

"I know," she breathed. His fingers spread as his hands moved to her back, up to her shoulder blades.

"Ellie's my girlfriend," he reminded her. As if she needed it.

"I know." Apparently her impressive vocabulary had deserted her. His hands slid back down, all the way to her butt. She put her hands on the dresser behind her, bracing herself.

"This isn't just me."

He'd said it as a statement, but she knew it was a question. She was feeling it, too.

"*I know,*" she whispered.

"If you want to run, I suggest you do it now," he told her.

"Why?" she asked, and he leaned in close.

"*Because I eat girls like you for breakfast,*" he hissed in her ear.

ABOUT THE AUTHOR

Crazy woman living in an undisclosed location in Alaska (where the need for a creative mind is a necessity!), I have been writing since …, forever? Yeah, that sounds about right. I have been told that I remind people of Lucille Ball - I also see shades of Jennifer Saunders, and Denis Leary. So basically, I laugh a lot, I'm clumsy a lot, and I say the F-word A LOT.

I like dogs more than I like most people, and I don't trust anyone who doesn't drink. No, I do not live in an igloo, and no, the sun does not set for six months out of the year, there's your Alaska lesson for the day. I have mermaid hair - both a curse and a blessing - and most of the time I talk so fast, even I can't understand me.

Yeah. I think that about sums me up.

Made in the USA
Las Vegas, NV
08 April 2022